KAT –

MISSING

ED JAMES

Copyright © 2016 Ed James
All rights reserved.

✽ Created with Vellum

For Len.

OTHER BOOKS BY JAMES

SCOTT CULLEN MYSTERIES SERIES

1. GHOST IN THE MACHINE
2. DEVIL IN THE DETAIL
3. FIRE IN THE BLOOD
4. DYED IN THE WOOL
5. BOTTLENECK
6. WINDCHILL
7. COWBOYS & INDIANS

CRAIG HUNTER SERIES

1. MISSING
2. HUNTED

DS VICKY DODDS SERIES

1. TOOTH & CLAW

DI SIMON FENCHURCH SERIES

1. THE HOPE THAT KILLS
2. WORTH KILLING FOR
3. WHAT DOESN'T KILL YOU
4. IN FOR THE KILL
5. KILL WITH KINDNESS

DAY 1

Tuesday
11th August 2015

1

'Come back here, you little bugger!' Police Constable Craig Hunter darted left to follow his prey into a room at the back of the house, his heavy boots clumping off the stripped-wood flooring. He stopped dead, his footsteps echoing around the stark room. White walls, old floorboards varnished mid-brown and a single bed in the corner.

No sign of him.

The sash window hung open. Chest heaving, Hunter ran over and leaned out to scan the sandstone walls of the old farmhouse. A towering oak tree blocked out most of the sunlight, the gnarled branches like fingers plucking at the sky.

Still no bloody sign of him. Where is he?

The summer breeze cooled his damp forehead, as he rubbed the sweat off with his forearm, soaking the thick hair.

Below, the walled garden was alive with colourful fruit trees pruned into perfect bowl shapes, all swaying in a ceilidh dance formation. Over the top of the wall, the Sphinx-like bulge of Arthur's Seat loomed in the distance, casting judgment on Edinburgh and the surrounding Lothians. Nearer, a white car bombed down the road, screeching as it pulled into a side street, Shawfair sprawling around them. Some politician's idea of a new town — the whole place was a building site and would only go downhill from there.

Hunter looked around the garden again. The front gate was hanging open, but no sign of Finlay there, either.

He can't have got away, surely?

Crack. A tiny branch tumbled to the ground, landing on a mossed-over flagstone.

He was climbing down the far side of the tree.

Hunter pushed out, propping his hands against the ancient bark, and looked for any footholds on the tree.

Not enough time to go back through the house without losing him. Bugger it — just ignore the twenty-foot drop.

Hunter rested his weight on the sill and touched one big boot onto the branch. The tree gave a muted creak, but it stayed firm. Seemed steady enough. Just about.

Hunter wedged his palms into the window casing and stretched out his left foot, giving the branch a good dunt as his fingertips tightened around the pane. A shard of old paint jabbed under his left thumb nail.

Just what I bloody need...

The tree took all of his weight, sixteen stone of idiot. At least they were mostly muscle. He held tight, getting his bearings. Felt like the branch could take another couple of idiots. Thank God for all those burpees.

Hunter inched forward, his stab-proof vest rattling. The tree moaned again.

Christ...

Hunter kept his body low and kept moving, his fingers tracing the knots on the bark, ready to grip at any second. A gust of wind blew through him and his peaked cap fell to the ground, spinning like a wheeling bird as it went.

Bollocks...

Hunter reached the trunk and hugged it close, the stab-proof vest pressing into him and digging half a dozen bits of equipment into his ribs. He looked around the garden, sucking in deep breaths.

Where the hell—

There he was, not far from the ground. *Christ.*

Halfway down to a thicker branch than the one Hunter stood on, was a sawn-off stump. He eased himself down, supporting his weight on his hands like an old man getting into the bath, and reached his feet down.

Careful... Keep it nice and steady... Not like your usual—

The wood creaked and the rough bark dug into his palms. Definitely a cut there.

He lowered himself, inches at a time, his upper arms and hands burning as he let the half-branch take his weight. He blinked as the sun disappeared behind the clouds, letting his eyes adjust to the light. Another blast of Scottish summer wind hit him, carrying a fug of distant cigarette smoke mixed with second-hand diesel and the deep mud stink of a building site.

Where the hell is the little chancer?

There. Standing near the edge of the branch, staring back at him, looking ready to jump.

Hunter lurched forwards and grasped with both hands.

'Mraowr!' The fat tabby cat squirmed in his grasp. It swung its hind legs up, scratching with its sharp talons and drawing blood. 'Hchhhhh!'

'You little shite!' Hunter pinched the scruff of the cat's neck.

It stopped raking with its claws and went limp, all four legs hanging loose. Rebuking eyes struggled to look at him.

Got you.

Hunter supported the cat's legs and looked around the garden. *Still no sign of—*

A sash window clattered open. 'Officer! Over here!' Mrs Carstairs was reaching out to him, the loose skin on her hands speckled with liver spots. 'Is my wee boy okay?'

'He's fine.' Hunter kept a firm grip on the cat's neck as he leaned forward, a gentle shove encouraging the little guy to move towards his distressed owner. The tree creaked. 'Here, can you take him?'

'Of course I can.' She took the squirming cat and hugged him close. 'Oh, Pickle, my poor wee angel.'

'I wouldn't let him out again, Mrs Carstairs.' Hunter tried to stand up, but near enough lost his footing. He crouched low and pulled himself tight to the branch.

That was close.

Hunter thumbed over the tall stone walls. 'It's a busy road there. Lots of construction traffic and he could get—'

'Of course.' Lost in the world of Pickle, she slammed the window with a rattle.

A "thank you" wouldn't have gone amiss...

Hunter inspected his hands. A red gash ran across one, like a new life line or whatever palm readers went on about. Blood dripped from his thumbnail. A latticework of smaller cuts ran over his wrist and up his forearm.

Little bugger.

Hunter sucked at the deepest wound as he crept back to the trunk. He looked down, trying to—

You're bloody kidding me...

A series of handholds was dug into the tree, running all the way to the ground, some worn and rusty, others overgrown and set deep into the trunk. Looked like more than enough to get down, though. He gripped the first one and lowered his left foot until it connected with something solid, dull metal ringing out into the warm afternoon. Then he started climbing down, accompanied by slow handclaps.

'The mighty detective at work.'

Hunter dropped the last few feet to the ground and stayed focused on the tree bark, sucking the fresh blood from his wounds. 'That cat was a vicious little bugger.' He swung round and rubbed at his thumb.

'Well, it certainly met its match.' PC Finlay Sinclair folded his arms across his chest, his standard-issue Police Scotland T-shirt turned up at the cuffs to show off his biceps. Disco muscles let down by the beer gut poking out of the bottom. 'Oh, and you lost this.' He tossed something over.

Hunter caught it — his cap. He battered the stoor out. Dust motes leapt off it and briefly danced in a flash of sunlight, before quickly dispersing in the breeze. He put the cap back on, pulling it tight. 'You cleared off sharpish.'

'Saw it was just a cat, mate. No point wasting our time. Can we get onto some more important police work now, please?'

Hunter nodded over at the sprawling Victorian mansion and the steading conversion going on behind it. '*She* thinks this is important.'

'Aye, well, not important enough to thank you.'

Hunter started back down the path towards their squad Focus. Shards of light bounced off the white paint, the blue-and-yellow regalia streaked with pigeon crap. The lower half looked like it'd been through a carwash that sprayed mud. 'You going to call it in?'

Finlay winked at him as he caressed his Airwave radio's screen. 'Got that interview, have you?'

Hunter plipped the car's lock and hauled the door open. 'That's just a rumour.'

'Aye, bollocks it is.' Finlay twisted his face into his usual gurn, cheeks pushing out to show too much gum and teeth, as he spoke into the Airwave. 'PC Sinclair to Sergeant Reid, over.'

'Receiving. Safe to talk.' Lauren Reid's plummy voice crackled out of the handset. Always sounded that wee bit more English over the radio. 'You finished with that missing boy yet?'

Finlay took his time lowering himself into the passenger seat, then rested his feet on the bleached pavement. 'PC Hunter has secured Pickle and returned him to Mrs Carstairs.'

'Hang on. Her boy was a cat?'

'Aye, sarge. Just heading back to the station for our piece. That okay?'

'Suppose it'll have to be.'

2

'And I'm saying you're a softy, Craig.' Finlay was leaning back in the passenger seat, doing almost enough manspreading to block the gearstick. 'I mean, a *cat*. Man alive.'

'I notice you just foxtrotted oscar when you saw what it was.' Hunter stopped the engine and yanked the keys out of the ignition. The underground car park was deserted, just a flickering light keeping the squad cars and unmarked detective jobs company. 'If you were any lazier, you'd be hibernating.'

'I'm not lazy, jabroni.' Finlay pulled his legs together and let his seatbelt whizz up. He brushed the back of his hand up Hunter's sleeve. 'Looks like you've been dragged through a hedge in all directions. Thought you'd want to keep yourself clean for your interview.'

Hunter's own seatbelt rattled up, the buckle glinting in the low light. The fresh cuts on his hands were still welling up. 'I tell you, it still bloody hurts.'

'Hurts, my arse.' Finlay ran a hand over his shaved scalp, more skin than stubble. 'A wee cat takes a dislike to you and you need Mummy to rub some Savlon on.'

'Don't get any ideas.' Hunter got out, the slamming door echoing round the car park, and set off across the concrete, his vest and equipment playing their usual rattling drum beat. The place stank of spilled diesel, stale fumes and the few cheeky buggers who couldn't be bothered to go to the designated smoking space. 'Do you want to sign the car back in?'

'No point, is there?' Finlay was practically tap-dancing to keep up with Hunter's pace, his shoes clicking off the concrete. 'The Princess will just have us back out after our piece.'

Hunter stopped by the stairwell door. 'Your call, Finlay.'

'Aye, well, maybe I'll just sign it back in.' Finlay snatched the Focus's keys and pushed through to the office.

Fat Keith was slumped in front of a computer, a half-eaten Krispy Kreme doughnut hovering between his teeth. He put it back on the plate and rubbed his podgy hands together. 'Oh, I'd better call the Chief Constable. The Brains Trust are back in the building!'

Finlay tossed the keys at him. 'That's Alpha six back in.'

Keith caught them and ran his other hand across his mouth. 'Do I need to check for any scrapes to it or adjacent vehicles?'

'Nah, you're fine.' Finlay picked up a glazed donut and bit into it, swallowing the mouthful without chewing. 'Been a while since Hunter's totalled a police vehicle.'

Hunter nudged the door further open with his boot. 'I've seen you make an arse of a three-point turn, so keep your beak out of it.'

'Brilliant.' Keith hung the key up on a latch and peered out of the mesh-glass window. 'In the name of the wee man, it's barkit! Where the hell were you?'

'At this old farmhouse by Shawfair.' Finlay snorted. 'That new village out by Musselburgh, just inside the bypass. Load of new-builds going up.'

'Musselburgh? Didn't think that was our patch.'

Finlay thumbed upstairs. 'We go where we're told.'

'Well, you could've avoided driving up the soil bings, you pair of chancers.' Keith nodded at the window. 'Any danger you could give it a wash?'

'Well, I would. It's just...' Finlay grimaced, his teeth gritting as his cheeks puffed out. 'We're due for a briefing with Sergeant Reid.'

'Aye, bollocks you are.' Keith collapsed into his chair and stabbed at the keyboard, frowning. 'Can you pair settle a bet for us?'

Hunter rested his hand on the stairwell door. 'Depends what it is.'

'Does the "I" in MIT stand for Major Investigation or Major Incident Team?'

'There's no "I" in MIT.' Finlay smirked. Then coughed to mask the lack of laughter. 'Mass Incest Team.'

'Aye, very good, Sinclair.' Keith's eyes were pleading with Hunter — guy would bet on anything with anyone. God knows how much was riding on something you could look up on the intranet. 'So, Investigation or Incident?'

'Investigation.'

'Ya dancer!'

Hunter opened the door, letting a clatter of descending footsteps into the room. Still a couple of floors above by the sound of things. 'Why are you asking?'

'Jimmy was saying it was Incident.' Keith picked up his donut and stared deep into its eye. 'Been a shooting up in Dumbiedykes. Way I hear it, some drug dealer got his comeuppance. Shot by a prossie.'

'*Shot?*'

'Aye, can you credit it?' Keith frowned, his red face almost glowing in the harsh light. 'Could be the other way round, mind.' He chomped down on the rest of his donut. 'Anyway, thought I'd remind you the old MIT are up on your floor.'

Hunter winced. 'Including...?'

'Aye, your old pal. Happy hunting...'

'HAPPY HUNTING'S GOOD, THOUGH, EH?' Finlay got in front and held the canteen door open, his metal sandwich box clinking off the frame. The sort of thing you'd see in an IKEA poster of workmen up an American skyscraper. 'Oh, in the name of the wee man...'

A long queue snaked around the canteen, way past the servery. All knuckle-draggers in cheap suits.

Hunter let out a sigh. 'Bloody MIT are taking over the station again.'

'Aye, and it's pea and ham soup the day.' Finlay scowled, like someone had put a hex on his first born. Not that anyone'd been stupid enough to breed with him. 'They'll have scranned the lot by the time I get to the front.'

'Let's just eat our sandwiches and see what's what, okay?' Hunter led him past the queue.

'Miaow!'

'Miaow!'

Hunter stopped dead by the end of the queue and looked round. Those two arseholes had the table near the front. Dave and Steve, shaved heads and scar tissue on their knuckles, like they'd come out of a vending machine for primetime TV beat cops. 'What did you say?'

Dave looked up from his soup, steam spiralling around his hook nose. 'Heard you got some pussy this morning, Hunter.'

'Well, you boys have always got each other, right?'

'Piss off, Hunter.'

'See you lovebirds later.' Hunter took his time walking over to a window seat, the only one free. The table was covered in at least two lunch sittings.

Dave was still scowling back at him. Hate doing that to such soft targets, but it's the only language they understand...

Hunter sat facing the window. Outside, Leith Walk was in deadlock, stalled by the major incident of a Scottish afternoon hitting twenty-five degrees. Centigrade, too.

He glared at Finlay. 'You had to bloody tell them, didn't you?'

Finlay shrugged as he sat, more interested in the clasps on his sandwich box. 'Well, you've got to admit—'

A tall figure obscured part of the sunlight streaming in, casting a long shadow across the table. 'Craig Hunter.'

Terrific. Him.

Hunter shut his eyes, so he wouldn't have to look at him.

Scott bloody Cullen.

Prick thought he was a male model, certainly slept around like he was one. Smooth baby's arse face, like he shaved every hour, on the hour.

Cullen dumped his tray down and scraped a chair back, grinning at Hunter. 'You all right, Craig?'

Hunter unclipped the top of his sandwich box but didn't open the lid.

'What's up, mate? Cat got your tongue?'

Hunter focused on him now. 'Who told you about that, Scott?'

Cullen was frowning between Hunter and Finlay. 'Told me what?'

Finlay raised his hands. 'Nothing to do with me, honest.'

Cullen tapped the edge of his tray. 'So, do you mind if I sit here?'

Hunter pulled a face and flexed out his fingers, just enough to tear open a scratch. 'We're kind of in the middle of something here.'

'Right.' Cullen snatched up his tray and looked around, giving someone a nod in the distance. 'See you around, Craig.'

Finlay's frown added a couple of ridges to his forehead. 'What's that all about?'

'Nothing. Just don't want to speak to that arsehole.'

'Did he steal your cheese or something?'

'It's your turn to get the water.' Hunter slouched back and watched Finlay waddle across the room towards the water fountain. Just behind it, Cullen was sitting with a pair of suits.

With a sigh, Hunter inspected his latest creation. A sourdough he'd baked the previous night, with Goat's cheese, beetroot and walnut, fronds of rocket reaching out the sides. Pretty much all still intact despite the rocky transport.

Finlay plonked two cups of water down and nudged one across the table, scowling like he'd stepped in dog shit. 'Hey, jabroni, is that food?'

Just a bloody toothpick away from a villain in a buddy cop film...

'No, Finlay, it's nuclear waste material.' Hunter picked up the first half of the sandwich. Didn't feel like eating it any more so just held it there. 'Want me to enlighten you on its contents?'

'No, just keep it well away from my nose, all right?' Finlay opened his box and a rancid stench wafted out, his eyes closing in bliss. 'Now this is a sandwich.'

Hunter winced at it, felt even less like eating his own now. 'Your egg mayonnaise still on the UN's official munitions list?'

Finlay chewed on his first morning roll — neon-yellow egg stuffed into a flap of flour, yeast and air — and beamed wide. 'Beautiful.'

Hunter opened his mouth to finally get started on his own lunch but didn't. 'My brother, Murray, got another couple of hens at the weekend. Lovely eggs.'

Finlay raised his half-eaten roll, the eggy mush dribbling out of the corners. 'Can't beat Farmfoods' cheapest.'

'If those were from my hens, I'd take them to the Vets. You do know about free-range and all that?'

'Aye, I just don't care.' Finlay finished chewing and slurped down some water, giving Hunter's sandwich a little nod. 'What's the deal with you and that Cullen boy? Look like you shat yourself.'

'Used to work with him at St Leonards.' Hunter didn't look up, just nibbled at the crust, the rocket burning his tongue. 'I was Detective Constable and he was Acting.' He tried a full bite, chewing slowly. 'Guy thinks he's a hot shot.'

'Caught a serial killer a few years back.' Half-chewed mush coated Finlay's tongue and teeth. 'Heard he's a DS now.'

Hunter dumped his sandwich back in the box.

His Airwave chimed. 'Sergeant Reid to PC Hunter, over.'

Hunter stabbed the button. 'Safe to talk.'

'Need a word with you in my office when you've got a minute.'

HUNTER KNOCKED on the door and stood back. Someone had stuck a handwritten sign under the names of PS Lauren Reid and PS Adrian McKay saying "Strictly NO Detectives after the hours of darkness".

Maybe that someone found it funny.

He checked his phone for messages — nothing, as per — then knocked again. Gave it a few seconds and cleared his throat, loud enough to get a decent echo in the corridor.

Feels like I'm fourteen years old again, waiting to go into the Headmaster's room.

Through the door, a phone slammed into its cradle. 'Yes?'

Hunter yanked the handle and pulled it open. 'You wanted a word, Sarge?'

Sergeant Lauren Reid sat at a computer, gymnast posture and a thousand-yard stare, her left hand resting on the keyboard, purple nails and a giant diamond on her ring finger. Expensive-looking watch on her wrist, the kind that hadn't seen a single day's active service on the streets. Black fleece zipped up, even in summer. 'Craig, right.' She focused on Hunter and sat back, resetting her dark-blonde ponytail, loose and frayed. 'Sorry, I was miles away. Thanks for coming down.' She waved at the seat in front of her. 'Sit.'

'Do I get walkies after?'

'Just sit.'

Hunter did as he was told, slouching on the creaking wood and resting his left shoe on his right knee. Scuffed half the leather off climbing that tree. 'What's up?'

She crossed her arms and sat back, shivering. 'It's freezing in here.'

Hunter stood up tall, hands in pockets. 'It's a lovely summer's day out there.'

'There's no such thing as summer in Scotland.'

'Well, I spoke to Facilities.' Hunter propped himself on the backrest of the seat in front of her desk. 'They'd kept the heating at Winter levels. That's why it's been so bloody hot.'

'Hot?' Lauren took a printed email out of a lime-green document folder and slid it across the table. 'Have a look at that.'

Don't cops just love their files?

Hunter scanned through it, picking out the words "PC Craig Hunter" and "Interview". 'What's this?'

She flicked up her eyebrows. 'And you used to be a detective...'

'No, I get what it is.' Hunter handed the page back, heart thudding in his chest. His mouth was so dry, it was like he'd eaten Finlay's sandwich. 'I just don't get *why*.'

'Because I put you forward for it after our one-to-one last month. You might remember it, as you were badgering me to get you out of uniform and "back doing something important".'

'I'd had a strong coffee, Sarge. I can only apologise.'

She tilted her head to the side. 'A "thank you" would be appreciated.'

'Cheers. I don't know what to—' Hunter sat up straight. 'It's not because you want rid of me? New broom and all that.'

She shook her head, that cheeky little grin flashing across her lips. 'No, Craig. It's because the MIT are looking for an Acting DC and you want to be one.'

'I want to be a full DC again, not an Acting one.' Hunter gripped the chair arms tight. 'I didn't spend six years—'

'—in CID only to be rescuing cats.' She rolled her eyes, the grin puckering to a pout. 'Yeah, I know, Craig. You should know what it's like in Police Scotland. I've only been here three months and I've already got the message, loud and clear.' She handed him the paper. 'Anything coming your way, you need to grab with both hands.'

Hunter loosened his grip on the chair arms, his tongue rolling around his mouth, trying to get some moisture back. He coughed again. 'When is it?'

'Tomorrow, at two o'clock.'

Hunter folded the sheet in half, then again. 'Thanks, Sarge.'

'The rest's up to you, Craig. There are a lot of people going for it.'

'I'll try not to let you down.' Hunter got up and stuck the page in his pocket next to his notebook. 'That all?'

'Not quite.' She leaned back and crossed her arms, a fresh shiver working its way up her spine, judging by the expression on her face. 'Afraid you and laughing boy need to attend a domestic in Restalrig.'

3

'Such a wee princess, you.' Finlay spun the wheel round, turning left into Mountcastle Green. 'Just get it out of your system.'

'Wish I hadn't bloody told you now.' Hunter turned away from the idiot, his knuckles white around the grab handle over the door.

The street was a load of boxy houses arranged in a grey court. No matter how shabby they were, though, they'd still cost three or four times what he could afford. The car trundled past the modern graveyard's wide expanse, regimented rows and columns of bling gravestones, like a spreadsheet of death.

'Should I really have to be interviewed for an Acting DC position?'

'It's a joke. Think it'll be worth the bother?'

'Doing something important would be a start.' Hunter reached into his pocket for his notebook, getting the folded-up interview email instead. He stashed it again and pulled out his pocket book, flicking through the pages. 'Number six.' He waved at a white-harled house covered in ivy. Triangular sixties detached thing, strips of painted wood at the front, grimy white everywhere else. A giant blue six was painted on the garage door. 'That one there.'

'The one with the private plates?' Finlay pulled in behind a Citroën Berlingo van in the drive. H185 DFF. 'HIBS DFF... What's that mean?'

'Well, other than being a Hibs fan...' Hunter shrugged. 'Usually initials, right?'

'Guess so. Boy must be doing okay for himself.' Diesel fumes filled the cabin as the squad car's engine clattered to a stop. 'Only had this thing two months and it's knackered already. I tell you, the way Dave rides that clutch, it'll soon be as clapped-out as his missus at the end of a week in Magaluf.' Finlay slapped his cap on, covering the fine-grain stubble. 'Anyway, got anything on this family?'

'You know I did a PNC check when we were driving over here. Don't you bloody listen? All three Fergusons are clean as a whistle.' Hunter got out of the car and stuck his own cap on.

'Just let me in! Pauline!' A man was thumping against the front door, wiry like an ex-boxer gone to seed but still clinging onto his Popeye forearms. An old purple Hibs away shirt lurked underneath paint-spattered navy dungaree overalls, "FERGY" poking through the straps at the back. Probably Mr Ferguson, but you never could be sure. 'Come on, Pauline! She's bloody lying!'

'Bit early in the day for this sort of malarkey.' Finlay stomped over the pavement and marched up to the man, swerving past a fresh lump of dog mess. He flicked on his Body-Worn Video, nodding at Hunter to follow suit. 'What seems to be the matter, sir?'

'The *matter*?' Bloodshot eyes darted around, struggling to focus on them. Fergy took a deep breath, clearly trying to control himself, and thumbed at the front door. His dark hair was greying at the temples, bristles of salt-and-pepper stubble dotting his jawline. 'The bloody *matter* is *she* won't let me in.' He gave it another dunt for good measure. Up close, the guy looked like he could handle himself, all tight muscle backed up by the snarl of a seasoned bar brawler.

'Can we start with your—'

A woman's voice tore through the front door. 'I've called the police, Doug! They'll be here any minute!'

Finlay took a step towards the door. 'We're here, Mrs Ferguson!'

'Keep him away from this house!'

Finlay nodded at Hunter to take over, like he'd had enough already, and crouched down to speak through the letterbox. 'PC Finlay Sinclair, ma'am. Can I come in?'

Hunter got between him and Fergy. 'Doug Ferguson, is it?' He waited for a brief nod and motioned away from the door. 'I need you to come with me, sir.'

Doug followed with slumped shoulders, eyes locked on the door as Finlay flapped the letterbox open to turn the conversation down from a shouting match.

Hunter clicked his pen and noted the date, time and location. 'Let's start with your full name, sir.'

'Doug Ferguson.' His eyes looked like they were trying to drill through the wooden door.

'Is that Doug or Douglas?'

'Douglas.' He shook his head, firing another salvo of daggers at the house. 'She's got no bloody right...'

'Do you live here, Mr Ferguson?'

'Course I bloody live here. And I pay all the bloody bills, an' all!'

'I understand, sir.' Hunter stepped closer, getting a face-full of paint fumes and second-hand smoke. No trace of booze, not even a masking mint or the clack of chewing gum. Maybe drugs? He tilted his head to the side, eyebrows raised. Doug's pupils looked a bit on the large side, but still within anyone's normal range. Ish. 'Can you tell me what's happened here, Mr Ferguson?'

'What do you bloody think's happened, you tube?' Doug was panting now, hard and fast, like an overbred show dog. 'She's booted me out of my own house!'

'Who has?'

'Pauline.' Another thumb at the house. Didn't look like Finlay was getting anywhere, least not inside. 'The wife.'

'And did your wife tell you why she's kicked you out?'

'Aye, she bloody did.' Doug snorted and started twanging the straps of his overalls, the Hibs badge masked by a splash of magnolia. 'Her daughter's saying a load of shite about me.'

'Not *your* daughter?'

Doug sniffed, then rubbed a hand across his nose. 'Steph's my stepdaughter.' He focused his fingers on kneading his forehead. 'Took the wee tart in and this is the bloody thanks I get?'

Hunter checked his video was still blinking away. Could never be too sure. 'Take it slowly, sir.'

'Was just making a sandwich in the kitchen, man, when I get an earful from Pauline.' Doug's eyes flicked from side to side, as if he wasn't comprehending what was going on. 'All this bollocks about this and that.'

'Can you expand on "this and that", please?'

'Speak to her.' Doug shook his head, eyes on the house. 'A load of nonsense, I tell you.'

'Stay here, Mr Ferguson. I'll see what's going on, okay?'

'Aye, no worries.'

Finlay was on his hands and knees in front of the door, pushing the floor-level letterbox wide open. 'Mrs Ferguson, I need you to let me inside.'

'How do I know you're proper police and not one of his mates, eh?'

'I've got a warrant card and a uniform.'

She paused. 'You're no' getting in 'til he's away from here.'

Hunter leaned over to whisper at Finlay. 'I'll take over here. Sure a wee chat with Doug in the car about Hibs' prospects in the Championship this season will settle him down.'

Finlay nodded and resigned himself with a deep shrug. 'Aye, sure.'

Hunter waited until Finlay had lured Doug round the other side of the van. 'Mrs Ferguson, my name's PC Craig Hunter. My colleague's taken your husband away.'

'He's no' my bloody husband after what he's done!'

'I understand.' Hunter left a pause, trying to listen for a key in the lock. Anything. 'Would you mind letting me in?'

A latch rattled loose and the door clicked open.

Pauline Ferguson stuck her head out, looking down the street in search of her husband. Eyes not so much ringed as dropped down a well. She wore a skirt without tights, sunburnt skin under a pale salmon blouse. Then she locked eyes with Hunter. 'In you come.'

PAULINE WEDGED herself onto a beige sofa next to a teenager, clasping her hands. 'This is Stephanie.'

The thin girl grunted up at Hunter. She was most likely sixteen, looking like she'd just emerged from her pupa as a full-grown goth. Shoulder-length hair, same brown as her mother dyed hers. Dark tights and white blouse under a navy gymslip. Purple school jacket lined with yellow, matching the tie, sarcastically tied.

Hunter stood a distance away from them, taking in the large living room. The white walls were covered in white-background action shots of Pauline, Doug and the teenager, looking like she was having fun despite herself. A pair of floor-to-ceiling windows overlooked the street — Finlay had got Doug to sit in the back of the squad car, his legs still outside the vehicle.

'Stephanie, this guy's here to help, will you at least look at him?'

Stephanie nibbled at her lips, eyes only for the TV, some white metal kids throwing shapes at the camera, the din on mute.

'Stephanie, my name is PC—'

She jabbed her thumb at the remote and a thrashy racket filled the room.

Pauline swivelled round to stare at her daughter, her long legs tapping in time to the music. 'Christ, Stephanie, what's got into you?'

The girl closed her eyes and dropped her chin onto her chest. Sunlight crawled up her skinny leg, catching some glitter on her lumpy knee. Despite the hunched posture she looked tall, like gravity had a different effect on kids these days.

'Do you want to speak to the police officer, hen?'

Steph shook her head, still transfixed by the metallers on the TV.

'Okay, love.' Pauline hugged her daughter close.

The girl recoiled and crawled over to the other end of the sofa, her eyes wide like the cat with his neck pinched.

Hunter smiled at Pauline and tried to lead her away from her daughter. He stood by the door, wincing at the thud from the TV.

Pauline grabbed the controller and turned the music down, just enough to stop blood pouring out of anyone's ears. She got up and trudged over to the doorway, her mouth hanging open. 'I've kicked him out.'

'Can I ask why?'

'She says Doug's been...' Pauline gave a quivering sigh, eyes shut. Then open again, jaw clenched, eyes back on the couch, where Stephanie was rubbing at her eyes. 'She said he's been *abusing* her.'

Jesus wept. Only this morning I'd been longing for more important work. Be careful what you wish for...

He swallowed hard and focused on the girl on the sofa, her mouth twitching in time with the music. 'Do you know how long this has been happening?'

'I've no idea.' Pauline scratched at her wrist. 'She won't say.'

'Do you believe her?'

'Of course I *believe* her. She's my daughter.'

And sons and daughters never lie...

'Okay. How old is—'

'Sixteen in May.'

Hunter paced across the room and crouched down in front of the girl, thighs burning as he held himself there. 'Stephanie, I need to ask you a few questions.'

She ran a finger across the palm of her left hand.

'I know this is difficult to talk about, Stephanie, and, if you want, you can tell me to go away.' Hunter paused for a few seconds, leaving a gap for her to fill. She didn't. 'I need you to take me through what you told your mother.'

Stephanie looked away, the sunlight catching her pale neck.

'I know this is difficult, but, if he's abused you recently, there are things we can do.' Hunter left another space. 'Has anything happened today?'

Tears streamed down Stephanie's face, drawing mascara stalactites under her eyes. Then she gave the world's smallest nod.

'Recently?'

An even smaller nod, if that was possible.

'Stephanie, I need you to help me here, okay? We need to get you to a doctor who will do what's called a Sexual Assault Evidence Kit. Once that's been processed, we'll be able to use the evidence to prosecute him.' He waited for another nod. 'Can you remember if he used a condom?'

Stephanie shook her head.

Jesus Christ...

Hunter returned to the doorway, fire burning at his neck. 'Mrs Ferguson, we need to get your daughter to the hospital to undergo some tests.'

Pauline ran a hand across her forehead. 'But she's got the school...'

'This is urgent. If she's been sexually assaulted recently, there will be evidence.'

Pauline covered her face with her hands. 'I can't cope with this.' Then she let her hands go, her jaw clenched, and glanced over at the window. 'What's going to happen with Doug?'

'We'll have a word with him at the station. Keep him away from here for a few hours. In the meantime, you might wish to consult a lawyer about legal proceedings.'

'I work for a solicitor.' Pauline nodded, the same mascara tears now lining her cheeks. 'Just do whatever you can.'

'The important thing is to be strong for your daughter, Mrs Ferguson.'

She gripped his arm tight. 'Don't call me that.'

'Of course.' Hunter stared at the girl, trying to get her attention. Nothing.

'IT'S ALL A LOAD OF SHITE!'

Outside, Doug was on his feet, jabbing a finger at Finlay, like he was abusing Hearts fans at an Edinburgh derby at Easter Road.

Hunter clenched his fists and started across the hall carpet. 'Wait here.'

∽

'I don't give a monkeys about the Rangers or Alan bloody Stubbs.' Doug only had eyes for the house and the twitching living room blinds. 'You hear what that wee—'

'Mr Ferguson.' Hunter marched over to the police car, straight for Doug, using his extra height to show he meant business. 'I need a word.'

Doug leaned back against the car, arms folded, and looked away. 'So she's going to let me in, right?'

'Not just now, Mr Ferguson. Stephanie has levelled some serious allegations at you.'

Another glare over at the house, shaking his head. 'That wee bitch is *lying*.'

Hunter motioned for Finlay to restrain him. 'Douglas Ferguson, I'm detaining you under—'

'No, you're not!' Doug launched his forehead at Finlay, thudding against his skull with a loud crack. Finlay dropped like a sack of tatties. Before Doug could sprint off, Hunter reached out, grabbed Doug's wrist and almost yanked his arm out of his socket. Doug stopped short with a grunt. He somehow managed to throw out a wild kick, his steel-toe-capped boot clipping Hunter's knee, freezing him for long enough to spin out of his hold.

Hunter stumbled forward, clutching his knee tight as he screamed out.

Doug hugged his arm to himself, gritted his teeth and made off down the road, tracing the chainlink fence along the graveyard in the shadow of a tall beech.

'Here we bloody go again...' Hunter got up and tried to dart after him, but his knee buckled and he dropped back down. He struggled to his feet, wincing in pain as he settled for a limping skip, gradually gaining speed as he closed in on the winded fugitive. Clearly not a runner.

Ignoring the pain in his leg, Hunter sprinted the last few yards and jumped, his forearm smacking into the side of Doug's neck. His legs caved and he tumbled over the old stone wall into the graveyard. Hunter's already damaged knee grazed the wall. He went down hard and lay on the pavement, chest heaving, red pain throbbing in his eyes. A shadow ran across his vision.

Doug was up, weaving through the gravestones like a zombie on fast forward.

Hunter hauled himself up and kept pace with Doug, hobbling along on the other side of the wall until Doug got within arm's reach. Hunter propped his weak leg on the wall and kicked himself up and over.

Ah, you bugger...

Feeling his balance go, Hunter launched himself at Doug and caught him in a headlock, tackling him to the ground.

Strong fingers scratched at his thighs, clamping around the muscle. Locked together, they rolled through the grass, stopping just inches from a grave. A jab to his side made Hunter let go.

Doug was up again, ready to run. Hunter, still on the ground, swiped at him with an elbow and caught Doug's right ankle, sending him sprawling backwards, his shoulder cracking off a gravestone.

Hunter grabbed Doug's wrist, twisting it behind his back a few more notches than was necessary. 'Douglas Ferguson, I'm detaining you under Section fourteen of the Criminal Procedure Scotland Act 1995.' He snapped his cuffs on the prone man's wrists. 'Anything you say—'

4

'Lawyer!' Doug Ferguson stood stock still in the car park, his voice cascading around the concrete space. 'I want a lawyer!'

Hunter rolled his eyes at Finlay across the car's roof. 'You okay to deal with this?'

'I will be now.' Finlay nodded back the way. Fat Keith was rolling his way across the scarred floor, belly hanging out as he chewed on another donut. 'After all, the cavalry's waddling in.' He shoved Doug towards Keith. 'Go and update the Princess, aye?'

'Lauren?' Hunter had to check they'd both turned their Body-Worn Video off. 'Thought I was the princess?'

'You're just a princess, mate.' Finlay slammed his door. 'She's the definite article.'

∽

LAUREN KEPT her gaze on her computer, fingers battering the keyboard like it'd wronged her in a past life. She locked her machine and slumped back in her chair, a frown twitching over her forehead. 'You okay?'

'Why wouldn't I be?'

'Young girl being abused by her stepfather. It's pretty traumatic, isn't it?'

'I'm fine.' Hunter tightened his grip on the chair back and shrugged. 'Just doing my job, Sarge.'

'Strap a tin suit on and I swear you'd be RoboCop.'

'Rather be the Peter Weller one than that remake a couple of years ago.'

She frowned. 'That was a remake?'

'You should check out the original. Or maybe not.' Hunter stood up tall again and stuffed his hands deeper in his pockets. 'Anyway, Dave and Steve are taking the girl and her mother up to the hospital. And we've got Doug Ferguson in custody downstairs. He's lawyering up as we speak.'

Lauren brushed a stray hair off the arm of her fleece. 'So, I take it there's something in this?'

'Like I said, the girl's a mess and her mother's not exactly helping.'

'And him?'

'Not being judgmental, but I've seen the type. The grass on the pitch sort.'

'Excuse me?' Lauren tightened her jaw. 'That's not a term I ever came across in Thames Valley.'

Hunter cleared his throat. 'Look, there's a certain kind of guy. They have this saying, something like "if there's grass on the pitch, you've got to play". Sick bastards, usually told with an evil grin in their eyes, you know? The sort of bastards we're finally managing to put away these days, at least more often than not.'

'Jesus Christ.' Lauren shut her eyes, her jaw tensing through the skin in a tight rhythm. 'I get where you're coming from, but let's not be too hasty here.'

'I'm just saying, that's my initial assessment, Sarge. Guy ran off when I tried to detain him.'

'Listen to me, Craig. We need to treat him as innocent until he's proven guilty, okay?'

'Come on, Sarge, that's—'

'No ifs, no buts. This man has been accused, that's all. We need to build up a solid chain of evidence against him. I don't need any knee-jerk reactions or any lynch mobs with faming torches and pitchforks.'

'All I'm saying is smoke and fire are never too far apart, Sarge.'

'And sometimes the cause of the fire isn't what you think it is.'

'This doesn't disgust you?'

'Of course it bloody does. Just make sure we get this man convicted, if he indeed did anything.' She curled a strand of hair around her fingers. 'Listen, we had a briefing from Inspector Buchan last week. You remember that case in the Omni Centre? Well, anything like that, we've got to work with the Sexual Offences Unit in Bathgate in the first instance.'

'Think they'll bite?'

'We just need to give them a nice juicy worm.' She pushed herself off the desk and stood up, the coil of hair falling in front of her left eye. 'Think this stepfather's juicy enough?'

Hunter exhaled, making his cheeks wobble. 'You have watched the BWV footage, haven't you?'

'That's why I think it'll suit their skill set more than ours.' She stared at her keyboard, placing her fingers in a triangle and thumping the DEL key. 'I'll raise it with Inspector Buchan. Can you get back up to the hospital while he waits for his lawyer?'

∽

FINLAY TOOK OFF HIS CAP, the hospital's strip lights bouncing off his shaved scalp. 'Bloody baking in here. Worse than the Princess's office.'

Hunter looked up from his sandwich and took a few seconds to finish chewing. 'There you are.'

'Here I am.' Finlay nodded at the lunch box. 'Lord Ponsonby-Smythe finally got round to eating his nettles and tarmac sandwich?'

'My stomach started eating itself.'

'Another hipster monstrosity. Ay caramba.' Finlay collapsed in the seat next to him and thumbed back at the ward. 'The girl been seen yet?'

'Just in the middle of it now.' Hunter stuck his lunch box on his lap as he finished chewing the last mouthful. 'Lauren's handing this off to the Rape unit in Bathgate.'

'Aye, good luck with that. Twats will only touch it if the boy looks like a future serial killer.' Finlay got out his smartphone, big and shiny, the sort of thing that cost half your monthly wage on a contract. 'Lawyer's still not turned up.'

'He's got one?'

'Aye, some big shot. Stuck in court just now.'

'Dirty bastard needs the best he can get.' Hunter peered over to the nurse's station, still empty. He got to his feet and dumped his box on the side table. 'Bugger it, I'm—'

'Craig Hunter.' A deep voice from behind, all too familiar.

He spun round and nodded. 'Elvis.'

'That again...' DC Paul Gordon stood there, rubbing his long sideburns, black triangles. He wore a dark grey suit, the pale grey shirt underneath matching his complexion. The sort of pot belly you could only get from eight pints of premium lager a night with Finlay Sinclair. 'The uniform suits you, mate.'

'I prefer a bit of camouflage, if I'm being honest.' Hunter glanced down at his black ensemble. 'This is itchy as hell.'

'Classic. Serves you right you being in uniform, Hunter.' Elvis stroked his chin, a few shards of stubble in among the clean shave. 'The MIT management must spend a lot of time working out how we could've let a talent like yours slip through our grasp.'

'Clearly don't know what they're doing if they've kept you on.'

'DCI Cargill said I'm a rising star.'

'Sure she didn't mean arse?'

'Just messing, mate. Long time no—'

A hand grabbed Elvis's shoulder from behind. 'Come on, Paul, the doc's...'

Hunter's heart fluttered.

Yvonne Flockhart. Tall, dark hair, scowling at Hunter. 'Come find me, Paul.' She let go of Elvis and stormed off down the corridor.

Elvis crouched down next to him. 'Another of your conquests, mate?'

'In a manner of speaking.' Hunter slumped forward in his chair, thick mucous sticking in his throat. 'What brings you here?'

'Proper work, you know?' Elvis shook his head at Hunter's uniform again, laughing anew. He pulled his jacket tight, frowning at Finlay. 'Pint tonight, Fin?'

'The Elm at the end of the shift, bud. I'll be propping up the bar.' Finlay gave a cheeky grin to Hunter. 'Saved a cat this morning.'

'Aye?' Elvis planted a hand on Hunter's shoulder. 'Keep up the heroics, maybe one day they'll notice that you too are full of promise, Craig. Who knows, you might even get to trade in the uniform for a cat suit.'

Hunter nudged him away before he stuck the nut on. 'Is Yvonne your carer now, or what?'

Elvis raised an eyebrow, his cheeks puckering into a dimple. 'You hear about that shooting in Dumbiedykes?'

'You're working that?'

'Sure am. Witness ended up in here. Someone clocked him on the head when he got home from giving his statement.'

'Sounds suspicious.'

'Aye, and then some.' Elvis's eyebrow danced up. 'What are you pricks here for?'

Hunter glared at Finlay. 'Domestic abuse case.'

'Nasty.' Elvis gripped Hunter's shoulder tight again. 'Sure you'll put the punk away.'

Finlay batted Elvis's hand away. 'Here, Craig, we've got a doctor to speak to once you're done flirting.'

∼

Finlay leaned against the window overlooking the car park and nodded at the doctor. 'Have you managed to examine Miss Ferguson yet?'

'Well. I've performed *most* of the standard tests, yes.' Dr Helen Yule got up from her desk, stethoscope dangling from her neck, folded arms cracking the starch of her white coat. She took her glasses off and blew on the lenses. Half of her right eyebrow was missing, an old scar intersecting it. She stood up tall and put her specs back on, the strip lights turning the round lenses into mirrors. 'I'm afraid the rape kit's negative.'

'Seriously?' Hunter slumped back against the wall and frowned. 'What do you mean by "most of the standard tests"?'

'Unfortunately, the girl wasn't particularly co-operative.' Yule pointed out into the corridor. 'She's at the more feral end of the scale of what we see in here. And the mother isn't exactly helping, either. She's supporting Stephanie's attempts to block the tests. Doesn't want anything to happen to her wee angel.'

Heard that too many times today...

Hunter let out a sigh. 'Are you saying she wasn't raped?'

'Look, it's not that clear cut. I got Stephanie to start speaking while her mother was out of the room taking a phone call.' Yule snorted and took a few seconds to think things through. 'She told me she'd had a shower after the latest attack.'

Hunter bit his bottom lip, tearing off a thin strip of skin. 'So there are no signs of rape?'

'That's still not conclusive. If Mr Ferguson didn't use a condom, then there should still be traces of semen in the standard test regions. I need to do more tests, but I'm not convinced it'll be easy.'

'Want me to have a word with her?'

'That'll be fine, so long as you get her to comply without trying to bite.' Yule held up her closed fist and flexed out the fingers. 'Luckily she's not made contact yet.'

5

The hospital room had that boiled-cabbage smell, as sweet as it was sour. *Christ knew where it came from.*

Stephanie lay back, staring at the ceiling, ignoring her mother. She was hunched up in a hospital gown, the bedsheets the same gleaming white as the walls. Hunter stood his ground in the doorway until she finally became aware of him and looked his way, though only for as long as it took her eyes to come into focus. Then they flicked back to the ceiling.

The glass of orange Lucozade by the bed gave off a peppery tang. Not sure how that'd help with a rape.

Pauline Ferguson was sitting on the chair next to the bed, withdrawn and dabbing a tissue at her eyes. She twisted round and spotted Hunter. 'Have you put him away yet?'

'I need a word.' Hunter smiled at her and beckoned her out into the corridor. Once she'd left the room, he closed the door behind him and leaned against it, blocking her re-entry, though not as subtly as hoped. 'How's Stephanie doing?'

'Her bloody stepfather's been raping her. How do you bloody think she's doing?' Pauline rested against the wall, her expression as foul as the hospital smell. 'My poor wee angel...'

Hunter got out his notebook and opened it, focus on Pauline. 'Have you witnessed any instances where your husband could've—'

'No.'

Hunter almost snapped the end of his pen as he pressed it against his notebook. 'You're sure?'

'Calling me a liar?'

'We need to establish a list of events where Ms Fe— where Stephanie confirms she was abused. All the who, where, when stuff. Okay?'

Pauline ran a hand across her forehead, smearing the beads of sweat. 'You need to give the lassie time...'

'Time is critical in this case.'

'And that Doctor keeps trying to do things to Steph...'

Hunter clenched his jaw and tried to stare her down. 'Dr Yule has been unable to perform a full physical examination on your daughter.'

'Should've done her job when she had the bloody chance.' Eyes locked tight, mouth twitching silent incantations. 'She must've got enough to put that animal away, right?'

'She didn't find any evidence.'

Pauline's eyes shot round, lips pursed tight, a snarl distorting her nose. 'After all that, she can't do her bloody job?'

'You weren't obstructing Dr Yule, were you?'

'What?' Pauline turned away from Hunter, her forehead creased. 'What are you saying?'

'I'm saying that, if we are to stand any chance of convicting Mr Ferguson, we need evidence to support Stephanie's allegations.'

'You saying my daughter's a liar?'

'I just need the truth.' Hunter let it sink in. 'We need to get a full statement from you. And one from Stephanie. We need them as soon as possible. And, perhaps most importantly, we need those stories not to merge together.'

'Fat chance of that.' Pauline focused on the shining floor tiles and wiped a tear from her blotchy cheek. 'She's not speaking to me.'

'Do you mind if I have a word with her?'

Pauline's gaze swept up again, water filling her eyes. 'Can't you see how traumatised she is?' She gasped, her lips quivering as she stared at the door behind Hunter. 'She just needs space.'

That's how she's playing it, is it?

Hunter tried the smile again. 'In that case, I'm afraid Stephanie's going to have to vacate the room.'

'You can't be... What? Why? She's been *raped*!'

Hunter nodded. 'Is there anyone who could give you a lift home?'

'What, you drove us here!'

'You'll need to make alternative arrangements.'

'Christ...' Pauline blinked hard and fast a few times, her shoulders slumping low. 'Ailsa. She lives next door to us. I can call her.'

'Might be an idea to get her to bring a change of clothes for Stephanie.'

'Sure, sure.' Pauline reached down for her handbag and retrieved a basic Samsung mobile. 'Just a second.' She wandered off, hitting buttons on her phone.

Finally...

Hunter re-entered the room and perched on the chair nearest the girl, letting her acclimatise to his presence.

Stephanie glanced over at him, her mascara now just a faint shadow under her eyes. She started fidgeting with her thumbs, pushing them together until one forced the other over, like they were no longer parts of her body.

'Stephanie, I need to ask you a few questions.' Hunter left a long pause, filled with the girl's short breaths. 'It's about what you told your mother earlier.'

Stephanie rolled over to face away from him, the gown crinkling and bunching up tight around her.

'I need to write down your account of events, which we'll have to present in court at a later date. It's important you tell me what happened as soon as you can.'

She curled up into a tight ball.

'I just want to help you, Stephanie. Then you can have some time to yourself. But I need to do this as soon as you're able to.'

No reaction.

'Is your mum stopping you from speaking to us?'

Her body loosened off. 'What?'

'I want to help, Stephanie. Whatever's going on, you can tell me. If your mother's—'

She let out a deep sigh and shuffled round to face Hunter, eyes brightened by tears, glistening under the strip lights. 'Mum keeps going on at me. Is it a lie? Am I lying? Keeps nipping at my head. I just need a break, man.'

'I understand that, Stephanie.' Hunter shifted back on the chair, close to falling off. 'Are you able to tell me what you told her?'

'I just want everyone to get off my back.'

'Stephanie, I'll give you all the space you need once you've told me what's happened.'

She blinked slowly, lost and scared, looking a lot younger than sixteen. 'What do you want to know?'

He got out his notebook and eased off the pen lid. 'Can you tell me what you told your mother at lunchtime?'

A long pause, like he'd lost her again. Then she gasped.

'Steph, Ailsa's going to give us a lift—' Pauline grabbed Hunter's arm and tugged him to his feet. 'What the bloody hell's going on here?' She barged him out of the way and reached over to massage her daughter's back. 'Are you okay, sweet pea?'

The girl flinched away from her mother's touch. He'd lost the eye contact.

Pauline twisted round and scowled at Hunter. 'Were you hassling my daughter?'

Hunter raised his hands, noticing Finlay in the doorway. 'I understand your concern, Mrs Ferguson. I managed to—'

'I told you to stop calling me that.'

Give me strength...

'To stand any chance of convicting your husband, we need to get your daughter's statement on the record, okay? She was just starting to open up to me there. You need to give me space and let me help. Do you understand me?'

Pauline slumped against the wall and gave a slight nod. 'What do you need from me?'

'Just keep away.' Hunter returned to the bed.

Stephanie was crying, the sheets rocking in time with her ragged breaths. Her glistening eyes stayed locked on her mother.

Hunter tried to make eye contact, but she wasn't playing that game any longer. 'Stephanie, can you continue?'

She shook her head.

'It's important.'

She shut her eyes. 'Is that true?'

Pauline paced over to the bed and started stroking her daughter's bare arm. 'Is what true, Toots?'

'He said he might not be able to put Dad— *Doug* away?'

'Don't you worry, petal. It'll all be fine...'

Stephanie was pleading with Hunter now. 'I mean it. Is he going to get off?'

'Stephanie, we've barely started this case.' Hunter swept his quiff over in a vain attempt to stop his hands shaking. 'We just need to be able to do our jobs.'

'Right.'

Hunter motioned for Finlay to join him in the corridor. He closed the door and peered through the safety glass. 'This isn't getting us anywhere.'

'You're telling me.'

'The mother keeps obstructing. You saw what happened, right? I had the girl talking.' Hunter leaned back against the door, arms folded. 'Finlay, I need you to—'

'So you're in charge of me, is that it?' Finlay stood there, hands on hips, face like a skelped arse. 'You're not my boss, jabroni.'

Here we go again...

'I'm not saying I am.' Hunter pinched his nose, heat rising up his neck. 'Look, we need to divide and conquer here, okay? I'll get the mother's statement. You stay here with Stephanie and make sure Yule gets the physical finished.'

Finlay shrugged, phone already out. 'How long you going to be?'

'As long as Yule needs. You okay to do it?'

'I'll keep an eye on her, don't you worry.' Finlay let out a wide yawn. Could practically see his tonsils.

Hunter stood up tall and smoothed down his T-shirt. 'This doesn't bother you?'

Finlay's eyes shifted around the glowing screen. 'What, taking orders from you?'

'No, what that girl's been through.'

'Seen it all, mate.'

Hunter spotted his sandwich box on the table at the side. 'Terrific. Almost forgot that.' He opened the door and entered the room.

Pauline was propped against the wall, shaking her head slowly and muttering to herself.

Hunter joined her, a tight hand on her arm. 'I'm going to take your statement now.'

∼

THE FAMILY ROOM looked recently decorated. Tasteful colour scheme, all beiges and browns, contrasting with a strong purple couch. Fresh flowers sat next to the box of Kleenex on top of the chunky oak table.

Nice to see someone still has money to spend these days.

Hunter nudged the tissues across the table, past Pauline's sleeping mobile. 'I know how troubling this time is for you and your family.'

'Do you?' Pauline stuffed a hankie up the sleeve of her jumper. Yellowed bruises encircled her wrist. 'Do you really?'

'Where did you get those bruises?'

She pulled her sleeve back down. 'Nowhere.'

'If your husband has been—'

'I was helping that doctor and Stephanie kept grabbing hold of me.'

The iceberg's in danger of tipping up here…

'I find that hard to believe.' Hunter crunched back in the chair. 'Has your husband been—'

'Where is he?'

Hunter smoothed down his notebook, adding the date and time. 'We've detained your husband ahead of a formal interview, so no further harm's going to come to Stephanie.' He clicked his pen and laid it on the blank page. 'But we need to take your statement and ensure it stays consistent throughout the process.'

She snuffled into a tissue. 'What are you saying?'

'I mean, you can't get Stephanie to change her statement to further incriminate your husband. It has to stay the same. And we need to substantiate the allegations to support a prosecution.'

'You think she's lying, don't you?' Pauline dropped the hanky on the table, where the tight ball slowly blossomed. 'I can see it in your eyes. You think she's made up a pack of lies.'

'I've got an open mind, I can assure you.' Hunter jotted the attendees on the fresh page, just him and Pauline Ferguson. 'I know this isn't easy.'

'I blame myself for what's happened.' She took out another hankie and blew her nose. 'Letting Doug into our house.' She dabbed at her nostrils, shaking her head. 'She's just a bairn and I've let her down.' She tossed the bunched-up tissue across the table. 'Stephanie's a bright girl, in the top class for everything. I want her to go to uni, get a proper job and not end up like me. Can't believe this...' Another honk on the tissue. 'Doug's been ... abusing her.'

'Did she say how long?'

'I got the impression it was at least a year.'

'So since she was fifteen?' Hunter drew two timelines on a separate page, one for that morning and the other going back years. 'How long have you and your husband been together?'

'Since 2010. Married the following year. I wasn't pregnant or anything, I just needed to settle down for Steph. She was ten.' Pauline stared into space, her eyes glazing over with a layer of fresh tears. 'Christ, that's almost half the girl's life.'

Hunter lay his pen down and rubbed his eyes, loosening a few sleep crystals with tired fingers. It had been a hard day already, and there were no signs of it getting easier any time soon.

How long has this really been going on? Up to six years. Look at it one way and you've got a predator hunting down a single mother and her young daughter. Playing a long game, getting himself trusted, then abusing that trust.

'What happened to Stephanie's father?'

'He died when she was a bairn.' Pauline reached for another tissue. 'Not long after her eighth birthday.'

Hunter added it to the timeline. Certainly explained a lot of her behaviour. Both their behaviours. 'How did you meet Mr Ferguson?'

'Through a friend. I thought he was...' She sniffled, fingers tightening around a fresh hankie. 'Thought Doug was a good man. Ran his own business, had a load of mates, seemed nice.' She balled up her fists, looked ready to strike them down on the table. 'Didn't think he'd do this to my Steph. How could he do that to my wee girl? What sort of mother lets that happen?'

You tell me...

Hunter let her soak in her melodrama for a few seconds.

Was it guilt? Shame? How much did she know? The ring of bruises... Complicity was common in these cases. And sometimes turning a blind eye seemed easier than facing up to the truth. Either way, it still didn't protect those who needed protection.

'Can you take me through the events of lunchtime today, please?'

The fire in Pauline's eyes died to a slow ember. 'Doug's a painter-decorator, comes home for his lunch most days if he's working locally. I work at the solicitors in Porty, means I can come home as well.' She ripped off another Kleenex and honked her nose in it. 'When I got back today, though, he was shouting through her bedroom door.'

Hunter looked up at that. 'Was it locked?'

'Steph was tugging it shut.' Pauline lifted a shoulder, barely putting any effort into it, and dabbed at her dark eyes. 'I pulled Doug back from the door and shoved him into the garden, so I could try to calm my daughter down.' She balled up her hankie and rolled it on the table. 'Then she let me in her room and... That's when she told me all about it.' She gasped out a cry. 'I can't believe this.'

'This is going to be hard, but do you honestly believe her?'

Pauline flicked the tissue away, eyes narrowing to slits. 'I believe her.'

'Has Stephanie ever lied to you?'

'Which girl doesn't?' The fire flared up again. 'But it's never anything serious. We're close, you know? Always tells me what's going on with her.'

So close she flinches away from your touch?

So close she tries to drown you out with music?

So close she tries to bite doctors trying to help her?

Hunter held her gaze for a few seconds. Little flickers of doubt appeared in her eyes — they shifted around too fast, blinked maybe a bit too quickly. 'Okay, so after she told you, what did you do next?'

'I locked him out of the house.' Pauline narrowed her eyes, like she was reliving the terror. 'And that's when he really started kicking up a fuss. Banging on the door, hitting the windows. He even kicked the window in the bloody conservatory. Thought he was going to smash the glass. So I called you lot.'

Hunter checked the timeline and drew a line under it. There wasn't much Stephanie's statement could contradict — it was all from the girl's perspective. 'This is definitely the first you knew of it?'

Pauline's eyes bulged. 'What are you saying?'

'Just answer the question.'

'Course it bloody is.'

'Is there anyone else your daughter could've shared this with before she told you?'

Pauline frowned. 'No.'

'Sure about that? What about friends from school?'

'Steph doesn't have many friends. Despite my best efforts, she's a bit of a recluse.' Pauline bunched up the latest tissue. The frown deepened, then pulsed. 'Well, she's got a boyfriend.'

'We'll need his name and phone number.'

'His name's Neil.' She looked around the floor, as if that's where his surname was hiding. 'Alexander, I think. He's a gentle laddie. Bit too soft, if you ask me. Don't have a number for him, though.'

Hunter noted it, his stomach starting to gargle up acid.

The water was muddying now. Not just an allegedly abusive stepfather, but a boyfriend. Teenage boys were even worse these days, nasty little bastards pressuring girls into the perversions they watched on their laptops and phones.

'Is this boyfriend at school with her?'

'He's older. Couple of years, I think...'

Oh no...

Hunter sighed, then quickly smiled in an attempt to mask his resignation. 'Is it possible he could've been abusing her?'

'Are you not listening to me?' Pauline almost threw herself across the table, eyes narrow as she reached for his arms. 'She told me Doug's been abusing her. Okay? Not Neil. *Doug.*'

And you're not putting words in her mouth, are you?

Hunter prised her fingers off his arms and sat back. He circled *Neil* and added a few notes around the name. 'We'll speak to him in due course.'

Or rather, the Sexual Offences unit will...

His mobile flashed up a text from Finlay. "Doc's finished."

Hunter pocketed his notebook and got up. 'In the meantime, is there anything else I should know about?'

'Not that I can think of.' Pauline scrunched up her face and let out a small gasp. 'Oh, Steph.'

'I know it's going to be difficult, but I need you to refrain from discussing the exact details with her. Please just focus on reassuring her and being there for her. I'm sure you're good at that.'

'Aye, aye.' She pinched her forehead again, letting a snarl crawl up her cheeks. 'Not good enough, clearly.'

6

Finlay was sitting in the chair outside the hospital room, pudgy fingers mangling his phone.

Hunter stopped and turned to Pauline. 'Can you wait here for a second?'

'I want to see my daughter.'

'You'll see her very soon, promise. I just need to verify a few things.'

'Well, I'll phone my pal.' Pauline started rummaging around in her handbag.

Hunter crept up on Finlay from behind, kept it casual, and stopped a metre or so behind him.

Idiot was playing some stupid game, archer towers firing arrows at orc warlords. Finlay hammered the screen a few times. 'Come on, you bloody bugg— Oh. Arse.'

A wave of goblins marched through the gate. "Game over" filled the display.

Finlay crunched back on the chair, eyes bleary.

Hunter gave him another second to contemplate the tragic fate of his imaginary friends, then leaned forward and whispered into his ear: 'Busy?'

Finlay jumped up, his face flushing a guilty shade of scarlet. He cleared his throat, glancing up and down the corridor. 'Didn't see you there, mate.'

'You're a bloody chancer.' Hunter thumbed at the door. 'Did Dr Yule get in there?'

'Aye, all done.' Finlay plonked himself back down on the seat. 'She bit Yule this time. Didn't break the skin. I think.' He locked his phone and stuffed it in his pocket. 'Not heard how she got on, mind.' He got up again and stretched out, then frowned. 'I'll go and supervise Mrs Ferguson.'

Unusual...

Finlay walked off, passing Pauline who was still speaking into her phone. Movement flashed in the corridor behind her as Lauren clomped along, giving Finlay a nod.

Terrific. Well, that explains it. Look busy when the boss is around.

Hunter straightened his back as she approached. Stood to attention, stomach in, chest out, head up, eyes straight ahead. 'Sarge.'

'Craig.' Lauren zipped her fleece up and rubbed her hands together. 'It's *freezing* here.' She blew into her fist. 'Good news, though. Buchan's been onto the Rape Unit in Bathgate. DI McNeill's taking this off our hands.'

Fun while it lasted... Well, hardly fun, but certainly meaningful.

Hunter's shoulders sagged a few notches. 'When does he get here?'

'She. And that's good news, Craig.' Lauren clamped his shoulder, like she was trying for a sports-jock pump. 'Means we can get on with what we're supposed to be doing.'

'Right.' Hunter shrugged off her hand. Felt like a block of ice. Behind her, Finlay was ushering Pauline into Stephanie's room. 'The doc's finished and I've got the mother's statement.'

Lauren flicked up her eyebrows. 'That's good work, I suppose.'

'You suppose?'

'You know what I mean.' Lauren stopped rubbing her hands together. Her eyes narrowed to fine points. 'They're here already.'

Hunter wheeled round.

A woman marched down the corridor, sharp steps matching her no-nonsense trouser suit. She was pale and thin, but as toned as she was tall. Could probably handle herself on a Saturday night on Lothian Road. She held out her hand to Lauren. 'DI Sharon McNeill. Sergeant Reid, is it?'

Lauren shook the hand. 'This is PC Hunter.'

Tempted to give her the old fake Masonic handshake. Gave her a nod instead. 'Ma'am.'

McNeill stepped aside to introduce her colleague. An Asian woman with striking cheekbones. Late twenties, at least her outfit said so. Seemed like she knew she was it. She took one look at his uniform and laughed. 'Craig Hunter, as I live and breathe.'

Wait, what?

'Chantal Jain?' Hunter frowned, his heart dancing. 'Not seen you since Tulliallan.' He gave her the once over, struggling to hide it. 'You've changed.'

She smirked at him. 'You've not.'

McNeill grimaced at Lauren as she patted Jain on the elbow. 'DS Reid, this is DS Jain.'

Lauren treated them to a flash of her smile. 'Well, you're outranking us.'

'That's not what I'm about.' McNeill nodded at the door. 'The girl in that room?'

Hunter folded his arms across his chest, tucking his thumbs into his stab-proof vest. 'She's back with her mother.'

Jain flicked up her perfect eyebrows, thin pencil lines, and shot him a cheeky grin. 'I take it she's been a bit of a nightmare?'

'I should give up poker...' Hunter nodded, his forehead creasing up. 'Not sure what her mother's game is, but she's been obstructing attempts at interviewing Stephanie.'

'She's been checked over, though, right?' McNeill was tilting her head to the side, her ponytail draping over her shoulder. 'Standard rape kit, aye?'

'Dr Yule's just finished. Haven't got the results back.'

'Okay.' McNeill nodded at Lauren. 'Let's you and me grab a cup of tea and get up to speed.' Then a nod at Jain. 'Chantal, can you and PC Hunter here have a word with this doctor?'

∽

HUNTER STARTED off down the corridor, shoes squeaking on the lino. 'So the cavalry's finally arrived, has it?'

'Hardly.' Again Jain arched an eyebrow, just about keeping pace with him. Her lipstick was a smoky shade of plum. She definitely didn't look like she should be stuck in a Scottish police station. Or chatting to an idiot in a hospital. 'Standard protocol and all that. You respond, we mop up.'

'Mop up, eh?' Hunter stopped outside Yule's door. Her voice droned through the wood.

'You know what I mean.' Jain caught his look and buttoned up her suit jacket. 'How's it going, Craig? Not seen you in years.'

'I'm doing ... okay, I guess.' Hunter bit down the anger. 'You seem to be doing well for yourself. Hardly recognised you.'

'The hair or the make-up?'

'Both, probably.' Hunter kept his gaze off her. 'So, Sarge, do you want to lead or...?'

Jain knocked on the office door and entered without waiting for a response.

Dr Yule sat in her office chair, twirling a pen in her thin fingers, phone handset clamped between her ear and shoulder. She gazed at Jain, then held up a single finger to Hunter and went back to her call, turning her back to both of them. 'And what do you expect me to do about it?'

Hunter took a seat in front of the desk and waited for Jain to join him.

She got out her notebook and an expensive-looking pen, black with brass finishes. 'I thought you were in CID?'

'I was.' Hunter let out a sigh. Tried to catch it before it escaped. 'DI Davenport at St Leonard's for a few years.'

'I was in Leith Walk. Wilkinson then Methven.' She brushed a hand over his uniform. 'When did you get this fetching number?'

'Couple of years now.' Hunter's thigh tingled where she'd stroked it. His mouth was dry as a Basra June . 'When they shuffled the deckchairs.'

'I got shunted onto the MIT. Worked with Sharon's ... DI McNeill's other half for a bit. Nightmare.'

'Not to be recommended?'

She smirked at him and started nodding. 'Thinking of getting back into proper police work?'

'Just want to do something important, you know me.'

'Have a word with a few people before you apply for anything. A ... pal of mine got stuck as Acting DC for a couple of years.'

'Brutal. What's his—'

Yule slammed the phone down and sat scowling at it for a few seconds. 'Bloody registrars think they're more important than front-line doctors...' She shook her head and nudged her glasses up her nose. 'Now, how can I help you?'

'This is DS Chantal Jain from the Sexual Offences Unit. They'll be taking over this case from us.'

'I'm glad to hear it.' Yule looked at Jain with an even expression, no emotion in it. 'I hope that means I can stop listening to that dreadful woman's moaning.' She tilted her head slightly. 'Do you know she was trying to raise an official complaint? Said her daughter might catch MRSA—'

'I can imagine.'

'Frightful woman.' Yule stared up at the ceiling, then down again. 'Can Sister get the bed back?'

'If you've finished the tests, I don't really care what you do with it.' Hunter opened his notebook. 'So, have you?'

Yule opened a paper file on her desk, a temple form covered in hieroglyphics. 'Sadly, young Miss Ferguson has no traces of semen.'

Jain glowered over at Hunter. 'Sadly?'

'You know what I mean.' Yule raised a knobbly finger, barely any fat on it. Teeth marks dug in around the knuckle. 'But I did find what I'd suggest are telltale signs of abuse. Bruising on her arms and legs. And I'd say the girl's ... demeanour shows severe mental trauma. Not to mention her weight. Definite candidate for anorexia. And I know there can be multiple causes...'

Hunter was struggling to scribble it all down.

Jain glared at the doctor. 'So we've got no evidence the stepfather has been abusing her?'

'That ship has sailed, I'm afraid.' Yule raised a shoulder. 'No way to tell without a positive on the rape kit. Though there are deformations in her vagina consistent with intercourse.'

Jain's smile was as quick as it was triumphant. 'That sounds a lot like evidence.'

Hold your horses...

Hunter let out a groan. 'She's got a boyfriend.'

'Oh, sweet Jesus...' Jain shut her notebook and folded her arms. 'I thought Stephanie told her mother he'd been doing this to her for a while?'

Hunter nodded. 'Probably since she was fifteen.'

'Well, that's certainly consistent with what I'm seeing here.' Yule rummaged through the report on her desk. 'But, the sad fact is, there's just no way of knowing who's been abusing her. Or even if it was abuse. The secondary bruising could be from school bullying, say.'

Or it could be from her stepfather holding her down on a bed and raping her.

'Anyway, Constable, I'm finished with her.' Yule held out her hand. 'She *bit* me, can you see?'

Jain sat back, nodding as she reopened her notebook. 'Is it worth checking the stepfather for bite marks?'

Yule clicked her tongue as she thought it through. 'That's not a bad idea. Better still, the duty doctor at whichever station you're based in would be able to perform that test. I can, of course, validate the outcome.'

'Appreciate it.' Jain produced a business card from a flap at the back of her notebook. 'Okay, can you send the report through to me? I'm sure I'll have a lot of follow-up questions.'

'I don't doubt it.'

7

'And, for a stepfather, it's a Schedule 1 Offence if she's under twenty-one. She's *sixteen*.' Hunter held open the door and let Jain head through first. 'So what do you think?'

'I've not even seen the girl, so how can I say anything?' Jain sashayed through the door, her short heels clicking off the floor and echoing around the bare walls. 'What do we know about this boyfriend?'

'Mother says he's older. Got the impression it was more than a couple of years.'

'Interesting. So he could be the one abusing her?'

'Could be. Or nobody could be.'

Jain stopped in the corridor outside a room with a pair of women hugging and crying. 'What do you mean?'

'What if the ... deformations are from rough sex. What if she's trying to frame her stepdad.' Hunter traced a line around his wrists. 'The mother's got bruises there. If he's beating her mother...?'

Jain blew air up her face, then set off. 'Just chaperone me back to your boss and we'll see what's what.'

'Right.' Hunter led her down the hallway and took the left-hand fork. 'So, you enjoy the SO unit?'

'Interesting work, plus I got made full DS a couple of months back.'

'Congratulations.'

'Thanks.' Jain turned the corner into another generic corridor, which seemed to go on forever. 'Long time since we were wet behind the ears and in uniform.' She grimaced. 'Sorry, no offence.'

'Aye, none taken.'

Well, not too much... though I wasn't wet behind the ears to start with.

Still no sign of McNeill or Lauren.

Jain waved a hand at Finlay, his thumbs bashing at the screen like he was back at his game. 'Fin been your partner long?'

'Couple of years. Feels more like a pet sometimes.' Hunter marched up and clapped Finlay on the shoulder. 'Wakey, wakey.'

Finlay slowly turned round, palming his phone like a street magician. 'Craig.'

'Sarge back?'

'Not yet. Still yakking with Bu— Sorry, Sharon.' Finlay gave a nod to Jain. 'Christ, Chantal Jain. How's tricks?'

'Fine, Compo. How's your bollock?'

Finlay gurned. 'Still get more use out of it than most with two.'

Hunter did a double-take. 'Compo? What?'

'You don't know?' Jain leaned in close. 'Finlay and I used to walk the streets together. Got hooked into a drug raid in Pilton. Your partner here took a bullet. Lost a ball. Made a killing in the compo, hence the name.'

Hunter frowned at him. 'You never told me that.'

'Aye, and put up with all the bloody jokes?' Finlay shrunk down in his chair. '1pac Shakur? Hitler?' He shook his head. 'Heard them all mate.'

Hunter crouched low. 'Why are you still working with all that money?'

'What—'

'Excuse me?' An overweight woman stood just down the corridor, bobbed hair flapping around as she tossed her head about. She carried a tote bag stuffed with clothes. 'I'm looking for PC Sinclair.'

Finlay got to his feet, frowning. 'Are you Mrs Ferguson's pal?'

'Neighbour, aye. Ailsa Crichton. I've come home from work especially.' She held up the cream bag. 'Pauline asked me to get some clothes for Stephanie.'

'Thanks for that.' Jain took the bag with a nod. 'Can you wait with PC Sinclair here? I'll check with my superior and keep you apprised of the situation, Mrs Crichton.'

Ailsa grabbed hold of Jain's suit jacket. 'It's just, I need to get back to work?'

'And I'll see what the story is.'

'Great.' Ailsa collapsed onto the chair next to Finlay, her short skirt riding up to reveal an extra inch of her flabby thighs. 'Do you know how much they charge for parking here?'

'We'll be as quick as we can.' Jain gestured at Hunter to go first.

He opened the door and slowly entered Stephanie's room. The window was open a crack, letting in a strong breeze. Had lost a fair few degrees in that time.

Stephanie was sitting up, her mother whispering into her ear and trying to stroke her back. Looked like she was going to get elbowed in the face.

What did I bloody tell her about speaking to the girl?

Hunter dumped the bag on the edge of the bed, making them jump enough to break apart their huddle. 'Here's some clothes for you, Stephanie. And Mrs Crichton's here to take you home.'

'Thank Christ for that.' Pauline picked up the bag. 'So we can get home now?'

'You can.'

'You've got all the evidence you need?' Stephanie looked up at that, eyebrows arching above eyes that burned with the same fire as those of her mother. The young girl coughed. 'You're going to get him, right?'

'It's not as straightforward as that.' Hunter raised his hands, trying to dampen the wildfire. He nodded over at Jain. 'DS Jain here will—'

'He *raped* me!' Stephanie kneaded her temples, fresh tears streaking down her cheeks. 'Nooooo...'

'There, there. It'll be all right, toots.' Pauline started rubbing her daughter's arms, not getting pushed back this time. Her glare left blisters on Hunter's determination to catch the animal that had broken this child. 'What did the doctor say?'

'Well, she's found no evidence. Like I said, DS Jain—'

'Bloody doctors.' Pauline kept glaring at Hunter. 'Don't know their arses from their elbows.'

'DS Jain will be taking over from me and Sergeant Reid.' Hunter stepped back, trying to distance himself. 'She works for the Police Scotland Sexual Offences Unit.'

Chantal crouched down between Hunter and Stephanie. 'We'll need time with yourself, Mrs Fer—'

'*Pauline.*'

'Of course. And with Stephanie. We'll come round later this evening to take her statement, if that's okay?'

Pauline scowled at Hunter. 'Here, how could they not find anything?'

Hunter glanced at Jain, who seemed like she was already regretting taking this case on. Bracing himself, he looked back at Pauline.

'The doctor hoped some evidence would remain from the last contact, but that's not the case.'

'You lying bastard!' Pauline was on her feet, prodding her nails into Hunter's chest. Would've hurt if he hadn't been wearing his stab-proof. 'You should've found his spunk! You lot should—'

'Mum...'

'—ashamed of yourselves, you—'

'Mum.'

'—ing bunch of cu—'

'Mum!'

Pauline jerked round, blinking hard at her daughter, now in floods of tears. 'Christ, Stephanie.' She spun back around and jabbed a finger charged with blame first at Hunter, then at her girl. 'See what you've made me do now?'

No. No way is this my fault.

Hunter crouched down by the girl. 'Stephanie, I need your help here, okay? The doctor couldn't find any physical direct evidence to prove what's been happening to you.'

She screwed her eyes tight. 'What?'

'When was the last time—'

'Is he going to get off with this?'

'Stephanie, when was the last time your stepfather abused you?'

She stared down at the floor. 'Yesterday. Last night.'

Terrific...

Hunter tried to cover another sigh. Failed, judging by her expression. 'Stephanie, you said it was this morning.'

Her eyes dropped to the floor. 'It was last night, late. I was in my room. He... He came in and... He...' She curled up into her ball again. 'He grabbed my arms and...' She tailed off, eyes clamped shut.

'You see what you're doing to my girl, you fu—'

'Stop!' Jain got between them. 'Let's park this for now, okay? I suggest we get you guys home and pick up again in a few hours.'

'I'm not happy with you treating my girl as a liar.'

'Nobody's doing that.'

'Make sure you get him for this, right?' Pauline clapped Stephanie's upper arms. The girl just about hit the ceiling. 'Right, Toots, come on.' She opened the bag and took out a springy purple top and some faded jeans. 'This is your favourite, Steph.' She held up a grey hoodie. 'Want me to stay with you?'

Stephanie shook her head, much clearer than before.

Pauline put the hoodie down and smoothed it flat, like she was ironing it with her hands. 'I'll leave the clothes here and you can get dressed, okay?'

The girl mumbled something. Seemed to be assent.

Pauline kissed the top of her head. 'Don't be too long, okay?'

∽

THE FAMILY ROOM door slid open and Ailsa bumbled in carrying two Starbucks cups. 'Here you go, hen.'

Pauline tore the lid off and sucked in the stale coffee aroma. 'You're a lifesaver.' She placed it on the table and blew across the surface. 'Ailsa, thank God you're here.'

'It's okay, honey.' Ailsa wrapped a hug around Pauline. 'You poor, poor thing.'

'It's Steph I'm worried about.' Pauline pulled a chair up to the table and dropped into it, burying her head into her shoulder. 'What have I done?'

Ailsa sat next to her and crossed her legs. 'You need to cut that stoat bastard's balls off.' She narrowed her eyes at Hunter. 'Then make him eat them. Then throw away the bloody key.'

'We can't do that, I'm afraid.' Jain flashed a grin. 'Much as we might like to.'

'Aye, well you need to bloody do something!' Ailsa's whole body shook with the force of her rage, coffee splashing through the lid of her takeaway cup. 'Get that animal off the bloody streets!'

Pauline clamped her eyes tight. 'Steph...'

'Shhh.' Ailsa clasped Pauline's hand, accidentally pushing her sleeve up and revealing the bracelet of bruises. 'How could he do this to you?'

Pauline tugged the sleeve back down again, almost covering her entire hand. She locked eyes with Jain. 'Will you do him for this?'

'I'll be honest with you. There's always a chance that they get off with something like this. The right lawyer, evidence disappearing by accident.' Jain wrinkled her nose. 'What's important for you is, whatever happens, you give Stephanie your full support, okay?'

Pauline took a long slurp of coffee, grimacing as she swallowed. 'What should I do if I don't believe her?'

'In cases where children ... fabricate such stories, there's usually some other underlying issue.'

'Are you saying I'm a bad mother?'

'Nobody's saying anything like that.' You could spark a fire on Jain's flinty eyes. 'If this is a cry for help, then Stephanie needs to talk about something else.'

Another long gulp of coffee. 'There's nothing.'

'All I ask is that you make sure there's nothing.'

'Here, you.' Ailsa crumpled up her cup, the cardboard not quite complying with the intended gesture of intimidation. 'Are you saying Pauline's lying?'

'I'm keen to deal with your concerns, Mrs Crichton, just as soon as I've spoken to the mother of the victim about the potential root causes of her trauma. Thank you so much for respecting that.'

Hunter checked his watch. Five minutes up. 'I'll just check on Stephanie.'

∽

Hunter marched down the corridor, keeping perfect time as he passed the open doors. In one, a teenage boy was leaning forward, crying like a newborn as a doctor stroked his back.

Poor kid...

Hunter swung round the corner and neared on Stephanie's room.

Not again... Stupid bastard...

Finlay was rocking back and forth on the chair, like a toddler needing the toilet, his fingers and focus on his mobile. 'Come on, you twat, I've got you now. I've—'

'Finlay.' Hunter gripped his shoulder and pulled him back, his shoulder thunking off the hard plastic. 'What the hell are you doing?'

'Just waiting on the lassie.' Finlay thumbed at the door as he pocketed his phone. 'How's the mother?'

'Troublesome. Is she ready yet?'

Finlay shrugged. 'No idea, jabroni.'

'You're a complete arsehead, you know that? Every time I see you, I hear circus music. Just waiting for you to throw a bucket of glitter on me.' Hunter scowled at Finlay as he knocked on the door. 'Stephanie, it's PC Hunter. Are you ready to go?'

No response.

He knocked again. Harder this time. 'Stephanie?'

Nothing.

Hunter grabbed the cold door handle and yanked at it. Bloody thing was locked. 'No, no, no...'

A metal door grinding open, dusty heat burning at his skin. The smell of fresh leather and burnt wood. His foot kicking at the door, pushing it wide. A girl's body swinging from a rope, gently spinning. Eyes popping out of her head, her swollen tongue almost touching her chin.

Adrenaline spiked in his veins, thumped in the back of his neck.

'No, no, no.'

'What's up with you?' Finlay was stepping back, fingers crossed like he was warding off a vampire.

'She's bloody killed herself!' Hunter kicked Finlay away and booted the door. 'Stephanie! I'm coming in!' He kicked at the painted wood and forced the door off its top hinges. It stumbled open, like a Friday-night drunk outside a kebab shop. Hunter piled into the room and did a one-eighty.

The bed was empty. Her gown was half on the bed, the other half dangling down to the floor. The bag sat next to the pillow, but the clothes were gone.

Hunter raced over to the window. Ground floor, no height for a suicide.

But no sign of her either.

She'd just run off.

Hunter's shoulders slumped and he breathed again. She must have left through the door. How the hell could this happen? How could that amateur sit outside and play on his phone when…

Never mind Finlay. I shouldn't have let the girl out of my sight. Shouldn't have let her do this to herself. Put herself at risk. Again.

Traumatised, confused, vulnerable… and now alone.

Or had she been taken?

8

Hunter raced down the corridor, leaving Stephanie's room behind him, and shouted into his chest-mounted Airwave: 'PC Sinclair turned his back for a minute, Sarge.'

Lauren groaned down the line. Could just about make out her footsteps as she paced away from someone, probably McNeill. 'Was he playing that bloody game?'

Hunter cut round the corner into the main concourse. 'We need to know where she's gone.'

'Hang on, we're just by the security room.'

Hunter rested against the barrier and scanned the area, chest heaving as he tried to get his breathing back under control. A wide, blank space filled with people, some supported by zimmers, some cradling newborns. The dark musk of strong coffee just about overpowered the hospital smell.

No grey hoodies.

No tall teenage girls.

You can catch a cat, but you lose a girl. When it comes down to it, you can't do it.

He wheeled around, scanning every face in the crowd. A man looked away from his uniform, stepped aside. Hunter got up close and eyeballed him. Got something in Polish for his trouble.

'Craig, you there?'

Hunter tapped his Airwave. 'I'm at the entrance.' He started across the concourse, passing the crowded newsagents and bumping into a man in a suit. 'You got anything yet?'

'There's a camera just outside her room.' Lauren spoke in a low voice, like she was trying to keep a lid on her rage. 'She just bloody sneaked past Sinclair. Can you believe it? Locked the door behind her, as well! He's going to pay—'

'Where did she go?'

'Right.' Lauren paused to clear her throat. 'She went down the corridor away from her room, then doubled back to the main hall. Just walked out of the front door.'

'Cheers, Sarge.' Hunter sprinted across the foyer and through the entrance into the car park, his rattling vest not even close to silencing his self-criticism. He trotted to a stop among the rows of parked vehicles, searching for a grey hoodie or a purple top between the multicolour metal.

Come on, come on. Where are you?

Trying to spot a teenaged girl in a hoodie was like identifying a gambler in a police canteen. None of the twenty-odd girls cleared six foot, let alone Stephanie's towering height.

'Any idea where she went next, Sarge?'

Rows and rows of cars, seemed like every make and model ever sold. A yellow van flashed on its reverse lights and slipped back into one of the few empty spaces. Back on the main road, a grey Peugeot with a matching roof box slalomed between two buses and powered past, a woman on the back seat huffing and puffing.

'There's a blind spot outside, Craig.'

What's the point in monitoring everyone's bloody movements if you can still lose people you need to track?

The massive expanse of the hospital sprawled behind him, hordes of smokers lining the designated area. Up on the hill in the distance, the last few towers of Niddrie stood like squat sentries, guarding the city's horizon.

Where would she go?

Hunter darted over to the bus area, the road closed off to cars and vans. A 49 heading for Rosewell crawled out from the stop, leaving just two old ladies dressed for winter in the shelter. He slid to a halt on the crossing and waved his hands in front of the bus.

It jerked to a halt, the driver's head almost connecting with the glass as he rocked forward in his seat.

Hunter mouthed an apology and skipped round to the hissing door, jamming himself between the railings and the bus. 'I'm looking for a girl. She's sixteen, tall.' He held a hand above his head.

The driver was already shaking his head. 'Sorry, pal. Just two old wifies and a dar— an ethnic gentleman.'

'Right.' Hunter stepped back and let the bus start up again. He swung around — just a steady stream of cars and vans coming in —

and stormed over to the bus stop. The two old women beamed at him like he was a cross between George Clooney and Jesus. 'I'm looking for a teenage girl. Sixteen, tall, dark hair.'

'I bet you are, son.' The woman on the left nudged her pal. 'Mary here's looking for John Lennon in his—'

Jesus wept...

Hunter spun around, trying to get a better view. 'This is important. You've not seen her?'

'Sorry, son.'

'Cheers.' Hunter stomped away from them, fists clenched. The next stop was empty, as were the small grassy hills behind.

Another bus revved over the crossing, aiming for one of the three stops on the far side.

A grey hoodie darted between two tall vans.

Hunter held his cap tight to his head and bombed over the road.

The hoodie paced towards the bus, thumbs sticking through straps in a green backpack.

Hunter pushed through a crowd of old men and grabbed an arm. 'Excuse me, miss.'

The hood twisted round. A young man scowled out, all piercings and thick stubble. '*Miss?*'

'Sorry, I've got the wrong person.' Hunter let him go and took a few steps back into clear space away from bus queues. He stabbed a finger on his Airwave, gaze drifting around. 'PC Hunter to PC Sinclair. Over.'

'Receiving, over.'

'I've drawn a blank at the front. Got anything?'

'Not a sausage, big ma—'

A hand gripped Hunter's bicep, tightening around the muscle. Bloody sore. He swung round.

Sharon McNeill stood there, eyebrows to the heavens, bunching up the skin on her forehead. 'Well?'

'Got to go, Finlay.' Hunter killed the Airwave call and gave McNeill a grim smile. 'Sorry, ma'am. There's no sign of her out here.'

Lauren was back at the turning, looking like she was going to strangle someone. Someone with the surname Sinclair.

'We checked the rear entrance. Nothing there, either.' McNeill let out a sigh and leaned against an empty bus stop. 'This is a disaster.'

'She can't just have disappeared, ma'am.'

McNeill raised her eyebrows even higher. 'You think I don't know that, Constable?'

'No, ma'am. Sorry.'

Lauren got between them, eyes like headlights on full beam. 'We can do all the arse-kicking we want later, ma'am, but right now, we need to find the girl.'

'Don't disagree.' McNeill twisted her neck to take in the full panorama of the car park. 'We can discuss your officer's failings at a later point.'

'She's not in immediate danger.' Hunter stuck his thumbs in his vest. Felt better that way. 'Her stepfather's in custody.'

'At least you're doing something right, I suppose.' McNeill did a slow one eighty across the car park. 'Assuming he's not got an army of his mates out putting frighteners into Steph.'

'Terrific.' Hunter tightened his grip around the stab-proof vest straps and huffed out a sharp breath. 'Hadn't thought of that.'

'Before we start running around like blue-arsed flies, I want to be abundantly clear.' McNeill locked eyes with Lauren. 'Most disappearances are resolved within forty-eight hours. I don't think this is a usual case.'

'Me neither.' Hunter did another visual sweep of the terrain, still nothing. 'I was worried she'd killed herself. Still am.'

McNeill's eyes burnt into Hunter, like he knew where she'd gone. 'Why?'

'Only thing I can think of is she got freaked out by us telling her mother that we had no physical evidence.'

'So she thought her stepfather would get off?' McNeill rubbed bony fingers into her eyes. 'Sure that's all?'

'I can't thin—'

'That's all for now.' Lauren's turn to grab Hunter's arm. He felt like a male stripper at a hen do. Not for the first time. 'We need a plan of attack here. DI McNeill, as ranking officer, do you—'

'No need to be sarcastic, Sergeant.' McNeill nodded at DS Jain who was approaching from the hospital entrance. 'First things first, Lauren. You and I are going to square this off with DI Buchan and our superiors. We're going to need budget and support to find this girl.'

'Agreed.'

'Next.' McNeill raised her hand and twirled her finger through a quick three sixty. 'I want someone getting hold of the CCTV round the hospital. Council should have it.'

'I'll get Finlay Sinclair on that.' Lauren unclipped her Airwave from her jacket. 'I've got a unit heading to the house, but that's assuming she'll go back there.'

'Good work.'

'I've got another six units on their way here, but she's got at least five minutes on us.'

'Okay, okay.' McNeill stopped by Jain and nodded at Hunter.

'Chantal, can you and PC Hunter have a word with the mother and see if she's got any friends we can chase up?'

∽

THE AIRWAVE CRACKLED AGAIN. 'That's still a negative from the house, Sergeant. Over.'

'Okay, thanks.' Jain stopped outside the family room and pocketed her Airwave. Her turn to grip Hunter's bicep. *Just need to stick a pair of socks down the front of some sequinned budgie smugglers, find a stage, get an agent. At this rate, I'll be quitting the day job in...* She stared straight into his eyes. 'I'm leading here, okay?'

Hunter shrugged her off. 'You're the Sergeant.'

Jain took a step back and planted her fists on her hips, glaring at him like an Exocet about to go off. 'Right...' She opened the door and entered, a remorseful smile plastered on her face. 'I'm afraid we've got some ba—'

'I know she's run off.' Pauline was slumped at the table, brushing her hands through her hair. 'What I want to know is what the hell you lot are doing to find her? Eh?'

Jain stood in the space between Pauline and Ailsa, hands deep in her pockets. 'We're doing everything we can, Mrs Ferguson.'

'Don't. Call. Me. That!'

'Sorry.' Jain winced, her smile slipping for a few seconds. 'We've got four units—'

'How could you let this happen?'

Ailsa patted her arm. 'Shhhh, it's okay, Pauline.' Her hair gleamed in the light, piggy eyes darting between Jain and Hunter. 'They'll find her.' She looked at Hunter, more of a threat than a glance. 'Right?'

'Of course we will.' Jain rubbed her hands together. 'Our best officers are out looking for her.'

'You need to find her. She's only a lassie!' Ailsa's gaze settled on Jain, like she'd spotted her for the first time. 'Who are you, by the way?'

'Detective Sergeant Chantal Jain, ma'am.'

'So this is your fault?'

'I'm accepting full responsibility, yes. We're doing everything we can to find Mrs F— to find Stephanie.' Jain crouched near the coffee table, locking eyes with Pauline. 'Do you have any idea why Stephanie might've run away?'

'Are you stupid?' Pauline sniffed, then ran the back of her hand across her nose. 'It's this stuff with Doug.'

'Mr Ferguson's in custody just now, so he's no threat to her.' Hunter watched Pauline for any signs. Her hands shook like an arthritic alcoholic, making her brass bangle rattle. 'Has she ever done anything like this before?'

'She's a good girl.'

'Is it possible Stephanie would contemplate suicide?'

'What? Suicide? Steph?'

'Is it possible?'

Pauline folded her arms tight across her chest, her sleeves rolling up. 'Not possible.'

'Are you sure there's nothing else that could've—?'

'What?' Pauline's eyes were back on fire. Seemed like an inferno was raging in her mind. 'It's this shite with Doug, you stupid Pa—'

Jain jolted to her feet and gripped Pauline's wrist. 'Be careful what you say.'

Pauline pushed her hand away. 'I'm sorry, all right? This is just…' She exhaled.

Jain gestured at her bare wrist, where the ring of purple bruises was still coiling round her skin. 'Where did you get those bruises?'

Pauline tugged her sleeve down and stared at her painted nails. 'I got my hand jammed in a door…'

Like I believe that. Last time she said it was her daughter.

Hunter clenched his jaw and switched his gaze to Ailsa. 'Did you notice anything unusual when you arrived?'

'Didn't see nothing. Well, other than that cop pissing about on his phone.'

Jain closed her eyes. 'When was this?'

'Just when I turned up. That doctor was in with Steph and he was playing a game.'

'Did you see anyone outside?' Jain opened her eyes again. 'Anyone you might've recognised from your street? Or school, maybe.'

'Lots of people. It's a big place. The car park's full…' Ailsa shook her head and sighed. 'Here, I'm still paying through the bloody nose for parking as it is…'

Hunter got between the two women. 'Do you know where she could've gone?'

Pauline grabbed a tight hold of Ailsa's arm. 'What about Neil?'

Jain's thin eyebrow coiled up, lining her forehead. 'Neil's the boyfriend, right?'

Hunter tried for a reassuring nod. Didn't look like it worked. 'He's on our radar. We've got a unit trying to pick him up just now.'

'Good work.' Jain nodded at Hunter, her eyes saying "Lying bastard". She shifted her glare to Pauline. 'Does Stephanie have any close friends?'

'The only one I can think of is this lassie called Olivia Pearce.' Pauline started fidgeting with a tissue, kneading the damp paper over and over. 'Steph does Maths coaching with her every Tuesday. Supposed to be there tonight.'

Not much, but worth a try.

'Have you got an address for her?'

9

'Come on, come on.' Hunter kicked down to second and blared past the queuing traffic on Duddingston Road, just a single white Range Rover sticking its arse out into the road. He swerved round it, getting a honk and a pair of palms in response.

Cheeky bastard.

'Going to slow down a bit?'

Hunter glanced over at Jain, pouting like she was on the cover of Vogue. 'Seriously?'

'Seriously. This isn't a blues and twos situation.' She hit a key on her Airwave and held it out, static crackling. 'Control, this is DS Chantal Jain. Any movement at the house in Mountcastle?'

'Still a negative.'

'Thought so.' She rolled her eyes at Hunter. Felt like the ice was cracking, if only a fraction. 'Can I get an update on the whereabouts of Neil Alexander?'

'Still struggling with that, lass. You any idea how many Neil Alexanders there are in Edinburgh? Got units out at all five teenagers with that name, both spellings of Neil. Want me to get onto the adults?'

'No, let's leave it at that for now. Thanks again.' She pocketed her Airwave. 'Bloody useless.'

Hunter bumped over a sleeping policeman by the High School's old tower, nine storeys of sixties hell. 'My alma mater there.'

Jain looked up from her Airwave. 'Your what?'

'I grew up here. Few streets over.'

'Right. I'm a Corstorphine girl. Much of a muchness, right?'

'Too right.' Hunter swerved round the bend, getting a clear run at the lights and powering under the railway bridge, his speed deterring the Lexus from chancing it. 'Building a replacement up by the Jewel.' He thumbed to the right, past the mansions of Brighton Place, all neatly laid out in a half-moon. 'Be very strange—'

'Craig.' Jain stabbed her finger on the screen of her Airwave and dumped it on the dashboard. 'Give me peace for a minute, would you?'

Hunter sprayed through the wave of traffic thinning out like the Red Sea. 'Sorry, Sarge.'

Jain let out a sigh as he swung right onto Portobello High Street, her thumbs beating an impatient rhythm on the screen of her personal mobile. 'You don't have to Sarge me.'

'Is Chantal okay?'

'It's fine.'

'Okay, then. Sorry, Chantal.' Hunter took the next left, a long row of villas blocked off from Portobello promenade by a row of Victorian flats overlooking the sea.

A short red-haired man walked hand-in-hand with a woman who was at least another foot shorter. Looked like a woman, anyway.

Hunter trundled down the road and pulled in on a free space. 'Here we go.'

Jain got out of the car first, stuffing her phone into her pocket.

Hunter joined her on the pavement, the harsh wind blowing sand in his eyes as he stuck his cap on. 'Christ, you forget how windy it is here.'

'I don't.' Jain looked back up the street, frowning at a drum kit in a lower-ground window. She wandered over to the flat door and knocked. 'And I'm still leading, okay?'

The door creaked open and a short girl looked out. Bookish, thick glasses, the same purple gymslip Stephanie had worn earlier. Her eyes flicked over to Hunter's uniform. 'Aye?'

'DS Chantal Jain and Constable Craig Hunter.' Jain moved up to the second-top step, warrant card out. Face like she meant business. 'We're looking for an Olivia Pearce.'

The girl swallowed. 'That's me.'

Jain nodded and climbed the last step. 'Can we come in?'

'What's this about?'

'We need to do this inside, if that's okay?'

'Aye, sure.' Olivia led through a dark hall to an even darker kitchen. Yellow melamine cabinets with brass handles. Pots and pans hung from an extractor housing. She jumped up and sat on the edge of the wooden worktop. Swung her legs back and forth.

A large wooden dining table sat in the middle of the room, covered in jotters and textbooks. Looked like at least two people working there. She shrugged and started stacking up her papers.

'Are your parents in?'

'Be back home soon.'

'Okay, Olivia, we're looking for Stephanie Ferguson.' Hunter took the seat nearest the door. Had a slight wobble to it. 'Have you seen her today?'

'Saw Steph this morning. She wasn't at school this afternoon, though.'

'That happen a lot?'

'Not with Steph. Her mum's a nightmare. She'd kill her if she bunked off school.' Olivia held up her smartphone, pretty much the same model Finlay had been playing with. 'I sent her a Facebook message. Got nothing back.'

'You were close with her, right?'

'Why'd you say "were"?' Olivia's legs stopped kicking. 'Has something happened?'

'I mean *are*.' Hunter smiled at the girl. 'You *are* close, right?'

Olivia made a love heart shape with her fingers and thumbs. 'Pretty much BFFs.'

'So she talked to you about stuff, right?'

'Totes. Justin Bieber, though he's gone off him. One Direction.' She rolled her eyes. 'Kim Kardashian.'

'I meant personal stuff.'

'Isn't that personal?'

'Look, she ran away this afternoon.' Hunter rested his elbows on the wood and cracked his knuckles. 'Do you have any idea where she'd go?'

Olivia nudged her glasses up her nose. 'Home?'

'She's not there.'

A toilet flushed and a door opened off the hall. Footsteps marched through, stopping dead at the kitchen door. A plump woman in her late twenties frowned at Hunter, then at Jain. Dark hair tied in a ponytail, chunky glasses filling her face. 'What's going on, Olivia?'

'Ms Tait, the police are looking for Steph.'

Jain flipped open her warrant card and slid it across the table. 'I'm DS Jain and this is Constable Hunter.'

'Call me Gaynor.' She didn't even look at the card, just dropped onto the chair opposite, the metal crunching. She patted Olivia on the arm. 'Can you make us all a cup of tea?'

'Aye, sure.'

Gaynor watched Olivia trudge over to the sink and start filling the kettle. Eyes back on Jain, leaning in close. 'What's happened to Stephanie?'

'She's run away.'

'That explains why she didn't turn up tonight...' Gaynor raised an eyebrow as she put a smartphone in her handbag. She waved around at the mess on the table. 'I'm supposed to be coaching Olivia and Stephanie some Maths on the side. Earn a few extra quid. Got a mortgage to pay, you know?'

Hunter took the nod from Jain as instruction to lead. 'How well do you know Stephanie?'

'Hard to say. How well can you really know kids these days?' Gaynor's eyebrows flicked up as the tap hissed on in the background. 'I'm her registration teacher. Last time I saw her was this morning.' She frowned, her teeth grinding over her bottom lip. 'I got a note from the school office saying she'd not returned from lunch. They said they were dealing with it, though.'

Hunter looked out of the tall windows at the back, couldn't avoid the thousand yard stare at the long beach leading out to the sea. When Jain cleared her throat, he refocused his attention on Gaynor. 'You haven't received a text from her or anything?'

'Like I said, we weren't that close. Kids these days are always on their phones, but it's not something I get involved in.'

'Did she ever confide in you about anything?'

Gaynor swallowed, gaze flashing between the two of them. 'Anything in particular?'

Jain crunched forward in her chair. 'Stephanie told her mother her stepfather's been abusing her.'

'Dear God.' Gaynor's eyes glazed over as she lifted a trembling hand to her glasses and dropped them onto the table. The kettle started hissing behind them. A teaspoon clanked against a cup. 'Jesus Christ.'

'Have you noticed any signs of abuse?'

'No... Jesus.' Gaynor put her specs back on and glanced behind her at Olivia, safe in the peaceful ritual of tea preparation. 'We're trained to look for it and raise anything. And I mean *anything*. But I didn't detect anything with Steph. I would've called it in if there'd been even the slightest sign.'

Anything, three times? Code red...

Hunter cleared his throat, catching Gaynor's attention. 'Are you sure about that?'

'Why, don't you think I care?'

'I'm not saying you don't care, it's just your language... The way you phrased—'

'Look, I've had kids in abusive situations before, okay?' Gaynor spoke with her eyes closed, like she was recounting some old horror. 'I know what I'm looking for, believe me.'

Hunter stared at her for a few seconds, trying to get the measure of her. Didn't seem to be lying. Couldn't see any reason she would. 'What's Stephanie like?'

'She's a good kid. Smarter than most here. She did really well in her Standard Grades. Think she'll do okay in her Highers.'

'Just okay?'

'She's only just started.'

'But she's slipping behind?'

'Why do you say that?'

'Well, she went from really well to okay. And apparently she's in need of coaching.'

'She's not been as focused since the summer.' Gaynor rubbed her forehead. 'Shite, it's the abuse, isn't it?'

'It's supposed to have been going on for a while. Did you know?'

'Oh my God...' Gaynor brushed away a tear. 'No. No, I told you I didn't know.'

'Can you think of any other teachers she'd speak to?'

'None spring to mind.'

Hunter gave her a slow nod. 'Do you have any idea where she could've gone?'

'Sorry, none at all.'

'Is it possible Stephanie would ... consider taking her own life?'

'I don't know.' All the puff and fire seemed to drain from Gaynor as her shoulders rounded, her thick arms hanging by her sides, hands disappearing below the table edge. 'I mean, maybe. She's talked about it to me, but it seemed more like an intellectual curiosity. You don't listen to the music she does without thinking things...'

'What bands?'

'You know, Goth stuff. The Cure, Joy Division, The XX. I'm not really into it.'

'Anything sinister in it?'

'Well. There was a girl in Musselburgh killed herself a few months ago. Steph was obsessed with it, kept reading all the stuff in the paper. There was a Facebook group about it.'

'I heard about that.' Hunter let her have some space, but she was just shaking her head. 'Do you know a Neil Alexander?'

Gaynor snorted back a tear. 'Who?'

'Her boyfriend.'

She shook her head. 'Never said anything about a boyfriend.'

Olivia plonked a cup down in front of Gaynor. 'Did you say Neil?'

Jain frowned at the girl. 'Do you know him?'

'He's Steph's boyfriend.'

'You know him?'

'Just met him the once. Few of us from school went bowling with them at Fountain Park. He didn't exactly fit in.'

'He's older than you, right?'

'Yeah...'

'Have you got a number for him?'

'Mum told me not to give my phone number out.' Olivia picked up her own cup and blew on it a few times, then gave the steam a brief respite. 'But I saw him on the bus a couple of days ago.'

'So he lives near here?'

'No, he was driving it.'

10

Hunter pulled into the right-turn lane towards the bus station. Car after car after car streamed past them, a blur of commuter traffic — Leith to Portobello or Musselburgh. He glanced over at Jain. 'What are you thinking there?'

'I'm thinking suicide's a lower threat now. Probably.' Jain clinked her Airwave off the passenger window a couple of times. 'This boyfriend, though… If he's mid-twenties… A ten-year gap isn't good at that age, is it?'

'It's legal.'

'But is it moral? He's almost twice her age.' She ran a hand through her hair, fingers disappearing in the sheer black as though she'd dipped them in ink. 'You've spent more time with her than I have. Does she seem mature for her age?'

'The opposite. Seemed like a wee girl.'

'Which makes it even worse.' Jain held her Airwave out in front of her, the plastic screen flashing in the sunlight, but it didn't look like she was focusing on it. 'She might be physically old enough, but… These scumbags don't always prey on children because they're young…'

'It's because they're weak, right?' Hunter inched forward, then hit the brakes to let an old man on a mobility scooter struggle out of the bus depot. 'Same with the scum who pick on disabled people, right?'

'Scum isn't a strong enough word.' Her knuckles were bone white against the matt grey of her Airwave. 'But let's see what he's got to say first before we start lighting the torches and sharpening the pitchforks.'

Hunter trundled forward, trying not to startle the old man. 'Any update on Stephanie's whereabouts?'

She huffed. 'It's supposed to be me chivvying you along.' She released her grip on the Airwave enough to dial a number, leaving it on speaker. 'Shaz, it's Chantal. You found her yet?'

'Still a negative.' Even the sweltering heat in the car was no match for the frost in McNeill's voice. 'We've only just been taken through the CCTV for the hospital car park. Looks like she got on a bus into town.'

Hunter glared at the handset, like that would transmit down the line. 'I thought we'd checked the buses.'

McNeill paused on the line. 'Well, clearly not your finest hour. You sure you want to be a detective when you grow up?'

Charming...

Hunter hared across an oncoming Audi and squeezed through. 'Ma'am, I suggest you redirect some units to search along the bus route in both directions. She could've got off.'

'We're about seven steps ahead of you, Constable.'

'Right. Good.' Hunter pulled into a disabled bay by the entrance. 'Well, we're at the bus depot just now.'

'We've got a lead on the boyfriend.' Jain craned her neck round to glare at Hunter. 'Do you want us to ask for the bus CCTV?'

'It'll save me sending that ... what's his name? Finlay? That clown's supposed to be in charge of getting hold of it.'

'We'll see what we can do.' Jain stabbed her Airwave, killing the call. 'Do you want to stop talking over me?'

Hunter stared over at the bus depot, dark grey concrete lit up by the evening sun. A squad of mechanics worked at the few empty buses that weren't on the rush-hour commute. Gulls wheeled around between the building and the firth of Forth beyond it, the tide encroaching on what passed for seaside in the capital's suburbia. 'Sorry, Sarge.'

'Look, it's not that, it's just...' Jain let her seatbelt whiz up. 'I'm not long in this role and I've got three DCs reporting to me. None of them are exactly ideal, so the heat's on, you know?'

∽

HUNTER REPLACED his cap and walked up to the security desk. Wood and laminated steel rather than glass and chrome. He smiled at the guard, generously ignoring that the man was just about a bottle of whisky short of the full Rudolph red nose. Whippet skinny, mind. 'Constable Hunter and DS Jain. We're looking for a Neil Alexander.'

'Just a sec, officer.' The guard hammered the keys of a computer, sniffing like he'd taken a gram of coke with his Irish tea. 'Well. He's not on a route just now.'

'So he does work here?'

'Aye, lanky streak of pi— Sorry, he's a tall lad, you know. The boys call him Rodney.'

Hunter leaned on the counter. It groaned like it might give way at any second, so he stood up tall again. 'Have you got an address for him?'

'No need, son. Just spotted the boy in the canteen. C'mon, I'll show you.'

Jain raised a hand. 'I need to speak to someone about CCTV.'

'Just you wait there, darling.' The guard gave her a wink. 'I'll take you there next.'

∼

'Now, LET ME SEE.' The guard opened a glass door and waddled into a wide room, dark as a gambling den. Groups of men crowded around long tables, some holding court, others reading books or staring at phones and tablets. He squinted around the space and jabbed his finger over to the far side. 'Aye, see him over in the window?' A tall man hunched over a paperback. 'That's him.'

'Thanks.' Hunter nodded at him and caught the guard's eye as he made for the exit. 'What's he like?' He waved his fingers between them and gave a conspiratorial grin. 'Just between us, you know?'

'Like I say, lanky streak of piss. Harmless, like.'

'Ever talk about his girlfriend?'

'Well, I never.' The guard's eyes widened. 'Thought he was a horse's hoof.' He shrugged and wandered back the way they'd come. 'That's a bet I'm not owning up to...'

Charming bastard...

Hunter strode through the space, conversations dying as he passed, nervous eyes sticking on him like dog shit. He stopped by the window table. 'Neil Alexander?'

'That's me.' Neil didn't look a day over twenty. Had the air of an art-school dropout — Heroin-thin, his dark hair swept over in a lank fringe, hoops in the top of his left ear. He glanced up, still chewing a mouthful of sandwich, and went back to his book. *"Postcapitalism"* by Paul Mason. Whatever that was. Whoever that was. 'Can I help, officer?'

'Constable Craig Hunter.' He sat opposite and picked up a sachet of sugar, started tossing it in the air. 'Need to have a word about young Stephanie.'

Neil reached for a plastic cup of water and took a sip.

That's how he's playing it, is it?

Hunter took out his notebook and turned to a fresh page. 'You do know one Stephanie Ferguson of Mount—'

'Of course I know her.' Neil dropped his sandwich in the tub and brushed flour off his fingers. 'Is she okay?'

'Are you her boyfriend?'

Neil carefully licked the tip of his left forefinger. 'What's happened to her?'

'Are you her boyfriend?'

'Fine, I am.'

'Have you spoken to her today?'

Neil gave a slight shake of his head. 'Last saw her on Saturday night. We went to the Filmhouse.'

Hunter raised his eyebrows. 'The Filmhouse?'

'You think it's funny that a young woman should enjoy going to an arthouse cinema?'

Woman?

Hunter flashed a grin. 'I'm sure you'd pass for her dad if she ever wanted to see a PG film, right?'

Neil ran the nail of his pinky through his canine teeth, followed it up with his tongue. 'What's this about?'

'Have you heard from her today? Texts, emails, Facebook messages, anything like that?'

'I'm not into all that stuff.' Neil held up his book. 'I'm a reader. Biographies, political books. I like to educate myself, keep my brain in shape.' He tapped a finger against his temple. 'I only use Facebook to see photos of my nieces and nephews.'

Hopefully fully clothed...

Hunter picked up another sachet of sugar, returning the other one to the jar. 'You don't have kids of your own?'

'Never had the time.' Neil sat up tall and cracked his neck. 'Anyway, being a bus driver suits me. It's great for thinking. The pay's okay, as well.'

Must be a good half-foot taller than me, though probably weighed a lot less.

'Thinking, right.' Hunter slouched back in his chair and took in the place. Ten pairs of eyes discovering the endless wonders of the cafeteria ceiling. He focused on Neil again, eyes narrow. 'Stephanie's gone missing.'

'Shite, what?'

'Have you got any idea where Stephanie could be?'

'None at all.' Neil stuck a bookmark in his paperback and carefully shut it, like he didn't want to crack the spine. 'What's happened?'

Hunter made a couple of notes, took his time doing it. He sat up and gripped the edge of the table. 'Mr Alexander, is she in your flat?'

Neil raised his hands, twisted his head to the side. He seemed to lose a few inches in height. Obviously been in a defensive position a few times. 'What? No, of course not.'

Hunter frowned. 'Does she have a key?'

'We're in a trusting relationship.'

'So I wouldn't find her if I went round there just now?'

'Look, if she's missing, then I share your concern.' Neil placed his hands palm down on the table. 'You're welcome to come with me to see if she's gone there.'

11

Hunter followed Neil up yet another King's Road stairwell, reeking of soiled newspapers and wet dog. The red paint was chipped and rolling off, coiling up at the corners. Could use the place as a kiln.

Neil stepped aside as a dog trotted down the stairs, soaked through.

'Come back here, Alfie!' An old man trundled down, carrying a faded beach towel and a dog lead. He did a double-take at Hunter's uniform as he passed.

Neil led up, his desert boots slapping against the puddles on the red staircase. 'Just in here.' He twisted his key in the lock and nudged the door open with his foot.

Jain trudged up behind them, just finishing a phone call. 'They're sending it over now, Shaz. Get Elvis on it, if you can.' A flick of her eyebrows let Hunter know he was in charge.

'Wait there, Mr Alexander.' Hunter placed a hand just in front of Neil's chest and entered the flat, happy to get away from the stink. 'Stephanie?'

His words echoed around the hall. It was rammed with books, floor-to-ceiling shelves lining both sides. Barely enough space to get through, just a thin strip of pale laminate flooring. Just like he'd said — Philosophy, left-wing politics, economics, popular science.

Enough to start up a bookshop.

Enough to start Amazon.

'Stephanie? It's the police!' Hunter looked around, already with a good idea of the flat's layout. The living room door stood open to the left, next to a closed door at the back — the bedroom, most likely. Another two doors reeled off — kitchen and bathroom. 'Stephanie?'

Still nothing.

Hunter opened the living room door and stepped inside. He heard breathing from somewhere. 'Stephanie?'

A ginger blur flew out from under a groaning bookshelf and tangled up around his legs. He caught his feet together and fell forward, just catching himself on a bookcase. Thing just about toppled over, a couple of books flying down from the top.

The cat swished around his ankles, rubbing its neck against his shin and calf.

Flirtatious little rascal. Clearly hungry.

Hunter flicked the light switch on and took a good look. Not really anywhere for her to hide in there. He walked over to the front window overlooking King's Road. A couple of neds were giving his squad car the once over. He had a clear view back to the hall as the cat scampered out. The room had a sofa bed and more bookshelves.

Nowhere to hide in there either.

He went back into the hall and opened the bedroom door. The cat sprawled on the bed like it owned the place. A pile of books lay beside the unmade bed, on the verge of tottering over. More bookshelves filled the wall opposite the bed, though it looked like fiction this time.

A laptop sat on a desk at the window, unmoved by the cracking view across the bus depot. Or perhaps it resented having to look at Fife, the Kingdom of boredom on the other side of the water. Anyway, a few speedboats were out on the Forth in the evening sun, and the droning engine noise brought him back to the here and now.

Stephanie wasn't there.

Back in the hall, he tried the third door. The bathroom, bright light gleaming through the glass. He opened the shower cubicle — empty. The tiles were bone dry.

Again, nowhere to hide.

The last door led to a small kitchen. The left half was filled with coffee-making equipment, an AeroPress sitting in front of a posh espresso machine and a wooden hand grinder. The cat darted through and started nibbling at an open sack of coffee beans lying in the space under the counter.

Hunter opened the cabinets and the washing machine door — all empty, certainly nothing big enough for a tall teenager to hide in.

So she wasn't there.

Bollocks.

Hunter went back to the flat door, where Jain's glower was just about burning holes into Neil's head. 'In you come, sir.'

'Very kind of you.' Neil thumped through to the living room, pausing halfway to scoop up the squirming cat.

Hunter stayed by the door, letting Jain wander around the rest of the place. 'Do you own this flat, sir?'

Neil collapsed on the sofa bed, surrounded by his crowded bookshelves, and started stroking the cat's long fur. 'Inherited it three years ago.' He tickled the cat, starting up a crackle of purring. 'When my folks died.'

'I'm sorry to hear that, sir.' Hunter waved around the room. 'I trust you spent a fair chunk of that inheritance on books?'

'Not as much as you'd think.' Neil stopped stroking as the cat lay down. He picked it up and dropped it at his side, then wandered over to the window, jangling keys in his pocket. 'So do you believe me now?'

Hunter tried to focus on his face, lost in the bright backlight. 'Did Stephanie ever talk to you about her stepfather?'

'A bit.' Neil ran a hand through his greasy hair and started bunching it up. 'Didn't have a good word to say about him.'

'She told her mother he'd been abusing her.'

Neil drummed his fingers on the window ledge behind him. 'Jesus...'

'You knew about this, didn't you?'

He collapsed against the glass. 'I said she could move in here.'

'You didn't think to call the police?'

'Look, I tried to persuade Steph to go to you. I couldn't force her, though.' Neil crouched down to stroke the cat at his feet. 'She thought her mum might not believe her and, even if she did, that she wouldn't do anything about it.'

'Why?'

'Pauline loves Doug. Steph said this would break her. Didn't want to have to make her choose.' Neil put his hand back in his pocket, leaving a clump of hair standing tall at the back. 'I just wanted to love her and help her get over it. I'm glad she's done this.' He shook his head, the hair flopping over. 'She's a smart woman, knows her—'

'She's *sixteen*.'

'Calm the beans, man.' Neil raised his hands, eyes wide. 'Steph's old enough to know her own mind. You seem to think she's a wee lassie. She's not. Reads a lot, you know. Smart stuff, too. She's no idiot.'

'How old are you, Mr Alexander?'

Neil folded his arms. 'Twenty-seven.'

Eleven year gap... Dear god.

Hunter tried to keep his face straight as he saw his disgust mirrored in Jain's face.

'Look, we haven't had sex, if that's what you're thinking, okay? We've not been going out that long. Just a few months.' Neil held up his hands. 'And she was sixteen when we met.'

Methinks the lady doth protest too much...

'Did Stephanie ever talk about suicide, anything like that?'

Neil nudged the swarming cat away with his shoe. He started scratching at his neck, like he'd just discovered a welt of acne there. 'Never explicitly.'

'What's that supposed to mean?' Jain stepped over to the window, getting close to Neil. 'She's talked about killing herself or she's not. Which one is it?'

'She's got scars.' Neil ran a shaking hand up his right forearm, then chopped at it like he was a TV chef slicing carrots. 'Very slight cuts up and down the arm. Those things are usually a sign, right?'

'But she never talked about suicide?'

'I asked her about it, but she didn't want to discuss it.' Neil shrugged. 'Not yet, anyway.'

'She ever mention running away?'

'Not to me.'

Jain took a look around the room and picked up a paperback from the windowsill. 'Where is she, Mr Alexander?'

'I've already told your colleague here, I don't know where she is.'

Jain stepped over to the bookshelf just past Neil, brushing his arm as she put the book back. 'If you know anything about where she—'

'You'll what? You'll abuse my civil rights?' Neil leaned back and shook his head. 'Forget it.'

Here we go...

Hunter stepped into the room and started narrowing the gap between them, fists clenched. 'What did you think when she told you about Doug Ferguson?'

Neil's hands went up. 'You're getting nothing out of me.'

'You never thought of battering him because of what he'd done to your girlfriend? Is still doing to her, if she's telling the truth? Did you never want to sort the matter out yourself? Save your damsel in distress? Be her knight in shining armour? Maybe cut the old bastard's cock off?'

'Me?' Neil flashed a grin at Hunter, his teeth little yellow fangs. 'I'm a lover not a fighter.'

Hunter raised his eyebrows and stopped his advance. 'Thought you didn't have sex—'

'Shite, sorry. You've wound me up. I get really nervous about stuff like this.' Neil huffed as he gestured at a clock on the wall, ticking away in the quiet flat. 'Listen, I want to help. Sorry, I've just had a long day at work. Sitting in a hot bus all afternoon isn't fun.'

'Did you ever think of hurting Mr Ferguson?'

'No way.'

'And you didn't think of going to the police?'

'Steph and I talked about it. She was coming round to it, maybe, but if I'd gone off on my own...' Neil exhaled slowly, seemed to shiver a bit. 'She would've stopped speaking to me. And she'd have blamed me if... If Doug had got away with it.'

Hunter held his gaze until he looked away. 'You've honestly no idea where she'd go?'

'Cross my heart. I love her, you know, but I don't know where she could've gone.'

'If I find out you've been—'

'What, lying? No chance. Her life's too precious to me.' Neil picked up an ancient mobile, a grey plastic thing that the Third World would turn down with a snarl. 'Listen, how about I phone around her pals. The ones I know about. See if I can find out anything.'

Hunter passed him a business card. 'Call me the very second you hear anything, and I mean *anything*.'

12

'Just heading back to the station now, Shaz.' Jain held her Airwave to her ear, making sure Hunter didn't hear anything from the other end.

He set off from King's Road, weaving into the right-turn lane and stopping at the red light. Never could work out what they'd gained by switching from roundabout to traffic lights.

He had to brake hard as a car decided it wanted to head right down Wakefield Avenue, pretty much the last rat run left in eastern Edinburgh.

The old car showroom was still derelict, no sign of the threatened Lidl. In the rear-view, he caught a glimpse of King's Road, with Neil Alexander's flat just out of sight round the bend.

What the hell was going on there?

I'm a lover, not a fighter.

Guy seemed to think he's living in a Woody Allen film, a joke allowing him free rein to do what he wanted. Eleven years was a huge difference when the girl was sixteen.

Meant she was, what, born in 1999?

Christ... The year I enlisted.

She's a smart woman.

She's a child. A little girl who's been abused by her stepfather...

You'll what? You'll abuse my civil rights?

You have no idea...

'Aye, Shaz, we'll be back soon.' Jain killed the call and pocketed the Airwave.

Hunter joined a column of cars trundling along the road for no apparent reason. He pulled out to check the oncoming lane, but a pair of buses bore down on them, a wake of commuters trailing behind. Bloody hell. He glanced over at Jain. 'So now you've met Neil Alexander, what do you think?'

'I don't like him. I don't trust him. And I certainly don't believe him.'

Hunter pulled out again, but another bus powered towards them. 'What about?'

'Anything. Any of it.' Jain reached up for the sun visor and pouted into the mirror, twisting her head like a teenager taking a selfie. Then snapped the visor back up. 'Problem is, we've not got a smoking gun. He could just be a dirty bastard with a teenage girlfriend. Doesn't mean he's done anything to her. Doesn't mean he knows where she is.' She looked over. 'That stuff back there, do you honestly think she might've killed herself?'

'It's the first thing I thought at the hospital when she didn't answer the door. Got a flash...' Hunter cleared his throat. 'Thought we'd burst in there and she'd be swinging from a rope.'

'And how would she get a rope in a hospital?'

'You know what I mean. Pills, something like that.'

'Maybe... Nobody's stepped in front of a bus or a train today, anyway.' Jain slumped back in her seat, almost disappeared into it. 'If she doesn't show up soon, I think we should bring Mr Alexander in for some proper questioning.'

'On what grounds?'

'There's enough there, Craig. Don't you think?'

'Maybe.' Hunter set off down Moira Terrace, giving it some welly as he overtook a slow-moving Mini. He tried not to look across the road but couldn't help himself. Someone had stuck up a tall fence around the front garden of the house.

Good luck with that in winter.

Hunter pulled in, the engine grinding, and pointed at the house. 'I used to live round the corner from there. Not in a nice villa like that, mind. A dirty council house.' He tightened his grip on the steering wheel. 'A mate of mine, kid called Angus, he lived there. He was a good lad. Used to go out on our bikes and play on his N64.' Hunter killed the engine, waiting for the death rattle to end. 'Then Angus changed, started being quiet. Probably when we went to High School, round that time. Anyway... Angus's cousin, Paul I think. Guy was twenty-five, something like that. Worked at a bank. Good job, owned a flat in Porty.' He cracked his knuckles. 'Well, it turned out this honest bank employee had been buggering Angus since he was nine. Supposed to have been babysitting him.'

Jain's breath hissed out, harsh as a winter gale across the promenade. 'What happened?'

'The cousin got arrested.' Hunter stared over at the house again, a sunflower waving over the top of the fence in the breeze. 'Four days before the trial, Angus jumped in front of a train.'

'Did you know about it?'

'None of us did.' Hunter dragged a hand down his face, shutting his eyes like a funeral director. 'Like I said, this was the start of High School. I drifted apart from a few other mates, you know, thought it was the same thing happening with Angus.' He shook his head and punched the steering wheel. 'Just felt so angry, you know? Still do to this day. What that kid went through. What that animal did to him.'

Jain was looking away, staring at the eighties retirement flats opposite Angus's old house, already lit up in the evening sunlight. 'Did he get off with it?'

'The cousin was on remand for ages, you know the drill. His lawyer, big posh guy from the West End, was trying to get the case thrown out. The day he was up in front of the judge, the cousin got stabbed inside. Never caught who did it. Only good thing about that whole thing.'

Jain was deathly still, her breathing deep and slow. She brushed her hair back and twisted round to face Hunter, holding her Airwave. 'You know... never mind, Shaz wants us to check in with the house.'

'Thought we had a unit stationed there?'

'We do. Just wants us to have a look all the same.'

∽

Hunter indicated left at the Machine Mart and cruised past Scottie's pub down Northfield Broadway, a long stretch past the graveyard he chased Doug Ferguson around. At the end, he took a left onto Mountcastle Green, the row of sagging trees now dappling in the mid-evening light. 'Jesus Christ. Look at that pair of arseholes.'

The squad car sat on the kerb, guarding the house as subtly as a seventies DJ in a playground.

Jain didn't wait for the car to do its dying spurt before she was out and chapping on the other car's window.

Hunter joined her and leaned back against Ferguson's work van. Steve and Dave were double busy stuffing their phones into their pockets. 'Tenner on Mourinho getting the sack first, was it?'

'Piss off.' A wall of BO wafted out of the car. Dave popped his cap on and smiled at her. 'Not seen anything here, Sarge.'

Jain was looking around, hand shielding her eyes from the low sun. 'You're telling me nobody's been here at all?'

'A DPD van pulled up about half an hour ago. Dropped something round the corner and pissed off sharpish.' Dave frowned. 'Oh aye, and that boy from Forensics pitched up not long before. One with the ponytail? Took the felly's computer.' He ran his finger down the length of his nose. 'Reckon they'll find kiddie porn on it?'

'As you were.' Jain looked at him long and hard for a few seconds. 'And I'd be sticking my money on Advocaat at Sunderland.'

'Sarge.' Dave slumped back in the seat and reached for the Evening News. The front page was filled with a mock-up of the new hotel going in next to Alba Bank.

Jain tapped Hunter's arm and waved towards the drive. 'Let's have a look round the back.'

'Pair of bloody chancers...' Hunter led her over the monoblock pathway to the boxy porch, a mid-nineties addition by the looks of things. He peered inside the house.

No sign of Stephanie, or anyone else.

Wait. A flash of movement at the back door, distorted in the glass. Something clattered behind the fence.

'You see that?' Hunter twisted the handle round and opened the gate with a loud thunk. He pushed it hard and the bottom scraped over the grey slabs, dotted with moss and bird crap.

A man in a black T-shirt and grey Adidas trackies was running across the back lawn. He looked round, his mouth hanging open, eyes wide. Then he was off again.

Hunter sprinted after him, his gimpy knee letting him shift for once.

The man vaulted up onto a trampoline and launched himself over the slatted fence. His shins cracked into the faded wood slats and he tumbled over into the next garden. The trampoline collapsed in on itself.

Hunter jumped over a smashed plant pot and stopped, trying to prise the fence panels apart. Must be set with bloody concrete.

'Keep on him!' Jain darted back towards the street, her voice echoing as she shouted over at Dave and Steve: 'Get your arses in gear! Suspect spotted in garden!'

Hunter swung around and searched the space. There — a plastic seat. He shoved it against the fence and bounded up, heavy boots clumping against the wood.

In the neighbour's garden, the man was trying to get through the next door's hedge.

'Hunter to Jain. Suspect is entering next garden. Over.'

'Received.'

'Am pursuing.' Hunter launched himself over, landing feet first on a wilted patch of tattie plants. His knee gave way and he took a hard, graceless fall.

This one's not getting away...

He got up, charged across the garden, neatly segmented by slats of wood, and tore into the rustling hedge. Leylandii scraped against his cheek, drawing blood on his ear as he powered out into a paved driveway.

The suspect crunched over a bed of chuckies surrounding a weeping pear tree, heading towards an eight-foot wall. He hopped onto a bench and clambered up onto a greenhouse roof.

'Get back!'

The man glanced round at Hunter's approach. Guy looked forties, had a lived-in face. Full of lines.

Hunter grabbed his ankle. Got a kick in the face for his trouble. He skidded backwards, trying to right himself, then slid in something and tumbled over. 'Ah, Jesus!'

When he looked back up, the suspect was stepping onto the wall. The top was covered in anti-cat glass, broken bottles glued into concrete. He kicked out with a heavy work boot and smashed the top of the greenhouse. Shards of glass snowed on the green tomatoes and red peppers, frosting the bare cement floor.

Hunter got to his feet and a jolt of pain seared through his knee. Bloody hell. He put a hand to his face, felt like that kick had split his lip wide open. He sniffed something rotten and twisted round. Dog shite smeared his trousers right up to his arse. Smelled freshly laid. 'Hunter to Jain. Suspect is now in *third* garden. Unable to pursue from here.'

'Receiving. Meet us out the front.'

'Will do. Over.' Hunter set off along the wall onto a path down the side of the semi-detached house. He barged past a Land Rover onto the street, surrounded by lock-up garages and lanes leading off in all directions.

Hunter jogged behind the next pair of semis, more squat boxes decorated by dull planks of wood on the front. Instead of a side garden, a narrow drive led into a car park, empty except for an ancient Ford Cortina.

He stopped by a silver Vauxhall and peered into the gardens. Looked like both semis were owned by elderly couples — they were all outside, the men barbecuing in isolation, the women yakking over the dividing fence. 'Excuse me!'

The nearest man looked over. Did a double-take at Hunter's uniform. 'Aye?'

'Looking for a man in a black T-shirt. Would've come this way through the gardens?'

The man took a pull from a bottle of supermarket lager. 'Not seen anyone, son. Sorry.'

'Thanks.' Hunter stomped back into the road just as another pair of squad cars pulled up, local uniform getting out onto the baking tarmac.

Jain jogged back from an empty lane, Steve and Dave wading into a garden behind her. 'Where is he?'

'Lost him.' Hunter stormed back over to the house with the Land Rover. The wall led to a tall garage, backing onto the graveyard. 'He's in the cemetery.'

Jain waved at a pair of uniform. 'Get in there and track him down.' Then at the others. 'You two, back round to Moira Terrace and flush him out from there.'

The nearest glowered at her. 'But, Sarge, there's a million—'

'Just do it.' Jain slumped against the first squad car and got out her Airwave. She sniffed the air and scowled at Hunter. 'What the hell is that *smell*?'

Hunter was scanning around the houses, trying to spot the suspect. 'Had a bit of an accident, Sarge.'

'You shat yourself?'

'No, I fell in dog muck.'

She shook her head, eyes shut. 'Right. I want you with me.'

'But, Sarge, I can—'

'But nothing. We've got another four units heading here. Whoever it is, they'll catch him.' She held the Airwave up to her head. 'Sharon says she needs your brains at the station.'

13

'I'm just not sure you should put the phrase "stoat" into your report.' Jain smirked at Hunter, then her face twisted into a scowl. 'You know you really stink.'

'Right.' Hunter eased himself out of the car and looked down the back of his trousers. Like a map of Africa in dog crap. He took the taped-together patchwork quilt of carrier bags he'd been sitting on and dumped them in another one. 'I'll just head upstairs and clean this off.'

'After you've burned those trousers.'

Hunter started taking off his stab-proof, making sure it was jobbie-free. A wodge of crap slopped down on the concrete. 'Aw, Christ.'

'Get them off.'

'I can't—'

'You'll cover half the station in dog shite, you arse.' Jain placed the bag blanket on the floor, then reached round and unbuttoned his trousers. With one motion, she'd got them down to his ankles. 'Step out of them.'

Hunter stepped forward, too surprised to say anything. Her shoes trapped the bottom and he stumbled away, his bare legs ending in clumpy boots. 'Do I need a shower?'

'What do you think?' Jain's nose puckered up. 'Some of that shite must've seeped through.'

'Just what I needed to round off another shite day in uniform.' Hunter glanced around the garage — nobody there, least of all Fat Keith. 'I'll see you up at the office.'

She looked him up and down, shaking her head. 'That's a very fetching look.'

Was she checking him out?

Hunter's skin prickled all the way up his spine. 'Are you being sarcastic?'

'Maybe.' Her eyebrows wriggled up, then her gaze shifted down. 'Bet it takes a lot of squats to get thighs like that.'

Hunter stuck his left toes into his right boot and kicked it off. 'Ass to the grass, baby.'

∽

HUNTER HELD up the bag with the dirty clothes and dumped it in the bin. He sat down on the bench, his wet thighs damp against the cold wood, and rested his head against the metal behind him. His knee was throbbing like a Perthshire rave, the max-strength ibuprofen still not cutting through.

No more squats until that was healed up.

The locker room still stank of shite. Not the only thing that did.

Sick to the stomach.

Hunter looked down and sucked his gut in. Surprised no stomach bile had leaked out.

What had made Stephanie run away like that? Where the hell was she? Was she safe?

Poor Angus never had that idea, never had that hope, however false it might turn out to be. Far too young.

But Stephanie wasn't even that much older. Still a child. And he still couldn't shake the feeling she was in a ditch somewhere, a knife in her stomach or a few empty packets of painkillers next to her.

Where had she run to?

Means and Opportunity, all due to Finlay's bloody gaming addiction. Stupid bastard. Aided and abetted by goblins and inept cops.

Motive, though. Why? Why run away? Was it just from Doug? Could it be from her mother as well? What if Doug was beating up Steph as well as Pauline?

And who the hell was that man in the garden? Nobody'd found him yet, but... His stomach tied itself in another knot.

Hunter rustled around in his new uniform stash and started hauling the fresh T-shirt on.

Still stank of shite.

∽

Hunter stepped into their office, brushing a hand through his damp hair. The vaguest whiff of crap still hung in the air. Place was quiet, though.

Finlay was in the far corner, hunched over a laptop, facing away like a naughty boy caught with his fingers in the sweetie jar. Not that he'd see it that way.

Jain was slumped in a chair near the door. She frowned at his trousers. 'None in your size?'

'I always thought I should try the skinny-fit jeans craze.' Hunter bunched up the trouser material, hardly any give in it. 'Doesn't quite suit me, right?'

'You've got rugby player thighs.' Jain leaned back in her chair, eyebrows raised. 'And that's going to be distracting as hell.'

Sweat started prickling on Hunter's clean skin as he sat next to her, the trousers' industrial-strength stitching just about holding. 'What is?'

'Those thighs and those tight trousers. Jesus.' Jain spun her Airwave on the desk in front of her. 'Our guy's still at large.'

The knot in Hunter's gut pulled itself even tighter. 'Come on, what's with all this innue—?'

'It's Sergeant Jain now, I gather.' Inspector Alan Buchan strolled in from the corridor and held out a hand, his movement slow and considered. Red hair, thin goatee, medium height. Had a face like a potato someone had left in the microwave for too long. 'Long time, no see.'

Jain grinned at him. 'Al, how you doing?'

'Well, I've had better days.' Buchan nodded at Hunter, nostrils twitching. 'Nice move, Craig.'

What the hell?

Then Buchan was grinning at Jain. 'DI McNeil would appreciate an update on operation Spanner, if you've got a minute.'

'Okay, sir.' A smile crawled over her face. 'Your office?'

'Indeed. Just follow me.'

Jain clapped Hunter on the shoulder, perhaps lingering a second longer than necessary. 'Going to see where we are with the CCTV?'

'Sure thing.' Hunter watched them meander along the corridor, like the best of friends. Then over at the arse-wipe working in the corner.

Chasing up Finlay Sinclair wasn't exactly using my brain...

Hunter paced across the room and tapped him on the shoulder.

Finlay jumped, clawing at his white earphones. 'Christ!' He clocked Hunter and his shoulders slouched. 'Shite, it's just you, you schmuck.' His nostrils shifted up a gear, twitching like a frightened rabbit. 'What the hell's that stink?' He looked up from the laptop, across the office space. 'Jesus, Hunter, did you shite yourself again?'

'Funny guy... Had an accident chasing someone.' Hunter pulled his trousers away from his legs. 'We got any in my size, do you know?'

'You've checked the store room, right?' Finlay was back at his laptop. 'Steve ripped the arse out of a pair last week. Think he's the same size as you.'

'With that belly?'

'Why don't you go have a look, instead of hassling me for fashion advice?'

Hunter perched himself on the edge of Finlay's desk. 'You're in a great mood.'

'Aye, I signed up to do community policing not mess about looking at CCTV.' Finlay slapped the spacebar and slouched back in his seat. 'What exactly happened to your trousers? Chantal tear them apart with her teeth?'

Hunter missed a beat. 'I wish...' He coughed. 'Long story involving a mysterious stranger and a garden.'

'Sounds like an average Saturday night for you, minus the romance.'

Hunter tugged at his trousers. Bloody things were itching like a bastard. 'What CCTV you looking at?'

Finlay waved up at the clock on the wall. 'Half six. Should be in the boozer by now, except for bloody Princess Cleopatra making us stay and cover your arse.'

'My arse? You're the one who let her go.'

'No I bloody—' Finlay flicked his hands at him. 'Right, whatever. I'm just thinking about the OT. All I need to do is get the Princess to sign it with her feather quill.'

'Aye, good luck with that.' Hunter got another whiff of dog muck. He took his fleece off and checked the back — thing was definitely clean. 'How's the CCTV going?'

'Shite.'

'Got anything at all?'

'Square root, mate. Can you not undress in the changing room like a normal human being?'

Hunter tossed the fleece over to his seat. 'Look, I've been asked to babysit you while the normal human beings have their update meeting.' He stared out of the office's back window. Annandale Street Lane was cast in deep shadows. A mother grabbed her toddler's hand tight and took care in looking both ways three times before crossing.

Had Pauline Ferguson ever been like that? Had she ever taken that much care with Stephanie? Or had the girl flinched away back then, too?

The new-build flats lurked behind, big cream things like a custard obelisk. 'Lauren lives over there, doesn't she?'

'If you squint, you can just about make out the ivory tower. Who'd want to live there?' Finlay's focus was back on the laptop screen. Must be a world record for him. 'Tell you, the bloody Training department's still shuttered. Waste of time and bloody money that was. I told everyone when they built this bloody station. Nobody listened to me, though, did they? Same as usual. Bunch of rubes.'

'Only you pair could make an arse of looking out of the window.'

Hunter swung round to the doorway.

Elvis was resting against the jamb, arms crossed. Need to rethink that nickname — Elvis had soul. Paul Gordon was more like Shakin' Stevens.

'You should get a slot at the Stand, amigo.' Finlay looked up from his laptop. 'Then we can throw rotten fruit at you for those deadbeat jokes.'

'I'm not the one everyone's laughing at, Finlay.'

'Even with those sidies?'

Elvis patted the left one. 'What's wrong with them?'

'If you have to ask, you'll never know.'

'I'm serious. I'm trying for a Wolverine look.'

'The X-Man? You look more like an extra in a seventies porno. Or like Elvis, but not in his Sun Records phase.' Finlay kept his gaze low but his smirk high. 'More like the nappy-wearing days.'

Elvis wandered over, trying to laugh it off, and leaned against Hunter's desk, his nostrils twitching. 'Heard about you pair making an arse of that open-and-shut case.'

'We didn't make an arse of it. The girl ran away.'

'Oh aye? You were guarding her, though, right?'

Finlay shook his head and hunkered down in front of the laptop.

Hunter gave Elvis the up and down. Trying hard not to punch him. 'You here to investigate the case of the missing paperclips or something?'

'Nah, just wanted to rub it in.'

Finlay smirked. 'Like you do to young lassies on the bus?'

'Jesus, man.' Elvis made a T-shape with his hands. 'Time out, aye? Save that for the bar.' He shook his head and tossed a key onto Finlay's desk. 'We've got your CCTV upstairs.'

Finlay slammed his laptop lid. Be lucky if the screen was still intact. 'I'm fine here.'

'You sure? Lauren asked my DS for it. You don't piss Cullen off.'

Cullen was getting his hooks in now...

Hunter got away from the window and picked up the key. 'Finlay, go and have a look, aye?'

'Here we go again.' Finlay eyed the key in Hunter's grasp and let out a sigh. 'Is there anything on it?'

'Well, way I hear it, your lassie got the bus into town.' Elvis had his phone out, giving the screen a good look. 'Got the rest of the route, plus footage from around each of the stops. Princes Street, Cameron Toll.'

'How many's that?'

'Thirty, I think. And that's just towards Princes Street.' Elvis winked. 'Might make you think twice about buggering anything up in future.'

Finlay caught the key from Hunter's throw. 'Like that's ever stopped you.'

'Classy.' Elvis made pistols with his fingers at Hunter. 'Chantal's a radge wee midden and no mistaking. Said you're to meet her in Buchan's office.'

~

HUNTER POPPED his head round the door and shifted his gaze across McNeill and Lauren. Jain was lurking by the glass cabinet, a few small trophies on display. No idea what for.

Buchan was sipping at a latte behind his desk. 'What's up?'

'DC Gordon said DS Jain wanted a word, sir?'

Buchan waved at the display case next to Jain. 'I'd offer a seat, but they're all taken.'

'Prefer to stand, sir.'

Buchan took a drink from his cup, covering his ginger moustache in brown foam. 'How did the tournament go?'

What the hell?

Hunter frowned. 'Sorry, you've lost me.'

'The chess? You were two up on Saturday lunchtime, weren't you?'

'I've never played chess, sir.'

'Are you sure?'

'Pretty sure, aye.'

'Sorry, that must be someone else.' Buchan wiped the foam away, leaving a thin sliver in the middle. 'Have you found him, then?'

'No, sir—'

'Just a sec.' Lauren got up and gripped Hunter's arm. 'Can you give us a second, sir? Ma'am?'

'Sure thing.' Buchan shrugged and stared into his cup. 'So who played chess, then?'

McNeill nodded approval, already lost in her mobile.

Hunter followed Lauren out and pulled the door to behind him. 'Here comes a standard-issue size six up my rectum.'

'Size five.' Lauren opened a meeting room door across the corridor and peered inside. 'In here.'

Hunter took the chair nearest the whiteboard, sucking in wafts of marker pen. Sweltering in here. He reached over to open the window.

Lauren grabbed his wrist. 'It's too bloody cold in here as it is.'

'Come on, Sarge, it's stinking like an Airfix shop.'

'Just man up.' Lauren sat at the head of the table and folded her arms, narrow eyes glowering at him. She smacked her hand at the door, like she was hitting a forehand at squash. 'They're calling this Operation Spanner. Are you happy with that?'

'Not really, Sarge.'

'I'm *livid*.' Lauren untied her ponytail and bunched her hair together, snapping a scrunchy around, much tighter than before. 'Your idiot partner has really dropped a bollock on this.'

'That's an unfortunate choice of words.'

'What is?'

'Never mind.' Hunter stared at the warped grain of the wooden tabletop. 'He's lost in that CCTV, so he can't arse anything else up for a while.'

Lauren shook her head at him and rubbed her palms deep into her eye sockets. 'Well, Inspectors Buchan and McNeill have been putting their heads together, haven't they?' She sighed. 'We are to focus on this under the SO unit's supervision.'

'Why can't CID or the MIT do it?'

'Because we've already got a trained detective working it.'

He frowned. 'Who?'

'Christ sake Craig. *You*.'

Hunter laughed. 'You're joking, right?'

She glared at him. 'Wish I was.'

'Sarge, they didn't want me two years ago.'

'So?'

Hunter's mouth was dry. 'Can't believe they're playing that card now. That's all.'

'Well, I don't care whatever card they're playing. We're working this case full-time. You and that idiot partner of yours are off normal duties until we find Stephanie. Am I clear?'

Felt like I met the devil at a bloody crossroads and all I got for my soul was this case. That and Finlay Sinclair.

Hunter picked up a marker pen and drop-kicked it across the room, sending it straight into the metal blinds. Sounded like a cutlery

Missing

drawer clattering to the floor. 'Are you going to tell HR I won't be going to that interview tomorrow?'

'We'd better have that girl in here giving a statement by then, believe me.' She waited for him by the door, jabbing her index finger into his polo shirt. 'You get back in there and contribute, okay? Buchan doesn't want us looking like ginger stepchildren.' She raised her hands. 'His words, not mine.'

∽

BUCHAN WAS PLAYING with his empty coffee glass, swirling the froth around in the bottom. 'Does anyone want another cup while we— Oh.' He nodded at Lauren and Hunter. 'Right, so where have you got to, then?'

Lauren perched on her chair again. 'PC Sinclair's going through the CCTV we got—'

'PC who?'

'Finlay Sinclair, Alan.'

'Have I met him?' Buchan snapped his fingers a couple of times. 'He's the chess one.'

'Are you sure?'

Buchan clicked his tongue, then lifted his eyebrows. 'Maybe not.'

'Anyway, PC Sinclair's looking at the CCTV from the bus company.'

'Okay, that's a start.' Buchan ran his finger round the lip of the mug and sooked at a lump of foam. 'So where is she?'

'We don't know, sir.' Lauren started scribbling in her notebook. 'We are looking—'

'Phones?'

'Well.' Jain glanced over at Hunter as he joined her in the window. 'I've got a trace on the girl's phone. She's not had it on since the hospital.'

'Typical.' More scraping at the bottom of the glass. 'Did she have it with her?'

'Think so.' Jain looked over at Hunter. 'It was on her bedside table, right, Craig?'

'I believe it was, Sarge.'

'And it wasn't there when she flitted?'

'That's right.' Hunter got out his pocket book with a fresh pong of dog muck. He winced and flicked through the screed he'd written while Jain had driven back. 'We should also check out her social networks. We know she didn't reply to a message her friend sent, but she might have messaged someone else, or at least logged on.'

Lauren winked at him and whispered: 'See, you've still got it.'

Hunter gave her a blank stare. Anger fizzed away in the pit of his guts. 'Bottom line, sir, we still don't know where she's gone.'

Buchan dipped a longer spoon into his glass and supped some more foam. 'You've been out speaking to the usual suspects, though, haven't you?'

Jain nodded. 'Got a few leads to chase down, sir, but nothing concrete. Think it looks like a dead end.'

'Which means we've got to approach the tigers.' Buchan's spoon clattered onto the table as he tilted his head at McNeill. 'Sharon, you and I should lead on that?'

She flicked her head around, frowning. 'Sorry, approach the tigers?'

'You know, the tigers.' Buchan smacked his lips together a few times. 'Was it Keith who played chess?' He ran a tongue over his teeth and frowned. 'Not sure.' Then nodded at McNeill. 'I mean the press.'

'Right, with you now.' McNeill checked her watch. 'If we get onto it, we might catch the evening news.'

'Wait, so this isn't with the tigers, already?'

'Not that I know of.'

'Sergeant Reid... Come on...'

'Sir, that decision was between you and DI McNeill as Senior Investigating Officers.' Lauren looked up from her scribbling. 'But before we slip down that rabbit hole, we need to consider the possibility that the girl might've committed suicide.'

'We've made a complete arse of this.' Buchan sucked on his spoon again. 'I don't want this girl to be another statistic. Either way, we've got to find her and soon.' He inspected a notepad on his desk. 'How's the suspect from the lassie's garden?'

Jain folded her arms. 'Still at large, sir. And no, we don't know who he is. Could just be a burglar.'

'I doubt it.' Hunter leaned back into the window frame. 'He could just as well be one of the stepfather's mates looking for Stephanie.'

'That's a very good point, Craig.' Buchan frowned at McNeill. 'Sharon, we're at your bidding here.'

'I'm thinking Stephanie's running from Doug Ferguson, but it's possible there's something else we haven't uncovered.' McNeill stayed focused on the Inspector. 'I'm thinking it's time for someone to speak to Doug Ferguson. He's suffered long enough as it is.'

14

Hunter stood outside the interview room, a cramped space which reeked of stale BO and fresh pies. Some bugger had eaten their piece in there. *No doubt to avoid the MIT...*
At least it doesn't smell of dog shite.

Jain was silhouetted in the dying light from the window at the end of the corridor, talking on her mobile with such focus that it blinded Hunter to the seediness of the surroundings, let him forget that the glass behind her was as splattered with soot and muck from passing traffic as was the entire building.

She pocketed her phone and strode over to the door. 'Let's do this.'

'You leading in here?'

Jain raised an eyebrow. 'What, you think I haven't noticed you taking over every time I've asked you not to?'

'Sorry.'

'No, you're not, are you?' She shook her head, the grin back. 'You're a cheeky wanker.'

Hunter's gut started churning again, his heart fluttering that little bit faster. Is she asserting her authority or...?

She clapped him on the shoulder. 'Look. You caught Ferguson this afternoon, right?'

'If by caught you mean that I had a wrestle in the graveyard as he ran away after battering my knee, then aye.'

'You did well in Buchan's—'

'Save it.' Hunter looked away, sighing.

'Ooh, touchy. Right, let's get this started, then, shall we?' She pushed through into the interview room, flattening down her hair as she sat.

Hunter took the chair on the left and set the digital camera recording. He made sure it was synced with the audio, then got out his notebook. 'Interview commenced at nineteen oh six on Tuesday the eleventh of August 2015. Present are myself, PC Craig Hunter, and Detective Sergeant Chantal Jain.' He nodded at Doug. 'Please state your name for the record.'

Doug snorted. The bare lightbulb shone on his head, shards of light breaking on the grey stubble as on metal shavings. His overalls had disappeared, only to reveal a worn-out pair of paint-stained jeans under his Hibs top. His left shoulder looked packed out with something, right where Hunter had cracked it off a gravestone. 'Douglas Francis Ferguson.'

Hunter nodded at the suit next to him. Though expensive, it was in dire need of a good clean. 'And you are, sir?'

'Hamish Williams of McLintock, Williams & Partners.' Vacant stare, Brylcreemed white hair, rimless specs. Morningside accent straight out of a fifties radio drama. 'It's been five hours since my client's unlawful arrest, and I would greatly appreciate it if you could see your way to releasing him from custody forthwith.'

'Not going to happen.' Hunter leaned forward and unzipped his fleece. Still had the vaguest whiff of dog mess. He switched his focus to Doug. 'Can we just get something clear, first?'

Williams started blinking furiously, holding his glasses halfway from his face. 'What?'

'Mr Ferguson's a painter-decorator, right?'

'That is, indeed, my client's employment sector.'

'And your firm is one of Scotland's most prestigious?'

'We have received numerous accolades over the course of our incorporation, correct.'

'So how can he afford your services?'

'I will thank you for respecting the fact that my client's means of payment are confidential, as are those of all our valued clients.'

'Tell me if I've got this right. Extortionate lawyer and private plates on his van – H185 DFF...'

'And? Do please move on, Constable. I would be honoured if we could keep this conversation relevant to the issues at hand.' Williams put his glasses back on, the lenses catching the full glare of the strip lighting. 'Why have you got my client here?'

'We received some serious accusations levelled at Mr Ferguson and we'd appreciate some answers.' Hunter switched his focus to

Doug. 'Mr Ferguson, can you take us through what happened at lunchtime today, please?'

'You assaulted me.'

'Mr Ferguson, you resisted my attempts to detain you under Section 21 of the Criminal Procedure Scotland Act.' Hunter's ears were burning. His voice dropped to a gravelly whisper — a smirk ghosted across Jain's lips. 'I'm referring to what Section 21 pertains to.'

Doug glanced at his lawyer. 'Do I have to talk here, Hamish?'

Williams tilted his head to counsel his client in private.

'Right, so it'll not harm my case?' Doug let out a deep sigh, shaking his head. 'What can I say? I'd been on a job just down in Leith so I headed home for some lunch. Thought I'd maybe catch a bit of the golf on Sky.' His tongue was rooting around between his teeth. 'So, anyway, I get in and Steph's in the living room, watching that bloody music channel. The one with all the shouting and that. Mosher music.'

'Did you speak to her?'

'Asked her if she wanted anything to eat, but she ran off to her room.'

'She didn't say anything?'

'Nothing at all.' Doug shifted his pinky nail to fiddle with his teeth. 'Thought she was just being surly. She's a teenager, right?' He finally struck gold and pulled his finger out of his mouth to inspect the yellowish muck. He flicked it on the table between them. 'So, anyway, I went to the kitchen and started making a sandwich. Had all the stuff out on the bunker when I heard her mother coming in. She dumped her bag down and gave me a kiss. Then she went to check on Steph.'

'She knew Stephanie was in?'

'I told her the lassie was acting funny.'

'You didn't know why?'

'Look, next thing I know, Pauline's in my face, shouting at us, telling us to go in the garden.'

Jain leaned forward, head tilted at a slight angle. 'And did you?'

Doug rubbed at his neck, the purple bruise like some footballer's tribal tattoo. 'Like I had a choice.'

'Wait a sec.' Hunter raised a hand to stop Jain. 'You weren't shouting through the door at Stephanie?'

'Eh, what?' Doug frowned at his lawyer, then at Hunter. 'Course I wasn't.'

'Sure about that?'

Doug rested on his elbows. His arm hair was like steel wool wrapped around kettle drums. 'Has my wife been telling lies about me?'

'Mrs Ferguson stated that you were shouting through the door at Stephanie.'

'Well, that's bollocks.'

'Sure about that?' Jain got up and walked around the table, then stuck her head between Doug and his lawyer so she could whisper to both of them at once. 'We've got two different stories here.'

'Aye? Usually the difference means one's a pack of lies, princess. And I'm no—'

'Detective Sergeant, please.'

'Whatever. I'm not a liar, all right?' Doug clenched his fists, thumbs squeezing forefingers. 'Anyway, I was out in the garden, wondering what the hell's going on. Next thing I know, Pauline's at the back door, locking the bloody thing. Started shouting the odds at us, saying Steph's told her I've been *abusing* her.'

'And I take it you have been, yes?'

'Eh?' Doug thumped the desk and swung his head round to glare at Jain. 'Christ's sake. I'm not a *paedo*. I raised that girl as my own. I've done *nothing* to her.'

'That's a different story to what we've heard from her.'

'She's a lying wee bit—'

'My client requests you recant the allegations made by his stepdaughter.'

'Not going to happen.'

Williams waved a hand around the grotty interview room. 'I'm afraid she's not here to provide a sufficiently detailed statement. You know you'll be unable to get anywhere near charging my client, let alone a conviction.'

'Your client's been abusing that girl for the best part of two years.' Jain moved to within an inch of Williams's ear. 'He's going to answer for that.'

'And the courts of this great land deal in evidence, Sergeant. Not lies and hearsay.'

Jain stood up tall and walked over to the corner behind Doug's sore shoulder. 'Mr Ferguson, do you understand the seriousness of the accusations levelled against you?'

'Look, I didn't do anything!'

'But you understand?'

'Christ, aye. Course I do. Think I'm a monk—'

'Have you ever had anything that could be construed as sexual contact with Stephanie?'

'Eh?' Doug looked like he was about to reach out and throttle her. 'No bloody way.'

'How much physical contact have you had with Ms Ferguson since you've been her stepfather?'

'Look, I'm not the most hands-on guy, right? But if she wants a hug, I'll give her one.'

'So you were close?'

'She's my *daughter*. End of, far as I'm concerned.' Doug gave a shrug, the Hibs shirt crumpling as he raised his bony shoulders. He glanced behind at Jain, then winced and started rubbing his shoulder. 'She treats me like I was her dad.'

'But you abused her?'

'She's my *daughter*, for crying out loud. I'd never hurt her in any way. I love that girl.'

Williams raised a palm like he was stopping traffic in the street. 'My client merely means a paternal love.'

'I'm sure he does...' She leaned in close to Doug, this time on the other side from Williams. 'But you've been abusing her since she was fourteen, haven't you?'

Doug got up and swung round, fists clenched like a boxer, hovering in front of his face. 'Stop this, you wee Pa—'

'Or? Or you'll hit me? Like you hit your wife?'

'Shut up.' Doug looked ready to lash out at her. 'Shut up!'

'Come on. Show me how hard you are.'

Doug drove his forehead towards hers, then froze and slowly looked her up and down. A breathless moment later he whispered something and slumped back in his chair, smiling to himself.

Now Jain looked ready to kill.

Hunter raised his hands at Jain and mouthed: 'Calm down.'

She sat back in her chair and forced herself to look at the lawyer. 'Mr Williams, you should know that I work in the Sexual Offences Unit. We're investigating this as a Category 2 case of grooming and a Category 1 case of Intercourse with Step-Child. Further investigation will be undertaken to determine whether the abuse commenced prior to Stephanie turning sixteen. We will charge your client accordingly.'

'I appreciate the courtesy, Sergeant, but he is innocent of all charges.'

'Christ's sake.' Doug stabbed a finger across the desk at them. 'What about Steph's boyfriend, eh? That pretentious wee shite. You should be speaking to him.'

'We've already spoken—'

'Ken how old the boy is? Do you?'

'We know—'

'*Twenty-seven*!' Doug shook his head, nostrils bared in a snarl.

'Steph's *sixteen*. How can he live with himself? Shagging a wee lassie like that.'

Hunter turned back a page and etched a couple of asterisks next to *Neil Alexander*. 'As I say, we've been in touch with Mr Alexander.'

'And have you charged *him* with anything?'

'We've nothing to suggest there's anything to charge him with. Have you?'

'You think him shagging a sixteen-year-old is *right*?'

'Whether I think it's right or wrong is immaterial. It's within the law. If indeed he was having intercourse with Stephanie.'

'Course he bloody was.' Doug shut his eyes, his forehead creasing up like the ridges on a Cornish pasty. 'That boy was dipping his wick way before he should've been, if you catch my drift.'

Hunter sighed and started drumming on the table. 'And you've got evidence to support this?'

'Not as such—'

'Used condoms? Video? Photographs? A witness statement you'd be willing to defend in court?'

Doug jabbed a finger like a featherweight boxer throwing a punch. 'He's got my lassie on the Jack 'n' Jill.'

'You mean the contraceptive pill?'

'Aye! She's *sixteen*!'

'Which is the legal age of consent in this country.' Jain ran a hand down the open pages of her notebook. 'Whereas we have allegations of rape regarding yourself going back way before Stephanie could legally consent. And even if she could, it's still an offence.'

'This is a load of shite!'

'Stephanie's your *stepdaughter*. It's a crime for you to have a sexual relationship with her before the age of twenty-one.'

'There is no— Was no— Look, I've not shagged that lassie!'

'Mr Ferguson.' Hunter let him fester for a few seconds, the anger rising as his eyes narrowed. 'Have you got anything to support these allegations regarding Mr Alexander having sex with Stephanie before the age of sixteen?'

'No, I haven't. But he was—'

'Who was scoping out your house, then?'

'Eh?'

'We visited there this evening.' Hunter gestured at himself and Jain. 'There was a man in the garden.'

'Did he look like Neil Alexander, by any chance?'

'No, he didn't. Not in the slightest. He was shorter than you.'

'Why do you think he's got anything to do with me?'

Jain motioned for Hunter to take over.

'Because Stephanie ran away from the hospital this afternoon.'

'What?' Doug swallowed hard. 'You serious?' He looked at Williams, then at Hunter. 'Christ on a bike, how the hell could you clowns let that happen? That's my wee lassie!'

'We're doing everything we can to find her, but I'm afraid we have reason to believe her life is in danger. Do you know who this man at your house was?'

'Do I fu—' Doug caught himself and stopped. He leaned over to his lawyer and whispered.

Williams beamed at Jain. 'Could you give us a second, please?'

∽

DOUG'S VOICE droned through the door into the empty corridor, but the timber sucked in both the words and their meaning.

Hunter put his ear to the door. Still sounded like it was underwater.

How could he? His own daughter. Dirty bastard. Not On Normal Court-yard Exercise, indeed. Just wait till some hairy-arsed murderer gets his hands on Doug's skinny—

A hand grasped his left bicep. 'You okay?'

Hunter nodded at Jain, blinking in the dim light of the corridor. 'This makes me sick to the stomach.'

'You're not alone.' Jain's cappuccino skin looked a few shades paler, not all of it from the strip lighting. 'You seriously think he's done this?'

'Fits the pattern, doesn't it? Mother with young daughter, that nonce moves in, waits a few years, knows all the patterns, then bang, she's got no choice.'

Jain raised a shoulder and exhaled. 'Maybe.'

'You don't think so?'

'I just hope he's working out a deal with that lawyer of his.'

'I've kind of missed this, you know? The long hours of the detective. Feeling like you're scratching deeper than the surface.'

'I see a lot of this shit in the SO unit, day in, day out.' Jain rested against the wall, rubbing her arms. 'Makes you want to save cats from trees.'

Hardly. At least I'm working a more meaningful case now... Sickening as it is...

Hunter grimaced at the image of Stephanie running away down the hospital corridor.

Maybe saving cats from trees wasn't so bad after all...

'Hello? Someone Home? Craig!'

'Sorry. I was miles away there. Anyway, what did Doug whisper to you?'

'Nothing I haven't heard a hundred times before.' She stared up at the ceiling. 'Called me a frigid... well, it begins with P and rhymes with baccy.'

'You serious?' Hunter put his hands on the door. 'I'm going to batter him.'

'He was smart enough to do it without any witnesses.' Jain grabbed Hunter's shoulder. 'If you—'

The door jolted open and Williams stared at them. 'Douglas is ready to recommence the interview.'

Hunter barged past him and started the machine running again. Couldn't bring himself to focus on the racist scumbag.

A slight lag on the audio, but he wasn't going to be able to fix it without some chump in sandals and a polo neck patronising him.

'Interview recommenced at nineteen twenty-six.' Hunter held out a hand to Doug, palm facing up. 'I believe you've got something you wish to say? An apology, I assume?'

'Fuck no.' Doug sniffed, lopsided and bitter. 'You know about what happened with her father?'

'Her natural father?' Jain looked as puzzled as Hunter felt. 'He died when Stephanie was eight.'

Doug tilted his head to the side, his forehead creasing. 'Where'd you get that from?'

Hunter's stomach lurched. He tried to clear his throat, but a lump just stuck there. 'Stephanie's mother told us.' Sounded like he'd swallowed a frog.

'Christ. She never stops lying, does she?'

Another cough and it was still there. 'Explain.'

'Prick's called Robert Quarrie. Proper sick bastard.' Doug bared his teeth. 'Don't know the ins and outs of—' He scowled and banged the desk, sending vibrations through the wood. 'Shite. Look, he was abusing her when she was really young.'

'Oh really?' Jain rolled her eyes. 'You expect us to believe that, do you?'

'It's the God's honest truth.' Doug clenched his fists again, ready to hit more than furniture next time. 'Pauline didn't like to talk to me about it. Kept blaming herself for what happened. You need to ask her.'

Jain looked over at Hunter. 'This feels like a diversion, Constable, what do you think?'

'Definitely, Sarge. I'm not sure I—'

'You pair know something?' Doug's mouth hung open, his tongue darting around his yellow teeth. 'The day the boy got out of prison, September fifteenth, 2012, I drove up there. The one by Alloa. Glenochil or something. Waited outside in the van and gave the boy a lift down to Stirling. Dropped him at the bus station and stuck twenty quid in his dirty fingers. I told that sex pest to keep away from Steph and Pauline. Said if I ever saw or heard from him again I'd batter the living daylights out of him. Me and the boys wouldn't even leave a trace.'

Hunter sat back and let the echoes die in the small room. Seemed like a sack of balls. 'Any proof of this?'

A shifty look at his lawyer. 'You might be able to check the van's SatNav.'

'Witnesses would be better.' Hunter cracked his watch off the table as he crossed his arms. 'Are there any?'

'Not that I can think of.' Doug had another whisper in the lawyer's ear, then rubbed his nose. 'Listen, that prick was lucky he didn't end up in a ditch off the A9, you know what I'm saying? Beasting a wee lassie like that. His own daughter. She was *eight*! He's lucky to be alive, man, I'm telling you. I've got all my work tools in the back of the van. Chisels and pliers and hammers. Should've done it, you know? Should've sawed his balls off. Stuck his—'

'Douglas...' Williams reached a hand over to cover his client's mouth. 'That's quite enough.'

Doug collapsed back into his chair, his nostrils twitching.

Hunter tasted blood in his throat. 'So why didn't you do all this to him?'

'Because I'm a human being.' Doug wiped the streak of saliva smearing his cheek. 'Long as that beast keeps away from Pauline and Steph, he can live his life. Some animal will no doubt find out who he is and—'

'Mr Ferguson...' Williams had his hand over the microphone this time, only letting go when Doug sat back.

Hunter narrowed his eyes at Doug. 'Did you know about this history before you started going out with Stephanie's mother?'

Doug scowled at his lawyer, then at Jain. 'What are you saying?'

'My understanding is you met Mrs Ferguson through a friend of a friend. A lot of repeat abusers get intelligence on vulnerable sons and daughters before they make a move on their mothers.'

'What are you talking about?' Doug was wide-eyed, snarling. 'I'm innocent here! I've never even *accidentally* seen the girl naked. I'm really careful about all that shite.'

'What was the name of this friend you met Mrs Ferguson through?'

'Boy called Alec Wishart.' Doug blinked hard a few times. 'Done a few favours for me over the years...'

'Got an address for him?'

'Course I bloody have. Look, you need to—'

'Was it Mr Wishart we saw at your house?'

'How should I know?'

'You didn't ask him to try and find Stephanie to maybe keep her quiet, did you?'

'First I knew about her running away was you telling us just now.'

'That's the truth?'

'Course it bloody is.' Doug scratched at the stubble on his head. 'Look, how the hell am I supposed to get word out to Alec, eh?'

'You could've used Mr Williams here.'

'That is a baseless accusation which sullies my good nature.' The lawyer puffed up his chest and stuck his chin out. 'I request a formal apology. Immediately.'

'You denying passing on any messages on behalf of your client?'

'I don't have to deny it. You've got nothing suggesting I acted accordingly, so you must recant your words or I shall be forced to seek an appointment with your superior officers.'

Jain reached forward, her dimpling cheek the only trace of a smirk. 'Interview terminated—'

~

'—AND I just don't know whether to believe him or not.' Hunter plonked down across from Lauren and let out a groan. 'At least that's us finished with the stepfather. For now. Racist bastard.'

'Racist?' Lauren stopped writing and started fiddling with her biro, the top half of the plastic casing cracked and falling apart. Christ knows how she could write with the thing. 'What?'

'We'll never be able to prove it...'

Lauren scribbled a note, the pen cracking up the seam. 'You okay, Craig?'

'What's that supposed to mean?'

'It means, you haven't been trained to deal with this sort of thing, so you might not be okay.'

'Thought I was RoboCop?'

'Even RoboCop had a person inside all that metal.'

'I'll live.' Hunter grimaced. 'The lawyers always just as bad as the bloody paedos? Keeping those stoats on the street is a crime in my book.'

'I hope you're not prejudging here?'

'I'm keeping an open mind, Sarge, don't you worry. Just wish he'd gone for a lawyer who I don't want to flush down the toilet.' Hunter let his stab-proof hang free, getting a good thunk from the buckle as it hid the chair arm. 'How's it been going here?'

'I've had better. My derrière's somewhat tender.'

'That bad?'

'Just Buchan...' Lauren groaned and dumped her pen down, another bit breaking off. 'Him and McNeill go way back. You're lucky you're not a Sergeant. And one that's only been here a few months.'

'Aye, tell that to my bank manager.'

The door clattered open behind him and Jain stormed in, followed by McNeill clutching her Airwave close to her ear.

Jain perched on the edge of the vacant desk and nodded at Lauren.

'Chantal, I'm sorry about what happened in that interview. Craig told me that Mr Ferguson—'

'It's fine.' Jain narrowed her eyes at Hunter. 'Are you getting anywhere with the address of this Robert Quarrie?'

Hunter checked his Airwave — no new messages flashing. 'Still looking for him. All they've been able to find out so far is that he doesn't own any properties in Scotland. Control had a look at his record on the Violent and Sex Offenders Register. Said he's been living in Stranraer. Supposed to be sending officers round to the address now.'

'Tallies with what Doug Ferguson told us.' Jain shook her head, eyes shut and teeth clenched. 'How the hell could the PNC not have what happened on file?'

'Name changes, court orders, I don't know.' Hunter shrugged. 'Could be anything.'

Lauren jotted down another note, her left hand cradling the pen to make sure none of the cracked plastic touched her fingers. 'Do you believe this story?'

'There's something there, I think.' Hunter thumbed at the door. 'He seems to know a bit too much about Neil Alexander.'

'You think they could be colluding?'

'Nothing to support that. Yet.'

'DS Jain?'

'Like PC Hunter says, nothing to prove it either way.' Jain nodded over at McNeill. 'Sharon's raising it with her boss to see if we can get the old case file.'

'Needs more than raising.' Hunter's Airwave chimed. He was on his feet before the other two were even aware of it. 'Receiving. Safe to speak.'

'PC Hunter, it's Mags. That request you had with the Dumfries and Galloway lot? Well, Mr Quarrie doesn't live there anymore.'

Hunter wheeled round. Lauren and Jain glanced at each other. McNeill stabbed a bony finger at her own Airwave. He held the handset up. 'Any idea where he lives?'

'Still looking for a new address.'

'Mags, he's a registered sex offender.' Hunter could've crushed the little radio with his bare hands. 'Whoever's in charge of this damn search, they'd better pull their finger out or I'll personally kick their sorry arse into the middle of next week.'

'I'll get the ViSOR team onto it.'

'Issue a Be On the Lookout for him, aye?'

'Will do.'

'Cheers, Mags.' Hunter pressed the call button and collapsed against the burning radiator. You bugger... He stepped away from the furnace, the backs of his thighs feeling seared. 'Take it you heard that?'

McNeill unbuttoned her suit jacket and hauled it off. Flushed, like she was as hot as Hunter in that office. 'Let's get a press release out regarding this Quarrie character.' She grinned. 'Sorry, speak to the tigers.' The smile was gone as fast as it had appeared. 'If he's back in the area, then it could explain Stephanie's disappearance.'

Hunter frowned at her. 'More than her stepfather abusing her?'

'As much.' McNeill looked at him like he'd just shat in her kettle. Then smiled at Jain. 'Chantal, can you and PC Hunter run this tale past Mrs Ferguson?'

15

Jain parked by the Ferguson house.

Doug's van still obscured part of the view, but there were some lights on downstairs, the rest of the street shifting from the fading daylight of a summer's evening to the harsh lighting of fluorescent street lamps.

The dying sun dowsed Edinburgh in an orange glow, casting long shadows from Arthur's Seat and the crags.

Jain gave Hunter the up and down, her gaze maybe lingering on his legs a bit too long. Again.

'What's with that?'

She frowned. 'With what?'

'You looking at me. Is it the smell of shite?'

'Must be that, Craig.' She coughed and twisted away to open her door. 'Could murder a glass of wine.'

'Give me a couple of bottles.'

'Do you—?' Jain's Airwave chimed out. 'Can never get too far from Sharon McNeill.'

Hunter got out and rested against the car. Back the way, the graveyard was bleached yellow, the Royal High primary school peeking over the wall. Place looked like a prison. Fitting, given some of the kids he'd butted up against at High School. Just a couple hundred metres away and it could've been his fate, too.

He walked over to the pool car, clocking Steve picking his nose and flicking the product at Dave. 'Evening, boys.'

'Mieaow.' Steve couldn't even be arsed to put his back into it. He stifled a yawn. 'Still nothing here, Catman. Your pal hasn't reappeared?'

'Our pal, unless all that mutual masturbation has made you two blind.'

'Nobody else saw him.'

'DS Jain did.'

'Mieaooooow.'

'How come you didn't even get close to catching him in that bloody graveyard?'

Dave winked. 'Assuming he was actually there and not just your cover story for falling into a jobbie, Hunter.'

Could still smell it.

Hunter looked around the street. An old CID pool Vectra was parked round the corner, a pair of local detectives manning the fort. 'So you've not seen anything suspicious?'

'Just you.' Dave's turn to yawn. 'Mum and her pal are inside. We had a word with her, but you'd need a nuclear warhead to get past her, I tell you.'

Hunter looked at Jain as she ended her Airwave call and wandered over to the house. Then he stuck his back into the car. 'You been through the girl's room?'

'Aye, Dave was sniffing her knickers—'

∽

AILSA STOOD in front of the living room door, blocking their entrance. 'Is there any news about Steph?'

'I'm afraid she's still missing, Mrs Crichton. We have issued a press release, though.' Hunter tried a smile to see if that was the key to a less belligerent attitude from her. 'We're doing the full News Conference tomorrow, which will hopefully get on national TV.'

'Is that why you're here? To get Pauline to go along with you?'

'Not our department. We just want to keep her updated and ask her a few questions. Now if you'll—'

'That prick with the rubbish patter says he's supposed to do that.' She scowled over to the kitchen. 'Makes a shite cup of tea, too.'

'The Family Liaison Officer will become more helpful over time, Mrs Crichton. Especially as we progress into prosecution.'

'Aye, well, get the boy to mash the teabag before he puts the milk in is all I can say.' Ailsa twisted round and yanked the door open. 'The cops are back.'

Pauline was standing in the hallway, arms wrapped around her torso. 'Have you found her?'

'I'm afraid not.' Hunter nodded at the FLO, a couple of pimples away from finishing puberty by the looks of things. He mouthed: 'Milk, no sugar.' He watched the kid traipse over to get Jain's order and took a wingback chair in the window. About as comfortable as a gravestone. 'Pauline, we've been given some information regarding Stephanie's father.'

Pauline scowled at him. 'Doug?'

Hunter waited for Jain to take a seat next to her on the sofa. 'No, Robert Quarrie.'

Pauline collapsed back onto the settee, deflating like a stabbed beachball. 'Christ.'

'This isn't the first time she's been abused, is it?'

'Jesus Christ.' Pauline settled into Ailsa's hug and started picking at the tissue in her hands, tearing the plies apart as though she was hoping to find the answer buried there.

Hunter shifted forward on his chair. Thing almost tipped over. 'Can you start by telling us what happ—?'

'Her own father. Jesus Christ.'

'There, there.' Ailsa rubbed Pauline's arms. 'It's not your fault, hen.'

'It bloody is my fault!' The old fire was back in Pauline's eyes, a snarl contorting her face. 'What's that saying? "Fool me once, shame on you? Fool me twice, won't get fooled again?" That's no' right, is it?'

'It's "Fool me twice, shame on me".' Ailsa stroked down a lock on Pauline's hair. 'And it's not your fault.'

'Of course it bloody is!' Pauline pushed away from Ailsa and stood up. She paced over to the mantelpiece and ran her finger along the top of an old carriage clock, looked like some old relative's retirement gift. Sod the pension, here's a shitty time piece to remind you it's running out. She blew dust into the air. 'Stephanie was *eight* when I caught him. Eight years of age.'

The room was as silent as a morgue, just the clock ticking and the kettle thrumming through the door.

'I changed jobs so I could be at home at lunch and after school for her. She was off school for a year after that happened. Didn't settle until I told her he'd died. The girl was a complete mess, and it's all my fault.'

Hunter sat back in the armchair, still uncomfortable, but it was hardly the chair's fault now. 'And Mr Quarrie was definitely her natural father?'

'*Un*natural father.'

Hunter caught the same look from Jain. 'So who was?'

'No, I just mean he's a lying paedo scumbag.' Pauline let out a deep sigh, which seemed to deflate her almost as much as her self-loathing. 'Robert's a nasty piece of work. Still is, I bet. Used to drink a lot. I didn't know what he was doing or where he was half the time.'

'What happened with Stephanie?'

'I'd been going to Telford to do a night class, get some secretarial qualifications, ken? Left school with nothing but a wiggle and a perky pair of tits.' She hoisted her bra up from the shoulder strap. 'Kept me good for a bit, working in bars and that, but then I got pregnant with Steph and my tits sagged and my arse... Well.'

Jain shifted forward on the sofa. 'And Mr Quarrie was abusing Stephanie when you were at these classes?'

'Didn't even wait till I was out the door a couple of times.' She shook her head and tossed the tissue into a bucket next to her. 'The time I caught him, I'd forgot my bus fare.'

Hunter looked around the room. 'Was this here?'

'This is my— Doug's house. At the time, we lived in a flat on Moira Terrace.' She went over to the coffee table and snatched another tissue from the box. 'He denied it, said he was just comforting the lassie, said she was upset at me going out all the time. He had his fucking cock out!'

Hunter gave her some space to settle. Then again, maybe he was giving himself some space. Nothing seemed to fit together. Like doing a jigsaw in the dark. Wearing gloves. And too many missing pieces to even count.

'I grabbed Steph and drove to Porty. We reported it to the police and they did all that shite at the hospital. Then they locked him up. Took longer than forever, I swear.' She tore off another hankie and dabbed at her nose. 'Eight-year sentence wasn't anywhere near enough for what he did to that girl. Let him out after five bloody minutes, from what I heard.'

Hunter dug his pen into his notebook. 'I take it you've not had any contact at all from him?'

'The cheeky bastard still sends Steph a Christmas card every year. And a birthday card. Won't let me forget he fucked the both of us. Sorry, that was crude...' Pauline tore another tissue from the box, then another, bunching them all up. 'I bin the cards before Steph sees them. Every bloody year. It's so stressful, you know? Just waiting for the postie to appear with an envelope for her with that bloody Stranraer postage on it.'

'This is going to be a difficult question, Pauline, so can you take your time thinking it through?' Jain was smiling at her, like Mother Theresa comforting a small child. 'After your history with Mr Quarrie, I assume you trusted Mr Ferguson completely?'

'No way. Took a long time before I could. Had a private detective go through his past. His tax returns, his bins, his previous girlfriends, everything. Couldn't find anything dodgy, but...' Pauline burst into tears, hands clawing at a fresh Kleenex. 'How could I miss this?'

Ailsa decided it was time to cradle her neighbour again. 'There, there, hen.'

Hunter cleared his throat and nodded at Jain. 'Any chance I could use your bathroom? Too much tea.'

Jain gave him a slight nod back. Blink and you'd miss it.

'That's fine.' Ailsa thumbed upstairs. 'First on your left at the top of the stairs.'

'Cheers.' Hunter headed out into the hallway and started up the wooden staircase, which gave way to cream carpet at the top. Looked like it'd seen much better days.

The first door on the left had a comedy picture of a garden gnome peeing into a bucket. Next to it, a white door was stencilled with "Steph's Den!" Pink letters in that comic font that those arseholes in HR always used to show how zany they were.

Hunter nudged it open. The room stank of fresh paint, couldn't have been redecorated more than a few days ago, if that. Rock band posters covered two of the walls. The classics of despair — Joy Division, Portishead, Nirvana — among some newer bands. The XX, Electrum and the Twilight Sad. Weren't they from Edinburgh?

The Manic Street Preachers' "Holy Bible" album cover screamed out from a third wall, a triptych of a morbidly obese woman in her underwear.

Hunter swallowed — his brother Murray had that on CD. *Used to listen to it with Angus while they beat each other up on that N64 game...*

The open window let in a breeze, flapping the red gingham curtains and cooling Hunter's neck.

Didn't look like Steve or Dave had even been in there. Didn't look like anyone had — the place was spotless. Piles of paperwork on the desk next to a sleeping MacBook, the sort that cost a couple of grand. Thing was brand new. A high-end silver stereo sat next to it, an iPod Touch plugged in. Rows of DVDs filled a cupboard.

Her wardrobe didn't have a door. A stack of jumpers teetered at the back, school shirts hung among designer jeans and T-shirts. Nothing even slightly suspicious. Just a hell of an expensive image crisis.

Made sense — the mother was throwing money at her guilty conscience, and the daughter was trying her best to be someone else, someone unaffected by her own traumatic past.

The bedside chest's top drawer was open a fraction.

Hunter snapped on a glove and eased it out. An orange blister pack sat on top of white knickers and bras, all designer labels. The first row and a half of the pack were empty, each line of plastic bubbles marked out with days of the week.

Hunter's stomach churned as his fists clenched. He shut his eyes and sucked in paint fumes.

Well, that proved what Doug had said... Steph was on the pill. At sixteen.

He thundered down the stairs and stormed into the living room.

'—can't get my head around any—'

'What's this?' Hunter held up the blister pack, like he was presenting evidence in court. 'Have you seen these before?'

Pauline squinted at it, her forehead ridged like it was made of coral. 'Aye, they're Stephanie's. What the hell were you doing in her sock drawer, you dirty pervert?'

Hunter held them higher. 'Care to explain them?'

'Look. I had to take her to the doc's a few months back. Poor thing was crippled by PMS. The doctor gave her them.' She covered her face with both hands and let out a squeak as she started crying. 'Oh, Steph...'

Ailsa got in Hunter's face. 'You see what you've done to her?'

Hunter gave her a hard stare. 'Sure she's not been aiding and abetting what Doug's been doing?'

Ailsa's acid spit sprayed across his face. 'Shut your mouth.'

'Excuse me?'

'How can you suggest—'

Hunter got out an evidence bag and dropped the pills in it. 'That's going into evidence.'

'You're way over the line here, sonny.'

Hunter's Airwave chirruped. 'Control to PC Hunter. Safe to speak?'

Hunter walked into the hall and nudged the door behind him. 'Receiving and safe to speak, over.'

'Can you get out to South Queensferry nick?'

'I'm kind of busy here.'

'Oh, sorry to interrupt. It's just that serial alpha have responded to your BOLO.' Mag's voice distorted through the speaker. 'They've collected Robert Quarrie and taken him to the station for you.'

16

'After you.' Hunter held the door open for Jain, South Queensferry Police Station towering above them. One-and-a-bit storeys of muddy brick with too many windows, the kind of building eighties Chief Constables thought would serve the cause better than the Victorian ones they'd sold off to property developers.

'Pretty much the only station left round here, this. Drylaw'll be chokka with bams from Pilton and Muirhouse.' Jain stopped just inside, hands on hips. 'Anyway, you've not said a word all the way over.'

'This case is making me feel sick.' Hunter released the door, let it bounce off his toecaps. 'How could she let that happen to her daughter twice?'

'It's no consolation, Craig, quite the opposite, actually, but I've seen it a few times. And I've only been in SO a few months.'

Hunter took in the empty concourse, built for a much busier time. A time before call centres and twitter accounts. Looked shut, but shouldn't be yet. 'Think Doug knows Quarrie?'

'It's worth asking.' Jain made for the counter, striding across the black rubber flooring with a sense of purpose that almost lifted his spirits. Almost. 'Might be something in the original case's paperwork that tallies with this one.' She rapped on the glass. 'Open up!'

The curtains pulled back. Old Colin sat behind the counter, looking a couple of days short of retirement. Or a heart attack. Whisky scar tissue lined his ruddy face. He squinted at them, then frowned. 'Craig Hunter? And in uniform too. Oh, how the mighty have fallen.'

'I'm hardly mighty and I've not fallen far.' Hunter avoided his gaze, focusing on the ned behind him as he was led out of sight by a hulking uniformed officer. Torn green hoodie and a split lip. Then back at Colin, who had eyes only for Jain. 'Gather you've got a suspect for us? One Robert Quarrie.'

Colin relayed the name to his keyboard, the plastic rattling off the beige melamine counter. 'He's in interview room two. Stale bread and water. Spat in of course.'

'Cheers.' Hunter swiped his warrant card through the security system and led Jain through, stuffing his cap under his arm.

'Old pal of yours?'

'Had a few dealings out this way when I was in CID.' Hunter ruffled his hair, the gel having reverted to that horrible form of sticky, and rested his hand on the door to interview room two. 'Stabbing in South Queensferry. And another in Muirhouse about six months later. My DI always used this station as a base. Closest to his golf course.'

'Old guy back there seems to have loved you.'

'He hated us. Caught Ally rocking the vending machine when his crisps didn't fall.' Hunter pushed the door open.

Robert Quarrie sat picking at the table's grain with a nail. Didn't even look up. He wore an MC5 T-shirt with a flying panther and his lank hair hung down to his shoulders, like it hadn't been washed in weeks. He was clean shaven, thin pencil sideburns just about touching his jaw. Obvious where Stephanie got her height from — even sitting down he had the look of a seven footer.

The custody officer gave them a nod. Poor guy looked bored rigid.

Hunter stayed on his feet and waited for Jain to sit first. 'Mr Quarrie?'

'That's me.' Still not looking up, just scratching at the varnish.

'My name's PC Craig Hunter. This is DS Chantal Jain of the Sexual Offences Unit.'

That got a look. Quarrie's bloodshot eyes widened. 'Aye?'

'We need to ask you a few questions.'

Quarrie swallowed. 'Lawyer-y sort of questions?'

'Depends.' Hunter slowly sat down. He took his time placing his cap on the desk. 'Have you done anything that'd necessitate a lawyer?'

Quarrie stared back at the table, scratching harder. 'What is it?'

'Little bird tells me you lived in Stranraer?'

'Live in Cramond now.' Quarrie lifted a shoulder. 'Been there a few months.'

'Cramond, eh?' Hunter nodded his head slowly. Wasted on a man like Quarrie. Seemed more interested in his fingers and the pile of varnish dust he was building up than in Hunter's psychological power play. 'Nice bit of Edinburgh. Other side of town from Mountcastle, though, isn't it? Used to live there, didn't you?'

'Few years back, aye. Had a flat on Moira Terrace.' Quarrie locked eyes with Hunter. 'Why did you bring that up?'

Hunter flashed him a smile. 'So you work in Cramond?'

'Working in the kitchen at the Almond. Pay's shite, but they rent me a nice wee flat down the road for below the market rate. Can't complain.' Quarrie shrugged and went back to his scratching. 'Why am I here?'

'Why do you think?'

'No idea.' Scritch, scritch. 'I've nothing to hide.'

Hunter nodded slowly, this time getting an audience as Quarrie looked up. 'When did you last see your daughter?'

Quarrie's head jolted up, dark eyes sunk into the depths of his sockets. 'Steph?'

'Have you got another one?'

'No.' Back to scratching the table. 'Last time I saw my daughter was when her mother kicked me out.'

'That's a few years ago now.'

'You're telling me.'

'And you've not seen her since?'

'You saying I have, eh?' A quick glance. 'Well, I've not seen her since 2007, must be. Feels like a lifetime ago.'

'We know why you were kicked out.'

Quarrie arched his eyebrows. 'Right.'

Hunter gave him a warm smile. 'You got anything to say about that?'

'What's there to say?' Quarrie swallowed and went back to his scratching. Didn't seem to mind that the police knew about his deviant history. His raping past. His incest. 'Expected Steph to be in court, but they used that video tape thing.' He stopped and blew away the little pile of grated varnish. It disappeared into the air. 'I've served my time. Paid my debt to society.'

Must be some bloody overdraft...

Hunter tried to look him in the eye again, but got nowhere. 'There were some strong accusations against you.'

'Aye, don't I know it.' Scratch, scratch. 'That ruined my life.'

'Some might think it ruined Stephanie's life, not yours.'

'Why have you got me in here?' Quarrie sighed. Fists clenched, resting on the tabletop. 'I need to get to my work.'

'Because Stephanie's run away.'

'What?'

Seemed like genuine surprise. Hunter exchanged a quick look

with Jain, then he went back to Quarrie. 'She disappeared this afternoon from Edinburgh Royal Infirmary. You don't know anything about it, do you?'

'What? Of course I bloody don't.'

'So you've no idea where she'd go?'

'As you know, my daughter isn't part of my life.'

'How does that make you feel?'

Quarrie flexed his fingers, staring into space. 'I'm not happy about it.'

'You abused her. For years.' Hunter left enough space for Quarrie to give him some eye contact.

Scratch, scratch.

'Mr Quarrie. Your daughter's run away. Don't you want to help us find her?'

'Of course I do.' Quarrie brushed the fresh pile of varnish away. 'Not sure you digging into my past's going to help, though. I've served whatever debt to society that jury decided I was due and I've not seen her since she was a wee lassie.' He pulled his shoulders tight, nibbling at his thumbnail. 'She'll be fifteen now.'

'Sixteen.'

'Ah, Christ.' Quarrie rubbed at his forehead, eyes squeezed shut. 'Steph...'

Jain rested her elbows on the table. 'Do you know a Douglas Ferguson?'

Quarrie's eyes opened. 'That's the prick who married Pauline, right?'

'Do you know him?'

'No.' Quarrie narrowed his eyes at Jain. 'Look, I've got to get to my work.'

'Have you ever had any contact with him?'

'You know something?' Quarrie leaned forward on his elbows, seemed to prop himself up on more than the table. Years of festering resentment? Dreams of revenge? 'That arsehole met me out of prison, said he was a taxi the prison service put on. Drove me to a wee country lane and threatened to kill me. Said he'd take his time hurting me.'

Jain got up and grabbed the back of her chair, keeping her focus on Quarrie. 'What did he do?'

'Nothing. Prick's not got the balls for it. Gave me twenty and dropped me at the bus station in Stirling. Said if he ever hears about me getting in touch with Steph or Pauline, he'll go at me with a hammer and a blowtorch. That's the last I heard from the shiteing bastard.'

'Mr Ferguson never came to visit you in prison?'

'That was the first time I met him, okay?'

'Sure about that?'

'You got some evidence suggesting I know him?'

Jain looked up at the ceiling for a second, then smiled at him. 'If we go through your prison visits, say, I won't find anyone matching his description?'

'I know what you're getting at and you can forget it, you little bitch.'

Jain scraped her chair back and reached across the table to grab a handful of his T-shirt. Looked like she was going to smash his head off the table. 'I'll batter seven shades of shite out of you, sunshine. You really want to do this?'

'Come on, then.'

Hunter was on his feet, trying to separate them.

'You think I don't know how to handle myself?' Jain was tightening her grip, pulling Quarrie close enough to whisper. 'You think I've not dealt with worse scum than you?'

Hunter got hold of her wrists and pulled her back. When she let go of the shirt, he gently guided her back into the corner. 'What the hell's going on?'

Jain gazed over his shoulder, her nostrils quivering. 'It's just ... hard. Being face-to-face with pure evil like that.'

'I think the bad cop/bad cop routine isn't working. Shall we try again with at least one good cop?'

'On you bloody go, then.'

'Just don't go all 1970s on him again.' Hunter took his seat, then waited for Jain to saunter over and sit next to him. 'Mr Quarrie, can you confirm whether you had any contact with Mr Ferguson while you were incarcerated?'

Quarrie licked his lips, slowly, like he was thinking something over. 'You know I could say, aye, he visited me inside. We were mates. Shared some stories. Met on some weird forum online or something. I set him up with Pauline.' He sighed. 'But I'm not going to. I never met the guy before he tried to kill me.' He ran a nail across the tabletop. 'I had a lot of time to think when I was inside. Made me question everything about myself, what I did to Steph and her mother.' He closed his eyes and rubbed at his cheeks. 'I just want to help you find her. I don't even have to see her.'

A likely tale...

Hunter drummed on the table. 'Where were you this afternoon from three o'clock onwards?'

Back to the scratching. 'I was working till half five. Then I walked home to my flat and watched a bit of telly. '"Neighbours", I think.'

Hunter exchanged a look with Jain. 'Is that still on?'

'It's on Channel Five these days. Starts at six.'

'What happened in it?'

'You really want to know?' Quarrie shook his head. 'Paige kissed Mark for the first time.' His red face was enough to commute the embarrassment of truth. 'That do you?'

Hunter nodded slowly, then let a frown settle on his forehead. 'One last thing. If you were working earlier, why do you need to get back tonight?'

'Double shift today. Been on since breakfast. Won't get off till midnight. Best case.'

Hunter put his cap on. 'How about we drop you off at work, shall we?'

∼

HUNTER TURNED LEFT at the Almond Arms, a tall Georgian building with two rear extensions stepping down to the busy car park. It was only a few doors down from the Cramond Inn, the village's other pub, an even older fisherman's boozer. He pulled onto the back street and parked behind a Saab. The engine shook with a few final coughs, then gave its usual theatrical rendition of death by asphyxiation.

Over the road, a glorious sunset burnt the sky deep orange, dusted with a few clouds.

Hunter gave Jain a nod. 'Are you okay?' Got a shrug in response, then looked at Robert Quarrie behind the grille in the back. 'Want me to keep an eye on laughing boy here?'

'I've got a call to make, so can you go inside?'

'Fine. Just keep him here.' Hunter got out of the car and crunched across the pebbles towards the rear atrium.

Looked like The Almond had moved up in the world from its days as an underage drinking den. The back door was wide open and the place was still heaving just before nine. Red faces from too much wine, plates clinking below the bellow of laughter and shouted conversation. The charcoal grill smelled like someone had left the smoking area's door open.

The noise cut dead as he entered.

A waiter in fine French attire stopped and tilted his head. Dicky bow, white shirt, black waistcoat. The sophisticated outfit marred by the ginger moustache and rounded shoulders. 'Can I help you, sir?' Purest Midlothian accent, trying to sound refined and expansive but falling a country mile short.

'PC Hunter.' He ignored the stares from the nearby tables. 'Looking for a Stevie Ingram.'

'That's myself.'

'Can I have a word in private?'

'Would it be possible for you to come back later?' Ingram waved around the room. 'You can see we're very busy tonight and my sous chef's called in sick. Ten covers still to do and people are getting impatient.'

'I'm afraid it's important, sir.'

'Follow me.' Ingram powered through the space, tottering like a ballerino, arms out, hips swivelling, radiant smile beaming at his customers. He stopped just past the kitchen hatch and opened a heavy oak door that led into a small room. Two dark-green Chesterfield sofas faced each other over a chunky coffee table. 'In here, sir.'

'Thanks.' Hunter perched on the arm of the settee and took off his cap. 'I need to ascertain whether a Robert Quarrie was working here this afternoon.'

Ingram scowled at him as he sat on the facing sofa. 'Why?'

'His daughter's missing. We want to know—'

Ingram clutched his hands to his chest. 'He's got a daughter?'

'You didn't know?'

'Well, no. Robert's not the sort to share.'

'I'll bet he's not.'

'Is that supposed to mean something?' Ingram couldn't take his eyes off the door, shaking his head slightly. 'What's he done?'

'I just need to check he doesn't know anything about his daughter's whereabouts.'

'Well, wee Gemma's off sick, so he's been covering in the bar.' Ingram stared at the coffee table. 'He helped with the lunches in the kitchen, then did a shift pulling pints in the afternoon.'

'When did he leave?'

'Robert was here until half past five. He's the reason I'm sweating like— The reason I'm so flustered.' Ingram checked his watch. 'He was supposed to be here an hour ago.'

'What about after half five?'

'Well, I walked home with him. My house isn't far from his flat.'

'And you rent this flat to him, correct?'

'I don't, personally, but the business does. They own a row of cottages which they keep talking about—'

'What time did you last see him?'

'Ten to six? It's not far. I wanted to see my kids before they went to bed.'

Hunter got up again. 'Thanks for your time, sir.'

'Listen, should I be concerned about him?'

'Unless you or he aren't telling the truth, no.'

'Are you implying something?'

'It would be useful if there was some way to back this up.'

'Can I think about it?'

Hunter passed him a card. 'Please do. And feel free to give me a call if anything comes to mind.'

Ingram nodded. 'Could I ask you to leave by the front bar, please?'

∽

BACK OUTSIDE, the din from the restaurant had returned to the original volume before Hunter had spoiled their fun.

Quarrie was standing by the car, nibbling at his fingernails and making sure to keep his distance from Jain. He made a beeline for Hunter, twitchy fingers smoothing back the wings of his hair. 'What did you tell him?'

'I just checked your alibi.'

'Have you messed anything up for me?'

'Your secret's safe with us. For now.'

Quarrie tilted his head to the side. 'Are you threatening me?'

Hunter got in his face, though his forehead only reached to Quarrie's chin. 'If you've got anything to do with Stephanie's disappearance, you'll see what it means to be threatened by me. Is that clear enough for you?'

'Look, son, what's your problem?' Quarrie shifted away from Hunter. 'I'm not doing anything wrong here.'

'So why haven't you signed the Violent and Sex Offenders Register?'

Quarrie took a great interest in his shoes. 'I'm doing it tomorrow.'

'You should've kept your local station in Stranraer informed as to your whereabouts. You know that.'

'I spoke to a lad there. He said it was okay.'

Complete bollocks...

Hunter jabbed him in the ribs with his index finger. 'Just keep away from your daughter and your ex-wife, okay?'

The back door swung open and Ingram tottered over. 'Robert, is that you?'

'Aye, Stevie. Sorry—'

'You're *late* and you've brought the police.'

'Sorry about—'

Hunter took a step back. 'Thanks for your assistance, sir.'

'Okay.' Quarrie wandered over to Ingram, his shoulders slouched low.

Hunter opened the car door and collapsed into the driver's seat. He had that burn in the pit of his stomach again. Eating away at his flesh. Robert Quarrie followed Ingram inside the pub, like a scolded child. 'This bloody case...'

'Face to face with a child abuser...' She clicked a painted nail off her Airwave's screen. 'Did you clear his alibi?'

'Aye, for now. Unless he's lying, the manager saw him till ten to six. Quarrie didn't pick her up from the hospital.'

'Have to take his word for it?'

'For now.'

She checked her watch. 'Could just about be our guy at the Ferguson house, timewise.'

'You saw the height of him. It's not him.'

'Right. Well, Sharon's called me back to the station.'

'Anything I should know about?'

'Just a briefing for her team.'

'And am I in it?'

'No.'

17

Hunter swung onto Ferry Road and turned the radio down, "Friday I'm In Love" fading to a whisper.

Hadn't Gaynor said The Cure were one of Stephanie's bands? That tune was pretty far from their gothest, but it had some eerie darkness to it.

He passed the low-rise strip mall, a failed American-style experiment on a failed Scottish housing scheme. Sun-seeking boozers surrounded the Ferry Boat Bar, looking like the set of a soap opera. Could only be a matter of minutes before the blues and twos piled in to stop a murder.

He cruised past as the sodium street lights blinked on and glanced over at Jain, arms folded and sulking in the passenger seat. 'Want to talk about why you keep trying to kick the shite out of men twice your size?'

'They won't last thirteen seconds with me.'

Hunter frowned. 'You an MMA fan?'

'A what?'

'Never mind.' Coincidence. 'So, what's going on?'

'It's like I said in that interview.' She looked over at him, her lips tight. 'Being face-to-face with evil. Seeing that dirty bastard sitting there, treating it as a joke.'

'Sure that's it?'

'No, it's not it, Craig.' She hit the radio's power button, killing Ocean Colour Scene before the DJ had finished talking over that infernal riff. 'I've been thinking about Stephanie and her disempowerment.'

'Her what?'

'Disempowerment. Want me to spell it for you?'

'Won't help me.' Hunter slowed at the lights to let a pair of skinheads lurch across. 'So, disempowerment... What do you mean?'

Jain sat up briefly, fiddling with her seatbelt, then slumped back as Hunter pulled off at the green light. 'I mean the suffering that poor girl's been through her whole life.' She thumbed back the way, aiming at South Queensferry. 'That animal abused her when she was a child, put her through hell. Sexual and physical violence to compound the emotional kind. Can you imagine?'

Hunter couldn't answer. Couldn't even look at her. Just kept his gaze on the oncoming cars thrumming past them.

'She's been subjected to the whims of men who didn't have a second thought about violating her. Or about what it'll do to her long-term.' She hauled at her seatbelt, pulling the material blade-tight. 'To men like Robert Quarrie and Doug Ferguson, she's just a vagina. Something they can shag. Someone they can control, someone they can abuse without repercussions.'

Hunter slowed at the arc of red brake lights ahead of them. 'So why not come to us?'

'Are you serious?' She let go of the seatbelt. 'Really?'

'Listen, I hear what you're saying. I just mean... why didn't she report this abuse earlier?'

'Because she's been conditioned to hide *everything*.' She looked over as Hunter pulled up at the Crew Toll Bridge, the red bike route arches spidering across the road. 'And the reason she's run away is because two male police officers pitched up in her hospital room saying there's no evidence of rape. Of course she panics. Jesus. All her life she's put up with that sort of thing.'

Hunter stared at his hands. 'I hadn't thought about it like that.'

'It's not your fault, but... Jesus.' She stared over at him, eyes looking like they were cast from rock. 'This is different from your CID days, Craig. Took me a while to get it, but the victims here aren't dead. They're alive and they get stuck with this trauma for the rest of their life.'

∞

'Well, we are where we are, I suppose.' Lauren clicked her tongue a few times. Leith Walk was dark outside the window, just a thin sliver of light catching the side of a passing bus. 'Finlay, what do you think?'

Finlay looked up from his laptop, bleary-eyed and blinking. 'Sorry?'

Lauren sighed. 'Constable, you've got us into this mess. The least you could do is pay attention.'

'Aye, sorry, Sarge.'

'Well?'

'Well what?'

'What do you think about Robert Quarrie?'

Finlay shrugged. 'You didn't let me out to play, so how should I know?' He snorted. 'Might be worth speaking to anyone who knew him inside, though.'

'Why?'

'See what he was like in there?' Finlay scratched the top of his head, his elbow pointing up at the ceiling. 'Getting locked up for fiddling his own daughter might've put him on the radar of some of the big lads in there. Boy could be angry at her for grassing him up.'

'While I don't approve of your terminology, that's not a bad idea.' Lauren nodded slowly. 'I'm impressed. For once.'

'I'm not as bad as everyone says.' Finlay went back to his laptop.

'I'll be the judge of that.' Lauren scribbled a note on her pad. 'Right, I'll see what I can get done overnight. Might be worth a trip up to Glenochil. I'll get someone to look into it.'

'Just as well we've got Craig Hunter on this.' Finlay smirked as he opened his laptop's lid. 'Going to need the Master Detective to find her, eh?'

'I suggest you leave the humour to people who are actually funny.' Lauren glared at him until he strolled over to the printer and started rattling the plastic casing, tip-a-tap, tip-a-tap, tip-a-tap. 'What about us visiting Stranraer?'

'Let's settle for a cosy chat once Dumfries & Galloway have their ViSOR records in order.'

'See? I'm not so bad, Sarge.'

Nobody could be that bad, could they?

Hunter collected up his things and got to his feet. 'That us, Sarge?'

'For now.' Lauren clicked her new pen and put it down. Looked like she'd spent a few quid to avoid blue fingers. Until her next case of frost bite anyway. 'Night shift are taking over this mess.'

'There's got to be something else we can do.' Hunter undid the clasps on his stab-proof. 'We got any update on the phone?'

'Still waiting on her phone being switched on. Other than that, I'm afraid the MIT's taking up all of Tommy Smith's time just now and his team is stretched thin as it is. This murder at Dumbiedykes requires a lot of extracts.'

'Come on...' Hunter dumped his stab-proof on the desk, the buckle clattering on the wood. 'It's just one phone, Sarge.'

'I know, Craig. I've tried to call in a few favours with the MIT to see if we can get the records sped up, but the quickest we'll get them is the morning.' Lauren pouted at him. 'I did manage to get some of Paul Gordon's time to help us with the analysis.'

'Elvis'll love that.' Hunter picked the vest up again, swinging it like a school satchel. 'What about social media?'

'Same story, except for him actually doing something on it. He's still not got anything from the Facebook team.'

Hunter blew air up his face. 'In my experience, you just have to go in there and print it yourself.'

'Well, in that case, we'll all need to roll up our sleeves and get stuck in.' Lauren looked across the office. A shaven-headed man was lurking in the doorway, like someone had just channelled lightning through a corpse. 'I'll see you at home, John.' He snorted and headed off.

Hunter got up and started pacing around the room. 'I want to get out there, Sarge.'

'What?'

'Stephanie's still out there and we're just sitting around chatting.'

'So what do you propose? Sitting in a car like you're in a Raymond Chandler novel?'

Hunter stopped by the window and looked at her. 'At least it'll feel like we're doing something.'

'Leave the hardboiled heroics to fictional detectives, Craig. I get your impatience, but what we need here is a softly-softly approach, okay?' Lauren sighed and rubbed her sleeves. 'Bloody freezing in here still.' A shiver sent goosebumps up her arms. 'Oh, there was something. Neil Alexander, the boyfriend, he's been out speaking to the few friends of hers he knows. He called in to say a friend of Stephanie saw her in Musselburgh.'

'He was supposed to call me.' Hunter hefted his vest up, ready to put it back on. 'Want me to—'

'No. You're off-duty as of now.'

'Come on, Sarge. If she's—'

'There's a reason we've got multiple shift patterns. Besides, East Lothian isn't our remit.'

'We should be digging into Neil's background a bit harder.'

'Fine, I'll get the back shift on that, as well.' Lauren scribbled another note and nodded at Hunter. 'How's it going with DS Jain?'

A chill ran down Hunter's spine. Felt like he was Lauren for a second or two. 'Has she said something?'

'I just need to know if you're getting on well with her, Craig, that's all.'

'We're fine. Make a decent team.'

'There's nothing I should know about?'

'Well, I'm feeling excluded from their meetings.'

'You don't want to be in them, trust me. DI McNeill's hauling them across the coals as we speak. I was lucky to get out of there.' She zipped her fleece up to her chin. 'I'll see you tomorrow. Fresh as a daisy, please. That means a daisy that hasn't had six pints.'

~

HUNTER ENTERED THE CHANGING ROOM, yawning. Empty, save for the faded benches and rows of grey lockers. He opened his locker and sat on a bench to untie his shoelaces.

Master bloody Detective...

Cheeky bastard.

He reached into his pockets for his keys. The blue Ford logo glimmered in the strip lighting.

Could just scout out a few places. Everything in the police took too long... Someone somewhere must know something.

This Alec Wishart character... Introducing Doug to Pauline. Very innocent and very Edinburgh on the surface. Friend of a friend.

But lurking below that surface could be a network of paedophiles preying on damaged single mothers and their innocent children. Violating them. Brutalising them.

Robert Quarrie would get off at midnight. Worth following him down the Almond from his pub to his flat, see if he gave anything away.

Maybe the man in the garden was back at Pauline Ferguson's house. Maybe—

The door tore open and Finlay bundled in. He tossed his vest on the bench and tugged off his T-shirt. 'Hey, jabroni. Wanna head over for some brewskis?'

Like I can be arsed with that...

Hunter frowned as he got his civvies out. 'Got a thing on tonight.'

'A thing?' Finlay opened his locker. 'Sounds pretty vague, mate. Come on, let's have some pints, shoot some pool.'

Hunter took his time taking his top off, breathing hot air into the black fabric. 'I've got Krav Maga tonight.'

'Sounds like a gay nightclub, jabroni.'

'It's a martial art.' Hunter pulled the T-shirt right off. 'Israeli Defence Force.'

'Ah, right. Doesn't stop punks battering you all day, does it?'

'Most martial arts are based on seeing your opponent coming.'

'Thought you flirting with men in pyjamas was on Thursday's?'

'It never ends with you, does it? All that latent homophobia... Sure you're not covering over—'

'Piss off.' Finlay's tongue swivelled across his lips. 'I thought you went to that fighting thing on Thursdays?'

'Instructor's on holiday this week.' Hunter put his left leg into his jeans, caught a whiff of dog shite in amongst the tang of half-hour-old Lynx spray. 'Have to go to one at Meadowbank instead.'

'Right.' Finlay tapped his watch. 'It's quarter to ten, mate.'

Hunter tucked his checked shirt over his head, trying to buy some time. 'It's at this guy's house. Pay by the hour.'

'I bet you do... Another time, yeah?' Finlay slammed his locker and twisted the key. 'Tomorrow night?'

'If we're still in a job by then.'

'Shut up, mate.' Finlay sighed as he zipped up his leather jacket. 'Think it's that serious?'

'What, you cocking up guarding a teenager? Aye, it's that serious.'

'It wasn't just my fault.'

'Finlay, that game... You've dropped a ... clanger on this, okay? She walked past you. What do you think'll happen to you if she turns up in someone's sex dungeon?'

'Come on, mate. That's not going to happen, is it?'

'What about that bloke I chased at their house?' Hunter shook his head. 'You really need to pull your finger out. You know what it's been like over the last two years. Sacking you might save someone's bacon.'

Finlay stepped into his loafers. 'You mean Buchan?'

'Maybe. I'm just saying. You've been a cop for twelve years. You should know you need to cover your arse or someone else will kick it. And you don't want to lose your pension, right?'

'Not going to happen, Craig.' Finlay rested his hand on the door. 'And on that uplifting note, I'll see you tomorrow.' He pushed out into the corridor but stopped halfway. 'Look, if your Krav Maga instructor pulls out, I'll be in the Elm, aye?'

'Sure.' Hunter pulled on his jacket and dumped his new uniform back in his locker, waiting for the click of the shutting door. He laced up his Timberlands and dangled his keys in the air. Time to do it.

Out in the corridor, he kept an eye out for Finlay checking his alibi. Even the most inept of cops should see through that one.

The door to the ladies' locker room juddered open behind him. 'Evening, Craig.'

Hunter spun round and took a step back. Jain, with a thin wool coat slung around her, hugging her curves. Lucky coat. 'Chantal...' He swallowed, his pulse racing. 'Have fun at your secret briefing?'

'Secret, my arse...' She stuck her head back and huffed. 'You're not still angry about that, are you?'

'Not really. It's just—'

'Save it.' She put a finger to his lips. 'I'm off the clock and you look like you are too.'

Hunter stepped back, his mouth tingling. 'Right. Sorry.'

'Look, I'm heading over to the Elm for a drink, if you fancy it?'

18

The Cask & Barrel was pretty much dead. Tuesday dead. Over at the bar, Jain was chatting to the bearded barman, her casual charm seeming to work on him, too.

Hunter nibbled at his right thumbnail. His left hand drummed a tattoo on the wooden table.

Not been this nervous since Kandahar…

Jain wandered over, eyes locked onto his, and dumped a pint on the table in front of him, the contents pale-brown and cloudy. 'I got you a Jarl. The barman says you can still drive after that one.'

'Think I can trust him?'

'Let's just see.'

Hunter took a sip, sharp and hoppy. 'Oh, that's lovely.'

Jain chinked her wine glass against his, a thin bead of red sliding down the outside. She licked her finger and caught it before it hit the stem. 'Thanks for letting me buy the drinks.'

'You earn more than me, Sarge, so…'

'Cheeky sod. It's not that much more, you know?' Jain held his gaze as she took a long drink. 'Ah, that's better. Could do without having been open for a week, but beggars can't be choosers.' She looked around the place. 'So why here?'

'I prefer this to the Elm.'

She tilted her head to the side. 'Sure that's it?'

'Well, Lauren's a regular in there. Lives round the corner.'

'I know a couple of regulars. A sort of ex of mine and the cowboy. What a pair of chancers.'

Hunter frowned. 'Do I know the cowboy?'

'Doubt it.' She took another sip. 'I'm still not buying that as the reason.'

'Maybe I wanted to get you alone?'

She pouted. 'That's not it, either.'

'You passed the test...' Hunter took another drink. 'Finlay asked me if I wanted a pint and I knocked him back. Said I had Krav Maga. It's a martial—'

'I know what it is.' Another sip of wine. 'And do you?'

'Not been for ages.'

She smirked, her eyes twinkling in the spotlights. 'You know how I used to work in the MIT? Well, I went and caught up with a few of them. Guess what they call Finlay?'

'Arseface?'

She shook her head. 'Well, Elvis has now started calling him 1pac, but that's a side matter.' She twisted her glass around, the lipstick mark swivelling to point at Hunter. 'Napalm.'

'That's good.' Hunter laughed and took another drink of beer. 'Tell you what, I don't like the smell of Napalm in the morning. Especially after he's had one of his garlic specials the night before.'

'You make quite the pair.' She grimaced. 'Well, he doesn't, of course.' She shook her head and sipped at her wine. 'So. You really saved a cat at lunchtime?'

Hunter gave another shrug, condensation dripping down the side of his glass. 'Just doing my job.'

'You're such a sweetie.'

'Am I?'

'God, yeah. I remember at Tulliallan, you always had a different spin on things.'

Wonder why that was...

'First four weeks on the job, that.' Hunter took a much bigger drink than he intended. 'I just like cats. Finlay was next to useless.'

'Have you got one?'

'Bubble. She's a bit of a handful. Thought of getting another one to keep her company, but I just don't have the time. Plus, I'm taking the piss with my landlord as it is.'

Her dimpled smile turned into a frown. 'Why are you still helping out with this case?'

'I've not got a choice.'

'You've got a Messiah complex.'

'Ten years getting kicked up the arse if you don't follow orders does funny things to a man.'

'What do you mean?'

'You know I was in the Army, right?'

'No?'

'Enlisted at sixteen and I was off to Iraq.'

'Jesus. I had no idea.' She sipped at the wine, gazing into space. 'How was it?'

'Hell. Just...' Hunter shut his eyes. 'Hell. That's the only way you can describe it. Never met the devil, but you could smell the brimstone. The shit we had to do, man... And the heat. It's like getting off the plane in Ibiza and walking into a wall of fire, only it's ten times drier.'

She pulled a face. 'I know I'm one of those foreigners stealing jobs and everything, but I can't stand anything hotter than eighteen degrees.'

'Yeah, it took me a while to realise I wanted to get out of that kitchen.'

'Ten years is a long time, though?'

Hunter stared into the depths of his beer. 'Didn't have the imagination to leave.'

'So, if you're really that set on following orders, why do you rock the boat so often?'

'Do I?'

'You don't want to know what they call you.'

'When you say "they", you mean Elvis, right? Guy's an arse.'

'That he is.' She toasted her glass in the air before taking another drink. 'Conan.'

'Conan?' He looked down at his creeping gut, still sticking out despite hours of the plank. 'That because I've got Arnold Schwarzenegger's physique?'

'Hardly. It's because you're a barbarian. All that farting and your BO.'

'I don't stink, do I?'

'You've cleaned up since Tulliallan.'

Hunter shook his head again. 'Bloody wankers up there, I tell you.'

Jain wrapped her hands around her glass. 'The cowboy said you used to work with him up at St Leonard's?'

'You're talking about Scott Cullen, right?'

'That's the one. So why are you in uniform now?'

'Wish I knew. Wasn't my decision.'

'Really? Cullen said you were a decent detective.'

'Well, that shows how little he knows.' Hunter stared over at the attract sequence on the fruit machine as it hooked in another solo drinker. 'I clearly wasn't if I got busted down to uniform. Maybe I should've taken a leaf out of the cowboy's book.'

'He's doing well. Rumour is he'll be a DI soon.'

And they say there's justice in the world…

Hunter took another swig. 'He's only just got his DS post. The guy's inept.'

'Come on, he's not *inept*.'

'Right, so he's ept?'

'Very good.' Jain swept a hand across her fringe, tucking it over. 'You know that chat we had earlier? Have you actually applied for a DC position?'

'Maybe.'

'But you've been in uniform for, what, two years?'

'They didn't want me, Chantal.' Hunter took another drink of beer. Already hitting his head like a train. 'Enough about my tale of woe. How are you doing out in Bathgate?'

'Changing the subject?'

'Naturally.'

She looked away. 'I'm okay.' She finished her glass.

Hunter nodded at her empty. The car key in his pocket dug into his thigh. He could drive now, scope out the territory, do a bit of undercover work. Or… He picked up his pint and drained it. 'My round.'

She grinned, the dimple puncturing her cheek. 'Is there an alternative?'

DAY 2

Wednesday
12th August 2015

19

'─── Where police are still searching for schoolgirl Stephanie Ferguson, who disappeared from Edinburgh Royal Infirmary yesterday afternoon. Anyone with any information as to her whereabouts—'

Hunter snapped off the radio and cracked another egg into the smoking oil, the clear substance flashing to white as it started bubbling in the pan. The toaster popped up and he flipped the first egg over, the white sizzling afresh.

Fluff swept round his legs, swishing against his ankles. 'Mieaow.' Bubble's food bowl must be empty.

Hunter separated the hissing and spitting eggs with a plastic spatula. 'Time to feed you, young lady—'

Arms reached around him from behind, hugging his bare chest. Kisses traced up his neck. 'How's my big constable?'

Hunter stood there, feet cold on the kitchen floor. The buttons on Jain's shirt rubbed against his back. 'I'm good.' He twisted round and wrapped his arms around her. 'How do you want your eggs?'

'You might've fertilised them last night.'

'Shut up. I used two condoms at the last count.' Hunter reached over to kiss her. 'I meant sunny side up or … the other one. Where you flip it over.'

'Over easy.' She grinned at him and pinched his cheek. 'Thought I smelled moisturiser. You know you've got more products in that tiny bathroom than I have in mine?'

'It's 2015. Eggs?'

'Over easy.'

'That's how I like them, too.'

'And burnt by the looks of things.'

'Terrific.' He tried to break off from her embrace. Failed.

'I'm not hungry.' She grabbed his balls through his shorts, sharp nails making him clench. 'There are definitely two here.'

'Funny.'

'You've got a choice, Hunter. Eggs or balls.'

'I'm running late.'

'Then so am I.'

'Come on, I've got to get into my uniform, you just need to chuck on your blouse and knickers.'

'And that's after I let you into them.'

'Christ, your chat's awful.'

'Come here.' Jain reached over and turned off the hob. She clasped his hand tight and led him into the hall. Then she broke off, spinning around and walking backwards into the bedroom, the bedside lamp lighting up her skin. She undid the topmost of the shirt's three buttons. Then the second. Then the last. And then she shrugged free of the garment, casually letting it fall on the floor. The morning light from the window outlined the graceful curve of her hips as she sashayed towards the bed, reclined on it, and ever so slowly spread her legs. 'I see you've made your choice, then.'

Hunter knelt on the edge of the bed and eased off his shorts. 'Going to have to brave the canteen's fried eggs with their little bits of bacon stuck in.'

'Yum.'

Hunter crawled up the bed on his hands and knees, taking his time. He pulled himself closer and ran a hand up her bare leg from the ankle to the knee, tiny dots of sharp stubble rustling. He kissed her on her inner thigh. 'Sure you don't want any eggs?' Another kiss. 'Got them from my brother's hens at the—'

'I don't want any eggs, Craig.' Her tight fingers gripped round his shoulders. 'Now, shut up and kiss me.'

∽

'Craig!'

Hunter pulled into Leith Walk's underground car park and cleared the barrier. 'What's up?'

Jain was almost sucked down into the fabric of her seat. 'I told you to drop me off a block away.'

'Ashamed to be seen with me?'

'It's not that, it's just—'

'So it is that?' Hunter parked his car and leaned over to kiss her. Long and hard. 'Ashamed to be seen with me?'

Crack. The window behind him.

Jain's eyes bulged. 'Shite.'

Hunter swung round.

Finlay was gurning in through the driver's side window, clutching a massive coffee beaker. 'Morning!'

'Terrific.' Hunter pressed the button and the driver-side zipped down. 'Morning yourself.'

'You two love birds out for a spot of early-morning dogging?'

'If we are, you're not joining in, Finlay.'

'Funny.'

The passenger door clicked open. 'I'll see you guys upstairs.' Jain practically ran across the concourse.

Hunter turned to Finlay, now resting on the door. 'Thanks for that.'

He smacked his lips. 'I'll say one thing for your taste in poontang, I'd smash her backdoors in.'

'Jesus, Fin, you're a bloody neanderthal. You can't say misogynistic bullshit like that.'

'Whatever.' Finlay leered at Hunter. 'Bet you have. Several times.'

'No comment.' Hunter pulled his keys out of the ignition. *Almost like he resents me for not getting pissed with him or heading out for some PI action last night.* 'If you must know, I spotted her on Leith Walk and gave her a lift up. Ever heard of being courteous?' He started winding up the window.

'Watch it!' Finlay had to jump out of the way, splashing coffee on the concrete. 'How was Krav Maga?'

Hunter got out of the car and zapped it. 'It was fine.'

'Fine, eh?' Finlay unfolded a stack of papers. 'Well, look lively, we've got a lead on the lassie.'

'What?'

'Princess said we're plainclothes today.' Finlay waved at Hunter's shirt and jeans, the same as last night. 'You can keep that Brokeback special on.' He tossed him a copy of that morning's *Argus*. 'We're famous!'

Hunter scanned it. A grainy CCTV shot of Stephanie at the hospital sat alongside "MISSING: EDINBURGH TEENAGER FLEES COPS". 'Famous? More like infamous. The kind of losers who get their own YouTube video reel.'

'I'll take it, jabroni. Anyway, Keith's giving us the big Saab for the day.' Finlay tossed the keys in the air and caught them with a smug pout you'd never tire of slapping. 'Come on, I'm driving.'

Missing

~

FINLAY STUFFED the coffee cup back in the holder, somehow managing to splash half the content over the upholstery. 'If that guy was shagging her... Can you imagine? Same with her old man.' He turned right onto St Andrew's Square, a tram rattling past them. He stopped at the first set of lights and twisted round, a stupid grin on his face. 'Tell you, this car is the shizzle.'

Give me Chantal any day...

Hunter rubbed his eyes, desperate for a cup of tea and some protein. 'So, what's this lead?'

Finlay gave him his best pervy leer. Can't beat natural talent. 'After you tell me about you and DS Jain.'

A slight tremor shook Hunter's hands, so he clamped them over his knees. Still throbbing, like he'd popped the cartilage out. 'Tell me about the lead.'

'You let her do the walk of shame, you dirty bastard.'

Hunter slumped back in his seat as they stopped at the second set of lights on the bit of Princes Street you could still drive on. 'I'm saying nothing.'

'Good effort, sir. Like I say, cracking—'

'Lead. Now.'

'Nice arse on her. Come on, did you shag her?'

'Finlay, you don't say things like that about another man's—'

'Girl?' A wide smirk made Finlay look even dafter than usual. No mean feat. 'So it's serious? How long's it been going on for?'

'Piss off, Napalm.'

Close to punching this clown. Put his head straight through the window. No need to open it first.

'What. Is. The. Lead?'

'Look, sorry I mentioned it, jabroni. Your secret's safe with me.' Finlay crossed his heart and took a slurp of coffee, sucking through the lid like a kid hoovering up the dregs of a milkshake. 'Been in since five this morning chewing up the work, man. That sighting in Musselburgh? False alarm. Girl looked a bit like Stephanie. Wasn't her...'

'So what is it?'

'Transpires young Stephanie did catch a bus.' Finlay set off from the traffic light, then licked his lips as he took a right just past the bus station. 'Me and Elvis found her walking right in here.'

~

Hunter accompanied Finlay across the canteen, then took a seat at a vacant table. 'I'll wait here for your mysterious contact.'

Finlay tapped his temple and marched off. Like he was in a clichéd spy novel and needed to find the microfilm before someone in East Germany got killed.

Hunter stretched out and looked around. The place was buzzing with early-morning depression, even though it looked like midday outside. Still got a few weird looks from the drivers. A few sniffs, too, never mind that his uniform was back in his locker.

A kingdom for a cup of tea and a week of sleep.

He picked up the paper and scanned through the news story.

If this was Buchan's tigers, they were at risk of extinction. What a shower of slack-jawed amateurs. The article wasn't so much trying to help find Stephanie as have a go at the police, but whichever keyboard warrior was responsible for it, they couldn't even get their teeth into it. All weak opinions and regurgitated platitudes.

How very Edinburgh.

Hunter stared out of the window across the bus station tarmac. A middle-aged woman in a lime-and-pink tartan suit was struggling with her massive suitcase, not far off her own size. Must be American. A shifty bloke in a billowy blouse and cut-off tracky bottoms ambled up and offered to help her. Looked like love at first sight.

Hard to believe that only yesterday Stephanie had been in the same spot... Aimlessly running from her abusers or desperately racing to some mysterious haven of safety?

'Over here, sweet cheeks.' Finlay clapped Hunter on the back and hot-stepped across the canteen, Hunter choosing to let him go ahead by himself. Better to come in heavy-handed later, lay on some extra pressure when the interview ran out of steam.

He grabbed the paper and headed over to a table near the back, aiming for a subtle vantage point on Finlay and his mysterious informant.

Finlay was all big gestures and bravado as he met his man, shaking hands as they took a seat. 'Tam McEwan?'

'Depends on who's asking.' Everything about the guy was grey. His slicked-back hair, the thin beard, the bus company suit covered in union badges. 'You the police?'

Finlay showed him his warrant card, like he was a seasoned detective. 'That I am.'

'Then, aye, I am he.' Tam slumped down and necked an energy drink. He opened a can of Red Bull. Looked like he needed them both — deep lines ran away from his eyes. 'Billy Pollock sent you, aye?'

Finlay pushed a photo across the table. 'We're looking to trace this girl.' He let Tam snatch it, waited for him to get a good look. 'Her name's Stephanie Ferguson. We understand she got on a bus you were driving last night.'

'Quarter to six through to Glasgow. Last run of my shift.' Tam dumped the photo back on the table. 'I drove twelve routes yesterday, you know that, right? There and back. That's a lot of people.'

'Your supervisor said you recognised her.'

'I did, but...' Tam stared at the image again, bleary-eyed like he was still half-cut. 'Buggered if I know anything else, pal. Sorry.'

Hunter took the negative body language as his cue, crossed the room and tossed the newspaper on the table in front of Tam. 'That's her there.'

'Easy, pal! You a cop, too? Hold on just a minute now... Shite, is that her?' Tam held the paper at arm's reach, like he'd never been face to face with a broadsheet before. 'Christ.' He finished his can and crumpled it, eyes locked on the page. 'Aye, I remember her now.'

The wonders of fame...

Tam nodded vigorously. 'Lassie was on her mobile, eh? Kept jabbing the bloody bell. Does my nut in.'

'Did she go through to Glasgow?'

'No, got off in Edinburgh. For definite. Stop for the zoo.'

20

Hunter pulled in by the row of Victorian townhouses opposite the zoo's entrance and glanced at the passenger seat, where Finlay seemed to be in a coma. 'You got anything yet?'

Finlay shot up and smacked himself in the face with the Airwave clamped in his hand. Grumbling some inane excuse, he switched the handset on and pressed it against his ear. 'Last I heard, Elvis was still looking.'

'Going to stick that thing on speaker?'

'Man, you're such a princess.' Finlay stabbed a finger on the screen, then held the device out. 'Paul, you're on with Craig Hunter.'

'Morning, Craig. Heard you shagged Chantal Jain.'

'And good morning to you, too.' Hunter glared at Finlay, mouthing: 'Was that you?'

Finlay waved both hands and shook his head.

'Aye, she was up here chatting to young Eva and Cullen.' Elvis cackled down the line. 'Says you've got a wee willy winky.'

Jesus Christ. What?

She was up there, talking about my ... Why?

Hunter held the handset at arm's length, tempted to smash the thing on the floor. 'Have you actually got anything for us?'

'Getting there.'

'Didn't think to check her phone records when you were asked?'

'One, there's this murder investigation going on. Two, Tommy Smith's only just given me access.' Elvis hammered the keyboard in the background. 'There you are. Found it.'

'So?' Hunter scowled at the phone. 'Who did she call?'

'Ghostbusters. Hang on.' Sounded like Elvis had dialled off. 'She didn't call anyone. She received one. Balls. Unknown caller.'

'Don't the network people know?'

'I'll try, usually want a RIPSA form or something.' More keyboard abuse down the line. 'You on good terms with your DI?'

Hunter sighed and looked away at the passing traffic. 'You know I'm in uniform these days.'

'Aye, I do that.' Elvis laughed again. 'Well, have a word with your Inspector unless you've pissed him off, as well?'

Tempted to chuck the bloody thing out of the window. Like that'd harm Elvis...

'Anything else in the tea leaves?'

Elvis paused for a few seconds. 'She was on that call for ages. Twenty-two minutes plus change.'

'That doesn't make sense.' Hunter clicked his fingers. 'Can you trace the location?'

'Now that I can do. Sort of.' Elvis's mouth breathing sent waves of distortion down the line. 'Right, here we go. She started the call at St Andrews Square, then it switched through a few towers to the one by Haymarket. Then another couple and we're at the one by the Holiday Inn next to the zoo.'

Hunter looked back at the big grey box lurking behind the trees. The Holiday Inn's conference centre extension sat squat at the side of the road, like a bunker on the front line. Jesus, where did that image come from? Was the whole of Edinburgh a war zone these days? Certainly enough traitors...

'Then the call swapped to the tower by PC World on Glasgow Road.'

'You sure?'

'Sure as eggs are disgusting when you leave them burning in the pan too long.'

Fan-fucking-tastic. What else had she told them?

Hunter pulled out into traffic and powered along St John's Road, a jungle of trees and generic Edinburgh houses. Most of the cars were heading into town. 'So Stephanie was walking?'

'I'd say.'

Hunter rolled his eyes at Finlay. 'Anything else on that?'

The purple PC World building crawled round the bend, lurking by low post-war houses.

Finlay shook his head. 'This is a long way to be walking, dude.'

'Aye, you're not wrong, my man.' Elvis yawned down the line. 'Hang on. The call switched to a mast in the park up on Corstorphine Hill. Ended there.'

Hunter pulled in at the side of the road, just by the roundabout. 'What, so she didn't get to PC World?'

'Doesn't look like it. If I was a betting man, I'd say she was walking up the hill.'

'Let's say you're right...' Hunter swung around to look at the wall of trees climbing over the houses on the skyline. 'Why would she go up there?'

~

'THIS IS IT?' Finlay put his hands on his hips and propped himself against the car. 'You're sure?'

'That's what Elvis said.' Hunter scowled across the green expanse of the park near the top of Corstorphine Hill, practically glowing in the early morning light. A few people stood by the bus stop behind them, the nearest woman talking on her phone as a dog pulled on its lead. Further over, modern bungalows and houses sprawled down the side of the hill. 'This is another needle-in-a-haystack job, isn't it?'

'You trusted Elvis...' Finlay shrugged. 'Useless bastard.'

'Pot, kettle.'

'What are you saying?'

'Just watch who you're calling useless.'

Finlay snorted and looked around. 'She could be anywhere up here.'

'So let's get looking.'

'We don't know she's still here, do we? She's not had any camping gear. It's not like she'll be sleeping rough.'

Hunter frowned. *Made sense.* 'So she's staying with someone?'

'You tell me, jabroni.' Finlay gave a wide gurn, the special one reserved for being particularly arsey, where his bottom lip almost covered the top. 'This case must make you feel like you're a detective again. Beats saving cats, eh?'

'This is why I joined the police, Finlay. I could've earned a shitload working the rigs or what have you, but I'm doing something for society.'

'I'm doing it for the money, pal.'

'The money? The police?'

'The pension, then.' Finlay shoved his hands in his pockets. 'Soon as my thirty are up, I'm selling up here, moving to Spain and drinking myself to death.'

'And that's not depressing?' Hunter stared at the houses behind them. Could be anyone in there. He got out his Airwave. 'Did Elvis say Tommy Smith gave him the info?'

Missing 131

'Think so, why?'

Hunter jabbed the dial button on his Airwave. 'PC Craig Hunter to Control. Over.'

'Receiving.'

'Mags, can you put me through to Tommy Smith in Forensic Investigations?'

'Sure thing.'

The Airwave buzzed in his ear. 'Craig Hunter?' A burst of laughter erupted from the handset. 'You still alive?'

'Aye, Tommy, I'm still breathing. How are you doing?'

'Can't complain. Well, I could, but hey ho.' Tommy paused. 'Take it this isn't you angling for an invitation to my Burns event next week?'

'It's business, sadly. You still remember that bottle of Dunpender I gave you a couple of years back?'

'Knew that'd cost me in the end…'

'Don't think you could do me a wee favour, could you?'

'Damn and blast. Should've just got me a Likely Laddie, then I wouldn't feel so beholden. What is it?'

'You gave a load of data to Paul Gordon, right?'

'That Elvis boy? Aye, what of it?'

'Unknown caller on there at quarter to six last night, something like that. Any chance—'

'Got it in front of me. That teddy boy said this Stephanie girl you're looking for had called her just before.'

'Her?'

'Says here the phone belongs to one Gaynor Tait.'

∽

'GREW UP ROUND HERE.' Finlay held his Airwave away from his head and scowled up at the block of ex-council flats, covered as much by satellite dishes as brown harling. Four storeys of misery. 'Christ, man. This lassie's a teacher and she's living here? So much for key-worker mortgages, eh?'

'Maybe she likes it?'

'Tell you, this country's going to shite, mate.'

'Says the man who wants to drink himself to death in Spain.'

'Man needs a goal in life.' Hunter pulled up at the T-junction, waiting for a mobility scooter to unblock the way. 'Where now?'

Finlay waved across the road. 'There.'

Hunter parked in a bay between two big work vans. He got out and crossed over, then marched up the path to a smaller box of houses. Just four flats across two floors. He put his cap on and knocked on the bottom-right door, a white plastic thing. Replacement, but it looked more like a private job than a council one.

No answer.

He knocked again.

'She's not in, mate.' Finlay was staring down the street, watching a young woman hoik up a thong as she carried her baby. 'Let's get over to the school.'

'I'm smelling a rat here.'

'Well, I'm smelling bacon and fags.' Finlay was still staring at the mother. 'Spilt milk and tears. Like that Jam song, right? "Town Called Alice".'

'Malice, you idiot.' Hunter sighed as he crouched down and flipped open the letterbox. 'Ms Tait, got a parcel for you!'

A floorboard creaked. Feet padded across the hall.

'Just a second!'

The door opened a crack. An eye peeked out into the daylight, guarded yet gullible.

Stephanie!

Her eye widened and she shoved back on the door.

Hunter gave it a good shove, knocking the girl backwards into the flat.

She tumbled over, landing defenceless on the hallway carpet. 'No...'

21

Hunter gripped the handset and looked back inside the flat. A coffin-shape of sunlight was crawling along the dark laminate flooring in the hallway.

Stepping into a coffin can't be a good thing, can it?

He tightened his grip on the Airwave. 'I still think we should try to bring the teacher in, Sarge.'

'And I hear you, Craig. Just keep Stephanie there.' Lauren sounded like she was jogging down a corridor, her breath coming in short bursts. 'You understand what I've just said, right?'

Hunter kept his eyes locked on Stephanie through the glass door. 'Aye, we'll keep her until you get here.'

'I don't want her running away again.' A car door slammed at her end. 'Go.' An engine revved followed by a blast of siren. 'We'll be fifteen minutes tops, okay?'

Not at this time of day...

Hunter killed the call and opened the living room door.

Stephanie sat on a green futon, discarded bedsheets bunched up at her feet. Arms crossed, mouth hanging open. Still not speaking.

Hunter stood next to her. 'Stephanie, you really need to speak to us.'

She shrugged and glanced at a desk in the corner of the room, the kind of chrome latticework IKEA sold by the van-load.

Hunter wandered over to the computer. Looked ancient, a grey monitor sitting on top of a grey box. The screen was logged onto Facebook. 'You've been keeping yourself busy, then?'

Another shrug. 'Bored as hell.'

'You've got your phone.'

'Battery's dead and I can't exactly go home for my charger.'

'And Ms Tait doesn't have one?'

Stephanie started bunching up the bedclothes.

'I said, Ms Tait doesn't have one?'

'Different type. She's got an iPhone.' Stephanie nibbled at a fingernail and took another glance at the computer. 'Wasn't posting anything. Just seeing what people are up to.'

'Stephanie, you told your mother what Doug has been doing to you. Then you started telling me at the hospital. Who are you running from, Stephanie? Is it Doug?'

For once, she met his eye. No make-up on today, made her look her age. Just a teenage girl. She sniffed and looked away again, sticking her thumb in her mouth, like a little child now. 'They're after me.'

'Who are?'

'Can't say.' She nibbled at her bottom lip. 'They'll hurt Mum.'

'Who will?'

'I can't say.'

'Stephanie, there are four police officers outside the house, twenty-four hours a day. Your mother is safe.'

The man in the garden...

Hunter tried to crouch down, but his knee blared out an alarm that must have been heard across the room, so he stood tall again. 'There was someone at your house last night. Has Doug got people looking for you?'

Stephanie shut her eyes. A slight shake of her head, barely enough to shift her hair.

'Has Doug got people putting frighteners on you?'

A vein in her temple started throbbing. 'Doug said he wants to take me away. Wants us to run away together.'

'Did you say you would?'

'Well, aye. I didn't want him to get angry with me. Didn't want him taking it out on Mum, either.'

'Does he do that a lot?'

'Time to time. Usually when he's been drinking.'

'What happened yesterday? Did you tell him you weren't going with him?'

She averted her eyes and stared out of the front window. The sun danced in the elms like it didn't have a care in the world. 'Mum came in and we were arguing. So I told her everything Doug's been doing to me.'

'That must've been difficult.'

'You can't imagine.' Stephanie covered her eyes, tears flowing down her cheeks. 'Why me? Why do they always pick on me?'

'It's not your fault.' Hunter reached out to console her but pulled back at her flinch. 'I wish I could say it's just bad luck, but there are some really nasty people out there. We need you to give a statement about what he's been doing to you.'

'But what about Mum?'

'She's fine, Stephanie.' Hunter crouched down, ignoring the pain in his knee while aiming for a more sympathetic posture. 'Are you concerned about your father?'

'You know what Doug's been doing to me.'

'I meant your natural father.'

She scrunched up, hiding her face. 'He's dead.'

Hunter frowned at Finlay, who held his hands up. He cleared his throat.

She jolted to her feet. 'What's going on?'

'Stephanie, you should sit down.'

She sat down with a thud and kicked the bedclothes away. 'Tell me.'

Hunter swallowed hard and wet his lips. 'Your father is alive.'

'No...'

'He's living in Cramond.'

'No, no, no...'

Hunter wanted to reach over and pat her on the back, try to calm her down. 'I'm sorry to have to tell you.'

'I thought he was dead... It...' She collapsed against the futon. 'No...'

'We know what happened between you and your father. Has he tried to get in touch with you?'

CRASH.

'Stay here.' Hunter nodded at Finlay as he darted over to the hall door and nudged it open.

Nothing in the hall.

He whispered at Finlay: 'We need to get her out of here.'

CRASH.

Sounded like it came from the kitchen.

Hunter peered back into the living room. 'Stephanie, we're going to take you to the police station. We'll get your statement on record and help put Doug away. Okay?'

'But they'll—'

'It's okay. We'll keep you safe.'

'Okay, okay.' Stephanie got up and grabbed a hoodie from the table next to the futon, then froze as the banging downstairs seemed to register with her.

Finlay sighed at Hunter and grasped her wrist. 'You won't mind—'

She recoiled, like he'd splashed acid over her hand. 'No!'

'Woah, it's okay.'

'I do mind.'

Hunter gripped Stephanie's squirming wrist and hauled her through the door, then hustled her up the path. At the end of it, he stopped and let go.

Finlay was back at the house, his baton drawn like a sword.

The street was dead, just a couple of small cars trundling off to work. Three sets of heels clicked down the far side, each to its own rhythm. Dolled-up women heading to the bus stop.

Not too far to the Saab, maybe twenty paces.

Finlay joined them, spinning round to take in the street. 'I'll go ahead to the car, okay?'

'Go.' Hunter grabbed Stephanie's wrist again and waited until Finlay had unlocked the Saab. 'Now.'

'You're hurting me!'

'I'll let go again as soon as you're in that car, okay?' Hunter started across the road towards the squad car, while Finlay jerked the back door open. 'In you go, Stephanie.'

She rested a hand on the top of the door and looked back at Hunter. 'Thanks.' Then her eyes bulged. 'Shit!'

Something cracked off the back of Hunter's skull. He toppled forward, the searing pain making his eyes water. As the car door shot towards him, his vision went blurry. Then faint. Then black.

22

Cold concrete against his cheek. The mangled stench of a sewer. Heels clicking towards him, like they were running.

Hunter opened his eyes and got up on all fours. Woozy, felt like someone had cracked open his head. He dabbed fingers at his crown, almost like he was touching his brain. His hands were covered in blood, dark and wet. It dripped onto the pavement like crimson rain.

Hunter used the squad car's door handle to winch himself up and leaned back against the car, his gut lurching forward.

What the hell hit me? Shit, Stephanie!

He looked around, struggling to focus and stay upright at the same time.

Finlay lay in a foetal position a few metres away, cradling the bottom of a low hedge, thick and lush. He was groaning, facing away from—

A red car blasted past, wheels spinning as it took off. Looked like a Hyundai.

Hunter spun his head to catch the number plate, bile shooting up his throat.

He could see the back of Stephanie's head inside the car.

No, no, no...

Come on, get the registration.

SA61...

And it was gone. Just a partial.

Stephanie's gone – taken *– and I don't have a bloody—*

'Are you okay?' A woman in heels clicked over to him, concern etched on her face.

'We're police, ma'am.' Hunter could barely keep his eyes open. 'Did you see that car?'

'Going too fast for a built-up—'

'Did you get a plate?'

'Sorry, no.'

Hunter stared down the street, the horizon keeling to the left, then sliding right.

Go after the Hyundai? Or help Finlay?

'Stay with him!' Hunter wrestled with the squad car door and got behind the wheel. The road swayed in front of him, blurring like a rifle sight out of focus. He fumbled with the ignition and twisted until the engine roared. The sound wobbled, threatening to cut out again.

Not now...

Hunter drove out slowly, wrestling his seatbelt down and clicking it in as he floored the accelerator. Too hard. The Saab jolted forward. He eased off and jabbed at his Airwave: 'PC Craig Hunter to Sergeant Lauren Reid, over.'

'Safe to talk, Craig.' The high-speed drone of the engine blended in with the wailing siren. 'What's up?'

Hunter slowed the car down as nausea blackened the edges of his vision. 'She's been taken.'

'We know that. You found her.'

Hunter pulled the car to the right, barrelling down a side street and fighting back the urge to throw up. 'No, someone's taken her. Assaulted me and Fin—'

'Shit.'

Hunter hit the brakes and skidded to a halt. The road ahead was blocked by bollards. He slammed the Saab into reverse and revved back onto the pavement, getting an earful from an old man walking his dog. 'I'm in pursuit of the car, a red Hyundai SUV, license plate beginning SA61.'

'We're just passing Haymarket, Craig. Can you keep them in sight?'

'Get other units out here, okay?' Hunter slowed at the T-junction across from a token-gesture park, his skull feeling like it'd been cloven open. To the right, a blur of red weaved between the oncoming traffic in the far distance, just by the lump of trees on Corstorphine Hill. 'Got sight of the vehicle again, Sarge.' He pulled off to the right, blues and twos blaring out into the morning air.

A row of old women at the bus stop followed his arc as he scythed through the traffic.

'Okay, Craig, I've got three units heading your way. Can you give us a better description?'

'It's like the car on the Walking Dead. You know, the one that didn't get a scratch?'

'Colourful as ever...'

'But red... Need to go.' Hunter stabbed his Airwave and burst forward in the right-hand lane, cars screeching onto the pavement at his approach. Another T-junction. He sped right, squeezing a silver Audi and a grey Mondeo aside. Ahead, the cars on the main road slowed, a 26 bus dragging a bow wave of slow traffic behind it.

Hunter let the Saab eat up the gap to the last car. He blared along the road, more like a country lane than a city thoroughfare, fields to the left, council houses and a once-posh hotel opposite. Round the bend, they were heeding his cry and pulling in.

Where the hell was the Hyundai? Was it even the same one?

Hunter slowed, checking every car as he passed. Not a single red car. He stopped at the mini-roundabout and looked around.

Right went deeper into Clermiston, ahead back down the hill to St John's Road. Which way?

Hunter darted forward, pedal to the metal as he ploughed down the hill, gaining speed like a rolling egg on Easter Sunday.

A bus on the right pulled out and jolted to a stop, blocking the oncoming traffic. Blocking Hunter.

Terrific.

He honked the horn. Nothing was moving. Wait. An old Sierra, an ivory-white museum piece, mounted the kerb, all four wheels on the grass verge.

Gave Hunter the inch he needed. He crawled round it, waving a distracted thank you, and powered on down the hill.

Red flashed to his left.

Hunter hit the brakes and slid to a halt, neck craning round. Too far — another wave of nausea crashed through his skull.

The red Hyundai sped out of the bus terminus, a tight roundabout doubling back the way, and cleared through Hunter's wake, heading back up the hill.

The bastard's keeping away from the main road...

Hunter slammed the stick into reverse and whizzed round, just touching a Passat as he stopped and bolted forward, retracing his path.

The traffic was still just about static, sitting off the carriageway. A few cars stirred, sensing their chance to get off to the office.

Still no sign of the bloody Hyundai.
Wait. There. Coming right towards him on the grass.
How the bloody hell did—

He pulled into the Hyundai's path, the Saab's front wheels clambering onto the grass verge.

The Hyundai feinted left and tore past his rear end with a crack.

Terrific...

Hunter engaged the four-wheel drive and slammed it into reverse again, screeching round. He swayed to the side, his vision blacking out.

Thunk!

The car rolled forward.

Hunter crunched on the handbrake and looked around. The back window's glass had fractured. He'd hit a streetlight, the concrete base. Sounded like it had torn off half of the rear end. He stuck the car in first and gave it some welly. The Saab came back to life with a raging growl.

Not to worry, Keith can fix it later.

The Hyundai was in his sights now, snowballing down Clermiston Road, the main route out of Edinburgh. Then it took a left, along a former country lane long swallowed up by the city's ravenous appetite to eat away at its own greenbelt.

Hunter followed, passing mossed walls guarding old stone houses as he bounced over a sleeping policeman.

The Hyundai swayed round a tight right turn and disappeared.

That's how you're playing it, is it?

Hunter pulled on the handbrake and skidded right, kicking down to second as he got to the apex of the turn and gaining a couple of metres on the fugitive.

The road was much quieter, just a lime-green Picasso using it as a rat run. Hunter slalomed through a chicane, tires squealing to the accompaniment of a squeaky blast from the Citroën's horn.

He sped up as he descended the hill, generic post-war bungalows blurring past. Ahead, the wide expanse of Edinburgh opened up, rooftops and trees all the way to the Pentland hills bulging on the horizon.

Through another chicane.

There it was, the Hyundai barrelling down the hill and—

Terrific.

An old man was pushing a brown bin across the road.

Hunter screeched to a halt, the whiplash filling his head with red-hot pain. The man shook his fist in the air as Hunter put his foot down and swerved around him. Just then his knee decided to get in on the act, screaming out and making him pull his foot up again. Seconds ticking away... He gritted his teeth and pushed the pedal down full.

The bungalows gave way to mansions on one side, trees obscuring most of them. He took a tough left turn as parked cars doubled up, ring-fencing the small hospital.

Slammed the breaks on as another T-junction came out of nowhere.

Corstorphine Road to the left, St John's to the right.

No red Hyundai in either direction.

23

Hunter pulled up outside Gaynor Tait's house, now surrounded by squad cars, and parked behind an ambulance. The engine coughed and spluttered, then juddered off.

Knackered another car...

Hunter got out and nudged the door shut. The day was far too bloody bright. He screwed his eyes up and blinked back tears of pain. His head wanted to cuddle his feet. A shake of it and it was better, maybe. His shoulders were aching, his knee twanged and his skull...

Man up!

Pain is weakness leaving your body.

Aye, might believe that shite tomorrow.

He shuffled round to the back of the car and had a look at the boot. Looked like someone had taken a golf club to it.

Or that bonus stage in Street Fighter II...

A female paramedic wheeled a gurney past Hunter, spirals of straw-blonde hair dancing in the early-morning light.

'Jabroni...' Finlay was on his back, struggling to keep his eyes open. 'Craig, my man...'

Hunter clenched his jaw. 'How's he doing?'

The paramedic locked the gurney onto the ramp and started pulling Finlay up. 'He's a heavy lump, for starters.'

Finlay stared up at the sky, eyes rolling back in his head. Guy was completely out of it.

'Will he be okay?'

'He's got a concussion and he'll need some stitches. Gave him a shot of morphine to stop him shouting.' The paramedic rolled her eyes at him. 'This is pretty far from the worst I've ever seen, put it that way. A length of pipe, though.'

Hunter rubbed at the back of his head. His hair was matted with blood. A thick clump came away in his fingers, moist and sticky. 'I could do with—'

'Hunter! Over here!'

Lauren's hi-viz glowed in the sunshine over by an orange Focus, the car almost as bright as her vest. McNeill and Jain rested against the car, faces that could turn milk into yoghurt.

Hunter trudged over to them, hands in pockets, and gave Jain a nod. 'Morning.'

Jain stood up tall and got out her Airwave. 'I'll go and check how the search is going.'

What was going on?

Hunter frowned at her, his heart descending to the pit of his guts. 'We've not found him yet?'

'Him?' Jain stopped and turned back round. 'You saw a man driving?'

'Didn't see anyone...' Hunter gave a shrug. 'You've not found the Hyundai?'

'Not yet.' Jain stormed off towards the house, overtaking a gaggle of Forensic officers with an urgency that seemed to be about more than the case. What the hell was going on?

Lauren grabbed Hunter's stab-proof and led him away from McNeill and the Focus. 'How are you doing, Craig?'

'I'll live.' Another experimental tap at his crown. Stung like a bastard as his matted hair pulled away from the wound. 'Finlay's not looking good.'

'So I gather.' Lauren's gaze settled on the paramedic wheeling him away. 'But then he can be a drama queen.'

'Didn't get off as lightly as me.'

'You're kidding, right?' Lauren's eyes darted all over Hunter's face. 'You've got blood everywhere.'

'Seriously?' Hunter rubbed at his neck, slick with blood. 'I'll get myself cleaned up back at the station.' He perched on a low wall, the cold brick chilling his buttocks. 'I'm sorry, Sarge. I tried to give chase, but there's too many ways he could've gone down there.' He punched the wall. Hurt more than it should've done. 'If only I'd caught him before—'

'You keep saying "him". Was it the same guy as at the house?'

'I didn't get a look. Could've been a woman.'

'Think it could be this boyfriend?'

'Not sure.'

'The father?'

'Well, she didn't know he was alive. I had to break the news to her.'

'With your notorious tact and diplomacy, I suppose.'

What's that supposed to mean?

'I doubt it's him.' Hunter patted his skull again. 'We spoke to Stephanie before ... this happened. I'd put money on whoever's taken her being connected to Doug Ferguson.'

'And is there a chain of logic tying this policeman's hunch to the material evidence of this case?'

Hunter nodded at the block of flats. 'Stephanie told us Doug wanted her to run away with him. I got the impression he was in love with her.'

'Oh, sweet Jesus.'

Hunter folded his arms. 'She said he was beating up her mother.'

'I didn't want to hear that.' Lauren rubbed a hand across her forehead. 'If that's true, all bets are off.'

'I've dealt with guys like that a load of times, Sarge. Usually got at least one screw loose. Christ knows what's going on in his head.'

McNeill joined them, leaning against the wall next to Hunter. 'If it's true, we've got a lot of work to do.'

'You heard that?'

'Enough.' McNeill gave him a nod. 'This is sounding more and more like one of our cases.' She pushed herself off the wall again, eyes switching between Hunter and Lauren. 'Do you know why the Sexual Offences Unit was set up?'

'To cut the number of rapes?' Hunter rocked back on the wall. 'Raise the conviction rate?'

'Partly.' McNeill gritted her teeth. 'Our primary focus is on serial abusers and rapists. That's how serial killers start out. It's all about escalation from that first rape and we want to trap them as early in their cycle as possible.'

Hunter's crown started throbbing like an IED had just gone off next to him. 'You think Doug Ferguson fits the pattern?'

'First he's knocking Mrs Ferguson around, then he's raping her daughter. Men like that usually have a few other women in their pasts, too scared to speak out. You wouldn't believe how brave Stephanie was.'

A woman's voice called from behind them, harsh and guttural. 'Sharon!'

Hunter swivelled round.

A skeletal woman limped up the hill, clutching a digital recorder in one hand, an ivory-handled walking stick in the other. 'Sharon, it's

Linda? Heard about the car chase and wondered if there's a story here? Looks like it?'

McNeill let out a groan, her eyes flickering. 'The rise of the bloody bloggers.' She stood up tall and smiled at her. 'Just give me a minute and I'll be over.'

'Aye, that's smashing?'

Hunter got up and shoved his hands in his pockets. Then stuck them behind his back, standing at ease. 'Want me going door-to-door, ma'am?'

'No, Craig.' McNeill looked along the street at Jain as she got into her pool car. 'This teacher's on her way in to Leith Walk. I want you and DS Jain interviewing her.'

'With all due respect, ma'am, I'm not a DC.'

'But you used to be, right?' McNeill raised one of her sculpted eyebrows. 'I gather you're building up a rapport with DS Jain.'

Do you now?

~

'Oh, in the name of the wee man.' Fat Keith patted the back end of the Saab, treating the crack on the bumper like a child with a broken leg. He glanced at Hunter, doe eyes brimming with disappointment, then his focus went back to the car. 'This is my pride and joy, son. I trusted you with her!'

'Keith, what can I say? She did me proud in the heat of battle.'

'Well, glad as I am to hear it, I don't want to have to fit another bumper to her. And that bloody boot...'

'She'll live.'

'Aye, to fight another day.' Keith looked over, eyebrows arched. Lone hairs spiralled up, caught in the low lighting of the car park. 'She did good, though, aye?'

'Almost helped me catch the suspect.'

'Aye, well, almost isn't good enough, right?' Keith blew air through his lips, sending shockwaves up his piggy jowls. Then he turned his back on Hunter and crouched down to the clapped-out old banger. 'We're no' done with you yet, hen? You hear me?'

Hunter dabbed at his head, his eyes watering as pain scored from his temple all the way down his spine. 'Is DS Jain back, do you know?'

'The wee Indian bird?' Keith didn't take his eyes off the car, his fingers tracing the dent on its back. 'Signed the Mondeo back in. Said she's away to interview someone?'

~

HUNTER OPENED the interview room door and looked around.

Jain was sitting on the near side of the table. 'Please state your name for the record.'

Gaynor Tait looked up from her examination of the interview room table and focused on Hunter. 'Gaynor Laura Tait.'

Jain didn't even nod, just acted like a sulking teenager. All that was missing was a smily-face Nirvana T-shirt. 'For the tape, PC Craig Hunter has entered the room.'

Hunter slouched into the chair next to her and tried to ignore his thumping chest. *Feeling like a spare thumb here...*

Jain nodded at the lawyer next to Gaynor, a welt of acne in a pinstripe suit scrawling on a yellow legal pad. 'And you are?'

'Alastair Reynolds.' He didn't look up from his note-taking. 'I request you release my client this instant.'

Who the hell are you to threaten us?

Hunter glanced over at Jain.

She was smirking at the lawyer. 'That's not going to happen. There are a number of questions your client needs to answer before we charge her.'

'Charge? What with? She's committed no crimes.'

Jain focused on Gaynor. 'Ms Tait, do you understand why you're here?'

'My client remains puzzled by the outrageous act of sending officers to her place of work to apprehend her in the car park – under the watch of her supervisor, other teachers and a large section of the school's students.'

Jain sat forward and rested on her elbows, ignoring the lawyer. 'The reason we're speaking to you, Ms Tait, is because you've been harbouring one Stephanie Ferguson.'

Gaynor swallowed, keeping her eyes on the table. 'Right.'

'Do you acknowledge the fact?'

Gaynor didn't reply.

'You're not going to try telling us that she broke into your flat, are you?'

Gaynor shook her head. 'Stephanie told me her stepfather was abusing her. So I called her. She sounded like she was in a panic. Said she was worried her stepfather was going to kill her mother.'

Hunter got in before Jain. 'We spoke to you last night at Olivia Pearce's house. I asked you *specifically* about this.'

'I'm sorry.' Gaynor ran a hand through her hair, the dark brown mess slowly but surely reconfiguring to the secretarial bob. 'This is moving too fast for me. She only told me about it last night. *After* I spoke to you.'

Hang on a second...

Hunter opened his notebook and flicked back a few pages. 'When did she call you?'

'Yesterday, about half past seven?'

'Not according to this. The phone company said you called her at quarter to six.' Hunter held up his notebook and tapped the page. 'Around the same time we spoke to you at Olivia Pearce's house.'

'She sent me a Facebook message just after I spoke to you.'

'That's not true, is it? She'd called you.' Hunter flared his nostrils. 'So why are you lying?'

Gaynor nibbled at her lips, chipping away at the dark-green polish. 'You know what Named Person is, right?'

'Sure, Children and Young People Act 2014. But what does that have to do with you lying about when she called you?'

Gaynor tilted her head to the side. 'Not just a pretty face...'

Hunter narrowed his eyes at her, trying to stare down her evasive flirtation. 'It's not in force until next August.'

'When it does finally kick in, I'm going to apply to be Steph's Named Person.' She inspected her nails, staring deep into the green gloss. 'If it was in now, this wouldn't have happened. You'd have heard from me. And you'd have had to act.'

'So I'll go back to why you've been lying to us.'

'Look, I've been a teacher five years. In that time, one of my students was abused by his father. Another two were in violent homes. Every single time, I've gone to the police and you made a mess of the conviction. All three ... *men* got off.'

'Stephanie's stepfather has been in custody since she made the allegations.' Jain sat forward now, smiling broadly, like she'd replaced the Nirvana shirt with the dress from Frozen. Hunter liked one as little as the other. 'If we'd known where Stephanie was, we could've commenced prosecution of her stepfather. We could've taken a detailed statement and put her in protective custody.'

Gaynor let out a deep sigh and nodded. 'Look, I don't—'

'As it is, Mr Ferguson is nearing the very end of the amount of time we're allowed to detain him. My boss is pulling all the levers she can, but despite the mitigating circumstances surrounding this case, we're probably going to have to release him.'

The room fell silent but for the drone of the digital recorder and the scratch of Reynolds' pen on his pad.

'You kept Stephanie in hiding. That's made things a lot more complicated for us. And for her.' Jain's smile wasn't having anything to do with her eyes. 'If you'd told us you had Stephanie, we could've charged Mr Ferguson by now. He'd have been in a bail hearing this morning and probably wouldn't have got it. As it stands...' She shut her eyes for a second, her jaw clenching tight. 'As it stands, Stephanie's no longer missing. She's been abducted.'

Gaynor collapsed into the chair. 'What?'

'We found Stephanie an hour ago.' Hunter steepled his fingers. 'Then someone attacked me and my colleague and kidnapped Stephanie.'

Gaynor looked over at Hunter again, frowning. 'What?'

'Someone put her in the back of a car and drove off. We don't know where they took her. Or who they are.'

'Jesus.'

'Do you?'

'No, of course I don't.'

'But you've lied to us already.' Hunter held up his notebook. 'Why should we believe you now?'

'Look. After I spoke to you, I finished up with Olivia. Just gave her some exercises to do until her folks came back. Page 131, that kind of thing. Then I drove home from Portobello. Must've broken the speed limit several times over.'

'And Stephanie had gone to your flat as suggested?'

'We were up till the wee small hours talking. This is when I was trying to persuade her to speak to you. I went to sleep at about half one. It took a long time to get Steph to open up.'

'And you saw her this morning?'

'She'd slept on my futon. I was in my bed. I gave her a cup of tea, but she still wasn't hungry.'

'Sounds like she was in a state of distress. Don't you think you should've called us?'

Gaynor was in the process of trying to separate her left pinky from its socket. 'You wouldn't understand...'

'Try me.'

Again she tried resetting her haircut. This time a tuft stayed up near the back. 'This is a girl who's been subjected to abuse throughout her life. You've heard about her ... natural father?'

'We've spoken to him.'

Gaynor moved onto the middle finger. It barely budged. 'Given that history, Steph wasn't going to come forward unless I persuaded her. I said she could stay at my house until she felt comfortable talking about it. She just needed time to get used to someone close to her being prepared to support her.' An almighty tug got her middle finger to click. Sounded like a dry stick cracking in the fire. 'It took all the strength in the world to tell her mother what her stepfather had been doing.'

'I've seen cases like this.' Jain settled back in the chair and nodded. Could almost see the long black sleeves of the Nirvana shirt come back. 'Don't get why she wouldn't come forward. This isn't the first time it's happened to her.'

'Steph and her mother aren't close. It's not like they don't get on, it's more the other way round. She controls her, dictates who she can see. Smothers her.' Gaynor took her glasses off and put them on the table, the legs still sticking out. 'She said Pauline dotes on Doug. Nothing like with her real father. Apparently she's firmly convinced that the sun shines out of his arse. So Stephanie doubted she'd believe her. And when she did... There's just no security for the girl. Nothing to support her.'

'Pauline called the police.'

'But did she really believe Stephanie? Would she have kicked Doug out?'

Jain sat there brooding, eyes downcast. 'Did she say anything about any threats against her, perceived or otherwise?'

Gaynor popped the index finger. Not a sound. She looked away, settling her gaze on the far wall. 'Last night, I got the impression her running away was about more than her mum not believing her. It was like she thought someone was after her.'

Hunter sat forward, his pulse jolting. 'Any idea who?'

Gaynor shook her head, her face pinched tight. 'I'd put money on it being her stepfather.'

'Anything to support that?'

'I wish I had.'

~

Jain stomped down the corridor a few metres ahead of Hunter. Sounded like she'd dislodged at least one floorboard.

He jogged to catch her up. 'You okay?'

'Mm.' She weaved past him. 'What did you think of her story?'

'You didn't try to strangle her.'

Jain stopped. 'What?'

'Yesterday, you tried to batter the shit out of Doug Ferguson and—'

'Right, aye. I get it. What are you trying to say?'

'Just that I understand your frustration.'

'Oh?'

Hunter reached for the back of his skull, but thought better of it. Felt queasy enough already. 'We had her. Found her. And someone's taken her. Makes me want to go off and do some of the shit I've been trained for.'

'Army shit?'

'What else?'

'Look, Craig, watch what you're doing, okay? You had a hierarchy there, you've got one here. Don't step out of line.' She marched off, arms tight across her chest like she was the top girl in High School.

Hunter got in front and stopped her. She tried to weave past but he blocked her. A couple of other uniforms were at the other end, frowning their way. He didn't recognise either of them. 'Chantal, have I done something wrong?'

Jain folded her arms and rested against the wall. 'You tell me.'

'Come on. This morning you're all over me and now I'm in the dog house?'

Jain looked deep into his eyes, her brows low. 'Craig...' She sighed. Sounded like she added a ton of CO_2 to the atmosphere. 'Look. I'm having a shite day and it's nothing to do with you.'

So why don't I believe that...

She looked him up and down. 'You look like someone's shat on your Corn Flakes. What's up?'

Hunter rubbed his eyes. 'I just want to know what the story is with us?'

'Is there an "us"?'

'Is that it? Do you not want to be seen with a lowly PC?'

Jain stepped back to let the two uniform past, her smile dropping again as soon as they headed off. 'Craig, now's really not the time.'

'Doesn't feel like there'll be another time.'

'You always this needy?'

'Forget it.' Hunter marched off, thundering down the corridor.

She caught him at the corner. 'Sorry I said that. Is something annoying you?'

'A few things.' Hunter stared over her shoulder through the window overlooking McDonald Road library. 'I heard you were talking about me to the MIT.'

'What?' Jain leaned back against the glass. 'Who told you?'

'Elvis.'

'Jesus, don't listen to that clown.' She gave him a dirty look. 'Of course I wasn't speaking to them.'

'Sure about that?' Hunter tilted his head to the side. 'Didn't speak to Scott Cullen about it?'

'What?' Her frown deepened, two squiggly lines tracing across her forehead. 'Trust me, Scott's the *last* person I'd speak to about my love life, okay?'

'And Eva?'

Jain closed her eyes for a few seconds. 'Christ.'

'Like I said, Elvis overheard it. Said you said I've got a small cock.'

'Elvis...' She pursed her lips and looked sidelong at Hunter. 'I've not seen him all day, so there's no danger he's overheard anything. Relax. I haven't talked to Eva or anyone about the size of your...' She looked down at his trousers and smirked. 'Manhood.' She winked at him and started off down the corridor. 'Anyway, it's what you do with it that counts.'

The back of his neck burned, like someone had put a cigarette out on his skin. 'What's that supposed to mean?'

'She reached over and patted him on the shoulder. 'You've got nothing to worry about. It's what you do with—'

'I get it.' Hunter felt like the burn was spreading to his ears. 'Look, I don't like people talking about me.'

'And neither do I, okay? Especially office romances.' Jain held a door open and stopped to let a uniformed Superintendent pass with a nod. 'If you listened to Eva, I've shagged half of this station.'

'And have you?'

'Just you and ... someone else.'

Hunter's heart sank below his gut. He swallowed. 'Cullen?'

'No, not Cullen.' Jain laughed hard as she walked. Then she stopped with a groan. 'Finlay. He saw us. Bollocks.'

'I told him I saw you walking in and picked me up.'

'I live off Easter Road, Craig.'

'How about you took your car to the garage in Seafield and the bus broke down?'

'Sounds pretty far-fetched, but okay.' She gripped his shoulders. 'Look, Craig, relax. Last night was fun.'

'Really?'

'Really.'

Hunter let out a halting breath. 'So, where do we go from here?'

Jain started off down the corridor. 'Have a think about it, okay?'

∾

LAUREN WAS RECLINING in her office chair, her desk phone clamped to her ear. She pointed at the free chair and Hunter let Jain take it, instead settling into the window space.

Elvis was opposite Lauren, fiddling with his mobile as he smoothed down his sideburns. Maybe he'd trimmed them a bit shorter. He craned his neck round to shoot a super-sized wink at Hunter.

Lauren huffed into the handset. 'If you're cleared for duty, Constable, then you're working.' She started windmilling her hand through the air. Either winding the call with Finlay up or getting her circulation working. 'Desk duty is fine. I'll see you at the station in twenty minutes. Okay. Bye.' She slammed the phone down. 'Never let it be said that Finlay Sinclair isn't a monstrous drama queen.'

Elvis looked up. 'He's a drag queen?'

'*Drama*.' Lauren shook her head. 'I take it you've got something on the CCTV?'

'Aye, well, kind of.'

Lauren bristled, lips pursing tight and eyes narrowing. 'What. Have. You. Found?'

'Calm the beans, Sarge.' Elvis raised his hands, the gesture diminished by the fact that he was still holding his flashy phone. 'Just been sitting with the CCTV guy up on the Royal Mile. Took an age of man, but he gave me the footage. Finally.'

'And?'

'And I've been through the cameras on Corstorphine Road and all the other names it has. St John's Road, Glasgow Ro—'

'I get it. What have you found?'

'Have a look at these, baby.' Elvis held up his phone, a gleaming thing with the sort of screen that used to come with a projectionist and a vat of popcorn.

A greyscale Hyundai filled the display. Looked like it was on Corstorphine Road, left of where Hunter had lost it. The license plate was obscured by a tall removals van.

'Wait, wait, wait.' Lauren held up her hands, eyes narrowed. 'You've got all this CCTV on your phone?'

'Relax, Sarge. This is how they do it since they outsourced it.'

'You'd better keep it secure.'

'Locked down tighter than—' Elvis coughed as he shuffled through the pictures. He swung round and showed off a still of Hunter in the battered Saab indicating right. 'You went the wrong way, mate.'

Hunter glanced around. 'Thought it was heading for the bypass.'

'Well, it didn't. Headed left back into town.' Elvis swiped to the next image, taken from a camera down a side street. 'The Hyundai took a right turn past the Holiday Inn onto Pinkhill.' He grinned. 'My gran used to live there.' He flicked to another photo. 'This is him, by the way. Lost his wing mirror when you clattered Keith's Saab into that street light.'

'Hang on.' Hunter picked up the mobile and swiped to the right. A notification popped up at the top —

"AGE OF GOBLINS: Fin69er challenges you to a duel"

Hunter handed the phone back. 'So this is him?'

'Looks like it.' Elvis flicked to another image of the car by Carrick Knowe golf course. 'Narrows it down, right?'

'All very interesting, Paul.' Lauren was on her feet, arms hugging her body tight. 'Where is it now?'

'That's the thing, Sarge.' Elvis sniffed. 'That's the last camera. Doesn't show up on anything after it.'

'So it's gone to ground?'

'Looks like it.' Elvis switched to another image and circled a vehicle at the bottom. 'See there? It's indicating left.' He flicked to a maps app and traced his finger down the long stretch by the golf course. 'Keep going down that street and you end up in Saughton, give or take a few wrong turns. Could be anywhere, so long as he keeps off the A71.'

'So, we're waiting until it's flagged on the ANPR?'

'*If* it's flagged, Sarge, aye.'

Lauren shook her head, then frowned. 'Are you telling us you haven't got the full plate despite all this CCTV?'

'Calm down. I ran Conan's— Sorry, PC Hunter's partial when it came in.' Elvis tapped his phone again. Looked like another notification popped up. 'This bad boy gives me the full shebang, not that there were many red Hyundais in Edinburgh.'

Lauren got to her feet and rubbed her arms. 'All very interesting, but have you run the full print?'

'That's right.'

Lauren gritted her teeth. Looked like she was fighting the urge to roll her eyes. 'So you've found it?'

24

Hunter stopped on Mountcastle Terrace, a back street full of bungalows built from the same post-war kit as those in Corstorphine. Low-rise fifties or sixties things, all with mismatching attic conversions.

Someone had burnt bacon not too far away. Someone else was baking bread — rye sourdough, most likely.

David Boyle's house was a semi-detached bungalow. A weeping birch rested in the middle of a monoblock drive, casting dappled shadows on the clay-red tiles. Place wasn't too far from the Ferguson's house. Might even back onto the same rat's nest of paths running behind the garages and houses.

Hunter jabbed at his Airwave and nodded at Jain, as she scanned up and down the street. 'Are all units in position, Steve?'

'If by all units you mean me and Dave, aye, we are.'

Cheeky wanker.

Hunter marched over the empty grey-and-red chessboard of slabs leading up to the pebble-dashed house. He stopped inside the porch at the front door. 'Well, just keep the engine ticking over and keep an eye out for any movement out the back.'

Sounded like Steve yawned. 'Sure thing, Craig.'

Hunter cracked the brass knocker onto the door three times. The sound rattled down the quiet street.

Nothing.

Another three cracks.

Still nothing.

Hunter took a step back down the drive and peered in the window.

Vertical blinds blocked the view. A thin crack in the middle showed Fake floorboards glowing orange in the mid-morning sunshine streaming in from the back garden. He glanced back at Jain, lost in her Airwave. 'Nobody's in, Sarge.'

'Come on, then.' Jain pocketed her handset and walked down the drive back to the street. She opened the next-door gate with a squeak and paced over the monoblock, pampas grass sprouting in the middle of a circle cut out of the brown bricks.

Hunter gave the doorbell a go. Bing bong sounds came from inside.

'Just a second!' A woman's voice, her distorted figure growing in the security glass, until just a single eye was peeping out. The door slid open and she tilted her head at them, shrouded in the smell of baking bread. A silver-haired woman in her sixties. Her apron was covered in yellowy rye flour, a slogan above a cartoon wine glass just about visible — "You try coping with a retired husband!" She looked them up and down. 'Yes?'

Took Hunter a moment to remember he wasn't in uniform. 'Police, ma'am.' He showed her his warrant card, felt like he was posing as a jaded FBI agent from some cheesy TV show. 'We're looking for your neighbour, Mr Boyle?'

'I've not seen him for a couple of days.' She slapped her hands together, half disappearing behind a cloud of dust. 'What's he done?'

'We just need a word with him. Is it normal you'd not see him?'

'Keeps himself to himself, ever since Nancy left him. That's his wife. Ex-wife.'

'Have you seen his car?'

'Not since yesterday. I think.'

'Okay, thanks for your time.' Hunter handed her a card. 'If he shows up, could you give me a call?' He trudged back to the street and took another look at the Boyle house. Still no sign of life. 'Well?'

Jain stood by the squad car, a rust-red Volvo estate, and got out her Airwave. 'Lauren, it's Chantal. The car's not here.'

'That's disappointing.' Lauren paused for a few seconds. 'Elvis is still drawing a blank on the ANPR. Meaning it's still inside Edinburgh.'

'Or he's dumped it. And Stephanie.' Jain swapped the handset to her other hand. 'Listen, we're in Mountcastle. We thought we'd pay the mother another visit. Tell Sharon, will you?'

'Sure thing. Out.'

Jain pocketed her Airwave. 'Come on, then, driver boy.'

'*We* thought, did we?'

'Always make it sound like there's a consensus behind your actions, Craig.'

'Sounds like Donald Trump.'

'The wisdom of Scott Cullen.'

∼

'I JUST THINK he's an arsehole, that's all.' Hunter rubbed at his crown as he walked up the short drive. Still stung like a bastard. 'Guy's a total cowboy.'

'I'm with you there.' Jain knocked on the door and stood back.

Hunter wished he could just leave his head alone, back to the heavy throb again.

Feels like I'm falling apart. Need a new knee, a new leg and God knows what else... A Judge Dredd helmet wouldn't go amiss.

The Ferguson's door slid open and Ailsa Crichton stepped out into the daylight. Smelled like someone had either burnt coffee. Or she'd already smoked twenty fags. 'Have you found Steph?'

'We need to speak to Mrs Ferguson.' Hunter straightened up and showed his warrant card. 'Is she in?'

Ailsa took a few seconds to collect her thoughts, just staring into space. 'So that's how the police treat a lady these days.' She led them inside and held the living room door open.

Pauline sat on her armchair, fidgeting with a T-shirt draped over the girl's laptop. Some rock band's logo emblazoned on it. She looked up, dazed eyes struggling to focus on them, and started to blink away her fug.

Neil Alexander stood in the kitchen doorway, having to stoop below the door frame. A frown danced across his forehead. 'Have you found her?'

'Good morning, sir.' Jain took the seat next to Pauline and gave her a smile. 'We'd like a word with Mrs— with Pauline in private. Is that okay?'

'Come on, son. We know when we're not wanted, eh?' Ailsa barged Neil out of the room but stopped in the doorway. 'Tea for the pair of you, isn't it? Milk and no sugar, twice.'

'Thanks.' Hunter settled against the window frame and stuffed his hands in his jeans pockets, while Ailsa tugged the door shut behind her, leaving him and Jain alone with Pauline.

Jain got out her notebook and pen, then stopped and frowned. 'Has Mr Alexander been here long?'

'Since, I don't know, eight?' Pauline picked up the T-shirt and started kneading it, like his cat milking her bed. 'Ach, Neil's a good laddie. Doug thought he was a dirty pervert when he started seeing Steph. Takes one to know one, I suppose.' She braved the bitter irony with a broken smile. 'But Neil just wants my girl to be happy. We're on the same side.'

'Is the Family Liaison Officer not here?'

Pauline set the T-shirt down next to her on the sofa. 'I sent him away. Laddie was making the place look untidy. Do I need him here?'

'Not all the time, no.' Jain finished writing something and smiled at Pauline. 'Well, I'll cut straight to it, then? PC Hunter managed to speak to Stephanie this morn—'

'You've found her?' Pauline's eyes darted between them. 'Is she okay?'

'We tracked her down to a house in Corstorphine, where she'd gone voluntarily.' Jain bit her bottom lip, then twisted it into a smile. 'Unfortunately, someone abducted her—'

'What?' Pauline slumped back and let the T-shirt fall to the floor. 'You let her go?'

Hunter leaned back against the window frame, getting a jolt as his crown tapped the glass where he didn't expect it. 'She was okay at half past eight this morning.'

'But someone's kidnapped her?'

'I'm afraid so.' Hunter swallowed hard. Wished his throat wasn't so dry. 'We're investigating a number of leads.' He glanced at Jain, scribbling in her notebook. 'Someone in a red Hyundai took Stephanie. Do you know a David Boyle?'

'Aye, I do. Nasty piece of work.' Pauline's face screwed up into a snarl. 'Cut from the same dirty cloth as my bloody husband.'

Pieces starting to click together...

Hunter blinked away a flash from Jain's pen, caught in the slanting sunlight. 'Have you had any contact with him recently?'

'Last time would've been Saturday night, when he walked Doug home from Scottie's. He was a bit ... out of it.'

'What about since Stephanie disappeared?'

'No.'

'Do you have a number for him?'

'Aye, just call the bar at Scottie's. What kind of stupid question is that?'

Jain locked eyes with Pauline. Teacups chinked in the background, punctuating the droning voices. 'When we visited here last night, before you came home, there was a man in the garden. Do you have any idea who that could have been?'

'None.' Pauline shrugged. 'Could be a friend of Doug's. Might be worth asking him?' Her glare was like nothing Hunter'd seen since Iraq. 'He's got more than a few cronies in that bloody pub.'

'Have any of them been in touch?'

'Not a single one. All standing by their man, as that sort do. Still like the Wild West in there.'

Jain gave Hunter a warning look, eyebrows raised high. 'Stephanie told us that Doug was beating you up.'

The snarl deepened on Pauline's face, new lines furrowing the tanned skin. 'What?'

'Was I not clear?' Jain kept her face straight and left a long pause. 'Has Mr Ferguson ever assaulted you?'

'Are you lot trying to deflect the blame here?' Spit hung from the corner of Pauline's mouth, her gaze shifting between Jain and Hunter. 'You've lost my daughter and now you're trying to pin some shite on me?'

'We're not trying to pin anything on you. Your daughter was abducted and two officers were assaulted in the process. Mrs Ferguson, she told us that—'

'Don't. Call. Me. That!'

Jain whistled out breath, her notebook splayed open in front of her. 'So, you're saying it's untrue? That Stephanie was lying?'

Pauline looked away and shut her eyes. Tears slid down her cheeks, quickly wiped away with the T-shirt.

'Tell me it's not true and that'll be it.'

Pauline raised her sleeve to the elbow. Above the ring of bruises on her wrist was a kidney-shaped bruise, yellowing round the edges. Covered most of her forearm.

'How long has it been going on?'

'A couple of years.' Pauline nibbled at her top lip, her eyes still shut. 'Doug's business has been hard. He likes a drink. Most men do.'

'That doesn't make it okay to beat you up.'

Pauline's eyes opened, flaring at Jain. 'He never touched Steph, okay? Not in that way.' She clenched her jaws.

'Stephanie told my colleague that Mr Ferguson has been abusing her for a while.' Jain pocketed her notebook and raised an eyebrow at Hunter. 'How could you not know this was going on in your house?'

'Don't you think I'm asking myself those questions?'

Jain paused. 'Your daughter is the subject of two separate cases of abuse. Are you sure that's nothing to do with you?'

'Are you saying I'm whoring her out?' The fire in Pauline's eyes was white hot. 'How can you think that?'

'I'm paid to do exactly that. I'm not suggesting you were "whoring your daughter out", but you seem to attract this type of man.'

Missing

The kettle started to whistle through the door.

'What bloody type?'

'Abusive men. Stephanie's father and now Mr Ferguson.'

Pauline staggered to her feet, weaving around like her morning coffee had come all the way from Ireland. 'How dare you?'

Jain stood up and stepped forward. 'I'd like to get you on the record about the abuse you received at the hands—'

'Find my daughter!'

'—at the hands of Mr Ferguson over the last few years.'

'Find my daughter!'

'Will you consent to that?'

'Leave.' The fire in Pauline's eyes had blinked out, the flames dowsed by tears. 'I need you to leave!'

The kitchen door slid open and Ailsa stomped into the room, teacups clattering behind her. 'What the hell's going on?'

Jain held up a hand and got to her feet. 'We're just leaving.'

'Aye, well, you could've told us before we'd made your bloody tea.' Ailsa sighed and wandered over to Pauline, looking more like she was going to prod her with a poker than comfort her. 'Oh, Pauline. What've they been saying?'

Pauline hugged her tight, eyes clamped shut.

Neil paced over to the living room door. 'I'll show you out.'

∽

NEIL CLOSED the front door and stepped out, his bare feet slapping on the concrete slabs.

Hunter shared a look with Jain. 'Just so's you know, Mr Alexander, that sighting of her in Musselburgh last night didn't pan out.'

'Christ.' Neil slumped against the wall, looking like he lost a few inches of height in the process. 'I'm sorry about that.'

'Why are you here, Mr Alexander?'

'I'm trying to help.'

'Sure it's that?'

'What?' Neil rested his foot against the front door. 'I'm just as scared as Pauline. Can't focus on anything but what's happened to Steph. She's a beautiful thing and I want her to be happy. I just want to help bring that scumbag to justice.'

'Where were you between eight and nine this morning?'

'At my flat.' Neil stared into the middle distance. 'I called in sick today. All this stuff...' He frowned at Hunter. 'Why do you ask?'

'We found Stephanie in Corstorphine. Well, Clermiston.'

Neil's mouth fell open. 'Is she okay?'

'She was. Someone attacked me and abducted her.' Hunter let the news settle in, watching his eyes go blank. 'You don't know anything about it, do you?'

'What? You think I took her?'

'It's crossed my mind.'

'Look, I swear I don't know anything. I haven't heard from her since Sunday.' Neil stared up at the greying sky, a wall of clouds weighing in from the west, then at Hunter. 'I've been here since just after nine. I'm as worried as anyone.'

Jain got between Neil and Hunter. 'Mr Alexander, did Stephanie ever talk to you about Doug beating up Pauline?'

Neil glanced over at her, his lank hair spraying out in a wide fan. He swallowed and rested against the side of the house, knocking off a chunk of roughcast. 'She'd mentioned it.'

'You never thought to go to the police?'

'Listen. I tried to persuade Steph, but she said, if it came to nothing...' Neil closed his eyes, like he was meditating, then gave a little shake of the head. 'Can you imagine what Doug would do to them?'

'Mr Alexander, I've seen what can happen if we *don't* investigate.' Jain stuck her hands on her hips. 'The days of "dropping the charges" like in an episode of EastEnders are over. If a child is witnessing that sort of abuse, then we can prosecute, even if the mother — or father — isn't willing to come forward. The Procurator Fiscal and the Crown want us to convict these monsters.'

'I should've come forward. I'm sorry.' Neil shuffled back onto the doorstep, towering above the pair of them. 'It's just... Steph's fragile, you know? Like a porcelain doll. If I touch her when she's not expecting it, she jumps as though I'd electrocuted her.' He thumbed upstairs. 'The only time I've been in her room, it was like I was with someone else. I didn't recognise her.' He balled up his fists. 'That's where it all happened, where Doug ... forced himself on her.'

'Even more reason to report this.'

'I wanted to help Stephanie to do it. It's what we were working towards. I just didn't want to make her do it when she wasn't ready yet. Didn't want to see her shatter under the pressure. She's suffered enough at the hands of domineering men.'

Jain looked at him for a good few seconds, then took a business card out of her pocket. 'Mr Alexander, I need you to report to Leith Walk to give a full statement, okay?'

'What for?'

'Stephanie told you things. We need to get a crystal-clear picture of what they are. Shall we say two o'clock?'

"I'll need to go into work after that, but... Of course.' Neil slunk back inside, slamming the door with more force than it needed.

Jain scowled at the shaking glass. 'What do you make of all that?'

'He's like Gandalf in that dwarf house.' Hunter started walking back to the pool car. 'Still don't get him.'

Jain stopped by the car and blushed, looking him up and down. 'He creeps me out.'

Hunter's Airwave bleeped. 'Sergeant Reid to PC Hunter.'

He put it to his lips. 'Receiving. Safe to speak.'

'Craig, that Dave Boyle character's turned up at Portobello nick.'

25

Hunter pulled past a queue of idling buses on Portobello High Street. In the distance, a new row of Miami-style flats had sprung up on the promenade where the amusements used to be. He trundled past the five-a-side pitches, a tribal battle between two sets of schoolkids breaking out.

Angus's tenth birthday party had been celebrated there, a frantic game of sixes. Truth be told, the boy had been lost among all the skill from his so-called mates… Already lost to the abuse from his cousin…

Hunter pulled in outside the police station and got out. His mobile blared the nuclear bomb warning sound. 'Buggery.'

Jain stopped by the station's back door and glowered at him. 'What the hell's that for?'

'Letting me know I've got an interview in two hours.' Hunter fished it out of his pocket and hit the cancel button. 'There's no way I'll get to that on time. Terrific.'

'What's the interview for? That ADC position in the MIT?'

'Might be.'

'Want me to have a word with Shaz? See what I can do?'

'Forget it, it's a dead rubber anyway.'

'You sure?'

'Positive.' Hunter pushed the back door open. 'Started working at this station, you know? Can't believe they're talking about killing this place.' He swiped his warrant card through the reader and nodded at the desk Sergeant. 'Shug, I gather you've got a Dave Boyle here?'

'Boy's through the back.' Shug stared at Jain, just short of licking his lips. He cleared his throat. 'Aye, laddie reported his car stolen.' He tapped at his computer, squinting at the screen. 'Red Hyundai.'

∽

'I DON'T LIKE THIS.' Hunter stopped outside the interview room and turned to frown at Jain. 'First, the car of one of Doug Ferguson's mates is seen abducting Stephanie, then that same mate reports it stolen.'

'You think he's throwing us off the scent?'

'Textbook.'

'You want to lead?'

'Just try stopping me.' Hunter opened the door and stepped inside. Then back out again.

'What's up?'

Hunter stabbed a finger at the guy sitting at the table. Medium height, dark hair in a centre parting, mouth hanging open like he was trying to catch flies. 'That's the guy from the Ferguson's garden.'

Jain's eyes bulged. 'Are you sure?'

'Of course I'm sure.' Hunter charged into the room, taking the seat directly opposite Boyle. 'Good morning, sir.'

'Still morning, is it?' Boyle looked up, slack-jawed as the day he was born. His teeth hadn't seen much cleaning this century. 'Been in here ages, man. What's going on?'

The good look Hunter got outside the Ferguson's house had clearly only gone one way. That or the guy didn't recognise him out of uniform. 'Mr Boyle, my name is Craig Hunter and this is DS Chantal Jain. We're working on a separate case we believe is connected to your car going missing.'

'Woah. Hold on a minute, guys.' Boyle raised his hands, his mouth flopping open even wider. 'You trying to fit me up for something here?'

'We just have a few questions for you.' Hunter got his notebook out of his top pocket and opened it, taking his time to write down the date and each attendee's full name. 'We understand you know a Douglas Ferguson of Mountcastle Green.'

Boyle stared at Jain, a nerve under his right eye twitching. Then he swallowed. 'Doug's a good guy. Why?'

'You own a red Hyundai, correct?'

'Aye and some bastard stole it.'

Hunter sat back in his chair. 'You expect us to believe that?'

'Look, my car got nicked last night. That's why I'm here!'

'Why are you only reporting it missing now?'

'Look, hen, I've got a van for my work.' Boyle ran his lolling tongue over his lips and sniffed. 'Didn't notice my motor'd gone till Nancy told me this morning.'

'Nancy's your wife?' Hunter frowned at Jain. 'We understood she'd left you?'

'You been speaking to that battle axe next door?' Boyle sniffed a frown onto his face. 'Nancy moved back in a couple of months ago. Things've been good since.'

'How do you know your car went missing last night as opposed to, say, the day before?'

'Because I took it for a spin yesterday lunchtime. Doesn't sit well that motor. Needs a daily birl up to Asda to keep it ticking over.' Boyle scratched his chin. 'Well, it could've been snatched this morning, right enough.'

'Do you know Mr Ferguson's stepdaughter, Stephanie?'

'*Step*daughter?' The mouth hinged open again, like the drawbridge on a medieval castle. 'Stephanie's not his kid?'

'That's correct. So you do know her?'

'A bit. Dougie had a barbie round at his for his birthday. Middle of June, I think. I went along.' Boyle chuckled, the first time his mouth had properly shut. 'Got pretty banjaxed, as it happens.'

'How did she seem?'

Boyle's jaw went slack again. 'Great wee kid. Full of the joys of Spring, you know?'

Hunter noted it down and looked up. 'Was that the last time you saw Stephanie?'

'Steph? No, she was at their house when I took her old man home on Saturday night. Boy was out of his tree.' Boyle shook his head. 'Can't believe she's not his real daughter, man.'

'Do you know where Miss Ferguson is just now?'

'Should I, pal?'

'You've not taken her for Mr Ferguson?'

'What? This is a load of bullshit.' Boyle got to his feet and snarled at them. 'I've not taken her nowhere!'

'Sit down, sir.'

'I can go, right?'

'You can, but we'll be around your house picking you up when we get the arrest warrant.'

'Arrest warrant?'

'Miss Ferguson has gone missing.'

'Well, I've had hee haw to do with it, you hear?'

'Sit.'

'Christ, man.' Boyle slouched on his chair, scraping it back halfway to the wall. 'She's gone *missing*?'

'We tracked her to an address in Clermiston.' Hunter licked his index finger and danced backwards through his notebook. 'Unfortunately, Ms Ferguson was abducted by someone driving a red Hyundai with plates matching your car.'

Boyle shifted his gaze around the room, his teeth making a vain attempt to meet without quite managing. 'What are you talking about, pal?'

Jain gave him a wide grin. 'Seems very convenient how your car went walkies and was later seen by my colleague here abducting your friend's stepdaughter.'

Boyle's lips started twitching, still giving a good view of his lolling tongue. 'Wasn't me driving.'

'But you were in it, right?'

'No way. No way at all.'

'Where were you this morning between eight and nine o'clock?'

'On the phone to my lawyer.' Boyle frowned. 'Buying a new house, mate. Joppa.'

'House phone or mobile?'

'Moby, why?'

'We'll need their contact details.' Hunter scribbled it down. 'And where were you between five and seven last night?'

'You honestly think I'm doing something here?'

'Just answer.'

'Working. I'm a plumber. How I ken Dougie.'

'Okay, so your customers should be able to back up your location?'

'Aye.'

'Aye, well, I wasn't on site. I was on the laptop in the conservatory. Had a load of jobs to price up.'

'Alone?'

'Nancy wasnae back from her work, so aye.'

'You didn't go out for a run or anything?'

'Eh?' Boyle's face twisted up like a sun-dried tomato. 'I had a beer with the work, that's it. Bottle of Peroni, if you must know. One of the big ones.'

Hunter noted it, not that it proved anything. 'How come I saw you outside Mr Ferguson's house?'

Boyle started panting hard, eyes shuttling back and forth between Hunter and Jain. 'Eh?'

'Doug Ferguson lives on Mountcastle Green, correct?'

'That's where the barbie was, aye?'

'Well, I saw you there last night.'

'What? Shite you did.'

'So if I go to your house with a search warrant, I'll not find a black

T-shirt and grey trackies, maybe covered in grass? Or a pair of boots with greenhouse glass stuck in the soles?'

Boyle snorted air out and stared up at the ceiling. He shook his head and locked his eyes back on Hunter. 'It wasnae me you saw.'

'You do know that Stephanie alleges Doug was abusing her, right?'

Boyle closed his eyes and his jaw hung fully open. 'What did you say?'

'Been going on for a while, apparently. You wouldn't know anything about it, would you?'

Boyle's hands fell to the table with a clunk from his wedding ring. 'You're shiteing me, right?'

'I'm not in the business of doing that, no.' Hunter dropped his pen and splayed his hands on the tabletop. 'Were you aware of this?'

'You're saying he's been beasting young Steph?' Boyle grunted a few times, like he was considering going on a quest for fire. 'I knew nothing about it, all right? It's not the sort of thing you bring up in the pub, is it? "Oh aye, I was just fucking my daughter." Give me a break.'

'So you're not in league with him?'

'In league? What's that supposed to mean? I wasn't playing pool with him, if that's what you're saying.'

'I mean, you weren't sharing videos or photos with him?'

'Are you calling me a paedo?' Boyle hauled his jaw up, lips just about meeting. 'Look, I was doing a mate a solid. That's it. If he's a…' He swallowed hard, his nostrils flaring wide. 'If he's a *paedo*, then I'll be at the front of the queue to boot the shite out of him.'

'So. Was it you in the garden?'

'I'm saying nothing, pal.'

'Have you had any contact with Mr Ferguson since yesterday morning?'

'No.' Boyle slurped at his lips. 'But…'

'Go on.'

'His lawyer did call us up…'

∼

HUNTER RESTED his head in his hands. He winced at the flash of pain from his crown. Managed to catch his breath again. 'Mr Ferguson, it seems to me that you'd benefit greatly from Stephanie's disappearance.'

'Whatever. Like I say, I've not seen the lassie since yesterday lunchtime.' Doug slumped in his chair with a squeak. Guy looked defeated and drawn, like he'd aged two years in as many days. 'You lot have had me locked up in here, so how could I kidnap my lassie?'

'You being here doesn't stop you getting a message out via certain channels.' Hunter glared over at Williams, the lawyer gazing at his legal pad.

'I don't appreciate the insinuation.' Williams didn't even look up, just kept on writing, slowly, steady and even.

Hunter gave an exaggerated shrug to Doug. 'Well, you'll be glad to know that Mr Boyle's now down a red Hyundai, but up a friendly paedophile.'

'You what?' Doug leaned forward, elbows on the table, hands on his face. 'Why the hell did you have to tell him about that shite, eh?'

'Don't you think he deserves to know that his friend's been accused of a serious crime?'

'It's just that daft wee lassie telling lies.' Doug pointed a finger at Hunter. 'You could ruin my whole bloody life here, pal.'

'As I'm sure you'll appreciate, it's Stephanie's life being ruined that has me worried right now. But speaking of your former friend Mr Boyle, he was lurking around your house, seemingly at the instruction of Mr Williams.'

'Constable, I ask that you defer from involving me directly in this case.'

'Only if you stop dropping yourself into it.'

'Au contraire! Dropping is what you should be doing, namely this tissue of lies. Immediately.'

Hunter held up a sheet of paper. 'I've got a statement from Mr Boyle saying—'

Williams snatched the page from Hunter and scanned it, lips moving as he read. Seconds later, he folded it in half and placed it in his document holder. 'Mr Boyle is clearly confused as to the contents of our conversation. I was extending my client's concern at the disappearance of his stepdaughter and enquiring as to whether Mr Boyle had seen Miss Ferguson or had any information which would lead you, the police, to finding her.'

'If that's the case, why did Mr Boyle think it was okay to hang about in their back garden? Why did he run away when we approached?'

'I am unable to comment as I do not represent Mr Boyle.'

Doug waved a hand in front of Williams. 'Look, Davie Boyle's a mate, okay? When I heard she'd gone missing, I just wanted Steph to be safe. Needed somebody I could trust to see what's what at the house. So I got a message out to the boy.'

'You expect us to believe that?'

'It's the truth.'

'Sounds like you've been stalking her.'

'Piss off.'

'Or attempting to coerce her into changing or recanting her statement.'

Williams stopped scribbling. 'You have evidence of any exchanges, hostile coercive or otherwise, hmm?'

'Mr Ferguson.' Jain rested on her elbows and started rubbing her hands together. 'Stephanie told us you wanted to run away with her.'

'What?' Doug scowled at her. 'Well, that's ... nonsense. She's just a daft wee lassie.'

'Didn't stop you abusing her, did it?'

'I did nothing with her. *Nothing*.' Doug sat back and shoved his hands in his trouser pockets. 'And there's no bloody way I'd ... run away with her. What do you think I am?'

'You should be aware of what we think you are, sir.'

'Well, it's complete bullshit.' Doug took his hands out of his pockets, then gripped his thighs tight. He stared over at his lawyer but got nothing in response.

Williams continued his documentation. Or maybe he was handwriting a novel. *Stranger things had happened.*

'Listen, I've been thinking about what you said, right?' Doug beat his wrists off the table edge, three times each in quick succession. 'That wee bitch is spreading a pack of lies about me. Christ knows why, I've only ever been loving and caring towards her.' Another three beats, harder this time. 'So, anyway, I've been thinking about how I can prove my innocence. She said I ... interfered with her on Monday night, right?'

Jain sifted back through her notebook, her focus still on Doug.

'Look, whatever, that's what you told my brief here.' Doug clenched his jaw and did another few beats with his wrist. Then flashed a grin at Jain. 'See, the thing is, I was with my pal all night.'

26

Hunter marched across the Logie Mill car park towards a two-storey brick building, an office someone had mistaken for a shitty retail development. A group of men stood outside, some sucking on vape sticks, most smoking old-school fags. He stopped and stared up at the logo. Summers Actuarial Services. 'What's actua—'

'My brother's an actuary.' Jain pushed through the group into the building, a wide-open space with just a few suits sitting round. 'It's something to do with insurance and pensions.'

'I love the precision.' Hunter walked over to the desk and got the attention of the receptionist, a woman in her early twenties whose drawn-on eyebrows were as obvious as her boredom. 'Looking for an Alec Wishart.'

The receptionist waved across the room. 'That's him over there.'

A man was sitting in the chair opposite, kneading his giant forehead, which seemed to stretch all the way back to his shirt collar, like a car with the sunroof open. His thin goatee was barely ten hairs radius around his tiny little mouth, and his suit looked like it cost at least four figures. 'I've told you on the phone, I've nothing to say to you.'

Hunter went over and hovered at the edge of the man's comfort zone. 'I can't force you to come with us, but your name has been given as an alibi and we need to obtain a statement from you.'

'I've nothing to say.'

Hunter crouched down next to him. 'Are you acquainted with a Douglas Ferguson?'

Despite himself, Wishart made eye contact, if only for a split second. 'What's he done?'

'We need to clarify his movements with you.' Hunter got back up, his knees popping like a champagne cork. An even sharper blast of sound surged from behind as a door opened. Radio noise and people shouting over it. 'Is there somewhere—'

'Here, Eck, what's this prick want?' A lump of muscle and hate loomed over Hunter, at least six six. 'You picking on him?'

'I just need to speak to Mr Wishart about—'

BANG.

A meaty fist clattered into Hunter's stomach. A second into his jaw. He tumbled backwards, clambering over Jain, the pair of them rolling over the floor tiles.

The man mountain stood over them, looking like he was away to stick the boot in. 'You leave him alone, all right?'

Hunter reached into his pocket for his warrant card. 'I'm a police officer, you stupid bastard.'

The bravado crumpled faster than he could say 'Aw shite.'

'You're getting arrested.' Hunter got up to his aching knees and helped Jain up. Then he jabbed a finger in Wishart's sternum. 'And as for you... We're doing this down the station.'

∽

STANDING OUTSIDE THE INTERVIEW ROOM, Hunter wolfed down a bite of a canteen egg sandwich. Bloody awful and no way to know how freerange the eggs were. No time to make anything and that piece box had gone missing...

You were never bloody safe in this game. Some lump of muscle was always lurking round the bloody corner, working in a mailroom but thinking he was Jack Reacher.

Big arsehole was going away for a little holiday after this one.

Another bite and his jaw clicked as he chewed.

'Did you get me one?' Jain stopped and rested against the interview room door.

'Cheese and tomato.' Hunter tossed a triangular box over to her. 'I spared you the egg.'

'Great.' She tore it open and bit into the first half, covering her mouth as she chewed. 'Alec Wishart's lawyer turned up yet?'

Hunter tapped a boot against the interview room door. 'Decided he didn't want one after all.'

'Bloody hell.' She swallowed down a mouthful, like that's all it deserved. Just fuel to keep hungry cops going. 'Sharon's happy with where we've got to, by the way.'

'I'm not.' Hunter finished his sandwich and put his hand on the door. 'I'll get this started, okay?'

'Aye, go on.'

Hunter entered the room and sat down. 'DS Jain will be in shortly.' He jotted down the date and time as he tried to stretch out his jaw. 'Then we'll get going, sir.'

'I can only apologise for Billy's actions...'

'I see. Paid minder, is he?'

'He's just a friend. Gets a bit boisterous at times.' Wishart ran a finger round his beard. If anyone looked like a tabloid paedophile... 'Listen, I really need to get back to the office. I've got a client—'

'Then the quicker we get started...' Hunter got the recorder playing. 'Interview commenced at twelve thirty-eight. I'm PC Craig Hunter.' He nodded at Wishart. 'State your name for the record, please.'

'Alexander Hamilton Wishart.'

'And you're an actuary, is that correct?'

'Work down at Powderhall. Summers Actuarial Services.' Wishart's smile just came off as nervous. 'What's this—'

Jain walked into the room, chewing furiously as she crumpled the sandwich box up and dumped it in the bin. She gave Hunter a nod — get stuck in, sunshine.

'DS Chantal Jain has entered the room.' Hunter waited until she'd got herself settled. 'Mr Wishart, are you acquainted with one Douglas Ferguson of Mountcastle Green, Edinburgh?'

'That's right. My brother worked for him. We hit it off at a party at his and we lived near each other. Used to drink together in Scottie's.'

'Used to?'

'Well, I don't drink anymore.'

Hunter noted it down and circled it a few times. 'So you're, what, good mates with Mr Ferguson?'

'Not great mates, but enough to talk about football or politics over a pint of eighty shilling.' Wishart coughed. 'Back in the day, of course.'

'I understand Mr Ferguson met his wife through you.'

Wishart flicked his tongue left to right. 'Well, Pauline's my sister's pal. Knows her from school.'

'Are there any other members of your family involved in this story?'

'Just Kath.' Wishart went back to scratching his forehead. 'Look, I drank with Doug for a few years in Scottie's. Kind of a local thing, right? You just show up and see who's there. Got chatting to him about the football one day. This went on for a few months until one Friday night, after a fair few pints and whiskies, he started going on about wanting to settle down.'

And the alarm bells start ringing again...

Hunter wrote it down verbatim and circled *settle down*. 'So you set him up with Pauline?'

'Kath'd been saying how Pauline was just getting to the stage where she wanted to think about dating again after her marriage fell apart.'

Jain flicked up both eyebrows. 'That's an interesting way of putting it.'

'What is?'

'Continue...'

'Anyway, Pauline made the poor bastard jump through so many hoops. Put him through hell, you know?' Wishart settled on smoothing down the thin band of dark hair circling his head. 'Doug eventually earned her trust and that was them. They're a great couple, though I haven't seen Douglas for a good while now.' He leaned back in his chair and yawned. 'Why do you want to know?'

'Do you know Mrs Ferguson's daughter, Stephanie?'

'Met her a couple of times at barbecues and the like.'

'Did Mr Ferguson ever talk about Stephanie?'

'Just how well she was doing at school. Guy was proud of her, you know? Treated her like his own daughter. That's how you're supposed to do it, right?'

'So I gather.' Hunter took a few seconds to let Wishart stew, started counting the beads of sweat on his forehead. Seven, eight, nine. 'The thing is, Stephanie's alleging that Mr Ferguson has been abusing her for a number of years.'

'Bullshit.' Wishart raised his hands in the air. 'No way. N. O.' He shook his head, frowning, giant ripples running across his skull. 'Doug's as straight as they come.'

'What makes you say that?'

'No reason, but...' Wishart swallowed and looked away. A bead of sweat dripped from his forehead. 'No way, man. No way.'

'Are you involved?'

'Christ, no!' Red blotches covered Wishart's face, his breathing thick and slow. 'Look, before I hooked them up, Doug stayed on my living room floor for a couple of weeks when he was between flats.'

'Do you live alone, Mr Wishart?'

'I'm married. Not long, as it happens. I met Marie at Christmas and we wed in the Spring.' Wishart rolled his bottom lip through his teeth. 'Look, when he was staying at my flat, I ... caught Doug looking at porn on his laptop once.'

Hunter scribbled it down. 'What sort of porn?'

'See that's the thing. It was granny porn. Forty-plus sort of stuff.' Wishart shook his head again. 'There's just no danger he'd be after young Stephanie. Doug likes ...' He looked at Jain and shut his eyes. Then whispered at Hunter: 'A bit of meat.' Then he wiped sweat from his forehead. 'You know what I'm saying? I mean, I'd—' He coughed hard, like his spleen might come up. 'I'll leave it at that.'

Hunter flicked back a few pages in his notebook. 'Mr Ferguson says he was drinking with you in Scottie's on Monday night.'

'Did he?' Wishart frowned. 'Well I wasn't there.'

'Of course, you said you don't drink anymore.'

'That's ... correct.'

'Sure about that?' Hunter sat back, letting the weight shift from his shoulders. Everything eased out. Then his jaw clicked and sent a spear of pain through his whole head. 'So you weren't there?'

'No.'

Doug Ferguson, you lying little toerag.

Hunter stood up, scraping his chair legs across the floor. 'Interview term—'

'Wait.' Jain grabbed Hunter's hand. 'Mr Wishart, will you stand up in court and testify to that effect?'

Wishart slumped back in his chair and let out a deep sigh.

'I said, would you—'

'I know what you said.' Wishart stared up at the ceiling. 'Look, I'm not supposed to be drinking.'

'Doctor's orders?'

'Marie doesn't like it.' Wishart ran his left hand across his damp forehead. 'But she was through in Glasgow on business. Staying over. If she catches me...'

Jain looked up from her notebook. 'Mr Wishart, during this case, you will be asked to appear in court and recount this tale. If you lie, that'll be up to seven years at her Majesty's pleasure. And we've got this on tape.'

'I know that.' Wishart swallowed hard. 'Aye, I was with Doug in Scottie's.'

∼

HUNTER PUSHED OPEN the interview room door and watched the custody officer walk Alec Wishart down the corridor. He stuck his head back in and nodded at Jain. 'I thought we were getting somewhere there.'

'No, we weren't. You just thought we were.' She put her hands on her hips. 'Doug's got himself an alibi.'

'So, what now?'

'I'm going to run this by Sharon, okay?' She waved her hands around the table at the interview equipment. 'Once I've sorted that lot out.'

'And what am I supposed to do? Wash your car, ma'am?'

Jain tapped her watch. 'You're going to that interview.'

27

Hunter stood outside the meeting room door, peering through the glass.

A woman sat at the table, scribbling in a notebook. Hair in a tight bun, wearing a trouser suit. Late thirties, maybe, and at least six months pregnant, judging by the size of her bump.

Kandahar Province has nothing on this...

Hunter cleared his throat. Gave it another good go. There we go. Then he knocked on the door and kicked it open. 'Donna Nichols?'

'Craig Hunter, I presume?'

'Sorry, I'm late. Had an interview.' He stepped into the room and stopped. 'A police interview. You know, a suspect interview.'

'I understand.' Donna glanced up at the clock on the wall. 'We're awaiting my co-interviewer, so if you'll just have a seat...' She waved at the seats across from her.

Hunter took a chair and tried to slow his breathing.

The door slid open behind him. 'Sorry I'm late, Donna.'

Hunter swung round.

Scott Cullen walked into the room, strutting around like he owned the place. 'That shooting's on its way to the PF's office, so I'm all yours for the next hour.' He frowned at Hunter. 'You taken up boxing?'

Hunter slumped back in his chair.

Terrific...

~

'—BEEN asking leading questions. Should the confession stand?'

Cullen was grinning like he just knew he'd snared him.

You complete wanker.

They're getting harder. Wonder who picked these questions?

Hunter cleared his throat again. 'I'd suggest that, under the PACE Act, it's the court's duty to exclude confessions we have obtained by coercion. And the lawyer should—'

∾

'ANY FURTHER QUESTIONS?' Donna smiled at Hunter. 'Anything at all?'

An ice pick and a quiet room.

Hunter tried clearing his throat again. Still something stuck there. Felt like a lump of coal. 'Just like to know which team this Acting DC role's going to be in, if that's okay?'

Donna smiled over at Cullen. 'Sergeant?'

'That's an interesting question.' Cullen spent a few seconds nodding, like the posy wanker he was. 'Can I ask why?'

'I'd just like to know who I'd be working for.' Hunter coughed into his hand. 'Should I get the position.'

'Okay...' Cullen smiled at him, eyes narrow. 'While the approval for this role goes back to last year, we've yet to find a suitable candidate. We've had to re-advertise.'

'Is the role working for you?'

'I'm afraid not, Craig. I've been on secondment to Operation Venus for the last fourteen months and, while I've just returned to the MIT as of today — I hope — the role's unlikely to be in my team. Besides, it's the DIs who take charge of team structure. As it stands, I took a number of officers with me to Venus and they'll be returning with me. Once we've finished supporting the conviction, I probably won't be allowed an Acting DC.'

'So is it likely to be with DI Davenport?'

'Is there a reason for that assumption?'

'Not in particular. I'd just ... rather work for another DI. To ... expand my skill set...'

'Well, I'm afraid I'm not at liberty to tell you who the successful candidate will be working for.' Cullen's smile inverted itself into pursed lips, but his eyes stayed friendly. 'Does that answer your question?'

'It does.' Hunter took a sip of water. 'And what's the tenure?'

'It'll be a year, maximum. Shape up or ship out.'

'Quite.' Donna reached over for Cullen's interview pack, barely scribbled on, and put it on top of hers. 'Now, is that everything?'

Hunter shrugged. 'That's all from me.'

'Cheers.' Cullen got up and wandered over to the other side of the table. He dropped his pen on the floor, a silvery Pilot thing, and reached down to pick it up, watching Donna leave the room. Then he settled back onto the desk and folded his arms. 'Let's have a chat about this at some point.'

'Right. Cheers.' Hunter sat back in his seat, hands stuffed in his pockets. 'Whenever you want, Scott.'

'Cool.' Cullen play-punched his shoulder and minced out of the room.

Hunter slumped back in his chair and groaned. His gut felt like someone had thrown a bowling ball into it. A dentist's trip might be in order. His knees needed to be replaced with ceramic joints. And as for his crown...

'Oh, hi Scott.' Jain stood in the doorway, waving Cullen off. 'You cowboy wanker.'

Hunter got up and sat on the table. 'That was a complete disaster.'

'You think?'

'Aye, made an arse of at least two of the questions. The one about coercing a confession?'

'Oh, Craig. Donna always asks that one. How could you not know?'

'Cullen was setting me up. Total arsehole.'

'Woah, angry much?'

'He's just...' Hunter slumped back on the table, his head clattering off the wood. Felt like he'd just reopened the wound. He sat up and gently rubbed at his crown. 'What's been happening in the real world?'

'Nothing much. Had a baked tattie for lunch. The tuna tasted off, but I still ate it.'

'And with the case?'

Jain got out her iPhone and unlocked it. A blog filled the screen, some sort of amateur site with all the wrong fonts and images stretched out of recognition.

"School girl taken by beast stepfather"

'Terrific.' He handed the mobile back.

'Aye, this is Sharon's blogger mate.' Jain pocketed her phone. 'Her charm offensive didn't exactly work.'

'How the hell did she get that, though? It's not common knowledge.'

'Or anywhere near accurate, as far as we know.' Jain helped him to his feet. 'Anyway, Sharon wants us to check Doug's alibi.'

'You've not done that yet?'

28

Hunter stopped outside the front door of the Scottie Lounge, a diagonal wedge cut into the sixties single-storey *thing* attached to the rogue Georgian two-storey building next door. At least the cream walls made it look cared for, unlike the grifty boozer next door, the sort of drinking den that either didn't like natural light or didn't want anyone seeing who was inside. A couple of rum punters supped on a pair of halves at a standard pub table and chairs outside.

Hunter thumbed at the chippy and Chinese takeaway further down the street. 'Everything a man needs.'

'Right.' Jain pushed through the door.

Still tasted of smoke ten years after the ban kicked in. No sign of anyone chucking crafty ashtrays behind the bar, though.

She propped herself up on the wood, looking like she was sizing up the beer pumps.

Just a Guinness as a safety drink in amongst the lager pumps, generic drinks you got everywhere that tasted less than the sum of their ingredients. The craft beer revolution was a distant dream, maybe the name of a band they'd have on a bank holiday.

A gruff guy in his late forties wandered in from a back room, white bristles sticking out everywhere in his face, like he'd been blasted in a carwash. 'Can I get you?'

Jain nodded at him. 'Looking for the manager?'

'That's me.' He held out a hand, enough gold hanging off it to replenish Fort Knox. 'Leslie Owenson.' He kept glancing at Hunter. 'So, who needs an alibi today?'

Jain smirked. 'Know a Doug Ferguson?'

'Not in a Biblical sense.' Owenson winked at her, then turned his attention to some clean glasses. 'But aye, Doug's a regular in here. What's he done now?'

'Now? What was it last time?'

'Nothing. Doug's one of the good ones. Drinks a skinful, gets some chips from next door and keeps himself to himself.'

'Was he here on Monday night?'

'Had the football on.' Owenson grunted. 'The English stuff, mind. Boy was putting the beer away, I'll tell you.' He pointed to the side door out onto Piersfield Terrace. 'Doug must've had a bet on the match, cos he got through a twenty-deck in the ninety minutes. In and out of here like a demon.'

'Okay...'

Owenson frowned at her. 'Sounds like I've given the wrong answer there, darling. Want me to phone a friend?'

Jain looked around at the other punters, a pair of old men losing themselves in their lagers. 'Is there any way of proving it?'

'Well, I've got CCTV.' Owenson thumbed at the door behind him. 'You lot made me put it in after a wee bit of bother during an Old Firm derby. Not that there's been many of those for a while.'

'Was he with anyone?'

'Well, he was with a couple of regulars. God, I can't remember the laddie's name. Well, he was with Alec Wishart. Boy's not been in for months. Thought he'd had a stroke.'

Terrific... Hunter's lungs emptied. 'Who was the other one?'

'Oh aye, and...' Owenson clicked his fingers a few times. 'Aye, that's it. Davie Boyle.'

Hunter shared a look of contempt with Jain, her lips forming a tiny circle, though not as small as her eyes. 'What's Boyle like?'

'Bit of a lad, but no better or worse than the rest of them, you know.'

Jain stood up tall. 'Let's see this CCTV, then.'

∼

HUNTER LEANED BACK in the chair and held up the greyscale screen grab from Scottie's, trying to compare it with the official version from the City Council.

No two ways about it, Doug Ferguson was at Scottie's on Monday night. Smoked enough to need a second mortgage on his house, by the looks of things.

Hunter dumped the sheets on the desk and looked across the

Observation Suite. On the main screen, McNeill and Jain were back interviewing Doug Ferguson.

Hamish Williams was scribbling in his legal pad as per. This time he looked like he'd found the golden ticket in his chocolate bar. 'My client has documented his whereabouts and you've validated them. That's the end of the matter.'

'Mr Ferguson, we're releasing you from custody.' McNeill's arms were so tightly folded it looked like she might turn inside out. 'We aren't releasing you because we think you didn't abuse your stepdaughter. You're being released because you have an alibi for the night Stephanie alleged she was last assaulted. Given her subsequent disappearance and abduction, it's our belief that you've either scared her off or are responsible for that abduction, albeit through a third party.'

Williams' pen flew across the legal pad and clattered into the microphone, producing a giant pop from the speakers. 'You cannot talk to my client like that, Inspector.'

'We're done.' McNeill got up and led Jain out of the room.

Williams clapped Doug on the shoulder. 'Good news, Mr Ferguson.'

'Aye. Cheers.' Doug slouched back in his seat and stared into space. More like he'd been given a death sentence than his freedom. He started whispering in the lawyer's ear, the microphone just picking up a dull rumble.

The Obs Suite door burst open and McNeill stormed in, pacing around like her first day in prison. 'I hope this doesn't bite us on the arse.'

'Shaz, we had no choice.' Jain perched on the edge of the table next to Hunter. 'We've got no evidence against him with Stephanie missing and nothing incriminating him.'

'Aye, and then some.' Hunter dumped a sheaf of papers on the table. 'Spoke to that Charlie Kidd guy up in Forensics. He's finished going through Doug's computers. No sign of anything remotely dodgy on them.'

Jain sat up straight. 'So no kiddie porn?'

'And no telltale signs of it, either. Stuff like TOR and all that.'

Jain rolled her eyes. 'Wish I knew what that was.'

'Trust me, you don't want to know.' Hunter frowned. 'Thought you lot would've been on that dark net course?'

'Next month.' Jain smoothed her hair behind her left ear. Made her look even more like a pixie. 'There's something weird going on here. You heard that Wishart guy. Sounds to me like Doug's been looking for an impressionable young mother.'

'Not sure that's exactly what he said. He said Doug's into granny porn, not kiddy.'

'No trace of that?'

'According to Charlie, it's the kind of porn you have to hide from your wife, but not from the police.'

'Well, he'd know.' Jain hid a smirk with her hand cupping her mouth. 'I think we should be following Ferguson.'

McNeill stopped her pacing and shook her head. 'We've got no budget for that sort of surveillance.' She stuffed her hands into her pockets, but it didn't seem to dull her frenetic movement any. Like she was at a rave and on her fifth E. 'Our priority's getting Stephanie on the record and—'

Someone knocked on the open door.

Elvis, lurking with his usual daft grin. 'Butch, got—'

'Never call me that, Constable.' McNeill stormed over, looking like she'd take him down if she could get away with it. 'Okay?'

'Aye, sorry.' Elvis nodded at Hunter. 'Thought I'd find Hunter in—'

McNeill shook her head at him. 'Has someone finally found a use for you, Elvis?'

Jain smirked. 'What, acting in granny porn?'

Elvis huffed. 'Quit it, would you?'

'Paul.' Hunter got between them and forced Elvis to look at him. 'What is it?'

Elvis thumbed out into the corridor. 'The lawyer said the dad had something else for you?'

∼

HUNTER WAS RESTING against the back wall of the interview room, standing behind Doug and Williams.

McNeill waited for Jain to sit, then took her chair. 'I gather you want to speak to us?'

'Aye, I've got something that might interest you.'

McNeill sighed and twisted round to grimace at Jain. 'And here was me thinking you were going to change your mind and confess.'

'It's... Listen, have you spoken to her father about this?'

Jain frowned at him. 'Robert Quarrie?'

'That stoat, aye. Have you spoken to him?'

'We have and he has an alibi for the time when Stephanie disappeared last night.'

'You told me that she went of her... What was it?' Doug looked at his lawyer. 'Own volition? Then you told us someone's taken her this morning, right? Like abducted this time.'

Hunter locked eyes with Jain across the table and saw his frown mirrored in her clenched jaw.

Oh, what...

'You've not spoken to him today, have you?' Doug pounded a fist onto the table. 'He'd be first on my list, not Davie bloody Boyle!'

'He is on our action plan to speak to.' McNeill didn't look like even she believed her words. 'If you've anything material to add...?'

'Look, Steph's father's been sniffing around the house for the last few weeks, looking for her.' Doug folded his arms across his chest. 'Her mother kept it from me. Didn't want me worrying, she said.'

'That's very kind of her, considering you weren't shy of knocking lumps out of her.'

'I...' Doug broke off, eyes shut. 'Look, I love Pauline.'

'You'll be speaking to a counsellor as part of your punishment, I suspect.' Jain licked her lips, emotion drained from her face. 'Do you know if her father managed to speak to Steph?'

'Not that I know of.'

'You expect us to believe that?'

'What can I say? It's the truth!'

'Anything to back this up or are you just fishing here?'

'Oh for God's sake! Pauline told me the other night, all right? I was going to head round to that pub he's working at and talk a bit of sense into him, if you know what I mean. Just never got the chance.'

29

Jain eased the pool Vectra down the hill towards the Cramond shore. Dark clouds were hanging low between the chimney stacks of the old fishing village, so low Jain was hunching her shoulders in the driver's seat. Or maybe she was still uncomfortable about last night. 'How's it going with the checks?'

'I'll just see, Sarge.' Hunter leaned back in the seat and stabbed at his Airwave. 'PC Hunter to PC Finlay. Over.'

The new fleece itched worse than the old one. *God knows where they got them from or what they washed them in — asbestos?*

'Receiving.'

'Have you or Elv— DC Gordon managed to get an extract of Stephanie's mobile records?'

'Just got it now, amigo.' Finlay huffed down the line, like he'd been out running. 'Nothing much on here, buster. I've got the house?'

Hunter glanced round at Jain as she stopped the car outside the Almond Inn. 'Surely not even Robert Quarrie could be stupid enough to call the house.'

'I'll check anyway. Tum tee tum...'

Hunter stuck it on mute. 'I swear that guy finds new ways to piss me off every bloody day.'

Jain ran a hand through her hair. 'I don't like Doug Ferguson being out.'

'Me neither. You didn't put up much of a fight, though.'

'I know when to push Shaz. That wasn't one of the times.' She checked her mobile and pocketed it pretty quickly. 'He could be anywhere, doing anything.'

The Airwave whistled out white noise. 'Aye, Craig? You still there?'

Hunter hit the mute button. 'Aye, we're here.'

'Still nothing on an address for Robert Quarrie.'

Hunter looked over at the pub. Have to brave Stevie Ingram again.

The Airwave crackled. 'Turns out she's been receiving calls from the landline at the Almond Inn. That mean—'

'What did you say?'

'I said the Almond Inn. Are you stupid or something?'

Hunter jabbed the end call button and let his seatbelt zip up. 'Come on.'

∽

Steve Ingram's face dropped as Hunter approached the bar. 'Oh, here we go again.' He rubbed his hands on his waiter's apron and started polishing a glass.

Hunter watched and waited. Let the man stew for a few moments. The place had that deep burnt smell you only got in really old buildings, like the soot had permeated the wood and stone. 'Can we have a word with Mr Quarrie?'

'I'm afraid he isn't in work today.'

'He's your chef, though, right?'

'Was, aye.'

Hunter frowned at Jain. 'You've sacked him?'

'What else could I do after you told me about his … history?' Ingram sprayed some Pledge on the bar and brushed at it with a cloth. 'He'd lied to me. His application neglected to mention a previous employer being Her Majesty's Pleasure. He said he worked at a hotel in Alloa, one that's conveniently ceased trading…'

'Have you confronted Mr Quarrie?'

'We had words, aye.' Ingram had one last go with the duster, then set it under the bar. 'He said he didn't do it, but I had to let him go. Nothing I could do.' He raised his arms like a third-rate mime. 'My hands are tied. Nobody lies to me. And besides, I'm not having him in here. We've got young kids staying here. I don't want him … interfering with them, you know? Sick bastard. He's lucky I didn't cut his—'

'You shouldn't be saying that to us, sir.'

'Aye, well. He's a dirty bastard, but at least he's gone. I gave him two days' notice on his flat, too.'

Hunter checked with Jain, her ice queen face back on, then at Ingram. 'Was this today?'

'This was last night. He waited around here after you went. I spoke to the police. They told me he's on the register indefinitely.'

'And did he put up much of a fight?'

'Not really. It's like he'd seen it all before. He just left, dirty tail between his legs.'

Hunter felt like his veins were going to pop. *He's got Stephanie...* Blood thundered in his ears, acid burnt in his gut. 'Did he ever talk about his daughter?'

'Aye, said he was trying to get in touch with her again. Bet she was disgusted with what he was put away for.'

'It was her he was—'

'Jesus H. Christ.' The Pledge can took flight across the bar. 'If I'd known that, he'd have had a steak knife in his—'

'We understand he'd been using the phone here to call—'

'What? He was noncing up his own daughter using my bloody phone?'

'I need his address.'

∼

JAIN STOPPED outside the block of flats and shook her head. 'You see this?'

'See what?' Hunter looked around. 'That these are way more expensive than a short-order cook could afford?'

'I mean that.' She pointed over the road at a lumbering new building, the sort of PFI monstrosity—

'He's staying opposite the bloody primary school.'

Sick bastard. Hunter stared up at the block. 'So the flat of a convicted child molester overlooks a bloody primary school?' He checked for his baton. 'Give me five minutes with him, Chantal, this is...'

Jain gripped his wrist, much tighter than he expected. 'Let's just have a word with him. Okay?'

Hunter tried to wriggle free, like being back in primary himself. 'You don't think he's taken her?'

'I don't know what to think.' Jain let go and paced over to the front door. She hit the buzzer for flat four. 'An hour ago, I thought one of Doug Ferguson's mates had taken her and he's fooling us. Now, I just don't know.' She sighed as the intercom hissed static. 'Let's just have a word and see where we've got to.'

'Is he in?' Hunter jabbed the button, catching her finger and shifting it onto the neighbour's.

'Ow.'

'Sorry.'

'Hello?' A woman's voice, slightly well-to-do. Typical Cramond.

He crouched in front of the intercom. 'This is the police. PC Craig Hunter and DS Chantal Jain.'

'So?'

'We're looking for Robert Quarrie. Does he live here?'

'I certainly think so, but I'm afraid he isn't in.'

'Well, we need—'

The door buzzed open.

Jain stormed up the stairs and round the bend. The sun shone off the grey flooring, almost blinding.

The door for flat three was ajar. It shut when the eye settled on Hunter and his outstretched warrant card.

Jain knocked on the door. 'Mr Quarrie, it's the police. Can you open up, please?'

Nothing.

Hunter sniffed the air. 'Can you smell hash?'

'Jesus Christ.' Jain shook her head and leaned back against the wall. 'And you call Cullen a cowboy.'

'That was you.' More sniffing. Definitely something like it. Strong and tangy. 'Sure you can't smell it?'

Her perfect nostrils twitched. 'Aye, maybe you're right.' She opened the letterbox and peered in. 'Definitely skunk. Isn't that a class A now?'

'Still a B, I think. You should check with your mate, Cullen. Fourteen months leading the war against drugs, right?'

'Craig. What do you want to do here?'

Hunter nodded over at the door. 'I want to batter that door down, then get in there and tie the bastard to a—'

'You can do the battering and getting in.'

'Fine.' Hunter took a step back and launched himself shoulder first at the door.

It didn't budge.

He slipped on the flooring and tumbled over, cracking his skull on the door. 'Ah, you bastard.'

'Are you okay?'

'I'll live.' Hunter got up on his knees and rubbed at his crown. A spatter of fresh blood ran across his fingers. 'Terrific.' He glowered at the door. 'Right, once more with feeling.' He took a step forward and kicked it just below the handle.

The door toppled back and trundled over the floor.

'Right, come on.' He got his baton from his belt and snapped it out with a solid thunk, cautiously stepping onto the dark laminate.

A long hall stretched into the flat, a few doors running off on either side. There was a light on behind the one at the end.

'Stay here.' Hunter inched forward, eating up the hall with each step, and nudged the first door.

A tiny kitchen. Empty.

The second door was a small bedroom, just a single bed stuck against the wall. Again, nothing.

The third was locked and the fourth was a poky bathroom. The shower was bone dry.

Hunter turned round and whisper-shouted: 'Clear up to here.'

Jain joined him by the final door, her own baton drawn. 'You first.'

'Right.' Hunter slipped on a pair of blue nitrile gloves and twisted the brass handle, getting a squeak.

The overhead light blazed out across the room. Beneath the window sill, a leather sofa was toppled over, the fake-silver feet sticking in the air. A pair of shoes poked out at the side.

'Terrific.' Hunter raced over and gripped the left-hand side. 'Help!'

'Give me a sec!' Jain finished snapping on her own gloves. 'Christ, man. Right.' She crouched down and braced the other end.

Hunter rocked his side back.

Robert Quarrie lay face down on the carpet, a circular pool of blood under his head, like a morbid halo. A knife stuck out of his chest, hilt-deep.

He coughed and moaned.

'He's not dead!' Hunter jabbed at his Airwave. 'Control, this is PC Hunter, requesting—'

30

Hunter stood in the living room doorway, his heart thundering in his ears.

A pair of Paramedics stood over the body, prodding and pushing and frowning and scowling and—

Giving up.

The male one got up and drew a line across his throat. 'We lost him.'

Hunter collapsed against the door frame. 'Did he say anything?'

'Nothing at all, mate. Sorry. Far as I can tell, it was the stabbing. Guy'd lost a lot of blood before we even got here.'

'Time of the attack?'

'This is between you and me…' He tossed his head from side-to-side. 'Been about an hour, hour and a half, judging by the blood coagulation.'

'That's helpful, thanks.'

'No worries. I'll call Deeley.'

Whoever the hell that is.

'I'll see what's what downstairs, okay?' Hunter gave him a final nod and barged past the female uniform guarding entry into the flat. 'Make sure you keep it tight, Joanne, okay? We just lost him.'

She grimaced. Looked like she'd been pulled straight out of a High School class. 'Shite, eh?'

Hunter trotted down the stairs and stopped halfway. He looked out through the windows, far across the dusky evening sky. Thick August clouds above the primary school, like they'd just come off the Atlantic

Ocean. It was raining, the water pooling on the pavement like the blood in the living room.

First time in a while. Years, even.
Doesn't get any easier, especially when the victim is still alive.
A dead victim to go with the living one. Assuming Stephanie still is...

Hunter started off down the corridor, teeth grinding together as he tasted the stale air. He grimaced at Jain, manning the crime scene entry point. 'Lost him.'

'Shite.' She ran a hand through her hair, then waved at a passing uniformed officer. 'Come here!'

The guy was even younger than Joanne, looked like his voice probably hadn't broken yet. 'Sarge?' Sounded like it, too.

'Martin, you are a trained Crime Scene Manager, right?' Jain handed him the clipboard. 'You weren't just trying to chat me up?'

Hunter did a double take. Boy's voice, but a man's cojones from the sounds of it.

The spotty oik gave her a nod. 'Done it last week, Sarge.'

'Good.' Jain led Hunter over to their pool car and leaned against it, staring up at the sky. 'You okay?'

'Seen worse.'

'Sure?'

'Maybe not.' Hunter joined her leaning on the wet car, the rain already soaking through his fleece and T-shirt. 'We almost had him. Can't believe he's gone.'

An orange Focus roared out of the mouth of the lane and screeched to a halt just next to them. Sharon McNeill scowled out from behind the steering wheel. Lauren looked battered in the passenger side, twirling a stray spiral of blonde hair. When the car stopped rocking, they got out, their doors clicking at the same time.

Jain stood up tall, dusting off her suit jacket, and drew a line across her neck. 'Stabbing.'

'Shite.' McNeill scowled over at the block of flats, now cordoned off with police tape. 'Chantal, I thought you said he was our number one?'

'If I'm not wrong, someone's got to him.' Jain shrugged. 'Either way, there's no sign of the girl inside.'

'That's all we need.'

'Good job securing this, though.' Lauren looked around the crime scene again. 'Buchan's in with DCI Cargill just now. Should be here soon.'

Hunter frowned. 'Cargill's MIT, isn't she?'

McNeill gave him a nod. 'And this is an escalation. We're not dealing with sexual assault or abuse any longer. What I want to know is who did it?'

Hunter held her gaze. 'Doug Ferguson wasn't in custody.'

'Okay. So let's get hold of him and find out if he was here.' McNeill frowned at him. 'Why would he kill Mr Quarrie, though?'

Hunter stared up at the teeming sky, letting the heavy clouds add weight to his answer. 'I can think of a good reason.'

McNeill scowled at him, holding his gaze for a few seconds, then nodded at Lauren. 'Sergeant, let's have a look inside. Chantal, can you two get statements from any neighbours?'

'Shaz, I'm a Sergeant.'

'And I'm an Inspector. Off you go.'

~

'Who does she think she is?' Jain knocked on the door to flat one. 'I mean, come on.'

'You're not still pissed off at having to do this, are you?' Hunter grinned. 'And you say I moan.'

'Quit it—'

The door thundered open. A man peered out and rubbed his eyes. 'Ah, you bugger.' He blinked hard and put a hand over his face. 'Shite, shite, shite.'

'Police.' Hunter showed his warrant card. 'Are you okay, sir?'

'Aye. Had my eyes lasered a few days ago. Bloody agony.' He sighed. 'Still, I can see without glasses. Means I won't have to fumble around for them when my kids wake us up at five in the morning.'

'Sure it'll be worth it.' Hunter let his fists go, still couldn't look at his eyes. 'Can I ask your name, sir?'

'Paul Vickers.'

'Have you been home all day, Mr Vickers?'

Vickers took his hands away from his eyes. Didn't look that bad, just a bit raw, like he'd been out on the piss for a couple of days. 'See this.' He pulled up his eyelid. A cut ran across the top of his cornea, blood red against the baby blue.

Jesus. Hunter's gut clenched tight. 'That looks sore.'

'It's nothing compared to about an hour after they did it. Still, didn't feel anything during.'

'So you've been here all day?'

'Aye, aye.'

Hunter folded his arms. 'Did you see anyone enter the building at about three o'clock this afternoon?'

Vickers frowned, blinking hard. 'Now, did I?'

'There was an attack upstairs.'

Vickers swallowed, frowning. 'What?'

'Do you know Mr Quarrie?'

'Had a beer with him a couple of months ago up at the Almond. Nice enough bloke.' Vickers slumped back against his door and focused on the floor, rubbing at his temples. 'Look, I don't know if it's anything, but I was out for a smoke at back of three. Saw a red car drive off.'

Hunter stared round at Jain. 'What kind?'

'Looked Japanese to me.'

Hunter reached into his pocket for one of Elvis's stills. 'Was it this one?'

'Aye, that's the badger.' Vickers took the photo and traced his finger over it. 'Queerest thing, mind. The wing mirror was missing.'

'Which side?'

'Driver's.'

Jain stepped forward, getting in front of Hunter. 'You definitely saw this?'

'Hand on heart.' Vickers stuck his hand to his chest. 'My eyes are just sore, they're not buggered.'

∼

JAIN STORMED out of the building's front door and looked around. 'Where the hell is she?'

A car pulled up with flashing ambulance lights and an overweight man got out. He approached Jain and stopped her. 'Chantal, I'd love to stop and chat, but do you know where the body is?'

'Upstairs, Mr Deeley. Flat three.'

'Catch you later, young lady.' He splashed through a puddle on his way to the Crime Scene Manager.

Hunter waved over at him. 'That's Jimmy Deeley?'

'I prefer my Pathologists slimmer and less annoying...'

'Got you.' Hunter looked around the wet crime scene. 'So, why are—'

'Bloody freezing here.' Lauren appeared between Hunter and Jain, rubbing her bare arms. 'Summer should last longer than a day, right?'

'You should move back to London.'

'It was Kent, but if the Met'd take me...' Lauren clapped Hunter's arm. 'The Pathologist's given time of assault as three o'clock today.'

'He's only just got here, though.'

Lauren shrugged. 'Don't question magic, Craig.' Her Airwave chimed out. 'Crap.'

'And Jimmy Deeley's the arch magician.' McNeill appeared on the other side of Jain, nodding at her but ignoring Hunter. 'Did you two get anything from the door-to-door?'

'We've got statements from two of the neighbours. Next door saw and heard nothing.' Jain pointed at the flats. 'Downstairs saw a red Hyundai matching the description. Still don't know who was driving it. We're lucky to get that much. The guy just had his eyes lasered.'

McNeill shook her head. 'He's not going to be a credible witness if he's just had bloody eye surgery.'

'He's giving a full statement to one of my DCs.' Jain waved over at the block of flats. 'He walked past the car. Used to own that model. A Hyundai Santa Fe.'

'We'll need to get a bloody surgeon in to testify before this guy.' McNeill frowned at Jain. 'It's the same car that attacked Craig and kidnapped Stephanie?'

'One and the same.'

McNeill stared up at the sky, shaking her head. 'Right. A kidnapping and now a murder. Superb.'

Lauren approached, tapping her Airwave. 'That was Buchan. He's finished with the SIO.'

'They're here already.' Jain jabbed a finger at a white Range Rover Vogue. 'Crystal Methven.'

An athletic-looking man from the driver's side, his wild eyebrows acting like antennae as his head swivelled around.

Cullen followed him out of the passenger seat, talking into his super-sized iPhone as he splashed into a puddle. 'Bollocks!'

'That'll be the MIT, then?'

'That's the MIT.' McNeill cupped her hands and shouted: 'Scott!'

Cullen stomped over, ending his call and pocketing his phone. 'Well, guess who's working this case?'

'It's a bloody mess in there, Scott.' McNeill turned her nose up. 'Looks like he spilled a bottle of Rioja.'

'The joys. Sharon, Chantal, can I get a minute with you?'

Hunter watched them traipse over to where the SOCOs were using their tent as a rain shelter. 'So we're just kicked off, Sarge?'

'We're better off out of it. Be grateful. This is getting worse.'

'And it's my fault. If I hadn't let—'

'Shhh.' Lauren put a finger over his lips. 'It's a murder. Let them worry about it, okay? We've done everything by the book.'

Hunter swallowed. 'Aye...'

'Haven't we?'

'Well, over and above Finlay twatting about on his phone, we didn't exactly get access to the flat by fair means. Thought we smelled skunk.'

'Was this you or your little friend?'

'Me, Sarge.'

'Bloody hell.' Lauren jabbed his chest with her finger. 'Make sure your notebooks are in complete alignment, understood?'

Hunter reached into his pocket for his. 'I'll get a head start, Sarge.'

'Good idea. Well, I'm off to make a nuisance of myself.' Lauren wandered over to the tents, rubbing her arms more frantically than ever.

Hunter got into the pool Vectra and took out his pen, leaving the door open. He jabbed the nib into the paper.

Bloody car, kidnapping people, killing people.

Bloody—

'Craig, you got a minute?' Cullen was peering round the car door.

Hunter closed his notebook. 'What's up?'

'I'm going to need you to brief my team.'

31

'Okay, that all looks good.' Cullen looked around his assembled troops, ten or so officers huddled together in the makeshift SOCO tent.

Hunter was at the very edge, getting the occasional spray of warm rain down his left leg.

Elvis was next to him, gradually nudging him further towards the outside.

'Sir.' Cullen nodded at the guy with the eyebrows as he barged into the fray. 'And we shouldn't forget that Stephanie Ferguson is still missing. She was last seen this morning, abducted by persons unknown.' Then he nodded at Hunter and Lauren in turn. 'We've got the resource from the preceding investigation allocated to this, at least for the time being. I want us to focus on suspects here.' He kept his gaze on Hunter. 'Craig, do you want to take us through where you've got to?'

Hunter waited until his breathing was back under control before starting. 'Okay, I'll start with Stephanie's stepfather—'

∽

'—THIS AFTERNOON.'

'Cheers, Craig.' Cullen was noting everything down on his phone. He looked up at Hunter, his forehead creased to show he was paying attention. 'One thing I don't get is why Doug Ferguson killed his stepdaughter's natural father?'

'They've got previous, Sarge. Ferguson collected Quarrie from prison on his release and made it clear he should leave and not come back, if you catch my drift. If he's done this, it's a vigilante action.'

'Seen a few of those in my time.' Cullen gave a smug laugh. 'So, do you think Mr Ferguson has got someone to abduct her?'

'It's possible. She was telling us about him and what he's been doing. That's put him on our radar.' Hunter raised a hand. 'And I mean Police Scotland's radar, not mine.' He expected a chorus of laughter but just got Elvis mouthing "wanker". He cleared his throat. 'We just need a statement from Stephanie and Mr Ferguson will be avoiding normal courtyard exercise for a couple of years. Then the pitchforks will be out wherever he goes.'

No laughter at that, either. Bastards.

Cullen held Hunter's gaze. 'You think he was abusing her?'

'I believe her.'

Lauren raised a hand. 'We've got units out trying to bring Mr Ferguson in.'

'Cheers.' Cullen pointed at two male officers on the far side. 'Stuart, can you and Si have a word with him when he pitches up?'

The skinhead snorted. 'Sure thing, Sarge.' Cockney accent, mangled with a bit of local flavour.

Was that Simon Buxton? How the hell had he got into the MIT?

Hunter nodded at Cullen. 'Another thing, Sarge, is that Ferguson got a message out to a mate through his lawyer. Hamish Williams.'

'I'm aware of his work.' Cullen groaned. 'What was the message?'

'We found one David Boyle lurking in their back garden last night. Gave chase, didn't catch him.'

Cullen scrolled back up on his mobile, his thumb flicking and flicking. 'This is the guy with the missing car, right?'

'Allegedly missing.'

'Sounds like it might be worth having another word with him.'

Buxton gave another nod.

Cullen slid his finger back down to the bottom of his phone's screen. 'What about the boyfriend? Neil Alexander, right?'

Lauren shrugged. 'He's been helping the investigation.'

'So?'

'So, what? He doesn't know where Stephanie is.'

'Right, well, we should speak to him again.' Cullen nodded at an elfin girl next to him, her hair a deep red. 'Eva, can you and Lauren do the honours?'

'Sure thing, Sarge.' Eva winked at Cullen. Turned Hunter's stomach.

Hang on... Eva. She's the one spreading rumours about—

'Cheers.' Cullen looked up from his phone, Lauren getting all the attention now. 'This teacher seems a bit weird. Why did she let the girl stay at her house?'

'According to her statement, she was giving Stephanie time, trying to persuade her to come in and talk to us on her own terms.'

'And you believe her?'

'You should've seen what Stephanie was like with my team.' Lauren tucked her fleece tighter. 'She just wouldn't speak. We were praying for a nod or a shake of the head, barely got anything. Seems like it was all she could manage just to tell her mum about the abuse.'

Cullen tapped a note into his phone. 'Well, let's make sure we speak to her about Robert Quarrie, aye?'

'That said, it's possible this death isn't connected to Stephanie's case at all.' Hunter cleared his throat, the lump of coal deciding to make another appearance. 'There's also Quarrie's boss. He wasn't impressed when I told him about his ... history. Turns out Quarrie had lied on his application.'

'Right, I'll get someone to have a word, but I'm not treating that as serious.'

'Your decision.' Hunter tucked his thumbs into his jeans. 'Of course, that brings up the fact that Quarrie was inside. He might've annoyed someone in there.' He thumbed at Elvis next to him. 'DC Gordon was looking into that.'

'Elvis?'

'Sarge?'

'Have you got anything?'

'I'll get onto it, Sarge. Sorry.'

Hunter leaned over to check what he was writing down. 'And Quarrie was living in Stranraer for a bit. Might be worth another chat with Dumfries and Galloway, now he's been murdered, aye?'

'Good shout.' Elvis narrowed his eyes as he stabbed his pen into his notebook. 'I'm sure I'll manage those, Craig.'

Cullen shifted his gaze from them to take in the rest of the group. 'Okay, let's talk wider strategy.'

∽

'—GRAB me if and when you need to, okay?' Cullen locked his phone and stuffed it into his jacket pocket. 'Let's get out there.'

Hunter stayed standing as the group disbanded around him, just a trickle of water dribbling down the collar of his fleece.

Cullen walked through, stabbing at his phone again.

Hunter grabbed his arm. 'What other help do you need from me?'

'Well, Craig, that's probably saved us a day of trying to work out what you've already investigated. You can just hang back for now, okay?'

'I want to—'

'Craig. We're trained for this stuff and it's our case now. Okay? Just need your operational statements and all the other paperwork you do in uniform these days.' He grinned at Jain as she marched through the tent towards them. 'Come on, Chantal, I'm short of a couple of skulls so let's you and me speak to this teacher. Be just like the good old days.'

Jain placed her hands on her hips. 'The shite old days, you mean?'

Hunter clenched his fists, fingernails biting into his palms. 'Any chance of a lift back to Leith Walk?'

∽

'I'M TELLING YOU, you need to speak to DI McNeill about that.' Hunter let his seatbelt ride up. The car park was quiet, just Fat Keith working away at the back end of the knackered Saab. He opened the door and put a foot on the concrete. 'I know how annoying it must be to be taking orders from Cullen again, so have a word with her. She's a DI, he's a DS.'

'Thanks for the advice.' Jain killed the engine. 'That I didn't ask for.'

Hunter put the other foot down and twisted round. 'Do you fancy a drink?'

'Craig…' She rested her forehead against the steering wheel and let out a deep sigh. 'I just need to get my head around this, so if you could just give me some space.'

It's like that, is it?

Hunter's mouth was dry. He tried to swallow, but nothing was shifting. 'Okay.'

'This is probably going to drag on and on tonight.'

Hunter stood up tall and leaned into the Vectra. She was facing away from him, practically hugging the door. No chance of a goodbye kiss. 'See you later.'

'Aye.'

Hunter traipsed across the car park. He got a warning glare from Keith so headed for the stairwell and the locker room.

The stair door burst open and Finlay stomped out, the upturned collar on his polo shirt standing at half-mast now. His face looked like he'd gone five full rounds of Mixed Martial Arts. 'Oh, hey.'

'You look like shite, mate. That can't be from the attack this morning, can it?'

'Is it that bad?'

'Looks like you got thirteen seconds of Conor McGregor's attention last night.'

'Feels like it.' Finlay patted the swelling over his left eyebrow. Didn't add much to his beauty. Then again, it didn't exactly take much away, either. 'Prick clattered my head off the pavement. Doesn't stop Lauren getting me back in here, though. Shouldn't be back on active service, I tell you.' He tugged his collar up again. 'You got Krav Maga again tonight?'

'Fancy a pint?'

32

Finlay supped at his lager, scowling around the pub like an old man in a miner's welfare. 'Hate what they've done to this place.'

Hunter stared into his glass, the Jarl's soupy head almost gone, even though it was still pretty much full. He looked around the Elm, a confused mix of off-duty cops and hipster students. 'It was a shit hole before.'

The heavily bearded barman poured a short glass of beer for a similarly hirsute man in skin-tight jeans. Behind them, another bearded man in a white chef's get-up put a burger on a chopping board onto the serving hatch and rang a bell. Burnt beef smells infiltrated their half of the pub.

'Maybe. But it was my shit hole.' Finlay supped a long draught of his lager, managing to dribble most of it down his chin. No reaction. 'Thought you'd stiff me again after last night.'

Hunter took a sip of his beer, tangy and sweet. 'What do you mean?'

'Krav Maga, my arse. You were playing hide the sausage with Chantal, weren't you?'

'No comment.'

'I saw you this morning, so don't you "no comment" me.'

'Like I told you, her car's in the garage on Seafield. I saw her on Leith Walk. The bus had broken down.'

'Aye, bollocks.' Another long drink, this one actually going into his mouth. 'Did she find your sausage in the end?'

'See when you lost that bollock, did—'

'Did you shag her?'

'I'm not telling you.' Hunter nudged his pint away until it clinked off Finlay's glass. 'See when you lost that bollock, you must've got a packet, right? Why are you still working?'

'It was only five grand, mate. Can you credit it?' Finlay finished his beer. 'Get half a mill for losing a leg. A half-empty scrotum and you'll be lucky to get change from a new kitchen.' He burped into his hand. 'Still haven't cooked in it yet.'

'Jesus.' Hunter reached for his pint and took another sip before pushing the glass away again. 'That tastes off.'

'Sure it's not you?' Finlay gave him a wink. 'Sure it's not because Cullen's sidelined you?'

'Maybe.' Hunter flattened his arms across the tabletop and rested his head on his hands. 'I thought I missed doing proper detective work, but I've had the shit kicked out of me, what, three times? And the shit Jain and McNeill deal with. Doesn't bear thinking about.'

'Speaking of which, how did the interview go?'

'How the hell do you manage to know everything that's going on and still be such a shite detective?'

'Professional secret, jabroni.' Finlay tapped his nose and nodded at his beer. 'You going to finish that?'

'Be my guest.'

'Cheers.' Finlay took a long drink of Hunter's pint. 'Not the best, that. How did it go, then?'

Hunter just shrugged.

'Whatever will I do without you?'

'Arse about on your phone…'

Clunk. 'Evening, boys.'

Hunter looked round to the left.

Cullen sat down at the next table, a burger and a bottle of Brewdog in front of him. 'Mind if I sit here?'

Hunter picked up his jacket and put it on his lap. 'Thought you'd still be on duty.'

'I am. Problem is, I'm barred from the canteen now. Guilt by association.' Cullen took a big bite out of his burger. Meat fat dribbled down his hands.

Hunter had to look away, his stomach churning at the sight. And the smell. Could almost taste it.

'Bollocks.' Cullen grabbed a handful of serviettes and started dabbing at his wrists. 'This should come with a health warning.'

'Right, boys, I'm off home.' Finlay thunked his glass down on the table and got up. 'That stuff's playing merry hell with those pills the doc gave us. Night.'

'See you in the morning, Fin.'

Cullen gave him a mock salute while he chewed another fatty mouthful. He swallowed it down with some beer and waved over at the bar. 'Napalm's your partner, right?'

'For my sins.'

'With a name like Finlay Sinclair, you'd expect him to be a Lord Advocate or something.' Cullen took another bite of his burger. 'Has to be one monkey in every family tree, right?'

'Right.'

'Skinky...' A wafer-thin skinhead loomed over Cullen, gave Hunter the briefest of nods. 'Thought I'd find you here.'

'The answer's no.' Cullen bit off half a chip. 'Now, what's the question?'

'This case you're working...'

Cullen dipped another chip in a pool of beef fat on the plate. 'You're getting nothing, Rich.'

'Come on, mate, you *owe* me.'

'I know I do, but not like this, okay?' Cullen bit another chip. 'Unless you find the girl, you're getting nothing.'

'Come on.'

'No.'

'But—'

'No.'

'You're a prick, Scott.' Rich stormed off, hugging his laptop bag around him.

Hunter's stomach tied itself into knots, sounded like it was gargling with mouthwash. 'Another member of the Scott Cullen fan club?'

'Can never have too many.' Cullen took another bite, seemed to ponder this one for longer than the cholesterol bomb deserved. Or he'd moved onto some unexploded ordnance in his private life. Must be enough women out there breeding from his toxic sperm. 'Journalist. Used to share a flat with him.' He chuckled. 'Not like that, Craig. I know how you think.'

Do you? You know people want to cut your balls off, do you?

Hunter took a drink of his beer. 'You need anything more on that teacher?'

'Chantal chummed me in there. Waste of time, but the woman's still in custody. Still don't get why she harboured Stephanie, but hey. That's more Sharon's side of this.' Cullen took another bite of the burger. 'This case really messes you up, though. That poor girl. Abused by her own dad and then her stepdad. Some dirty bastards out there, mate.'

'Aye, don't I know it. Good riddance to her old man.' Hunter couldn't tear his eyes off the Brewdog bottle. 'I've a mind to speak to the Custody Sergeant and get ten minutes alone with Doug Ferguson when we get him back in.'

'I'll pretend I didn't hear that.'

'Scott, are you telling me you wouldn't do it?'

Cullen ate the last of his burger and mopped up the fat on his chin. 'That's what juries are for, and it's why we don't kill people on the street.'

'Some days I wish we could.'

'You need to be one hundred percent sure with that vigilante shite, but I know what it feels like.' Another swig of Brewdog. 'Anyway, it's immaterial, as we've still not found him. Chantal's leading the hunt.' Cullen swirled his bottle round and drained it. 'You think he did it?'

'What, abused his daughter?'

'No, killed Robert Quarrie?'

'Like I said, I don't get the why. More like the why now. Could've done it when he got out of prison or any time since.'

'Wants to redeem himself, maybe?' Cullen gripped the bottle tight but didn't raise it, just kept in on the table. 'While you and Ipac have been in here shortening your lifespans, I went through the transcripts of your interview with Ferguson. He said he collected Quarrie from the nick, right?'

'Said he was warning him off. That's what's interesting. What if he wasn't warning him? What if they're in cahoots?'

Hunter leaned back on the bench. Nothing keeping me, talking to this prick... 'We've had nothing to suggest they might be.'

'Maybe we need to dig a little deeper.' Cullen bit into a chip. 'Weird having Chantal working for me again. Forgot how annoying she can be.'

'She's not that bad.'

Cullen winked at him. 'Got a soft spot for her, have you?'

Fire burnt under Hunter's collar. 'Just been working with her for the last day or two. She's all right.'

Cullen swigged more beer. 'Aye, she's okay.'

How could that prick just sit there like nothing had happened?

Hunter stared at him for a few seconds. 'Like Yvonne was okay?'

Cullen held his bottle in front of his face. 'Come again?'

'DC Yvonne Flockhart. Remember her?'

'She works in Ally Davenport's team. I borrowed her to make sure Elvis didn't bugger up the CCTV.' Another chip. 'What about her?'

Hunter sighed. 'Quit playing that game with me.'

'It's not a game. Has she annoyed you or something?'

What's up with him?

'We were engaged.' Hunter rocked forward and gripped the edge of the table. 'Then I caught you shagging her. Don't tell me that's just conveniently slipped your mind.'

Cullen's beer bottle toppled over. He righted it and started mopping at the spillage. 'What?'

'Remember Ally's Christmas party in 2010? You went back to a flat and shagged someone.'

'Wait, what?' Cullen finished mopping the beer. 'I ... had sex with Yvonne?'

Hunter gripped the edge of the table. 'From behind, if I recall.'

Cullen slumped back in his chair and rubbed his forehead. 'Look, I was plastered and it was a long time ago. I was a bad boy back then, I'll be the first to admit, but I'm in a ... stable relationship now.'

'You're lying.'

'Craig, trust me, I'm not. Jesus, I can't even remember it.'

'You don't remember me kicking you up the arse and pushing you down the stairs?'

'Craig, I stopped drinking for that reason. Did a lot of shit when I was blootered, and it seems like I forgot a lot of it, too.' Cullen chinked his nails off his beer. 'This is alcohol-free.'

'Jesus.' Hunter stooped to look out of the window. 'Think I just saw a pig fly past.'

'Better believe it. Over a year and a half on the wagon.' Cullen shrugged. 'Give or take.'

'You shagged her and we split up.'

'Look, I'm sorry. I've got a drink problem and...' Cullen swallowed, his stubbly neck bobbing. 'Jesus, no wonder you've been giving me the cold shoulder.'

'You're lucky I haven't kicked you down another staircase.'

'Craig, it's... What can I say?'

'Sorry would be a start.'

Cullen drained his bottle and pushed it across the table. 'I'm really sorry, Craig. I'm not going to defend my actions. You were a good mate to me and you deserved better. A whole lot better.'

'You're an arsehole, Scott.'

'I don't disagree.' Cullen picked up a chip and bit it in half. 'You did well in the interview, by the way.'

Like that gets you off the hook, you prick.

Hunter looked over. 'Does that mean I've got the job?'

'Can't tell you that, can I?' Cullen shook his head. 'And Donna Nichols is a stickler for process, if nothing else.' He frowned. 'What happened to you, Craig? Thought you were going places.'

'So did I. Fell out with Davenport, didn't I?'

'The role's in his team.'

Hunter slumped back in the chair. 'Right.'

'Look, I can put a good word in for you. See if Bill Lamb or Colin—'

'Don't bother.'

'Sure? You're a good officer.'

'Wish other people thought so.'

'You want to keep fishing for compliments or just take that one?'

Hunter couldn't help but grin. 'Cheers, Scott.'

'No worries.' Cullen finished his burger and got to his feet. 'Anyway, I'd better get back.'

Hunter grabbed his arm. 'Do you mind if I help?'

'Calm down, Craig. You're off duty.'

'I know, but come on, Scott... You really owe me one.'

'Look, if I broke up your engagement, you've got my apology. But I'm not letting you blackmail me, okay?'

'I'm not going to run amok. I just really don't want that scumbag out there, you know?'

'You and I both. But you've been drinking. Get yourself home, watch some football and chill out, okay?'

33

Hunter crept down the corridor, slowly and calmly. Nobody about, just the hissing of a kettle somewhere deeper in the station. He stopped by the door to the MIT's Incident Room and peered in.

Jain was sitting by the window, hammering her laptop's keyboard. Apart from her, the room was empty.

Hunter walked over and sat next to her. 'Hey.'

She glanced around, bleary-eyed and blinking. Then groaned. 'What the hell are you doing here?'

'Helping. Cullen said it was okay.'

'Did he?'

'Didn't take long to set this up.' Hunter waved around the room. The walls were already covered in photos from the crime scene in Cramond, the standard template on the whiteboard. Actions and suspects, all that jazz.

'What can I say, the MIT are a slick machine.' Jain tugged her scrunchie free and let her hair hang loose. 'Did Scott really say it was okay?'

'Didn't say it wasn't.' Hunter picked up a document from her desk. 'Is Doug Ferguson in custody yet?'

'Come on, Craig... If Scott's DI finds out you're snooping around, I'll be for it. You know that, right?'

'How about I was helping provide background?'

'Stinking of beer?'

'Didn't even have one pint.' Hunter started flicking through the document on the desk. Looked like it was summarised from his notes so far. 'Have you found—'

'Go home, Craig.'

'Come on, Chantal.'

'Is this what last night was about?' She slammed her laptop lid. 'Get in my knickers and I'll speak to my mates in the MIT? Maybe get you that job?'

'It's nothing like that, Chantal. I really like you.'

'Please—'

'I mean it. Liked you for years, just too much of a mess to say or do anything about it.'

'Craig, I swear.' Jain opened her laptop again. 'If you're trying it on, I will kill you.' She tied her hair up again. 'Now piss off.'

∽

HUNTER GOT out of his car and looked down Sandport Street, a pizza box tucked under his arm. Place was still damp from the rain, but at least it had stopped. The air had that clean smell, like everything had been washed away and we could all start over again.

Two buses hissed past each other at the end, spraying a few pedestrians on Commercial Street.

Hunter twisted his keys in the lock and entered the building. The marguerita tang hit his nostrils as he climbed the stairs. Better than the smell of half-feral cats from number one. He opened his flat door and walked into the tiny little space — most bedsits would be ashamed to share the name.

'Mieaow.' Bubble immediately started swarming round his legs, then stopped to hiss out into the hall at some invisible threat.

Hunter pulled the door shut and picked her up. Barely weighed anything, but she looked as healthy as the day he'd got her. He carried her into the kitchen and plonked her on the counter, making sure to put enough space between her and the pizza.

His eggs lay burnt in the pan, tiny nibbles taken out of the crisp whites. He put his nose against Bubble's fur. 'Have you been eating my eggs?'

'Miaow.'

'Dirty little bugger.' He picked up her food bowl and dumped in a pile of biscuits from the tin. 'Here you go.'

'Mieaow!' Bubble squatted down on her haunches and started munching through the bowl, as he filled the kettle and flicked it on.

He got a teabag out of the cupboard and put it in yesterday's mug, just a vague brown stain at the bottom. Didn't look too bad. Boiling water would kill any bugs anyway.

He got his phone out and checked for messages. A text from Jain.

Sorry for being a bitch. Girls don't like clingy men.

Terrific.
What to do...
He tapped out a reply as the kettle started to rattle and hiss.

I thought they wanted to be serenaded.

The kettle came to the boil and he poured the steaming water over his teabag.

Her reply flashed up on his screen.

Well, this one doesn't. You have gone home, right?

He got a spoon out and started mashing the teabag against the side of the cup, tapping out a reply with his free hand.

Getting something to eat while my cat molests me. Sorry about earlier. Don't let not being able to help.

The message had sent with that typo in it. *Bugger.* He typed:

*like not let. Bloody phone.

He yanked the teabag out and left a little trail of dark brown droplets as he carried it over to the compost caddy. He reached into the fridge for the milk — still in date — and tipped it in, turning the liquid just the right colour.

Cup in hand, he took the pizza over to the TV, all of two metres away. He collapsed into his chair with a groan and started supping the scalding tea as the screen warmed up with a crackle. Got a bit of pain from his knee. Nothing a slice of fat and salt couldn't cure.

He opened the box and let the aroma drift up. Mushroom, pineapple and banana. Heaven.

Netflix popped up. "Better Call Saul" was the first on "Continue Watching for Craig".

'Mieow!' Bubble sproinged onto Hunter's chest, making him drop the slice of pizza onto the cardboard.

'You wee bugger.' He tried to nudge her away. 'You've got your own food.'

'Mieow!'

The nuclear warning klaxon blasted out of his mobile.

Bubble spread herself low and hissed.

'It's okay, cat.' Hunter checked the phone and answered it. 'Hey.'

'Hey.' Jain yawned into her handset. 'Sorry, I'm really tired. Look, helping the case means being stuck in here.'

'I wouldn't mind being stuck in you.'

'Quit it with the cheese, Hunter.'

'Ah, go on. You love it. Anyway, you getting anywhere with that cock-block of a case?'

She sighed down the line. 'In the thirty minutes since you last pestered me, the case hasn't moved forward.'

'Seriously, nobody's seen Ferguson? He can't just have disappeared, can he?'

She spoke into the phone, like there was someone near. 'Cullen's worried you'll take some vigilante action against him.'

'What?'

'They call it extra-legal violence these days. You ex-squaddies with your PTSD and cupboards full of stolen guns.'

Hunter ran a hand down Bubble's spine as she sniffed at his pizza. 'I've not got PTSD.'

'What about the guns?'

'Ha. Ha.' Hunter picked Bubble up one-handed and lifted her away from the food. 'Look, that's not funny, you know? Took me years...'

'Shit, do you...?'

Jesus... Not like this. Not over the phone with a feral cat and a roaring belly.

'In Iraq, an IED went off next to me, killed my squad mate. Two years of therapy later, the police took me in. And I'm on antidepressants for the rest of my life.'

The line crackled for a few seconds. 'Shite, Craig.'

'The Combat Stress charity really helped me. Helped put all that shite in the past.'

A long pause before Jain coughed. 'It's not just ex-squaddies that get it.'

'I know that. But why bring it up at all?'

'You're thinking of going after him, aren't you?'

'No, I'm not.' Hunter yawned and took a sip of scalding tea. Just right. 'When are you finishing?'

'Midnight at this rate.'

'Do you want to come round here?'

'I'm shattered and I need to feed my own cat.'

'Well, Bubble's stuffing her skinny little face. Maybe I could see you there?'

'Good night, Craig.'

The phone clicked dead. *Charming...*

What to do, what to do.

Hunter closed the lid of his pizza box and picked up his car keys. He pecked the cat on the top of her head. 'Sorry, Bubble. Daddy's got to go out to play.'

Hunter put the last pizza crust in his mouth and chewed slowly, still getting a hit of the caramelised banana.

He took a sip of water and looked around the street. No sign of Alec Wishart or his wife, if she even existed. And no sign of Cullen's uniform unit, either.

He dumped the pizza box on the back seat and rubbed the grease off his fingers.

What if the wife didn't exist? What did he call her? Marie.

Assume Marie doesn't exist, what does that leave us with?

One, a lying bastard.

Two, a lying bastard who's a close friend of an alleged child molester. Said friend who introduced said child molester to the mother of a previously abused girl.

Three, that'll do.

Hunter got out of the car and walked across Mountcastle Terrace. Other than the distant drone of traffic, the only sounds were the gate creaking open and his feet splashing in the puddles as he approached the door. He hit the bell and stood back.

Nice street, though probably full of older people whose—

'Can I help you?' Harsh Northern Irish accent, Belfast area. Tall, raven-haired, eyes that could pierce armour.

'I was looking for Mr Wishart?'

'Aye, he's not in. And you are?'

'PC Craig Hunter. Are you Mrs Wishart?'

'Ms Marie Henderson.' She looked him up and down. 'Where's your uniform?'

'I'm working plainclothes for a case.'

'Right, right. Well, like I said, he's not here.' She crossed her legs like she was a small child needing to go to the toilet. 'Is this about that stuff with Doug Ferguson?'

'Have you seen him recently?'

'Not for a while, sorry. Not on my Christmas card list.'

'Well, thanks for your time. Good night, then.' Hunter trudged back over to his car and got in, slumping low in the seat.

So she did exist. Where are we now?

One, he's not a liar.

Two, he's still friends with an alleged child molester and—

A car pulled up two ahead of him, grinding round a tight parallel park. The door clicked open and Alec Wishart got out. He looked up and down the street, his gaze jumping in steps. Then he knocked on the back window.

Doug Ferguson got out, keeping himself low to the ground, shoulders hunched.

Hunter eased his door open and put his foot on the damp pavement.

Another door slammed behind him. 'Here, you!' Footsteps splashed through a series of puddles. 'Your own bloody daughter?' Dave Boyle was sprinting down the street, much closer to them than Hunter was. 'How could you?'

More doors slammed and heavier footsteps thumped along the pavement from the other side. Two twenty-stone skinheads.

Terrific.

'Police!' Hunter darted across the road and tried to get between Boyle and Doug, pulling his warrant card out of his pocket. 'I need you to—'

Thump. A fist caught Hunter's crown. He hit the ground, wet tarmac digging into his cheek.

Footsteps went the other way.

'Here, get back, you!' The heavy footsteps thundered off. 'You paedo cu—'

Hunter got up on all fours. A boot cracked his ribs and he was down again.

Fourth time in two days...

'Here! That paedo bastard's getting away.' Boyle crouched down by Hunter and grabbed him by the collar. 'You lot should've put that prick away when you had the chance, you hear me?'

Hunter swung round and cracked his left boot into Boyle's knee.

He tumbled forward, just missing Hunter. 'Ah, you bastard!'

Hunter clambered to his feet and rubbed his knee. No sign of the skinheads.

'Help!' Sounded like Doug Ferguson. 'Ah! No!'

An engine started up and a car pulled off, screeching along the dead street. A red Hyundai tore past, swerving between the parked cars.

Doug Ferguson was in the back, hammering at the glass, screaming his lungs out.

34

'Stand still!' Hunter twisted Boyle's arm up his back and gripped his neck, pushing him down onto the car's bonnet. 'Quit wriggling!'

A hand gripped Hunter's elbow from behind. 'Craig, you can let him go.' Steve, wearing his uniform and grinning away. 'The cavalry's here, big man. It's okay.'

'Right.' Hunter let Boyle go and stepped aside.

Steve wrapped his cuffs around Boyle's wrist. 'Come on, you.' He dragged Boyle over to a waiting squad car and nodded behind him. 'Oh, there's your lover girl. Thought her motor was in the garage?'

Hunter swung round, Airwave out.

Jain's car pulled up, fresh darts of rain making the puddles dance.

'Receiving.'

'Aye, Control, it's PC Hunter. Have you got an update on that red Hyundai, license plate SA61—'

'Still a negative on that, Craig.'

'Right. Cheers.' Hunter pocketed the Airwave and stood his ground, watching and waiting.

Jain got out of the car first, pulling her hood up over her hair, followed by Cullen.

Hunter set off across the tarmac. 'Sarge, back-up are taking Ferguson's mates into custody.'

'Good effort.' Cullen ran a hand through his wet hair. The grey was less obvious when it was damp. 'I gather you didn't see who was driving?'

'Sorry about that. Keeps happening...'

'It's okay. At least you saw it was Ferguson in the back. Opens things up a bit.'

'How so?'

'Well, he's probably not taken Stephanie, don't you think?' Cullen was grinning at him.

'Wouldn't be too sure about that.' Hunter had to look away. 'Boyle had a couple of big bastards with him. Proper SDL types. They must've run off.' He stifled a yawn. 'I need to go through the timeline. Ferguson got Boyle to help. Say he took her for Ferguson and he's keeping her somewhere. But he found out what the real story is, what Stephanie told us, and well...'

'I can buy that.'

'I tried going after them, Scott, but I had my hands full with Boyle.'

'Big pair of bastards won't be hard to find, surely?' Cullen looked up and down the street. A few curtains were still twitching. 'What were you doing here, Craig?'

'Trying to help.' Hunter lifted a shoulder, could barely put any defiance into it. 'So, what now, Sarge?'

'Given you don't seem to like being told to head home, I want you and Chantal interviewing these clowns.'

∽

ALEC WISHART PRODDED HIS JAW, swollen up even bigger than his bulbous head. 'This hurts more than it looks.'

'Well, it looks pretty bad.' Hunter got up from his seat and joined the Custody Officer by the door, propping himself up against the tattered wallpaper. The only position that didn't hurt like he'd been through a blender. 'Mr Wishart, we just want to know what you saw at the crime scene.'

'Nothing.' Wishart kept his fingers on the black and purple skin around his mouth. 'Someone smacked me one. Knocked me out, pretty much.' He tried to smile, but it switched to a grimace halfway through. 'Ah, Jesus.'

'So you didn't see anyone?'

'Just heard some shouting, then they clattered me. That was it.'

'What about before that? You collected Mr Ferguson from here earlier, right?'

'Aye, downstairs.' Wishart's fingers traced his jaw, not wanting to press too hard. 'Just being a mate to Dougie, you know?'

'Did he mention anything to you?'

'Doug wasn't speaking much. Could get like that. See if the Hibs lost, or Torquay or Elgin City buggered up his accumulator... Man.'

'He's the silent type?'

Wishart shrugged. Even that seemed to hurt. 'Can be. Likes to brood.'

'Did he ever get into a fight at the pub?'

'No, but...' He tailed off with a pained gasp.

'Go on...'

Wishart shook his head. 'It's nothing.'

'Try us.'

'Well, Davie Boyle, right?' Wishart's head dipped, like he was in confession. 'I've seen him assault people in the pub before. Saw him work a boy with a pool cue. Guy ended up looking like something from *Fight Club*.'

'And you reported this to the police, yes?'

Wishart looked away, started trying to click his jaw. 'Bar policy is to let the fighters sort it out among themselves.' He slid his hand across his bulbous forehead. 'You know the drill... Stripped to the waist, fighting on the cobbles. No need to involve the police here, gentlemen. We can look after our own.'

Hunter tilted his head, gave him an appraising look. 'I'm not a big fan of people taking the law into their own hands.'

'Aye, me neither.' Wishart covered his mouth with his hands and shut his eyes for a few seconds. 'Look, he kicked the shit out of a boy a few months back. Really battered him, ended up looking like an orc from *Lord of the Rings*.'

'Who was this guy?'

'Someone said he was a paedo.'

'And was he?'

Wishart rolled his shoulder. 'Doesn't make any difference to Davie.'

～

'No. Comment.' Dave Boyle slumped back in his chair, his mouth hanging wide open. Like a toilet bowl needing flushed. 'You corned beef, or something, darling?'

'There's nothing wrong with my hearing, Mr Boyle.' Jain tucked her hair behind her ears, as if to emphasise the point. 'We're going to charge you with assault.'

'Eh?'

'You attacked Mr Wishart.'

'No I never.'

'Don't start. We've got witnesses.'

'Here, I'm a hero. Taking some paedo scumbag off the street. Should be giving me a medal.'

'We tend to take a dim view of vigilantes, Mr Boyle.' Jain started flicking through a blank sheaf of paper. 'Tends to make our jobs a lot harder and people often get the wrong end of the stick without a proper evidence trail.'

Boyle battered his thumb off the table a few times, quick and tight, a scowl just about keeping his mouth locked tight. 'What the hell do you want to know?'

'Let's start with the Ferguson's garden last night?'

'What about it.'

'We know it was you.'

Boyle's mouth hung wide open again. 'What if it was?'

'Did Mr Ferguson ask you to raid the house?'

'Look, Doug asked me to see what's going on there. Said he's worried about Steph.' Boyle sniffed and ran his wrist over his nose. 'Now I know why. Doug wanted us to get close to Steph, find out if she was grassing on him for noncing her.' He stretched his arms out wide. 'That was me in the garden, aye. Wish I hadn't helped him, now. Stoat just wanted me to cover over his dirty trail.'

Hunter took his seat again and made a show of scribbling a note. No idea what to charge him with, if anything... 'Does the name Robert Quarrie mean anything to you?'

'Should it?'

'He's Stephanie's father.'

'Right. Never knew the boy's name.' Boyle shook his head, nostrils curled up like he'd stood in dog shit. 'When Pauline told Doug that her ex had been calling, he was raging. Full on Begbie. Said he wanted Quarrie taken out.'

'When was this?'

'Monday night. In the boozer. Watching Man City tonk West Brom.' Boyle's tongue flicked around his exposed teeth. 'Why are you asking about him?' He frowned, his mouth wide open. 'Wait, has something happened to the boy?'

'I'll give you three guesses.'

'Aw, shite.' Boyle buried his head in his hands. 'Look, I didn't kill the boy, okay?'

'We'll need to check alibis.'

'Don't doubt it, princess.' Boyle looked up through his fingers. 'I didn't slot him.'

'How did you know he was stabbed?'

'Shite.' Boyle sank even lower in his chair. 'Shitey bollocks.'

Hunter let him sit there, panting away, a wad of spit dribbling down his chin. Not going to get any more out of him now... Not on this, anyway. 'Do you know where Stephanie is?'

'Eh? What?'

'Did Doug ask you to abduct her?'

'No way, man.' Boyle raised his hands. 'I'm not going to kill for a paedo scumbag like Doug bloody Ferguson.'

'Sure you didn't find her this morning, assault me and kidnap her?'

Boyle sat up straight. 'Of course I bloody didn't.'

'And you didn't fall out with him when I told you—'

'What?'

'—Mr Ferguson had been accused of—'

'No, no, no.'

'I don't believe you.' Hunter tapped at the table. 'See, those two knuckle-draggers you were with at Alec Wishart's house haven't been found yet. They're not in on the act with you, are they?'

'No way.'

Hunter sighed and turned to nod at Jain. 'What do you reckon?'

'I believe him.'

'Really?'

'Craig, back down, okay?' Jain twisted round to smile at him, winking with the eye Boyle couldn't see. She switched the grin to Boyle. 'Mr Ferguson passed a message to you through his lawyer, correct?'

'I've told you this.' Boyle frowned, then clicked his fingers. 'Some boy called me up. Posh sod, Williamson or something.'

'Hamish Williams?'

'Aye, that's the punter.'

'And you took that as an instruction to root around in their back garden, correct?'

'It was pretty clear, aye.'

'Did you receive any other messages from Mr Williams?'

Boyle sniffed a few times.

'We're checking your phone records as we speak, Mr Boyle.'

'Fine, the boy called us this morning. Cannae mind what he said...'

'Thanks for that.' Jain stood up and put her hands in her pockets. 'Mr Boyle, I'm detaining you under the suspicion of murdering Robert Quarrie.'

∼

'You are besmirching my good name, Sergeant.' Williams straightened out his suit collar. 'Not to mention that of McLintock, Will—'

'Mr Williams, you committed a criminal act.'

'I did nothing of the sort.' Williams spluttered a gob of saliva onto the table, a little pool forming on the wood between them. 'How dare you bring my name into disrepute in such—'

'Did you or did you not pass on two messages to Mr Boyle.'

'I did nothing of the sort.'

'So you deny passing any information to David Boyle?'

Williams slumped back, his lips twitching. 'Well.'

'We're searching for phone calls between you and Mr Boyle.'

Williams started paying close attention to a button on his suit jacket. 'Of course, you have the text of this message?'

'We've got a witness statement from the man we believe carried out the attack on Mr Quarrie. Our understanding is this message was an instruction to murder.'

'What?'

'This message may have led to the murder of one Robert Quarrie.'

'Listen to me very carefully.' Williams tugged his suit jacket wide. 'I have not knowingly passed on a message of such a nature to a contact of any of my clients.'

'What about if it read as something pretty innocuous?'

'I don't know what you mean.'

'Did Mr Ferguson get you to pass on a message to Mr Boyle?'

'It was just a note to an acquaintance of his, that's all.' Williams flicked through his legal pad, covered in enough arcane inscriptions to look like an original language copy of the bible. 'The message was "Daddy can't come home".'

You stupid, stupid bastard.

Hunter folded his arms. 'That doesn't sound to you like a message about Mr Quarrie?'

Williams stared into space, frowning. 'What? I assumed my client was merely – and innocently, I hasten to add – referring to the fact that, due to your unfounded insistence on his continued detention, he was indisposed and could therefore not return–'

'Mr Quarrie is, as you should know, Stephanie's biological father. As for "can't come home", well, don't you think that could be read as a kill order?'

~

'Good work, Craig.' Cullen thumped Hunter on the shoulder. Made his jaw rattle. 'We'll certainly follow up on this.'

Hunter tried to shift away from him, but Lauren's office was a small space and he had him cornered. 'So you really think Boyle killed Quarrie?'

'It fits.' Cullen glanced at his phone and shook his head. 'That message can be construed as an instruction. Wishart told us Boyle's got previous as a vigilante. He's then gone and assaulted Doug Ferguson, looked like he was trying to kill him.'

'You think he's taken Doug?'

'His two mates are still at large, aren't they? And we *still* don't know where Stephanie is.' Cullen got up and let out a theatrical sigh. 'Wouldn't be the first person who's tried to pull the wool over our eyes.'

'I don't like it.' Hunter thumbed over to the office door. 'Given what Williams has just told us, I'd like to get back in there with Boyle.'

'Tomorrow, maybe.' Cullen gripped his shoulder tight, gave it a good matey squeeze. 'Get yourself home, Craig. Back in at seven tomorrow, okay?'

'Right.' Hunter hauled himself to his feet, felt like he was lifting a sack of tatties. 'I'd like to—'

'Craig, I'm really sorry about Yvonne, okay? I didn't know I'd done that.' Cullen shook his head. Looked like it was aimed at himself, the disgust of discovering the deeds of your drunk Mr Hyde. 'Especially not to a good mate. I thought we'd just drifted apart, like friends do.'

'Accepted. See you tomorrow.' Hunter bundled over to the door, rage twisting his gut, and went out into the corridor, his pace picking up as he put distance between himself and the reason for his failed engagement.

Drifted apart... Like me and Angus. You don't just drift apart... There's always something behind it, some hidden misery.

Shame on me for not confronting you about it. For keeping my misery hidden.

Hunter opened the stair door and nearly bumped into Jain. Dark rings under her eyes, much darker than the rest of her skin. 'Good night, Craig.'

Hunter stopped and frowned. 'Thought you might want to grab a drink?'

'Sorry, but no.'

The pit of Hunter's stomach fell away. 'Is that it?'

'No, it's just ... Not tonight.'

'Tomorrow?'

'Craig... Look, just back off.'

DAY 3

**Thursday
13th August 2015**

35

Hunter dropped to his hands, then lay face down, panting hard. Pushed back up and stretched his aching body out. Tucked his knees under his chest and planted his feet on the carpet. Then kicked up to standing and stabbed the button on his phone, sitting on the bed next to him.

'In ten seconds, do one burpee.' The music blasted out of the speakers, the sort of tinny dance tune pissed-up squaddies went mental for.

One. Last. Time.

'Three, two, one.'

Hunter dropped onto his hands, then to lying face first on the carpet again. Pushed, jumped upright, and stabbed the phone.

'Congratulations, you've now completed the burpee pyramid. One hundred burpees in twenty-two minutes fifteen seconds.'

Hunter collapsed onto his bed, sweat pouring off him in thick rivulets. He gulped tepid water, spilling half the glass down his chest.

Why do I do this to myself? Can barely feel my knees, there's so much ibuprofen in my system...

'Mawr?' Bubble pounced on him. Her paws slid along his sweaty chest, like she was ice-skating for the first time. 'Mawr!' She fell back down onto the carpet.

Hunter sat up, still panting, his throat burning. 'You okay, Bubble?'

She was sitting back, propping a paw on the floor as she licked at her tummy. 'Mawr...' Barely opened her mouth, as per usual.

'Come on, then.' He walked through to the kitchen, stretching off his chest as he went.

Jain's striptease flashed in front of his eyes, slowly taking off his shirt as she walked backwards.

That couldn't be it over, could it? One night?

Hunter picked up his phone from the charger and tapped out a text.

You up yet?

Hunter got a bowl out of the cupboard and rummaged around in the drawer for his whisk. He got out the last three of Murray's eggs and cracked them into the bowl, tossed in some rosemary and started whisking away, hard and fast. Spilled a load of eggy mess onto the counter.

Crap...

'Mieaow!' Bubble looked up at him, her left paw raised like that should mean something to him. 'Mieaow!'

Hunter bent down to fill up her bowl, then stuck the heat on under the pan, the ceramic element glowing red hot within seconds.

He picked up his phone. The little dots were dancing on her side of the chat. His text was marked as read, time-stamped one minute ago.

The little dots disappeared. He waited, but no text came through.

∼

HUNTER TUGGED on his work boots, black and shiny as if he was due for a kit inspection at oh seven hundred. He tied each knot twice, hard enough to feel them in his feet.

His torso was covered in bruises. Really should get the doc to look at that stomach. He hauled on his T-shirt as someone barged into the locker room.

'Hey, jabroni.' Finlay's face had swollen up even more since the previous night, like he'd been infected by a zombie plague. 'Back in uniform today, is it?'

'Not heard anything to the contrary.' Hunter straightened his T-shirt out and stood up. 'Sure you should be here?'

'Like I've got a choice.' Finlay slumped down on the bench and patted his head. 'Doc says I can't get signed off sick and Lauren'll know I'm at it if I do.'

'You're always at it.'

Finlay winked at him. 'Speaking of which, how's the fragrant Ms Jain?'

Hunter put a hand on the cold door and froze. He exhaled through his nostrils, slow and deep. 'I wouldn't know.'

'You didn't shag her last night?'

'I'll see you in Lauren's office.' Hunter barged through the door and started off down the corridor.

'Hunter!'

He swung round and frowned into the blinding light from the window at the end of the corridor. 'Sarge.'

Lauren stepped forward, still in her civvies but cradling her Airwave. Looked like she hadn't slept. 'Glad to catch you. We're needed at Cullen's briefing.' She checked her watch. 'And we're already late.'

~

HUNTER STOPPED outside the Incident Room, panting slightly. He tried to catch his breath as he listened to someone drone on. Didn't sound like Cullen, but he did have that annoying telephone voice…

He pushed into the Incident Room, attracting a few glares from the cops near the back. Dave and Steve shared a snarky comment, the only other uniforms in the room.

The guy with the eyebrows from the previous afternoon was leading the briefing, stopping to inspect Hunter for a couple of seconds, before barrelling on. 'And as I was saying, the forensic analysis will take some time due to the backlog we created in Dumbiedykes.' He nodded to the side. 'Sergeant?'

'Sir.' Cullen wandered over to the middle, clutching his iPhone, and stopped to look around the crowd, like he was a tech CEO showing off the next gadget.

Hunter took it as an opportunity to take a seat by the laser printer. Added a whiff of ozone to the BO and coffee in the room. Couldn't really get comfortable…

'Given the delay, we're focusing on the present threats, namely the whereabouts of Douglas and Stephanie Ferguson.' Cullen tapped at the screen of his phone. 'As we speak, David Boyle is being interviewed again by DCs Law and Murray.' He grimaced. 'Sadly, Mr Boyle's two associates from the site of Mr Ferguson's abduction last night are still at large. Consequently, we're treating them as prime suspects in the abductions of Doug and Stephanie, and are putting all efforts into locating them.' He did another one-eighty around the room. 'Anything else?'

Nobody was sticking their hands up. Looked like Jain might, though she was more likely to ask anything after the event.

Bugger it. Hunter cleared his throat. 'What about Neil Alexander?'

Cullen nodded at Hunter. 'Didn't see you there, Craig.' He grinned at him, like they were old friends who wouldn't let anything as common as adultery stand between them. 'What about him?'

'We should be treating him as a suspect.'

'And we are.' Cullen marched over the room to the whiteboard and jabbed a finger at an unflattering photo of Neil Alexander from his work pass. 'What do we know about him?'

Si Buxton tore through his notebook. 'He's had some history with the Transport union. Some sort of militant faction. Done sit-down protests over pay and conditions, but never anything violent.'

'So he's on our radar?'

'He is, but then so's every taxi driver in Edinburgh. As far as we know, he's not dodgy. Not the merest whiff, Scotty.'

Hunter twisted the strap on his stab-proof a few times. 'He's a suspect in my book.'

Buxton nodded recognition at Hunter. 'I'll be taking his statement as to his whereabouts once he turns up.'

'That's cool, Si. I want PC Hunter to be first in there with him when he pitches up.'

Great.

Jain's turn to clear her throat. 'Scott, he's in room three downstairs.'

36

Neil Alexander's gaze darted between Hunter and Jain. The gangly giant looked like he'd been up all night partying. Skin was a shade or two paler than usual and a rash of stubble covered his face, almost reaching his eyes. 'It feels like you think I've done something.'

'We're treating you with suspicion, Mr Alexander, because we have reason to be suspicious.' Hunter glanced down at his notebook, still pretty much just an empty page. 'We're investigating three related crimes and we need to identify your whereabouts for each of them.'

'Feels like you're fitting me up here.' Neil swept his lank fringe over. 'Steph's still missing, *abducted*, and you're sitting here with me.'

'Nobody's trying to do anything other than get the truth out of you.'

Neil smirked. 'And the truth can never be twisted, right?'

'I'm not interested in that.' Hunter waved to the side. 'And neither is DS Jain here.'

Neil started rolling up the sleeves of his bus driver's uniform. The shirt was nominally white but looked like it'd been washed with a Hearts strip a few times, giving it a pale maroon tone. 'Don't you think you guys should be out there finding Steph?'

'We have units out searching for her.' Jain nibbled at her bottom lip, her fists clenched tight, like she was going to lurch across the table and crack him one. 'It would be nice to know if we're in the room with the person who's taken her.'

'Me?' Neil gave a narrow-eyed smile. 'I've not taken her.'

'So prove it.'

'Definitely sounds like I should have a lawyer in here.'

We're getting nowhere with this punk.

'Mr Alexander—'

The interview room door opened with a crunch and Cullen stormed in, face like his beloved Aberdeen had thrown away a five-goal lead. He perched on the end of the table. 'My name's DS Scott Cullen and I'm the Deputy SIO on this case. Can I call you Neil?'

'Prefer Mr Alexander, but I'll let you away with it.'

'I work in the murder squad. We call it the Major Investigation Team internally, but I'm sure you can imagine what major investigation we're carrying out?'

'Aye, Robert Quarrie's murder.' Neil's raised eyebrow was just visible under his fringe. 'Which I had nothing to do with.'

'It would help me out greatly if you could exclude yourself from suspicion.' Cullen leaned close to Neil. 'Where were you yesterday afternoon at three?'

Neil adjusted his green Oxfam wristband, then nodded. 'I was working.'

'Driving the bus?'

'That's right. Number 12. I was struggling to cope with what's happened to Steph and I thought it might take my mind off not finding her. It didn't.'

Cullen walked over the other side of the table and spoke in an undertone: 'I'll get Lauren and Si Buxton to take over here. You pair know his supervisor, so can you confirm this alibi?'

Jain snapped her notebook shut. 'Whatever you say, boss.'

∽

THE BUS STATION canteen was morning-shift busy, reeking of charred meat fat and the sweet stink of tomato ketchup. Two drivers at the next table were tucking into breakfasts barely contained by their large plates.

Hunter stretched his legs out. Even just thinking about the hammering his knee had taken over the past two days made it seize up. 'We're merely trying to pin down Mr Alexander's whereabouts at around three o'clock yesterday afternoon. Do you recall–'

'How many times do you want me to go over it?' Jim Archibald's voice was barely audible above the bus station canteen's almighty din. The effect of the uniform wasn't as strong today. 'Why are you asking that?'

'Because it'll help rule Mr Alexander out of our enquiries.'

'Will it now?' Archibald dropped his roll onto the plate and a flabby slice of bacon dropped out, half-eaten and smeared with red sauce. 'Are you listening close? Cos I can go slow if you need me to?'

Hunter looked at him sidelong and raised both eyebrows. 'Just get on with it.'

Archibald wiped his hands together, dusting them off. 'The boy *was* working yesterday afternoon. Supposed to be out on the first run this morning as well to make up for the time he's had off, but then you lot got him to go into the police station.' His tongue darted around his sharp teeth, searching for that elusive shard of bacon. 'Had to drive young Ian out to Musselburgh so he could take over. Complete shambles, if you ask me.'

Hunter was close to grabbing Archibald's union tie and smacking his head off the table. 'So what route was he on yesterday?'

'Usual one. 12.'

Hunter checked his notebook. It tallied. Bugger. 'Which direction would he have been travelling in?'

'At three?' Archibald took another bite and chewed slowly, staring off to the side. 'He'd have been going through Corstorphine towards the Gyle.'

Wait a second... Corstorphine wasn't far from Cramond. Three miles, tops.

'So, where exactly was he?'

'I know exactly where he was.' Archibald chomped on the roll, chewing a couple of times before swallowing. A big splodge of butter and red sauce smeared his lips. 'He'll have been at the big Tesco in Corstorphine.'

'You can prove—'

Hunter's Airwave chimed on his chest. 'Control to PC Hunter.'

Terrific.

Hunter got up and walked off to a quiet corner before tapping the answer button. 'Receiving. Safe to talk.'

'It's Mags, Craig. I've just got a call in about a red Hyundai matching your plates at the Shawfield building site.'

37

Hunter powered down the damp street, the trail of rain blowing red in the rear-view. 'So, did you get my text this morning?'

Jain looked over from the passenger seat. 'Now's not the time, believe me.'

Hunter drove on, passing a row of new-build houses, partway through construction, just a couple protected from the elements. An orange glow flickered ahead, surrounded by the blue swirl of sirens. He pulled in and got out, storming across the muddy road.

Flames tore at the Hyundai's already blackened shell from one side, water jets from the other. The fire was clearly winning.

The fire service Watch Manager was standing a few yards back, observing the spectacle and shaking his head at the flames, his white helmet gleaming in the thick smoke.

Jain jogged over and flashed her warrant card. 'DS Chantal Jain.'

'Jim Heaton.' He didn't take his eyes off the blaze. 'You lot are quick getting here.'

'We were in Portobello and the old "blues and twos" still clears rush-hour traffic.' Jain shielded her eyes with her hand. 'What's happened?'

'Not had a chance to get a look at it.' Heaton pointed at the burning car. 'For obvious reasons.'

'Funny.'

'All right, all right. You lot are always the same.' Heaton shook his head and finally settled eyes on her. Gave her a good going over. 'Anyway, I'd say it was torched.'

'How can you tell?'

'Because the fuel tank's not gone up yet.' Back looking at the fire. 'Just got to make sure it doesn't set any of these houses up. Assuming it's not a diesel, of—'

BANG.

The fire exploded into life, the flames climbing into the mid-blue sky to the height of the surrounding house carcasses.

Hunter stepped back. The air felt like it was ablaze.

The air stank of roasting goat, coming from all directions. The sun felt like it needed factor five million to stop burning.

Movement to the right caught his eyes.

A man wearing a hoodie, with the hood pulled up. Tall and lumbering. He clocked Hunter and froze.

Neil Alexander.

He sped off down a lane between two half-built houses.

'Chantal!' Hunter darted after him, a blast of pain lancing his knee and slowing him to a trot. 'It's Neil!' He stopped at the edge of the plots, a pile of mud someone would eventually turn into gardens.

The light from the fire tore across, catching Neil's loping stride just before he disappeared behind the silvery wall of a new house. Seconds later, metal rattled.

You're not getting away, pal.

Hunter rounded the building and sprinted forward. He clattered into a metal fence and tumbled backwards, landing arse first in the wet mud.

'Get up, you idiot.' Jain reached under his armpits and hauled him up. 'Where'd he go?'

'Over that.'

She scanned up and down the chain-link fence. 'Boost me.'

'What?'

'Just do it!'

'Right, right.' Hunter knelt down and splayed his hands together.

Jain rested her boot on them, lighter than he expected, and she clawed her way up the fence links, cat-like. Even landed on her feet after vaulting over the top. 'Come on!'

'Easy for you to say.' Hunter gripped the fence and stuck his feet into the links. Then upwards, one fistful of steel at a time until he was at the top. He dropped down and his knee gave way. He slid forward, smearing mud up his trousers right up to the arse. Again.

'Buggeration.'

He hoisted himself up and started jogging, mud flying off his boots like he was mountain biking. Then through another gap between two houses much closer to completion, just missing their roof slates. Onto the tarmac of a new road, houses stretched in both directions, tiny boxes rammed together.

Jain clattered over the tarmac towards him. 'We've bloody lost him.'

38

Hunter leaned against Jain's car and let the water soak through his thin jacket, an attempt to shift some of the mud. 'It's Neil Alexander, this whole thing. Everything.'

Jain didn't look over, just stared at the ground. 'What?'

'He's the one who took Doug Ferguson.' Hunter thumbed back the way. 'He's the one driving that red bloody Hyundai.'

'Neil Alexander's in the station, Craig.' Cullen took another go at sorting out his hair, then gave up, leaving a tuft at the back. 'Your boss is still interviewing him. We need a really detailed statement from him.'

Hunter slumped back against the car and stared up at the sky. Drops of rain fired down on his face. 'That can't be right.'

'Sure it wasn't one of those skinheads you saw?'

'Scott, it was Neil Alexander.' Hunter shifted his hand back and forth between him and Jain. '*We* saw him, right? Chantal?'

'I saw a tall guy in a hoodie.' Jain shivered in the rain. 'Could've been Neil Alexander, but I didn't get a look at him.'

Cullen grimaced at her. 'Sounds like one of your skinheads, Craig.'

'I don't bloody believe this...'

Cullen raised his Airwave. 'Want me to call Lauren?'

Hunter held his gaze and shrugged. 'Might be an idea.'

Cullen stabbed a button on the device, shaking his head. 'DS Scott Cullen to DS Lauren Reid. Over.'

'Receiving. I need to—'

'Lauren, can you confirm the whereabouts of one Neil Alexander?'

'He's not here.'

'What?' Cullen looked away, rubbing his forehead. 'Where the hell is he?'

'Finished the interview half an hour ago. I'm shatter—'

'Right. Thanks.' Cullen stared over at the blaze for a few seconds, licking his lips. Then he locked his gaze on Hunter. 'Have you got anything on him?'

'A thanks wouldn't go amiss.'

'Craig, drop it. Look, I don't like this. Feels too easy.'

'Why don't you admit that you just don't believe me?'

Cullen smiled at Hunter. 'Look, Craig. I just need you to prove it.'

'No, you need to believe me and we need to find this guy.' Hunter took a step forward and widened his eyes at Cullen. 'Come on, Scott, I know you. You're the one cop I know who does the right thing regardless of the possible cost to himself.'

'Had my arse chewed a few times since we worked together, mate.'

'You don't believe me, do you?' Hunter took a step closer, got a good look in those blue eyes. 'Neil Alexander's abducted Doug Ferguson. He's most likely got Stephanie or is torturing Ferguson to find out where she is. If he's got her, then God knows what he's doing to her.'

Cullen ran his tongue over his lips and almost snarled. 'Prove. It.'

~

HUNTER STOMPED across the road to the pool car, splashing rain water up his legs. His bottom half was caked in mud, like he'd been wrestling in it. He got in and slammed the door, sending a rainstorm of droplets out. The windows started misting up already.

Cullen was ordering some other arsehole about, pointing everywhere and sighing. Always bloody sighing, like the whole world was a disappointment to him.

Was he telling the truth about him and Yvonne? How could anyone not remember getting kicked down the stairs mid-coitus? Maybe it happened so often to Cullen that they all just merged into one, his skinny arse bouncing off half the tenements in Edinburgh.

And show a colleague up in front of the rest of the squad. Sowing seeds of doubt everywhere...

It's Neil Alexander. Of course it is. Stupid lanky git standing by the burning car, watching his handiwork.

Need to play the game, though... Prove Cullen wrong.

He shut his eyes and tried to drown out the noise around them, focusing hard.

Pauline. 'Not Neil. He's a gentle laddie. Bit too soft, if you ask me.'

Olivia. 'He didn't exactly fit in.'

Doug. 'He's twenty-seven! Steph's sixteen. How can he live with himself? Shagging a wee lassie like that.'

Neil. 'What can I say? I love her.'

'You think it's funny a sixteen-year-old woman going to an arthouse cinema?'

'We're in a trusting relationship.'

'I just wanted to love her and help her get over it.'

'I'm a lover not a fighter.'

Hunter opened his eyes again. There was a tell in that line, like a poker player hiding a two to seven off suit.

'Steph's a beautiful thing. I want her to be happy.'

Jesus Christ. It just had to be him.

He hadn't helped the case in the slightest, but had he hindered it? The only thing they had from him was the false sighting in Musselburgh. Everything else was vague, opaque or conflicting. Or, worse, Neil worming his way into the investigation.

Hunter reached into his soggy pocket for his notebook, still dry, and started flicking through it. He tore off a blank page and drew a timeline, starting on Monday night, the last alleged attack.

Stealing Dave Boyle's car.

Assaulting Hunter and Finlay when he abducted Stephanie.

Killing Robert Quarrie.

Figuring out, like Hunter, where Doug Ferguson would be, striking when the opportunity arose.

Neil's movements were sketchy at best, unverified at the worst. At work, then at his flat, then back at work. The only corroboration was when he was with Pauline Ferguson and that still left a mile-wide gap before it. Never in custody.

Why did he do it?

Why would he have done any of it?

'I just want to help bring that scumbag to justice.'

Kidnap Stephanie and show her Doug Ferguson meeting medieval justice. And the same to Robert Quarrie...

Another look at the timeline. Neil had an alibi for killing Robert Quarrie. They'd just bloody checked it.

Hunter threw his notebook into the passenger seat, the card cover cracking off the door handle. He slumped back in the chair and pulled down the sun guard. In the mirror, he looked even worse than he felt. Cuts and bruises on his cheeks and jaw, dried blood tracing an intricate web of pain from the crown of his head down to his collarbone.

Hunter stabbed at his Airwave, direct-dialling Elvis's badge number.

White noise crackled out of the handset. 'The Night Hunter.'

Shouting and clinking in the background — sounded like Elvis was in a pub.

'The what?'

'You need a nickname.'

'I'd prefer one that didn't make me sound like an eighties cop show.' Hunter spotted Jain dawdle over, Airwave to her ear. 'Are you at the station?'

'Why?'

'Need a favour?'

'Only if I get to call you the Night Hunter.'

'Fine, whatever. I need a check on the CCTV at the Tesco at Corstorphine. Three o'clock yesterday afternoon.'

'Give me a second.' Sounded like he was hitting a keyboard. Maybe not in the pub after all, or he'd taken a laptop into the Elm's back room. 'Right, it's taking an age of man here.'

'While you're waiting, have you got an update on the ANPR search for our car? The Hyundai.'

'Come on, man. What's the priority here?'

Jain got in the driver side, rocking the car ever so slightly.

Hunter unclipped his Airwave and put it to his ear. 'Both of them.'

'Jeez. Right. Let me see.'

'Also, I need you to check on any car ownership in the name of Neil Alexander.'

'Hold your bloody horses, Conan.'

'Thought you said I needed a nickname?'

'Ah, shite.' Hammering at the keyboard in the background. Then a mouse dropping from a great height. 'Just checking that last one while the other two think about it... Aye, here we go. Looks like there's nothing registered in his name.'

'Sure about that?'

'Unless I'm misspelling Neil and Alexander.' More clattering. 'There's certainly nothing on King's Road, either.'

'That's not exactly conclusive.' Hunter wiped rain from his forehead. 'How's the ANPR doing?'

'Never bloody ends with you...' Elvis huffed, a big blast of distortion spitting out of the speaker. 'Still nothing. Oh, we're rocking with the CCTV. I've got the front of the Tesco. Three this afternoon, you say? Here we go. Christ, look at the ti—'

'Need it by the bus stop.'

'Right. Jeez, don't get many of them to the pound...' Elvis mouth-breathed into his handset. 'Can't see anything, certainly not this big bloke.'

'You're sure?'

'Aye, there's a big bus blocking everything.'

Hunter slumped back in his chair and stared up at the fabric on the roof interior. 'That's what I'm looking for.'

'Cool beans. It's a 12, heading to the Gyle by the looks of things.' Elvis snorted down the line. 'It's not going anywhere, though.'

'What?' Hunter's leg started jiggling. 'Should just be in and out.'

'It's sat there. That's ten minutes now.'

'Wind it back till it arrives.'

'Right-o.' More keyboard abuse. 'Aye. Pulls in and it doesn't look in a good way. Big plume of black smoke out the back. Like Finlay after the curry club. Doesn't even make the stop.'

'Anything else?'

'The passengers are getting off. She'd get it, I swear. Oh hang, on. The driver's getting off. Looks like a bloke, though you can't be too sure these days, right? Big greasy twat. Tall.'

'That's him. Where does he go? Into the shop?'

'Nah, the boy's getting into a car.'

'What?'

'Man alive.' Elvis groaned down the line. 'It's a bloody Hyundai. Missing a wing mirror and all.'

Hunter glanced over at Jain — looked like she was wrapping up her call. Sounded like it was with Sharon McNeill, wherever the hell she was. He got out his personal mobile and tapped the Google Maps icon. It flew over to west Edinburgh. He pinched it and zoomed in.

Corstorphine to Cramond... Go by Maybury, then Drum Brae. Or... round by Davidson's Mains... Maybe that little rat run through Barnton. Would have to hit the main road, though...

Hunter picked up the Airwave again. 'Can you check for ANPR hits on the A90?'

'Nothing on the A90.'

'Eh? Have you looked?'

'No, mate. There aren't any cameras there. They're at the Forth Road Bridge and Dean Bridge.'

'Wouldn't even need the rat run...'

'What are you havering about?'

'Never mind. Cheers, Elvis. Can you send that image through, please?'

'I'd say don't mention it, Conan, but then you never—'

Hunter ended the call and dialled another number.

'Aye?' The dead sound of a small office.

'Mr Archibald, it's Craig Hunter again.'

'I'm kind of busy here, sir.'

'Just got something I need to check with you.' Hunter clocked Jain kill her call. 'You said Mr Alexander was at Corstorphine Tesco.'

'Aye?'

'You didn't tell us his bus broke down.' Jain's eyes shot out wide. 'Did it get fixed?'

'Slipped my mind. I swear.'

Lying bastard...

'Did it get fixed?'

'Aye, took a while to get the van out there at that time. Bloody rain plays merry hell with my schedule, I tell you. Buses breaking—'

'When did the van get there?'

'The laddie got out there at the back of five, if my memory serves.'

'And was Neil there?'

'Why wouldn't he be?'

'Thanks for your time.' Hunter killed the call, his gaze settling on Jain. 'We've just got ourselves a two-hour window round Robert Quarrie's death...'

~

'See?' Hunter held up the Airwave and showed it to Cullen and Jain. 'This is him getting into the Hyundai at Tesco.'

Cullen grabbed the Airwave and stared at it. 'Go through your logic from the start.'

'Okay. Wind back to Tuesday.' Hunter tried to keep his words and thoughts in the same country. 'He stole Dave Boyle's Hyundai from outside his house. Then, yesterday morning, he's abducted Stephanie from outside Gaynor Tait's house. Fast forward to the afternoon and he's driving the bus, and he's knackered it at the big Tesco in Corstorphine. Then he gets—'

'Wait, back up. What?'

'The bus broke down by the Tesco.' Hunter jabbed a finger at the Airwave. 'Elvis has him driving to Cramond after getting into the Hyundai, which he'd dumped there after my scrape with him in the morning.'

'What, so he killed Robert Quarrie and drove back to the bus?'

'That's what I'm thinking. He's next seen at Mountcastle last night, where he's waiting in the car outside Alec Wishart's house so he can keep an eye on Doug Ferguson.'

'How did he know that Ferguson would go there?'

Hunter shrugged. It's 'doable. I worked it out by myself.'

'You did, all right.' Cullen twirled his umbrella around, flicking raindrops off. 'I don't get why he's taken Stephanie, though.'

'Neil's torturing the men who abused Stephanie. He killed her father and now he's got Doug Ferguson.'

'He's killed the girl's father, the guy who abused her as a child, and now he's got her stepfather.' Jain was frowning, her eyebrows rising far enough to line her forehead. 'Is he trying to impress her or something?'

'Could be.' Hunter glared at Cullen. 'You've met the guy, right? He's not right in the head.'

Cullen stared off into the middle distance. Looked like the fire was just about out as he stood there, letting the officers get close to hear his analysis. He raised his eyebrows. 'Okay, that's good enough for me.'

39

Hunter took a step back onto King's Road. A pipe had burst high up, sending a shower of water down that was merging with the rain at street level and gushing down to the seafront.

'Aye, Mags, I know I've still got four units out trying to find those skinheads.' Cullen held the Airwave to his head as he hit the buzzer. 'I know you're stretched. It was clear when we drove down... Look, can you shove two of them onto finding Neil Alexander?'

Hunter nodded at Jain, but she looked away just as quickly.

'Well, tell Finlay Sinclair to get his arse out. I don't care. He works for me on this case.' Cullen hit the buzzer again and swept the rain out of his hair. 'Get him to speak to Lauren Reid. Cheers.' He glared at the intercom. 'Why does everything take ten times as long as it should?'

Jain pulled her collar up high. 'Any chance you could get us inside this week?'

Cullen pressed the buzzer for the flat next to Neil's.

The buzzer crackled. 'Aye?' Male voice.

'Police.'

'It's a bit early for this shite, isn't it?'

'It's an emergency, sir.' Cullen put his mouth next to the mic. 'We're looking for Neil Alexander.'

'Not seen him for a few days, like.'

'That usual?'

'Not unusual.'

'Right. Have you seen or heard from him either this morning or last night?'

'Heard someone on the stairs about half an hour ago. Not sure it was Neil, mind.'

'Thanks, sir.' Cullen stood up tall and spoke close to the microphone, like he was trying to get it louder. 'Can you let us inside, please?'

'What are youse planning on doing, likes?'

'Nothing other than trying to speak to him.'

The intercom just crackled, maybe gave the slight sound of mouth-breathing. 'Aye, come on up, then.'

The door buzzed open and Cullen barged in.

Hunter followed him up the stairs. Someone had been using too much Persil, judging by the stink that wafted down from a flat on the middle floor.

At the top, the door across from Neil's flat was open, a beady eye peering out. The guy with the runaway dog from the other day. The door clicked shut.

Cullen waved at Neil's door. 'Craig, do the honours.'

Hunter took a step back and launched his foot against the wood. Didn't budge.

Cullen shook his head. 'I meant knock?'

'Right, well, it's stuck.' Hunter rubbed at a smooth patch underneath the handle. 'He must have some drug-dealer security shite in there. No way we're getting in there without an Enforcer.'

'You didn't see this, right?' Jain got a credit card out of her wallet and slid it behind the Yale. The lock popped and she did a magician's wave at it. 'Open sesame!'

That's me shown...

Cullen twisted his neck to look back down the staircase. 'Craig, you first?'

'Sarge...' Hunter snapped out his baton and entered the flat, careful to not creak the floorboards.

The flat was dark, just a feint glow from the two doors on the right, the side facing the sun. All the other doors in the flat were open.

Hunter paced along the hall and checked the first. Empty box room. Then the second. Empty bathroom.

He swung round and waved for Cullen to approach.

Across the hall, he opened the bedroom door. Nobody there. The bed was made, tucked in tight like in a hotel. Or in the army. The pile of books by the bed had been halved and—

Wait.

He shot over to the other side of the bed. There was a bin bag on the floor. He snapped on a glove and sifted through it. A grey T-shirt with "Pinker is ~~left~~ right!", completely smeared with blood. 'Shite.' He held it up to Cullen. 'Need any more proof?'

~

Hunter swung into the Asda car park at the Jewel. It was pretty empty. A couple of shady pimped Corsas were parked door to door over at the far side, doing something they shouldn't. The morning shoppers hadn't turned up yet, just a couple of van drivers stocking up on Coke and Lucozade for the day.

He parked by the bus stop and looked around, trying to ease more caked-on mud from his trousers. The foot rest was splattered with the stuff.

'Aye, Scott. I know. I know. He does, doesn't he?' Jain looked over and rolled her eyes. 'You'd think so, aye. No, we're just doing a tour of the car parks round here to see if he's gone anywhere. At the Asda now and we've done the Fort.'

Hunter turned the heating up full blast and the fan up to eleven. It drowned out her call but didn't seem to make much difference to his caked trousers. He pulled off and swung out in a U-turn, taking it slow as he scanned the area around the supermarket.

At least five shopping trolleys were taking a dip in the Niddrie burn. Rain battered the trees on both sides. A jogger in Day-Glo running gear swerved past a ned and his grunting Staffy.

Hunter sped up and cut across the roundabout past the idling cars bound for Edinburgh. The B&M car park was completely empty, not even a stray tramp out in the rain.

He pulled back onto the A1, driving against the swelling tide of traffic heading into the city. Looked like a brutal accident halfway along by the new Queen Margaret's campus. He tapped his Airwave. 'Control, can you give me an update on Neil Alexander's location?'

'I beg your pardon? Can't hear you, Craig.'

Hunter turned the heating down. 'Have you found Neil Alexander?'

'Had nothing since you last asked. Two minutes ago.'

'Right, cheers.' Hunter ended the call and indicated left to descend down to the Old Craighall roundabout, a pair of cheeky Audis trying to nip round and cut out the logjam on the A1.

'Aye, bye.' Jain stabbed at her Airwave and stuck it in the door pocket. 'This car stinks of smoke.'

'It's actually you and me that stink.' Hunter swung past the services for the Millerhill turning. 'How's Cullen?'

'Pissed off. He's got to brief three Inspectors on Operation Spanner.'

'We'll get our man.'

'Sure about that?'

Hunter shrugged as they passed the Jewson, the car park out front filled up with lorries and work vans, then a row of old cottages. 'Maybe.' He took a right, then another one, and they were back on the road to Shawfair.

Abandoned work equipment lurked behind steel fences, guarding the timber-framed shells of future houses. The workers huddled under a tarpaulin in one, sipping on bottles of Coke and beakers of coffee.

'This is where we lost him, right?'

Jain looked over with a sigh. 'Where I lost him.'

'We were both there.' Hunter pulled in behind an idling squad car. He got out into the pissing rain and took another opportunity to try washing all the mud off, while keeping a beady eye on the building site for any trace of movement.

Jain walked over and stared up at him. 'Is this you punishing yourself? Out here in the rain?'

'I just want to know where's he gone? I almost had him.' Hunter held his hands up and tried to wash the last streaks of mud from his palms. He nodded over at a dark old building. 'See that farmhouse? That's where I saved that cat the other morning.'

She grinned at him. 'I still think that's sweet.'

'Glad someone does.' Hunter ran his hand through his hair and fired a slick of water through the air. 'You didn't reply to that text this morning.'

'I was busy.'

'What's going on with us?'

Jain stared off into the distance, her petite nose in profile against the grey sky.

'Come on, Chantal. I can't seem to win here. One minute I'm flavour of the month, the next I'm praline and dog shit.'

She looked back round, tears merging with the rain. 'I've been a bitch to you.' She let out a sigh. 'I can only apologise.'

Hunter took his turn looking her up and down. 'Chantal, what's your story?'

'My story?' She twisted her body round like a football hooligan reacting to an insult to his team, eyes blazing and nostrils flaring. 'You think there's a story?'

'Going apeshit on Quarrie and Ferguson. Hunting for Stephanie. What's driving you to do this?'

'My job?'

'That's not it... I look at you and I look at DI McNeill. You're like Ms Chalk and Miss Cheese. She's all cold indifference, whereas you're like a volcanic spring in Iceland, bubbling away in all that frozen wilderness.'

A grin flickered on her lips. 'I'm sure Shakespeare wishes he'd written that phrase.'

'Bet you even get the flashbacks, right?'

'What?'

'Last night, on the phone, you said something like even non-Forces people get PTSD. Right?'

'That rattling sound is all those straws you're clutching at hitting the sides of the bottle.'

'Chantal, what gave you PTSD?'

'I don't have it.'

'Bullshit. I know the signs. Sat in enough group therapy sessions with civvies and squaddies.' And had enough run-ins to know who to keep away from and who not to... 'You're quick to anger, bordering on violence. Clear signs of repression. You had a nightmare when we slept together.'

She looked away, deep into the rain.

'What happened to you?'

'Nothing happened.'

'I can help.'

She turned back round, her gaze burning into him. 'You think you can fix me? You think you can change what happened?'

'I can help. Maybe. At least let me try.'

'You shag me once and you think we're together forever?'

'Look, just let me in.'

She stared at the bubbling puddle of mud between them. Raindrops exploded on the surface, the rings widening until they merged. Like Robert Quarrie's blood on the floor, pooling under the sofa.

She shut her eyes and snorted. 'My uncle raped me when I was twelve.'

'Shit.' Hunter stared at her, paralysed by indecision. What to do? Hug? Keep his distance? 'I'm sorry, Chantal...'

'It's the reason I joined the police. The reason I stayed in the SO Unit after Cullen shunted me there.' She brushed a hand across her eye, smearing her mascara. 'He got put away and someone stabbed him in prison. It gave me pretty big intimacy issues, I can tell you. Started using sex as a weapon. Thirty-one and I've never had a serious boyfriend. You know how many guys I've shagged and ran away from?' She stared back at the puddle, now rippling with the hard rain. 'I got a counsellor and I worked with her and overcame that whole thing.' The other eye got smeared. 'The problem is, I still can't trust anyone.'

He moved a step closer. 'You can trust me.'

'That's sweet, Craig, but you hardly know me. Four weeks at Tulliallan is no basis for a relationship. I'm a bloody mess.'

'And I'm not? Me with my PTSD? Thirty-two and I'm stuck in uniform.' He reached over and pulled her close, fighting against her resistance. 'Look, Chantal, I quite like you.'

She pushed back and tilted her head down. '*Quite* like me?'

'You know what I mean.' He reached over and kissed her forehead. 'I want to—'

Hunter's Airwave blasted out. 'Finlay Sinclair to all units! We've got him!'

~

HUNTER PULLED up by the parked squad car and jumped out. Jain was a few steps ahead of him, running across the road.

'Over here!' Finlay stood outside a new-build house, close to being a show home. Looked pretty much finished.

Hunter sprinted over, almost tripping twice. 'Where is he?'

'Went inside.' Finlay touched his baton to the door. 'Joanne's securing the back door.'

A female uniformed officer appeared from the back, the same one who had manned the crime scene in Cramond. Still looked like she should be at school. 'Back door's locked, Fin.'

Finlay waved his hand round the side of the building. 'Get back round there!'

She darted off.

Hunter snapped his baton out and nodded at Jain. 'You're the ranking officer here. What do we do?'

She looked back down the street. A complete lack of any flashing lights. 'Are Stephanie or Doug in there?'

'Just him.' Finlay tapped his baton on the windowsill. 'Think he's running from me and wee Joanne.'

'Right, I'll guard here, okay?' Jain got out her Airwave. 'You two get in there and apprehend him.'

'Sarge.' Finlay put his hand to the door and winked at Hunter. 'The dream team are back together, eh?'

'Lead on, Napalm.'

Finlay opened the door and stepped inside.

Hunter followed him in, clocking four doors off the open-plan hall, part living room, part kitchen. One of them was the back door, Joanne's silhouette visible through the glass. No sign of movement.

Finlay thumbed upstairs. 'I'm going up there, okay? You check down here.'

'You sure?'

'You saying I can't handle him?'

'Just don't think it's a great idea.'

'Need to get back in the Princess's good books somehow, jabroni...' Finlay started up the stairs, tapping his baton off the unvarnished wood as he climbed.

Hunter unlocked the back door and let the female officer in. 'Joanne, right?'

'Smith. What's up?'

'Help me check these doors.'

She pursed her lips and frowned. 'Sure I should leave this door?'

'We need to hurry. You take the two nearest here.' Hunter headed over to the furthest one, getting a stink of paint and sawdust. It opened onto a utility room, four washing machine-like things stacked two-by-two against the wall. What the hell were—

CRASH.

Hunter ran back into the main room.

'Need some help up here!'

CRASH.

'Stay here!' He waved his baton at Joanne and raced upstairs into a long hall, a strong breeze blowing in his face.

Neil had a knife on Finlay, edging him closer to an open space where a window should be. He swung round and clocked Hunter. 'Stay there!'

Finlay swung out with his baton. Neil dodged the blow, letting it glance off his shoulder, and stuck the head on Finlay.

Hunter raced over, baton raised, ready to lash out with it.

Neil pushed Finlay. Made him tumble backwards. Arms windmilling as he fell out of the gap.

Neil rushed Hunter and shoved him against the wall, his crown cracking off the partition board.

'Stay there!' Hunter froze. Trapped between an impossible choice.

Neil was already running down the stairs.

Hunter got up and stepped over to the open window. He stared down, his breath squeezing itself out of his lungs.

'No, no, no...'

Finlay lay on his back, screaming, his torso twisted round like a pretzel.

40

The air felt like it could burn your skin, even though the tall buildings hid the sun. The smell of roasting goat was everywhere, like they were all at it.

'Down here, Jock.' Terry led the way into a narrow lane, lined above with drying washing, though it was far from clean. Other lanes reeled off every few metres. 'Can almost taste the little bastard, can't you?'

Hunter followed him, his kit bag digging into his aching shoulders, his L85 rifle rattling as they jogged. 'It's definitely him?'

'Sure as eggs is eggs, mate.'

Terry's radio crackled. 'Permission to engage. Use lethal force if necessary. Over.'

'Roger.' Terry grinned like the devil, then set off down a corridor, distant footsteps clacking off marble. 'Got him, there.'

Round the corner, a shadowy figure raced away from them, spindly legs partially concealed by a long cloak.

'Standard tactics these days, Jock. Young lads pretending to be old women in full-on Burqa get-up.' Terry stopped at the corner and raised his weapon, safety catch off. 'On three.'

Hunter got on the other side. 'Three.' He kicked the door open with one go and entered, his rifle pointing into all corners of the room. Another opening led deep into the building, its door swinging on a squeaky hinge.

Terry went for it, tugging the door open.

'Craig!'

Hunter followed him up a staircase and stopped outside another door.

'Craig!'

Terry kicked the door down and entered, L85 pointing dead ahead. 'Come on, sunshine, hands in the air.'

'Craig!'

Their prey stood in the middle of the room, hands up. No other doors, nowhere to go.

His thumb on a dead man's switch.

It flicked off, pointing upright.

BOOM!

Hunter was blown backwards, like a hurricane in his face, infinitely hotter than the air outside. He cracked his back against the staircase, metal digging into his skull, his pack catching against something and ripping wide open. Gear clattered all over the marble.

'Craig!'

Hunter sat up, blood pouring down his face. Screaming white noise in his ears. Dizzy. His L85 was skipping down the stairs, like a child taking his first trip down a helter-skelter.

'Craig!'

In the room, Terry's boots were still standing. No sign of the rest of him.

All he could smell was bacon.

∽

'Craig!' Down below, Jain was kneeling beside Finlay. 'Are you okay?'

Hunter braced himself against the window. He caught sight of Finlay, face contorted and in so much pain he couldn't make a sound.

No sign of Neil.

'Where is he?'

'Shite.' Jain was on her feet, looking around.

Hunter punched the bare partition board, then stabbed at his Airwave. 'Officer down! Need immediate medical assistance to… Shawfair.'

Shit.

'Where in Shawfair?'

'Last location of PC Sinclair, Mags.'

'Got you. On its way.'

Hunter looked out of the window. Still no sign of flashing blues. He darted back the way and took the stairs four at a time, stumbling halfway down. He braced himself against the wall.

Heat burned his skin. Choked on that awful bacon smell. Terry's boots, smoking in the blasted room.

Not again…

Hunter stabbed at his Airwave. 'Mags, where the hell is that back-up?'

'There's another smash on the A1, Craig. This bloody rain. Both carriageways are out.'

Hunter set off down the stairs, fists clenched, and burst into the living room.

Joanne was on her side near the back door, groaning. She blinked hard as she got up, rubbing at her temples. Two police batons lay next to her. Must be Finlay's. 'What happened?'

'Where did he go?'

'Who?'

Bugger...

The back door was wide open. Hunter raced over and burst out onto the bare lawn. Finlay lay a few metres to the side, screaming now.

Jain was on her knees, unsure what to do. 'Fin, can you feel your legs?'

The screaming got louder.

'We've bloody lost him.' Hunter wheeled around, scanning the buildings. 'He can't have got far.'

A flash of movement over the road, just by one of the houses without slates. The front door clicked shut.

Hunter pointed across the street. 'Did you see that?'

'See what?'

Hunter took a few steps, clutching his baton tight, keeping it slow and quiet. A blue flash down the far end of the road. 'Follow me.' He crept up the mud garden of the house next door and got down on his hands and knees. He crab-walked the last stretch on fingers and tiptoes, sinking into the mud up to his wrists and ankles, and stayed there, rain battering off his back, his knee groaning with renewed frustration.

He listened closely. Nothing.

Then: 'Is he still here?' Sounded like Neil Alexander, but the glass muffled it.

Hunter peered into the window, obscured by swathes of whitewash. A small light lit up the far corner, like a phone flashlight app, picking out some figures. Couldn't make them out.

Hunter crawled over to the front door and stood up tall. His arms were crying out in pain from the burpees, the rest of him too sore to worry about at this stage — his head, his knee, his... Carefully, ever so carefully, he extended his baton, muting the crack with his hand.

Splash.

Jain was at the next house, holding a hand in the air. Wait!

Hunter held up his fingers, then counted down. Three, two, one. He opened the front door and stepped inside. Stood there, listening hard.

'Right, my friend...' The rest was muffled.

Hunter crept along the fresh laminate flooring, still tasting of the salt-and-vinegar tang of silicone. He nudged the living room door open and stepped through, baton raised.

Doug Ferguson sat on a chair, battered and bruised, his mouth stuffed with white socks, half dyed red. He lolled around, his left eye swollen to twice the normal size.

Standing in front of him was Stephanie, aiming a knife at his gut. Not so much a hostage as—

She swung round and her eyes widened. 'Neil!'

'Stop.' Neil stepped out of the shadows by the door and held out another long knife, pressing the cutting edge into Hunter's throat. 'Move and he gets it now.'

41

Hunter's hand tightened around the baton's grip. Just one flick and—

'Drop it.' Neil nudged the door shut and scraped Hunter's Adam's apple with the sharp blade. The man's hand was shaking, sweat or rain dripped from the bottom of his fist. 'Now.'

The knife Stephanie was holding in front of her stepfather... was it within his extended reach if he swung for it with the baton? 'Don't do it.'

'I said drop the baton.' Neil's knife dug into Hunter's throat. Didn't feel like he'd broken the skin. Definitely in the post, though. 'You want to be next, cop?'

'Stephanie, don't do it.'

'She's going to do it, Constable.' The blade nibbled at the stubble on Hunter's neck. 'It's her turn.'

'We know you killed Robert Quarrie, Neil. Had us going, but we know.'

'Whatever. The job's only half-finished.' Neil glanced over at Stephanie, then back at Hunter. 'Now, I'm telling you to drop the truncheon.'

Stephanie's hand wobbled in the air, not far from Doug's stained vest, yellowed with sweat, bloodied like Robert Quarrie's floor.

Too big a risk...

Hunter let his grip go and the baton toppled onto the laminate. 'Stephanie, it's your turn to drop the weapon.'

She shifted the blade to Doug's gut, almost touching the cotton. Her shoulders were tight, arms shaking, knife hand trembling.

'Steph, listen to me.' Neil's acid breath hissed in Hunter's ears as the blade notched into his damp skin. 'That bastard has abused you since you were fifteen. This is what he deserves.' He looked over at her again. 'Go on, Steph. Now.'

Stephanie looked around at Hunter, tears streaming down her face, the knife shaking in her grip. 'I can't.'

'You've got to, Steph. We *agreed*.'

Stephanie dropped the blade onto the floor. 'I can't.'

Neil pulled the knife back from Hunter's throat. A trickle of blood ran down his neck, thinning out in his damp clothes. Time to move—

Neil kicked at the back of his right knee.

Hunter toppled forward and landed on his baton, the metal crunching against his cheekbone. He grabbed it, rolled to the left and swung out.

Slashed through clean air.

Neil was already over by Doug, blade raised high.

The door clattered open. 'Drop it!' Jain held out her own baton.

Neil plunged the knife into Doug's chest and pulled him forward. Doug landed on the floor, the knife buried to the hilt. Blood poured out onto the laminate.

'No!' Jain jumped forward and lashed out with her baton. Just missed Neil as he skipped to the side. He grabbed Stephanie by the arms and pushed her at Jain, hard enough to make both of them stumble backwards. She landed on Hunter, squeezing the air out of his lungs like an accordion. Jain's baton rattled like a child's toy as it skidded across the floor.

Footsteps raced through the house.

Hunter got out from under the two and tried to stand up. His knee lurched, wobbling like a jelly peanut. Another go and he was up.

Stephanie crawled off into the corner, freaking out. Fingers fanning out her hair, rocking back and forward.

Doug groaned and toppled over into the crimson pool.

A trickle of blood slid down from the corner of Jain's mouth.

Hunter shook her shoulder. 'Chantal, wake up!'

Nothing.

'Come on!' The shaking got harder, lifting her torso up. 'Chantal!'

She groaned and more blood spilled out.

'Come on!'

She blinked a couple of times, then opened her eyes. 'What the—?'

'Stay here!' Hunter reached for his baton and limped over to the door, the stupid bastard knee finally locking. 'Secure Stephanie!' He jog-skipped through the house and hobbled out of the swinging door into the pissing rain.

Neil was ahead of him, running through the building site, twisting back to look at Hunter.

'Stop!' Hunter pounded after him, but he was only at half-speed, if that.

Neil burst into a house, three storeys of thin silver sheeting over wood. Rain battered off the tarpaulin covering the roof. Sounded like African drummers clattering sticks off drum skins.

Hunter entered the building baton first. Footsteps clomped up a ladder in the middle of the open area, propped up where a staircase would eventually be.

He put his baton between his teeth and started climbing. Hauled himself up onto the first floor and scanned around.

No sign of Neil.

Hunter knelt on the bare chipboard and slowly got to his feet, snapping out his baton. Tried to ignore the throbbing in his knee.

A punch hit his kidney and Hunter squirmed forward, trying to roll away. A kick caught him in the side. He caught the boot and tried to twist. It shook around, tearing his fingers away.

Hunter rocked himself back to sitting, arms flailing in front of him.

Neil stepped towards him, his blade glinting in the light coming through the window gap, raindrops flying in. 'You should've stayed back.'

Hunter reached for his baton and held it up. Tried to flip himself upright, but his knee wasn't having it.

Neil lashed out with the blade.

Hunter parried with the baton and sent the knife scurrying across the bare wood. He rolled onto his knees and raised his baton like a lucky charm.

Neil feinted left and darted right, punching Hunter's hand and sending the baton flying. He followed through with a swift right to the throat.

Hunter tumbled backwards and landed on his back. Chest heaving, he pulled himself up to standing.

Neil was halfway up the second ladder.

Hunter picked up his baton again and lashed out, just missing Neil's foot, the metal clinking off the wood and vibrating up his arm.

Neil raced up to the roof. Nowhere to go but—

Bollocks...

Hunter gripped the ladder and started climbing up, quick as his knee and back would let him. He pulled himself through the opening and rolled over the floor, getting up in one fluid movement.

No sign of Neil.

The top floor was a wide open space, not yet partitioned into rooms. The roof tapered up to a point above his head, rain cannoning off the tarpaulin as it flapped in the breeze.

Thunk.

Movement by a window hole at the back.

Hunter jogged over the boards. 'Stop!'

Neil stood gripping the silver sides of the hole, facing Hunter. He looked behind him, his tongue flicking over his lips.

'You honestly thought you'd get away with this whole thing?'

'I've nothing to lose.' Neil took a step back into thin air.

Hunter jumped forward and grabbed Neil's trailing leg. He fumbled at it, but the foot slipped out of his grasp. Neil fell backwards, the yank on his leg flipping him over as he tumbled through the window gap one floor down.

Hunter got up and ran back over to the ladder. He slid down the outside, fireman-style, stumbling over as he landed.

Neil was on his feet, lurching towards the ladder to the ground floor while gripping his left arm, all mangled and bloody.

Hunter ran over and caught him with a kick to the spine, sending him sprawling against the silver wooden frame. He grabbed Neil's arm and twisted it behind his back, digging his knee into the prone man's spine and pinning his other arm down.

'Neil Alexander, I'm arresting you for the murder of Robert Quarrie. You do not have to say anything—'

42

'A long time.' Hunter pushed Neil out onto the street, cuffed and defeated. 'A very, very long time.'

Neil stumbled over and fell face first into the mud. Didn't move.

Here we bloody go again.

'The joys of being in uniform, eh?' Cullen got out of a battered bottle-green Golf. Surely not the same one he used to drive? He waved at two uniforms behind him, Dave and Steve. 'Secure the suspect and take him to Leith Walk.'

'Sarge.' Dave sniffed. 'Getting him up's going to be a bit of a challenge. He's a floppy fucker, isn't he?'

'There's another two units on their way.' Cullen dug his key into the lock and twisted it, peering into the car like he was checking all the locks were down. 'Get them to help if you need it.' He wandered over, shaking his head, and took Hunter to the side. 'You did good here.'

'Right. Thanks, I suppose.'

'Like old times. You and me catching some proper arseholes.'

Keep telling yourself that.

Hunter folded his arms. 'Except last time, you worked for me.'

'Is that what this is all about?'

'No, Scott, it's about you shagging my fiancée.'

'I don't expect you to get over that, but I'm not the same guy, okay?'

Hunter couldn't look Cullen in the eye, just kept focused on Dave and Steve's efforts to get Neil on his feet. 'How's Finlay?'

'Broken back.' Cullen waved over at a receding ambulance, giving a blast of siren as it powered past a load of rubbernecking workers. 'Doesn't look good. Paramedic's face went white. Said he'd snapped at least four vertebrae.'

Hunter collapsed back against the car. Jesus Christ... Bile burned his throat, his gullet kept popping. He swallowed the lump down.

Finlay... Jesus.

Hunter stumbled forward, catching himself on the top of the car. *The guy wasn't the best, but... Did he deserve that?*

And it's no one's fault but mine. Him going upstairs alone... Idiot. Should've secured the downstairs, then...

Then Neil Alexander could've shinned down the scaffolding and got away. Wouldn't have seen where he'd gone. Doug Ferguson would look like he was in a butcher's window instead of being in hospital. Stephanie might've killed him and had real blood on her hands, rather than secondhand fingerprints.

'That's another one on me. I should've stopped it. Christ.'

'It was you or him, mate.' Cullen slapped him on the shoulder, swallowing hard. 'Had something similar happen to me a few years ago. An ADC got stabbed as we caught this guy.' He shut his eyes. 'Not a day goes by when I don't...'

Hunter wiped at his mouth. Needed a gallon of water to get rid of the taste.

'How's Stephanie?'

Cullen thumbed back down the road. 'Chantal's secured her. Another squad car's going to take her back to Leith Walk.'

An ambulance pulled in by the house, the blue lights flashing and reflecting in the puddles.

'And Doug Ferguson?'

A gurney emerged from the house, two paramedics speeding down the drive.

'He's still breathing.'

Hunter snorted just as Neil Alexander was finally hauled to his feet. 'Turns out he wasn't very good at this stabbing lark.'

'Just about good enough for Robert Quarrie. How you doing, Craig?'

'I'll live.' Hunter stretched out his leg. 'Knee's knackered, but I'll live.'

'I meant about seeing—'

Hunter shook his head and tightened his stab-proof. 'So, what's going to happen now?'

'First, you need to get changed. You look like you've been mud-wrestling.' Cullen zipped up his jacket. 'Then you're going to come back to Leith Walk and we're going to get to the bottom of this bloody mess.'

∼

HUNTER PARKED the pool car and got out, spilled diesel burning his nose. The flickering of a strip light caught on the shiny hide of a black Range Rover next to him.

'Craig, there you are.' Lauren stormed over from the stairwell, lugging a sheaf of papers. Looked like she hadn't slept in weeks — red eyes and dark rings. She frowned and checked her watch. 'I'm just off to the hospital.'

'I'm accepting full blame for what happened to Finlay. Nobody deserves that.'

'You mean it was his fault?' Lauren snorted. 'If he endangered himself, then you can't cover for him.' She zipped up her fleece. 'Anyway, Stephanie and Neil are still awaiting their lawyers.' She handed him the paper. 'And Elv— DC Gordon has been looking through Stephanie's emails and Facebook messages.'

You really do love your paper...

Hunter started sifting through the stack. Looked like an extract of the Facebook messages between Neil and Stephanie.

Lauren tapped at a page halfway through. 'See this here? They were talking about running away together.'

Hunter exhaled. 'She told us Doug wanted her to do that with him.'

Lauren snatched the pages off him. 'And this one here.' More prodding at the paper. 'She sent him this message first thing yesterday morning. "Police here! Help!" That make any sense to you?'

'Terrific.' Hunter rubbed at the back of his head. His crown had crusted over but still ached like a bastard. 'She was on the computer when we broke into Gaynor Tait's flat.'

'Well, Neil replied "Be there soon." So he turned up and attacked you.'

'And took her.'

'Well, she went with him by the looks of things. It's more of a rescue. And there's this.' Lauren flicked to the last message, the metadata showing three o'clock that afternoon. 'See this? "Worked like a charm. He thought I was you, babe." That's when Neil killed Robert Quarrie.'

Hunter snatched the document off her, just as a car trundled along behind them, the engine rattling to its death. 'This is a good start, but it's not enough.'

'No, but this might be.' Lauren picked out a print of some CCTV footage, the greyscale image burnt almost white by the sunlight. 'Neil Alexander arriving at the flat in Cramond...'

'That'll do. Cheers, Sarge.'

'I'll be about an hour.' Lauren opened the car door and stopped. 'Craig, this car is a cesspit.' The driver's seat was as soiled as a cat's litter tray. 'This is going to need a valet to get that whole lot clean.'

'Sorry, Sarge.'

'I'll have to take my own bloody car.' Lauren marched off through the car park, shaking her head.

Hunter stared down at his legs. Most of the mud had washed off, but it looked like he'd been fly fishing without waders. *How quickly Hollywood chases gave way to dirty trousers and stalled careers...*

A car door slammed on the other side. 'Craig? You okay?'

Hunter opened his eyes and looked over.

Jain was frowning at him as she crossed the street. Dave and Steve were in the front of the squad car, both pointing fingers at him and laughing.

'Chantal...' Hunter rubbed his eyes and averted his head. He hefted up the papers. 'We've got enough evidence to put Neil away.'

'That's all fine and good.' She grasped his bicep, barely getting halfway round, but her fingers digging in all the same. 'What happened in the house?'

Hunter stopped and leaned against a pillar, far enough away from those two pricks, their wagging fingers, and their *banter*.

'When Finlay fell out of the window, you just stood there. You had a flashback, didn't you?'

Hunter sighed, his breath getting stuck halfway out. 'Thought I was past them, you know?'

'You never get over it. You just learn to cope with it.'

'What happened to Finlay... Reminded me of my squad mate in Iraq. Big lump from Leytonstone, Terry Saunders. Big Cockney guy, bit of a twat, but, you know...' Hunter shivered, feeling it all the way down his spine. 'I was back there. Could feel the heat on my neck. Smell the roasting goat.' He screwed his eyes tight, trying to squeeze the last drop of tears out. 'I could smell Terry's burnt body.'

She wrapped a hug around him, snuggling her head into his chin. 'It's okay.'

Hunter swallowed deep, sucking in the smell of her hair. The rain had freshened the shampoo scent, some distant herbs tasting like mountain air. 'You were right.'

She looked up at him, frowning. 'I'm always right.'

Two car doors slammed within a second of each other and Hunter broke off. 'I meant about Stephanie. Neil was controlling her.'

Jain sighed as Dave and Steve wandered past. 'It's not bad enough that Doug Ferguson and Robert Quarrie did what they did to her, he's got to make it worse. Controlling her like that, it's just twisting the knife in her guts.' Her turn to wipe at her cheeks. 'She can recover from what's happened to her. Given time, counselling and a shitload of drugs. Catching her in this revenge-murder plot... You don't come back from murdering someone.'

'You think she's innocent here?'

'What, you don't?'

'The more I think about it, the more it all falls apart. She approached Neil. She told him what Doug was doing to her.'

'Craig, she's the victim here.'

'I'm not so sure.' Hunter started off across the concrete. 'But we need to find out.'

∾

'Is THAT so?' Hunter left his seat and stalked around the interview room, rounding the giant figure of Neil Alexander, slumped forward in the chair. He locked eyes with Jain and returned to his seat. The attempt at intimidation didn't seem to have made any difference to Neil. 'We know you stabbed Doug Ferguson, Mr Alexander, because we saw you do it. It's touch and go whether he lives or dies, but, either way, you'll be going away for a very long time.'

Neil smirked at him. 'Really.'

Hunter waved a hand at the lawyer next to him, the sort of dead-eyed Legal Aid vulture who'd represent an open-and-shut murderer at the drop of a hat. 'Your lawyer here's seen the evidence. You murdered Doug Ferguson and Robert Quarrie. We will be throwing a lot of crimes your way.' He started counting off on his fingers. 'Abduction, resisting arrest, providing a false alibi, motor theft. One murder and one attempted murder. Trust me, you're going away for a very long time.' He gave him some space. Just the sound of the lawyer writing and Neil's foot tapping on the floor. 'Did you kill Robert Quarrie?'

Neil looked at his lawyer and shook his head. Then back at Jain, then Hunter. 'Fine. I killed him. Happy?' He shrugged his slouching shoulders. 'I don't regret a single thing, other than you stopping Steph from killing Doug Ferguson. I just wish it was a double murder charge.'

'I don't get it. Why did you do it?'

Neil reached across the table, running his tongue around the tip of his lips. 'Listen, you're a police officer, right?'

'Well spotted.'

'Don't you get fed up with the way the world is?' Neil raised his arms like a preacher. 'All the work you do, back shifts and night shifts. Watching your back on holiday in case someone you put away spots you. And all you're doing is scraping away at the surface.' He put his fingers together in a steeple. 'When I was younger, I used to be an idealist. In the union, out canvassing every day. Vote Labour, then vote SWP, then it's for independence. But it just wasn't enough. Trying to get the world to change, trying to get it to be a better place. But it just gets worse. I'm just one man. Even with a political party, you can't change things. You can't change America or Russia or China or the EU.'

'Is this stuff you've read in your books?'

'My books... Everything I've read makes me realise you can't change anything. You can't fix the world, not on your own. The politicians are making the world worse for everyone. Everything's for the one percent. The zero point one percent. They all stick their money in tax havens, while us who can least afford pay more than our fair share. They're hiding money away, money which should be contributing to schools and hospitals and the police force.'

'We could've charged Doug with abusing Stephanie if you'd let us.'

'Aye? And he'd have got, what, four years like her old man? Four years for ruining that girl's life.' Neil paused, spit dribbling down his chin. 'I've read about the Black Panthers, Nation of Islam and the IRA. It was all academic until I read about the Revolutionary Front in Sweden.' He slid his fingernails through his long hair, combing it back. 'They took action against fascists, vigilante action and property attacks. I've been involved in Anti-Fascist groups since I was sixteen, but it's toothless. Just campaigning and sit-down protests and shouting in the streets.' He nibbled at his fingernails. 'This was my chance to do something. To make a difference in the world. To change one girl's life for the better.'

43

Hunter sat back and nodded at Stephanie's solicitor, same as Gaynor Tait. 'State your name for the record.'

'Alastair Reynolds.' He yawned, just about covering his mouth. Didn't look much older than Stephanie. 'Can we get going, please?'

'Sure.' Hunter waited for the nod from Jain, then smiled at Stephanie. 'Miss Ferguson, I'd like to start with asking why you've been hiding from us?'

She tugged at a long strand of hair. 'I'm not hiding from you.'

'Well, that doesn't stack up with the events, does it?' Hunter flicked through a pile of paper in front of him, but kept Stephanie from seeing any of the contents. 'You ran away from the hospital.' He passed the first sheet over, a time-stamped still from the CCTV footage. 'For the tape, I'm showing P dash oh one oh. This shows you running away from your hospital room.'

She glanced at it. 'That cop was playing a game on his phone.'

Hunter felt a sting in his guts, digging deep in. 'Nevertheless, you still ran away. Why?'

'I heard what you said to Mum. The doctor didn't find anything. Doug was going to get away with it.' Stephanie rubbed her cheek, a single tear sliding around her fingers. 'It took everything I had to tell Mum. Everything and you were going to let him go.'

'Yesterday morning, I found you at Gaynor Tait's flat and you ran away again.' Hunter scratched his scabby crown. 'After I was assaulted.'

Stephanie started twirling it around her fingers, knotting it like an old telephone cable. 'You know I was abducted.'

'Who abducted you?'

Stephanie let go of her hair and it bounced up before settling in front of her left eye.

'It was Neil Alexander, wasn't it? I assume he took you to that house in Shawfair from Corstorphine. Is that right?'

'It wasn't him.'

'So who was it?'

'I told you I never saw their face. They were going to kill mum! I told you it must've been one of Doug's mates. Dave or that pervy one with the huge head.'

'David Boyle is in custody and Alexander Wishart was released from hospital this morning. It wasn't them who attacked myself and a colleague outside Ms Tait's flat. It was Mr Alexander, wasn't it?'

'I told you. I never saw his face!'

'You did. He gave you a knife and you were going to stab Doug Ferguson with it.'

Stephanie shut her eyes and wiped at a stray tear. 'Neil kidnapped me.'

'Really?' Hunter slid the Facebook messages across the desk to between her and the lawyer. 'In that case, I'd like you to explain message fourteen there. Marked at three eighteen yesterday afternoon.'

'I've never seen that.' Stephanie didn't even look at the page.

'We got that off your laptop. It's from your Facebook account.'

'Well, someone's hacked into it.'

'If that's the case, what else did they do there?' Hunter let the silence grow in the room. 'No, whoever it was sent a message taking great joy in the death of Robert Quarrie. Your father.'

'No.'

Hunter stabbed a finger at the page. 'This kind of suggests it.'

'That's it?' Stephanie looked up, peeking up like a rat in a hole. 'That's all you've got?'

'Well, there's this as well.' Hunter slid over the page of CCTV footage. 'This item shows Mr Alexander getting into a red Hyundai outside the Tesco in Corstorphine.'

'What are you talking about?'

'Ten minutes later it was here.' Hunter produced a second sheet, taken in the gloomy rain and almost catching the school playground in the distance. 'Just outside your father's house in Cramond. And that's at five past three.' He left another long pause. 'Right about when he was stabbed.'

Stephanie kept staring at the evidence, breathing fast and loud. She reached over to whisper in her lawyer's ear.

Reynolds shook his head, hands raised, eyes bulging. 'No. That's not a good idea.'

Stephanie slumped her shoulders and fell back, arms folded.

Hunter took the sheets back. 'We understand you instigated your relationship with Neil, is that right?'

Stephanie twisted her face to the side. 'Who told you that?'

'We got it from a couple of sources. You didn't approach Mr Alexander and suggest killing your father, did you?'

'Neil started it.'

Reynolds reached over and grabbed Stephanie's sleeve. 'I really—'

'It was all—'

'Stephanie—'

'Neil—'

'No, you can't—'

'Neil was behind it.' Stephanie shrugged off her lawyer's warning grip. 'It was all his idea.'

Reynolds slouched low and tossed his pen onto the desk. 'Great...'

'When I told Neil about what... About what Doug had been doing to me, he just got so angry. I've never seen anyone like that.'

'So Mr Alexander suggested you kill your father and your stepfather?'

'He didn't suggest anything.' She snorted. 'He just said we're doing it.'

'And you went along with it?'

'Didn't feel like I had any choice. I loved him, but he...' She ran a hand through her hair. 'He was too intense for me. Kept saying I was older than my age, but ... sometimes I feel like I'm about six years old.'

'I understand that.' Jain gave her a smile. 'Stephanie, you've had a very difficult life. Being abused by your father when you're a child, it's a lot to happen to anyone and you clearly need to speak to someone.'

'I've got a counsellor.' Stephanie raised her shoulders. 'But she's rubbish. Doesn't help any of the...' She bunched up a sheet of paper, crumpling it into a tight ball. 'She doesn't help with what happened to me. What Doug did to me. What my own father did to me...'

Jain placed a hand on the table, not too far from Stephanie's, but nowhere near touching. 'I understand...'

'How the hell can you?' Stephanie nibbled at her lips and glared at Jain. 'You know something? My father called me up out of the blue. One day when Mum and Da— Mum and *Doug* were out. He said he was sorry.' She shook her head, fire burning in her eyes, the same as it would with her mother. 'How can you be sorry for shagging your own daughter? For pinning me down and raping me when I WAS SIX YEARS OLD!' She sat there, panting, then wiped spittle from round her mouth. 'He might've served his time, but Robert Quarrie deserves everything he's got.'

'You're saying he deserved to die?'

Stephanie thumped the table. 'I was *six* when he started it. Do you know what that feels like? The man was a beast. They should've locked away the key when they put him away.' She shook her head, nostrils flaring. 'But no, they let him out, didn't they?' She stared into space for a few seconds, her eyes twitching. 'Mum didn't tell me he was out. Said he was dead. Had to find out myself on the internet.'

'Did Neil kill him?'

'I wasn't there.' Stephanie picked up the picture of Neil outside Quarrie's flat. 'You can see that, right?'

There goes the accessory to murder charge…

Jain steepled her fingers in front of her. 'Doug denies abusing you, Stephanie.'

'What? He fucked me! Over and over again.' Stephanie thumped the table again, sending ripples across the surface of her water. 'Any time Mum was out, his fingers were all over me. Inside me. Everywhere!'

'It's just your word against his.' Jain tilted her head to the side. 'We don't have any evidence to support your claim.' She held Stephanie's gaze as long as the girl would allow. 'Stephanie, did Mr Ferguson abuse you?'

'How dare you?' Tears started flowing down Stephanie's cheeks. 'Of course he did. He made me go on the pill so I didn't get pregnant.' She shook her head. 'He was just the same as my father. Worse. Doug has a temper, especially when he's had a drink. I thought he was going to kill Mum, I really did. And then I'd be next, wouldn't I?' Her focus tightened around Jain. 'Doug was beating up mum before he started abusing me.'

'I know it's hard, but I appreciate your honesty, Stephanie.' Jain reached across the table and gripped the girl's fingers tight. For the first time, Stephanie didn't flinch, just let her do it. 'The problem is, Mr Ferguson has an alibi for Monday night when you said he raped you.'

Stephanie yanked her fingers away. 'What?'

'Mr Ferguson said he was in the pub all night. We've backed it up with some regulars there and CCTV. It's why we had to let him go yesterday.'

'But…' Stephanie attacked a stray frond of hair, pulling it until it was straight. She was panting like a dog after a long run. 'Look. He came into my room when he got home from the pub. Mum was in bed, whacked up on her Valium. Da— Doug came into my room. He-he-he stuck a hand over my mouth and pinned my arms down, just like...' She collapsed forward, her torso racking with each heavy sob. 'Just like Daddy did...'

'I believe you, Stephanie.' Jain gripped her fingers again, tight. 'We're going to prosecute Douglas Ferguson. But we'll have to investigate you for your part in this.'

'It was all Neil... All of it.' Stephanie looked up and nodded. 'One thing I want you to know... I didn't start this. Any of it. I tried to stop...' Her hair was plastered to her forehead. 'I tried to stop Neil. Tried to persuade him not to do it. But he just shut me up. Like they all do. Just said we're doing it. That's it. I said I didn't want to murder anyone... Neil said my dad's out of prison now. Been out for years. Said it'll be the same with Doug, if you even manage to prosecute him. They never pay in full. Never enough.' She gasped. 'He's just like them. Just forced me to go along with what he wanted, didn't care about me and what I need.'

Hunter looked round at Jain, a thick lump catching in his throat. She'd been right. Silenced and bullied and abused, her mind and soul as much as her body. Stephanie was a victim in so many ways.

Is a victim.

Not a dead body but a real person carrying this shit through the rest of her life.

Every single day.

～

Mountcastle Green was deadly quiet outside. Dowsed in bright sunshine, the summer back after a brief interlude. Could almost believe Edinburgh was a nice place.

Hunter sat in the chair in the sitting room and smiled at Pauline Ferguson. 'Stephanie is giving my colleagues a detailed statement regarding her abuse at the hands of Mr Ferguson.'

'Right.' Pauline lay back on the sofa and snarled. 'That boy who was here, the one that makes the shite tea, he said Neil stabbed Doug. Is that right?'

'That's correct.'

Pauline scowled over at the window, the tears soaking her cheeks shimmered in the second-hand glow. After a few seconds she shook her head. 'Are you going to prosecute Steph?'

'I don't know. She was Mr Alexander's accomplice.' Jain sighed. 'She should've given us a statement on Tuesday. As it stands, it's just

Stephanie's word against Mr Ferguson's. Even so, we intend to prosecute Mr Ferguson and we have the support of the Procur—'

'Is she lying?'

Hunter glanced over at Jain. Her expression could curdle cheese. 'I don't believe she is, no. Mr Ferguson was—'

'See that stuff Steph said about Doug? When was it?'

'Well, Stephanie told us Mr Ferguson abused her on Monday after he came home from the pub. Is that true?'

'Doug was out at the pub watching the football. I didn't hear him come back.'

'She told us he... visited her room.'

'Jesus.' Pauline swallowed. 'I heard something in the middle of the night. A whimpering. I thought it was next door's dog.' She gulped. 'It was Steph...' She crumpled into a heap, elbows clanking off the table, chin tucked into her wrists. 'Oh, Steph...'

Hunter gave her a minute, letting her pour all of the rage and disgust out of her body. Poor woman was falling apart. The bits of string holding her up were frayed and torn, had to break sooner or later. Like a broken Judy puppet, battered by Punch one too many times.

'Pauline. Stephanie told us that Doug has been physically abusing you.'

She sat upright and swept her hair back. 'Never started like that.'

'How long has he been doing it?'

'Never did it until his business started getting into trouble a few years back, then he took it out on me. A slap at first after a few whiskies. Then it got worse. And it didn't stop when his work picked up again. He just started taking on more people, expanding. Whole thing gave him more stress. Started drinking more.'

'Why didn't you leave?'

'I couldn't afford a mortgage on my wage. Nobody else was going to take me and Steph in, were they?' She tore at her lips with her teeth, stretching the skin tight. 'I took the ... beatings, thinking it would at least save Steph.' She brushed at her eyes. 'I tried to keep Steph away from it, make sure he never beat her.' She closed her eyes and snorted through her nostrils. 'But then I find out what he's been doing to her...'

All Hunter could do was get up and pace through the back of the room.

Angus thumped at the controller, the little green elf kid slashing out with his sword.

'How could you do this?' Hunter leaned against the back of his chair, glaring at Pauline. 'After you caught your first husband abusing Steph?'

'I thought this was different. You've got to understand, I tried to change him...'

'And when he started beating you up?'

Jain reached forward. 'I understand—'

'Do you? Do you really? Are you telling me you know what it's like to let two beasts into your house? To have them ... *fuck* your daughter? Their own flesh and blood, give or take...'

'I know what's going through Stephanie's mind. I know what it's like not to be believed by your own mother.' Jain clenched her jaw. All she could do to keep it under control. 'I know it's difficult for you, but think about your daughter and what she's been through. We need you to think through the events of the last two years and track down any instances where you believe Mr Ferguson *could* have abused her.'

'Is he going to get away with this?'

'If he lives, I hope not.'

'Stabbing's too good for him.' Pauline spat the words out. 'Should've been tortured and had his nuts cut off first, that sick bastard. Stick in a big bucket and shat on and pissed on and...' She shook her head. 'I hope he never wakes up.'

'It'd be helpful if we had other charges to level at him.'

Pauline rubbed a hand across her cheeks and glared at Hunter, her eyes glowing from the tears. 'I want to press charges for battery against Doug.'

44

'Should you not have a lawyer, one will be appointed for you.' Hunter stood next to the hospital bed, the crisp sheets seeming sarcastic next to Doug Ferguson's battered and bruised face. 'Do you understand?'

Doug huffed out breath with a whistle. A little flicker sparked in his eyes, then it was gone.

Hunter leaned in close. 'I said, do you understand?'

Doug rubbed his nose, smoothing his fingers across the skin.

Hunter looked round at Dr Yule. 'He should be understanding me, right?'

'He's just not playing ball.' The strip light flared in her glasses, her eyes opaque through the lenses. 'He's incurred no mental injuries during his ordeal.'

'Well, he's got a right to remain silent, I guess.'

Yule led him away from the bed. 'Being attacked like that, on top of the abduction, well, it's traumatic.'

Hunter just about picked her up and slammed her against the wall. 'Traumatic for him? You know what he's been doing to his stepdaughter, don't you?' He almost threw her at Doug. 'Well, he's going to be undergoing the trauma of a court case.'

'That poor girl.' Yule nodded slowly, her lenses clearing to give sight of her dark eyes. 'The only thing going for Stephanie is she's young. She'll cope with enough time.'

'I'm sure she'd much rather this hadn't happened.'

∼

'I'M NOT sure what sense you'll get out of Mr Sinclair.' Yule paced down the corridor, her crocs squishing on the floor, her coat flailing behind her like a cape. 'He has been heavily sedated. The consultant will be in shortly to advise on surgical options with his next of kin.'

'Finlay's old man lives in Portugal these days.'

'He's not married?'

'Afraid not.' Hunter gritted his teeth, trying to keep control. 'I assume he'll be in a wheelchair?'

'Only for a few days, if it goes well. The most likely option will be to fuse the vertebrae together in pairs, though it'll mean taking bone from his hip.'

Hunter shook his head as they walked. 'That sounds pretty bad.'

'It's a relatively easy operation these days.' Yule held the door open and let some of the stale air out. 'He's in here. I'll give you a minute.'

Hunter gave her a smile, then entered the room.

Finlay lay on the bed, back raised to forty-five degrees, and covered in thick white bracing. His arms were splayed up at the sides, the support stopping at his elbows. He held his phone close to his face, a lopsided grin on his face. 'Got you, Elvis, you big twat.'

'And here was me worrying about you...' Hunter grabbed the chair and slid it next to the bed. 'You winning?'

'Aye, about a hundred grand once the lawyer has a word.'

'I meant the game, but I suppose this is Compo striking again.'

Finlay rested the phone down and settled back in the bed. 'I'll be off on the bird's beak for three months, at least. Then it'll be office duties for six.'

Hunter's mouth was dry. 'I'm sorry about it.'

'Why? You shouldn't be, mate.' Finlay clicked his thumb off a button. 'This is awesome morphine in here.'

'I should've gone up there with you.'

'I went up on my Jack, okay?' Eyes back on the phone, his thumb hammering away. 'Lauren said you caught the boy?'

'He's locked up. Safe and sound.'

'Then it's a good thing.' Finlay stabbed the button again. 'We'd probably get a commendation for this, but it's my fault we let the lassie go.'

Hunter grabbed the bottle of ginger Lucozade from the bedside table and poured it into a spare cup. He took a drink and nodded. 'I wish I could disagree with you, but I just can't.' He tipped out another cup and handed it over.

'Always tell it like it is, Conan.' Finlay took a sip from the cup. 'That poor lassie, man. Jesus. What's going to happen to her?'

'Well, hopefully nobody'll abuse her again, but she's got a long process to go through before she clears her name.'

'How did that interview go?'

What interview?

Oh, that one...

Hunter slouched back in the chair and sighed. 'Never mind, mate.'

'Sure you'll get away from punks like me. Back to being a proper cop, eh, jabroni?' Finlay hit the button again. Then again. And again. 'Ah, knickers.'

∽

Hunter took a sip of beer. Could barely taste it. The Elm was quiet, just the four of them taking advantage of the lunchtime lull.

Cullen and McNeill were sitting close together, almost touching.

Hunter leaned over to Jain. 'Are they a couple?'

She smirked at him. 'You didn't know? Jesus, Craig.'

'That's his other half?'

'Why? Don't think she's good enough for him?'

'No, it just... explains a lot, that's all.'

Lauren stomped in, face like she'd just gone twelve rounds with Thor. 'Elvis said you'd be here.'

'Methven approved time off.' Cullen lifted his bottle of Brewdog Nanny State. 'His card's behind the bar.'

'I'd kill for a G&T.' Lauren collapsed into the bench between Cullen and Hunter, the leather squeaking. 'You saw Finlay, didn't you?'

Hunter took a sip of beer and barely tasted it. 'Not sure he sees it that way, though.'

Lauren nodded. 'Kept asking me how much the compensation was.'

'To good old Compo.' Jain raised her wine glass. 'Jesus wept.'

Lauren scowled at her. 'That's not in very good taste.'

'And since when was anything Finlay Sinclair said in good taste?' She got up, shaking her head at her. 'I'm getting another, anyone want anything?'

'That G&T would be super.' Lauren shrugged off her fleece. The hairs on her arms stood on end.

Hunter raised his almost-empty pint glass and watched Jain wiggle her way over to the irritated hipster behind the bar. He nodded at Lauren. 'She doesn't mean it.'

'I know. It's just ... hard. I can't believe what's happened to him on my watch.'

'I was there, Lauren.' Hunter finished the pint. 'Should've stopped it.'

'I don't disagree.' Lauren rubbed her hands together. 'What that girl's been through…'

Hunter stared at Jain, her secret rattling in his skull. Problem halved or doubled?

'She did what she felt she had to do.' He spun his pint glass around the table. Gas was already building up in his gut. 'I feel sick.'

'Join the club, Craig. Join the club.'

Hunter got up and collected his empty. 'I'm going to help Chantal.' He wandered over to the bar and stood a decent distance away from her. 'Hey.'

'All right?' She handed him his pint. Far too much foam, but he wasn't in a complaining mood.

He sipped it, trying to lubricate his mouth. 'What you said in the rain earlier…'

'Every one of these bastards I put away helps.' Jain took a sip of her red wine and stared into the middle distance. She swallowed and looked back at him, exhaling through her nostrils. 'It helps…'

'I want to help.'

'Listen, I don't know why I told you.' Jain glanced over at McNeill. 'Sharon doesn't even know about it.'

'Seriously?'

'Aye. And I don't want you to treat me like some sort of charity case, okay?'

'I'll treat you however you'd like to be treated.'

'You silver-tongued twat.' She sighed. 'Look, Craig, I'm shite at this relationship stuff, okay?'

'I'm not much better. Doesn't mean I don't want to try. With you.'

'What a pair we'd make.' She winked at him. 'Fuckbuddy cops.'

'I like the sound of that.' Hunter looked back at their table, all three of them staring into space. 'So, how about we get out of here?'

Jain nibbled at her lip. 'You need to be discreet, okay?'

'You really don't want to be seen with me, do you?'

'It's not that… Look, discretion or it's off, okay?'

'That's my middle name.' Hunter zipped up his lips. 'Mum's the word.'

'I'll finish my wine, leave and go around the block. Then you meet me by the chip shop on Montgomery Street. My flat's just up the road.'

'Deal.' Hunter clinked glasses with her and led back to their table, sitting next to Lauren and handing her a glass of white wine.

'Psst.' Lauren leaned over. 'We're all impressed with your work on this case.'

'Thanks.' Hunter shrugged, fire burning its way up his neck. 'Is it too late to withdraw the application for that ADC job?'

'Don't you want it?'

'I don't want to work with Davenport again.'

Lauren sat back on the bench. 'You need to get over your past, Craig.'

Hunter looked at Jain, already halfway through her wine. 'I'm trying.'

'You know, there's an opportunity just appeared somewhere else. And given you've passed a DC interview today...'

'What, I passed?'

'I got an email from Donna Nichols this evening.' Lauren gave him the thumbs up. 'Flying colours.'

'Cheers, Sarge.' Hunter clinked glasses with her. 'Well, that is good news.'

'What is?' Jain finished her drink and got up. 'I'll see you all tomorrow.'

'Aye, cheers, Chantal.' Hunter checked his watch.

Time to tan a pint in five minutes.

DAY 4

Monday
14th September 2015

Four weeks later

45

Hunter pulled up the pool car alongside a pair of high-end Audis, gleaming in the September sunshine. 'This it?'

Jain nodded. 'That's right.'

He executed a swift reverse park and killed the engine. 'You okay, Sarge?'

'I'm fine, Constable.' Jain reached over and picked at his jacket. 'That's a lovely suit, by the way.'

'Well, you chose it.'

'It'll be a shame to ruin it.'

'Not on my first day, surely?'

'Relax.' She pecked him on the cheek. 'Come on, let's do this. Three days of statements from this punk and we're done. He'll be off to the nick and we can move on.'

Hunter got out his briefing notes and started flicking through. 'He's done a lot of horrible shit. Sure he's going to comply with us just turning up?'

'He is.' Jain got out of the car and marched up the stairs to the Georgian townhouse, three storeys of red stone. She knocked on the door and waited for Hunter to join her on the top step.

The door slid open and a wall of muscle and gristle towered over them, face like a wrecking ball waiting to be launched. 'Aye?'

Jain smiled at him as she unfolded her warrant card. 'Police.'

He kicked at the door, pushing it in Jain's face and shutting it with a loud slam.

Hunter reached down to pick her up. 'You okay?'

'God by dose.' Blood trickled down from both of her nostrils. 'Ged him!'

'Right.' Hunter barged through the door and followed the clumping footsteps up the staircase, Jain's following him like a shadow. The sound led into a back room overlooking Dunfermline.

He was on the windowsill, just getting ready to jump out of the window. A thick tree loomed in the drying green behind.

Hunter stopped dead and groaned. 'Terrific. This again.'

CRAIG HUNTER WILL RETURN IN

"HUNTED"

(Craig Hunter Book 2)

Out Now

DC Craig Hunter of Police Scotland's Sexual Offences Unit. Ex-Army. Back doing the work that drives him, that makes a difference.

Private Sean Tulloch. Squaddie. Monster. He charms women. Moves in, dominates them, abuses them. Under investigation by the Sexual Offences Unit and the Royal Military Police, his partner Paisley Sanderson receives a threat. Soon she's in hospital and Tulloch is in the wind.

Now, Hunter and DS Chantal Jain must hunt Tulloch down before he can strike again. Where is he? How did he know they were investigating him? A simple trip to Portugal soon grows out of control. Will Hunter take down Tulloch before his already horrific crimes escalate? Are the Army Police really on their side? Is DI Bruce really hunting a missing child or do his intentions lie closer to Chantal? Can Hunter and Chantal overcome their very different but very similar demons? And, in Sean Tulloch, has Hunter finally met his match?

Subscribe to the Ed James newsletter to keep on top of upcoming releases —
http://eepurl.com/pyjv9

AFTERWORD

Well, I hope you enjoyed that...

For new readers, I hope you enjoyed reading this book and it introduced you to the world I've been building up over the last four and a bit years.

For old readers, I swore I wouldn't do another Cullen book for another year and this has sort of let me have my cake and eat it. I hope I've not diminished Cullen in your eyes by letting you see another side to him...

I plan more books in this series, just got a little bit of a delay until the second one due to contracts and so on. Should be Feb/March next year, I hope...

Thanks for dev editing help go to Russel D McLean, Rhona Lindsay, Pat Lynch and, as always, Kitty.

+1 thanks goes to Len Wanner for all manner of editing help throughout the book and probably blinding yourself during the process...

One final note, if you could find time to leave a review where you bought this, I'd really appreciate it — reviews really help indie authors like myself.

-- Ed James
   East Lothian, May 2016

MEET SCOTT CULLEN...

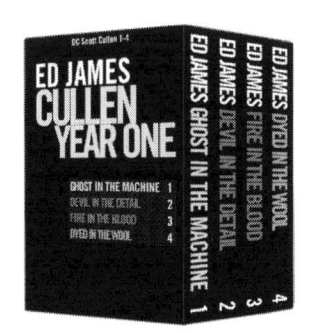

The first four novels for a bargain price...

- Amazon UK — http://bit.ly/EJYear1
- Available through all other Amazon channels — http://mybook.to/CYear1

ABOUT ED JAMES

Ed James writes crime-fiction novels, primarily the DI Simon Fenchurch series, set on the gritty streets of East London featuring a detective with little to lose. His Scott Cullen series features a young Edinburgh detective constable investigating crimes from the bottom rung of the career ladder he's desperate to climb.

Formerly an IT project manager, Ed began writing on planes, trains and automobiles to fill his weekly commute to London. He now writes full-time and lives in the Scottish Borders, with his girlfriend and a menagerie of rescued animals.

Subscribe to my newsletter at http://eepurl.com/pyjv9 (news on new releases and miscellany)

Visit edjamesauthor.com for my blog and news on forthcoming books

Follow me on Twitter at twitter.com/edjamesauthor
Like me on Facebook at facebook.com/edjamesauthor
Email me at ed@edjames.co.uk - I don't bite!

Printed in Poland
by Amazon Fulfillment
Poland Sp. z o.o., Wrocław